RED ON GREEN

Steve Ellis

Grosvenor House
Publishing Limited

This book is published by
Grosvenor House Publishing Ltd
Link House
140 The Broadway, Tolworth, Surrey, KT6 7HT.
www.grosvenorhousepublishing.co.uk

This book is a work of fiction. Any resemblance to
people or events, past or present, is purely coincidental.
In some cases, where true-life figures are mentioned,
all are now deceased.

A CIP record for this book
is available from the British Library

Paperback ISBN 978-1-80381-226-7
eBook ISBN 978-1-80381-227-4

Also by Steve Ellis

Silent Suffering (Trafford 2005)
Havercake Lad (MediaAble 2017)

Contact: steveellis641@gmail.com

Kathy

This one's for you

INTRODUCTION

Red on Green is set in the turbulent aftermath of a bloody civil war in what was then East Pakistan, now Bangladesh, in 1971. But the relationship between a Bangladeshi woman and British man, and the events that unfold, have echoes and relevance for today.

Aid worker Ben Altringham meets medical student Ayesha through her father, Dr Abdur Rahman. He volunteers to help in the nearby camp bursting with what international aid organisations call 'internally displaced persons': effectively refugees inside their own country fleeing persecution.

Ayesha and Ben's developing relationship is a dangerous liaison at this time of febrile nationalistic fervour. Increasing the peril, Ayesha's life-long friend, Khalida, desperately needs to escape the clutches of a government minister and his son. They are conspiring to coerce her into marriage.

Ben is asked by Ayesha to help Khalida – but their rescue plan is fraught with danger.

Sadly Bangladesh's nine-month 'War of Liberation' did not free the population from poverty, disease and natural disasters, nor endemic corruption, nepotism and discrimination.

Former 'freedom fighters' took revenge against those accused of being traitors and collaborators during the conflict.

Blood continued to flow into the new nation's lush landscape.

*

Before the age of mobile or smart phones, personal computers, apps, internet and instant global connectivity, phone calls in the 1970s were often made through an operator based at a telephone exchange.

International calls from the Indian subcontinent had to be booked in advance.

Air-mail letters to and from Bangladesh took between ten and fourteen days to arrive, although approximately one in four was never delivered.

*

Spelling is used as then. Dacca, now Dhaka; Calcutta, Kolkata; Jessore, Jashore. Others are by choice. Sari not Saree; dal not dhal; chapati not chupatti; cha not chai.

Steve Ellis
August 2022

ONE

Showering with frogs was a new experience for Ben. Many scurried away when he stepped under the tarnished brass showerhead and turned the tap. It wasn't hot water, merely warm, and the flow was slow, dribbles rather than a deluge. There was no danger of the creatures' delicate skin scalding. The more stubborn frogs however, around ten of them, didn't appreciate soap suds trickling down Ben's body. They joined the evacuation, hopping and crawling across the cracked concrete floor, securing their escape by scrambling through gaps in the wall.

Although grenades and tank shells had caused severe damage to more than half the bungalow, Abigale had been reassured the remainder of Dak Cottage was structurally safe.

Monsoon heat and humidity rendered a shower almost a waste of time. Within seconds of slipping on a fresh shirt, Ben felt wet with sweat and almost as grubby as before. Nothing would, nothing could, dry out properly at this time of year in the sodden atmosphere of Bangladesh. The winds had turned north to bring their payload gathered from the Bay of Bengal. Almost every day from June to early October it rained. Rained is too soft a word, a deceptive description. Rain caused pain: spears of water stung skin like splinters of lightning.

Unlike the thousands of people in the crowded camp surviving inside flimsy tents, makeshift shacks and lean-to shelters, Ben would have the bungalow roof to sleep under. For some, in the lower levels of Mohpur camp, even if the rain failed to penetrate their roof of canvas, corrugated iron or banana tree leaves, by mid-evening the water level would rise to their knees. More drainage ditches were desperately needed. Abigale had decided organising a work party should be Ben's first task.

'Benji, are you ready?' Abi raised her voice to penetrate the bathroom door.

'One minute. Nearly done.'

'Get a wiggle on. It'll be dark soon.'

'Here I am, ready for the off,' he said, although still vigorously towelling his hair.

Ben stepped into Dak Cottage's living room, the only room habitable after last year's war. It also served as Action Delta's administration office, meeting area, kitchen, store room and the bedroom. Both single beds doubled as seating during the day for camp staff, volunteers and visitors.

'This tour could wait until the morning, Benji. The camp's not going anywhere. It's still pouring down.'

'I need a walk after being in the Land Rover all day. It's a long drive up from Chittagong. I'd like to get a sense of the place. And what's a bit of rain?'

'Besides a brolly you'll need your torch. I've got mine.' To prove it, Abi playfully flashed the beam into Ben's eyes. He grabbed his and up-lit his face pulling a spooky face. 'Bet we'll have a power cut soon, Benji. Most nights after a downpour the electricity packs up here. Doesn't come on again until the early hours. Sometimes not at all for a day or two. Frigging nuisance.'

Moonlight, interrupted by dark, angry, scudding clouds, provided enough ambient light for Abi and Ben to see the way, their torches only needed for shadowy nooks and crannies. The rain stopped as suddenly as it had started, eight hours earlier, around midday.

Abi took Ben to the main tented area, perhaps half a mile south of Dak Cottage. It would be here where more ditches needed to be dug. Many of the ghostly-grey canvas tents were torn or worn transparently thin. Tents with light inside, even a single candle, projected a person's silhouette to the world outside. At tent tagged D121, Abi asked if they could come inside. She had to repeat her question. On hearing a gruff response, *haan* in Urdu, she raised the flap and stepped inside. Ben followed. Where the canvas dipped at the edges, weighed down by pools of rainwater, he nor Abi could stand upright.

Both adult occupants stood, stick thin, silent and still. He was naked, apart from his lungi, a sarong-like cotton wrap from his waist to shins. Her sari allowed easy access for the baby to feed. But she was so emaciated, her breasts small and sagged, Abi and Ben doubted that a morsel of milk was forthcoming. The baby boy, unclothed, just months old, already displayed the distinctive signs of malnutrition: pot-belly, tight thin skin, hollow eyes and sunken cheeks. Perhaps the mother was sixteen. Tough to tell: hard life hardens skin, dulls eyes, makes the young old.

The girl displayed no sign of embarrassment at her exposure in front of strangers. Like many occupants at Mohpur, as Ben and Abi had witnessed elsewhere in poverty-stricken areas of the world, the girl had nothing more to lose, including her dignity. She lived as if in a trance, an almost permanent state of shock. Both aid workers knew it was the girl's way of coping with the horror of her life, its present, its past, its future. Don't think. Don't feel. Don't hope. Alive, but not living.

Abi pleaded with her to see the doctor in the morning. She didn't respond. Mother had eyes only for her baby: fixed, dilated in the semi-dark, despondent. But the husband flipped his head signalling that his wife would attend the clinic.

'Dr Rahman will be there from eight o'clock,' Abi said in Urdu. Her ability to speak the language had come on a lot since Ben last heard her three months earlier. 'We might also have powdered baby-milk delivered in the morning.'

The husband, presumably the baby's father, perhaps only in his forties, but looked sixty with his white hair and untidy bushy beard, again side-nodded acknowledging Abi's words.

'I bet they won't turn up,' Abi scoffed as they trudged through the mud to the lower end of the camp. 'Too frigging proud. Won't want to show everyone his wife can't feed their baby properly. And the next infection the baby gets will kill him, if the poor mite doesn't starve to death first.'

'We can only do what we can only do,' Ben sighed. 'What the…'

3

Ben stopped stone still – shocked.

'Sorry, Benji,' Abi giggled. 'Meant to warn you. Rats often swim across here at this time. Think the rising water level forces them out of their runs. Expect to see the odd snake too.'

Minutes later Abi and Ben found themselves knee-deep splashing through a soup of sewage.

'Abi, this stinks.'

'Thanks for stating the bleedin' obvious, Benji. Raw crap and piss and puss and… well, you know. Hopefully it will have subsided by morning, assuming we don't get any more rain overnight. Seen enough?'

'For one night, Abi, *haan*.'

'Ah, so your Urdu's improving.'

'Only a few words and phrases, I'm afraid. Not as good as yours.'

'With so few English speakers around, I had no choice but to learn pretty-damn fast. Camp workers help. I ask them to just speak Urdu, at least at first. It's a great way to learn the language – when you're frigging-well forced to.'

Approaching the bungalow, their legs caked in debris, Ben said gloomily, 'I need another shower. I've crap between my toes.'

'Me too,' groaned Abi. She looked at her feet and grimaced. 'Sandals need a wash too. But may I take this opportunity of reminding you, Mr Benjamin Altringham, that it was you who insisted on looking around the camp tonight. I'd have been happy to spend the evening eating and drinking without the trip to sewage city.'

'Oh so sorry, Miss Abigail Benvin,' Ben said, echoing her jokey mood. 'I didn't realise you'd prepared a five-course meal accompanied by a selection of fine wines. Or is there a Michelin-starred restaurant near here?'

'Stop fantasising, Benji. We will be eating the standard Mohpur meal. But don't complain. You have a choice of rice and dal or…' Abi waited for Ben's response.

'Or?'

'Dal and rice.' Abi laughed. 'There's a further choice.'

'Yes?' Ben feigned enthusiasm. 'Can't wait to hear what it is.'

'You may have one ladle or two. Three would be pushing it.'

'Of dal and rice?'

'No, don't be ridiculous, Benji, just rice. We have to ration things. We're never sure when the next food delivery will turn up. But don't despair. I do have a delicious accompaniment – my secret supply of Bell's. Black Label okay?'

'Beer?'

'Sure, I've a few bottles, but who wants warm beer? The fridge broke last month. Beyond repair. Anyway, look, as predicted the frigging electricity's off.'

Dak Cottage stood bathed in blue moonlight, half demolished, skeletal-like with twisted rods of iron stripped of concrete pointing in all directions.

'Abi, can I ask you a question?'

'Sure, but only if I know the answer.'

'Ever since I've known you – what's that, seven, eight years? – you've always liberally used "fucking". Now you're saying "frigging". Explain.'

'Easy. I don't want to offend anyone here. Whether they speak Bengali, Urdu, Hindi or some other language, they all know the fuck word.'

'But "frig" means the same – and more. If anything, it's ruder.'

'Sure, but it sounds more polite.'

Abi and Ben mounted the four concrete steps to Dak Cottage's veranda and front door. The moon cast enough light to show details of the property's scars of war. Bullets had peppered the walls, chipping off chunks of plaster, brick and breezeblock. A tank shell had destroyed both bedrooms and the kitchen. Most of the rubble had been salvaged by camp residents: when you have nothing, even broken bricks and beams become valuable, for building or burning.

After sunset voices became muted, even those of the children, as if darkness dragged a thick blanket over the area. At night most camp residents – Biharis, an Urdu-speaking ethnic minority group that many Bangladeshis considered collaborators with the former Pakistani regime – remained inside their canvas tents. They felt safer, although they realised they were far from safe. New arrivals, who hadn't yet been provided with a tent, made small shelters from scraps of plastic, usually discarded fertiliser bags, propped up with bamboo sticks. A few had built thin walls of mud with their bare hands, but these usually needed daily repairs following heavy rain. Branches and broad banana leaves formed a slanting roof. During darkness and downpours, many cooked on kerosene stoves, when fuel was available or affordable. The poorest of the poor burnt twigs, dried leaves and dung in scrapes in the ground, anything to heat rice or keep tea warm.

AFTER CURRIED LENTILS and boiled rice, cooked on a one-ring camping stove, Abi and Ben slumped into two of the office armchairs. So damaged, back in Britain they would have been scrapped, unworthy of sale in a junk shop. Abi refilled their tumblers with Bell's, the bottle already half empty. The night was hot, humid, oppressive, sapping the energy to talk.

Lacking electricity, the ceiling nor desk fan had the power to push air around the room. An occasional draught would have provided some respite, but the air did not stir. The oil lamp supplied low light, although its yellow flame added more unwelcome heat. Batteries were too expensive to use for long periods, and in short supply. Abi was convinced the ones she'd bought loose from the local stall-holder in nearby Tungipur town had been used before, despite his assurances.

A mosquito ring burned to repel the malaria-carrying bugs. But a few evaded the rising column of smoke, flying in low to extract dinner from Ben's ankles. Swollen with blood, the mossies would make tasty meals for the wall geckoes. It seemed every property in Bangladesh housed more lizards than people. Outside, in this flat damp land of many meandering rivers, ponds and ditches, thousands – nay, billions – of frogs, toads and cicadas formed a cacophonic orchestra. The volume rose and fell conducted, Ben believed, by the movement of clouds interrupting the bright blue moon. But he was still sober enough to realise it was probably the whisky doing the thinking.

'I don't believe we're doing any good here,' Abi said suddenly, slowly, breaking a period of drink-induced mellowness.

Her statement shocked Ben. Since freshers' week at King's, seven years earlier, Abi had been a vociferous campaigner against poverty in

6

developing countries. At the first meeting he attended with her, Abi had insisted on using the phrase 'de-developed countries', arguing many had been exploited and set-back as nations by colonialists. What those countries had, she reasoned, had been taken away. It's an insult to call them undeveloped or under-developed. Abi also rejected the term Third World, declaring there is only one world.

'Benji, we're getting even less food and medicines now in the camp than ever. We're told there's more coming in the country. But corrupt bastards are skimming off truckloads of supplies. Two miles up the road in Tungipur, all over the country, especially Dacca, they're selling aid food openly in the market. Traders don't even bother to put the stuff in their own frigging bags, even the corn soya milk powder.'

Since his arrival in Bangladesh three months earlier from Action Delta's aid work in Nigeria, Ben had seen sacks of CSM powder on sale everywhere – at street markets, shops, off the back of trucks, bullock carts and rickshaws. The stars and stripes logo of America's humanitarian aid agency, USAID, clearly emblazoned across the sacks. Doubtless the US government hopes to win hearts, minds and influence in exchange for its altruism. Whatever President Nixon's motive, CSM from the US was keeping hundreds of thousands alive. And making illegal traders rich.

Abi continued sounding defeated, contrary to her usual high-octane enthusiasm and optimism. Ben listened, still surprised – and concerned – by her change in attitude, her despondency. Perhaps it was the depressing impact of too much alcohol in too much suffocating heat.

'When I've challenged the frigging traders,' Abi slurred, 'they claim they've filled up empty USAID sacks. But no CSM comes into Bangladesh commercially. It's exclusively aid. None of it should be sold.'

Abi took another slug of Bell's, swilling it around like mouthwash before gulping it down. She could normally drink most people under the table. But tonight it got to her. Or perhaps alcohol had opened the door to release her true feelings.

'The police shrug their shoulders,' she said, sounding even gloomier. 'They look at me as if I'm mad, Benji. You can see them

7

thinking "You crazy English – *Ingreji*. Of course goods gets stolen, you stupid cow. That's the system here. Everyone takes a cut". And the cops are as corrupt as everyone else. Worse.'

'Surely not as bad as Nigerian cops.'

As if Ben hadn't spoken, Abi continued. 'We've about seven thousand Biharis here in Mohpur. Many of the local Bangladeshis hate their guts – and resent us for trying to help them. They're too scared to leave the camp. Every day groups of twenty, thirty, sometimes more, roll up. They need shelter, food, everything. But we can't feed or shelter all of the poor buggers already here. You know there's ten people to one tent in most of the camp out there. Just enough floor space for them to lie in – that's if the floor isn't flooded. And when it is, they just stand or squat. All bloody night, Benji. All bloody night. Standing. Squatting. Frozen in fear and apathy.'

After minutes of silence, as if those harsh facts needed time to be absorbed, Abi asked, 'Benji, am I going mad? I am, aren't I?'

'No, of course not. Just tired. Exhausted. You've been here coping with all this mess alone for months. All the stress and strain and conditions, it's bound to have affected you.'

'Yup, knackered, for sure. And as pissed as a newt.'

'Let's see what tomorrow brings.'

'The thing... the thing about tomorrow, Benji, is that... is that it's just another day with more opportunities to fuck things up. And do you want to know something else?'

'You're gonna tell me.'

'Damn right, Benji, I am.' Abi struggled out of the broken sofa and stood unsteadily, throwing the remaining whisky down her throat. 'Most of the world's frigging problems politicians pretend to solve are problems caused by frigging politicians in the first frigging place.'

'I wouldn't say "most",' Ben responded limply. 'But certainly many.' It was too late in the night and both too inebriated to argue over a word, however significant.

Abi staggered across the room, accidentally kicking the empty whisky bottle. It spun like helicopter blades across the floor smashing into the wall. Shards of shattered glass splayed everywhere.

Approaching her bed Abi fell on her knees, her upper body flopping unconscious onto the thin mattress, her head face down.

Ben couldn't leave her slumped like that. But it took all his strength to lift her dead-limp body fully onto the bed. Before unravelling Abi's mosquito net, Ben, as a precaution, manoeuvred her into the recovery position. Just in case. At college they both knew a student who drowned in her own vomit after a pub crawl in Cambridge. After checking Abi's net had no gaps for the mossies to sneak through, Ben extinguished the lamp and swayed across the room to his bed. Like Abi, he was too drained to undress – or sweep up the shards of glass strewn across the floor.

TWO

Shrapnel caused Dr Abdur Rahman's limp. He had been treating casualties while a battle raged outside. When the rocket-propelled grenade smashed through the window and exploded he was rendered unconscious. His assistant died instantly. Junior surgeon Dr Abu Hasan was stood in front of Abdur and took the full force of the blast. Such is fate. Nobody tells a grenade where its fragments strike. Red-hot metal piercing your leg lets you to live; to the head, you die.

Their patient, a girl aged about eight, whose rubble-crushed leg they were forced to amputate, died too. There was no-one left conscious in the makeshift operating theatre, in the carcass of a bombed-out school, to stop her bleeding out.

The war had killed at least a million. Perhaps two. The new government claimed three. Nobody knew for sure. Nobody could know for sure. Many girls traditionally were never registered at birth. And when whole villages are obliterated, there is no-one left to count the dead. Or know of the dead. Or even care about the dead. Fire, flood and decay had destroyed records. Men of power in the old regime burnt files too, like Nazis trying to hide their crimes in concentration camps twenty-six years earlier. No inventory means no accountability. No proof, no prosecution. No eyewitnesses, no-one to bear witness.

'Abi, my dear, good morning,' said Dr Rahman, with his infectious smile and wave of hand. 'I see our queue for today's clinic is longer than ever.'

'I'm so sorry, Dr Rahman, we took in another batch yesterday. About thirty. Half of them looked in a pretty bad state. Soldiers turned them back at the Indian border, near Darsana they said.'

'Never mind, my dear. As always we'll do what we can do. Did the medicines and other bits and pieces arrive?'

'Thankfully, yes, an hour ago. Masaad is unpacking the boxes now in the office. He'll bring the medicines and dressings in a few minutes.'

Sixty or so patients had started queuing at sunrise, nearly two hours earlier. They had little else to do, apart from struggle for survival, and nowhere to go. It was dangerous to venture far from the campsite. Five months after Bangladesh's 'War of Liberation' ended, Biharis still faced hostility from some locals. Revenge attacks remained rife.

The women waited standing or squatting in ragged saris, the men in cotton lungis and white shirts or vests. Their children and the orphans played nearby. There was little shade from the dazzling sun, now high in the sky. Even where a tree or building broke the sun's rays to cast shade, there was no hiding from the energy-sapping humidity. During monsoon season the clammy moisture penetrated every crevice and corner day and night without respite.

Dr Rahman's routine was to walk along the queue selecting those he felt needed the most urgent treatment. Triage, he called it. He gently steered the most needy to the front of the line. Sometimes those not selected started to protest. Everyone's condition is, to themselves, the most serious. But Dr Rahman's quiet and polite manner invariably managed to assuage their frustration. 'I promise I will see you,' he said. 'Please be patient.'

Dr Rahman was born in East Bengal under British rule. But having lived and studied medicine in Karachi, West Pakistan, he spoke Urdu as fluently as Biharis in the camp. He was one of the few Bangladeshis Biharis trusted. There was however growing resentment in Tungipur, mainly from disaffected young men, about the doctor helping 'traitorous' Biharis. These 'collaborators' should be back in India or go to Pakistan, they said. Or dead.

Mohpur camp's clinic was the size of a two-car garage, its former function, built to the side of Dak Cottage. It had miraculously survived the war unscathed. Masaad, Dr Rahman's 'medical assistant' – he hated being called a nurse, believing it lowered his status – had already opened the doors and brought forward a chair and trestle table for the doctor. Towards the back of the clinic stood two free-standing screens, on loan from a hospital in Dacca, Bangladesh's capital, twelve miles to the south. Behind the screens the doctor conducted any necessary intimate examinations. With female patients, Faiyaz, whose pharmacology studies were interrupted at the outbreak of the war in March 1970, would accompany Dr Rahman. For women and girls who did not want a male doctor examining them, Faiyaz would carefully and sensitively inspect the patient and report her observations to Dr Rahman. Diagnosis by proxy was better than no diagnosis at all. Faiyaz would meanwhile be dispensing medicines, if supplies hadn't become exhausted. She would also explain to patients how to dress wounds, apply ointments and take their medicines correctly.

Many patients would, to the medical team's frustration, take their tablets in one go instead of every four hours, or twice daily, or as instructed. It was widely rumoured that swallowing all the tablets together would fight the disease better. One man threw five day's supply of antibiotics into his mouth as he walked away from the surgery. Faiyaz chased after him, but it was too late. Fortunately he didn't suffer any adverse reaction, apart from severe stomach pain and vomiting. Some patients sold their medicines, often to those who didn't need them, or for a condition the medicine would not help. Money, to buy cigarettes, paan to chew, or a little extra food from traders walking around the camp's perimeter selling coconuts or bananas, was placed ahead of their own health. These misplaced activities put an extra burden on Faiyaz and 'medical assistant' Masaad: it became necessary to dispense medicines daily at the clinic and see they were taken correctly.

Abi noticed the young mother she asked the previous night to visit the clinic was not in the queue. 'I'll leave you to it, Dr Rahman, I need to find someone whose child needs urgent treatment. And by the way, Ben's arrived at last. I'll bring him to meet you later.'

'That's very good, my dear, another pair of hands to help you will be much appreciated. Cheerio for now.' Dr Rahman rested his stethoscope on the table and called forward his first patient of the day.

He listened to the recessed chest of a tall, skeletal man, whose ribs could be counted easily. Not that Dr Rahman needed to count ribs to confirm his diagnosis. He'd witnessed thousands of cases of tuberculosis and it was a growing infection amongst the poor generally. But he needed to assess the extent of the damage to the man's lungs and other organs. Even if they had antibiotics, they were increasingly less effective against TB because of growing resistance. Dr Rahman was angry at the common practice across the country to dole out antibiotics for almost every ailment. 'So many people think they're a cure-all,' he often complained. 'I've even admonished colleagues for prescribing ABs for viral infections. I know of patients who bought them for headaches.'

Antibiotics should be prescribed by a doctor, according to the law. But almost every pharmacy across the subcontinent ignored the rule and sold them openly over the counter. Dr Rahman had also come across vitamin pills which had been repackaged and labelled antibiotics.

Abi arrived at tent D121 seeking the young mother. The girl nor her baby were there. Her husband was resting on his bedroll. Without sitting up, seemingly indifferent to what was going on, he told Abi that his wife was collecting water. Annoyed at his laziness, Abi wanted to ask why *he* wasn't collecting water. Or at least caring for *his* son. But she held back. He'd say it was his wife's duty, women's work. Abi was also aware that because hundreds of women in the camp had been raped – by fighters on all sides – some men doubted any recently-born child was truly theirs. A number of men *knew* the child couldn't possibly be theirs. But because of the shame they felt, and for appearance's sake, they carried on.

At the standpipe, with child in one arm and holding a plastic bucket in the other, the girl was near the back of the queue. Abi grabbed the bucket and asked the women in front if she could use the pump next so they get to the clinic quickly. They obliged with kind gestures and looks of concern. It took only a few pushes on the pump handle to draw sufficient water to fill the bucket. After leaving the water inside the girl's tent, with no word of thanks or acknowledgement from the motionless husband, Abi escorted the girl and baby to the clinic.

Dr Rahman examined the infant immediately. Behind the young mother, with her head down looking at her son, the doctor looked at

Abi and shook his head slowly. Knowing the girl could not understand English, Dr Rahman told Abi that even if they could fly the baby to Great Ormond Street Hospital in London, where he'd worked for two years as a registrar, or another specialist children's hospital in the US or Germany, the child couldn't be saved. The baby wouldn't survive the flight. His key organs had deteriorated too far to recover. Only hours left, I'm afraid, not days. Strangely, to Abi at least, the baby didn't appear distressed. Lifeless, before the loss of life itself.

As Dr Rahman discharged his last patient of the day, Ben approached the clinic. He'd returned from the lower camp surveying where best to dig new drainage trenches. Abi hurried to intercept him out of earshot of the doctor.

'Will you walk home with Abdur?' she whispered. 'He often walks instead of driving. It's good exercise, he says. But I wish he'd drive all the time.'

'Why? Does he need help? I see he's limping.'

'No, it's not his leg,' Abi said. 'He's been threatened by local yobs. He pooh-poohs them. But I'm not so sure. I'm told – not by him – his house was daubed with red paint a few days ago. A blatant threat. Intimidation at least.'

'I know some Bangladeshis have made revenge attacks on Biharis for siding with the former regime. But surely they wouldn't attack one of their own.'

'They do here and elsewhere if they're helping Biharis. That's why I've been walking back with him recently.'

'What, acting as a guard?'

'We have pleasant chats. But, yes, he's sussed out what I'm up to. But I think he'd enjoy your company. And it would stop the stupid gossip.'

Ben wrinkled his brow, intrigued, questioning.

'Some of the yobs we walk past shout that I pay for his medical services here with sex. Crap, of course. They're just trying to make trouble. Abdur is a lovely, generous, kind family man who wants to help. But I see it upsets him. And rumours spread like smallpox in this country.'

Abdur Rahman approached extending his hand. 'Ben, I assume. Delighted to meet you. Abigail has been taking on far too much by herself. I have no doubt you will greatly reduce her burden helping to run the aid programme.'

'We employ about twelve helpers, Abdur,' said Abi, adopting his first name now he was off duty, as he'd requested. 'So I'm hardly single-handed.'

'Yes, yes, my dear. But it's so much better to have an old friend with you with whom you can speak frankly and share life's little problems. Abi tells me, Ben, that you were at university together.'

'That's right, doctor. We first met swimming in the River Cam one evening with some mutual friends. That was – what? – seven years ago now.'

Ben omitted to say it was a raucous alcohol-soaked pot-smoking skinny-dipping session behind Clare College. Abi shot a knowing look at Ben, relieved he didn't elaborate.

'And you have also worked in the aid business with charities for a while.'

'Only two years, doctor, since 1970, working in Nigeria after the Biafran uprising.'

'Ah, another man-made tragedy,' said Dr Rahman, shaking his head slowly. 'Such a shame people can't resolve differences without resorting to violence. Just like here. East Pakistan against West Pakistan. Bihari Urdu speakers against we Bengali-speaking Bangladeshis. As your former prime minister Sir Winston wisely said, jaw-jaw is always better than war-war. But, alas, one key lesson of history is that we rarely learn from it.'

After a short pause for reflection, Abi lightened the mood. 'Ben would like to walk into Tungipur with you this afternoon – to have a look round the place.'

'Oh Abigail, my dear, you don't fool me,' Dr Rahman gave a little laugh. 'I really don't need anyone to ride shotgun to and from my home.'

'But…'

Dr Rahman raised the palms of both hands to stop Abi saying more. If Ben genuinely would like to see Tungipur, he would be delighted to show him its key features. But he didn't need a bodyguard.

He explained to Ben that the 'empty threats' came from a few disaffected Bangladeshi freedom fighters in the area. They're called Mukti Bahini. Contrary to their expectations, these former guerrillas haven't benefitted from the war. For most FFs, as Dr Rahman called them, if they were poor before the war, they've remained so afterwards. Those who already had good political connections have moved further up the greasy political pole. And the wealthy have become wealthier. What's new? Dr Rahman asked, not expecting an answer.

Dr Rahman and Ben set off to town, clearly enjoying each other's company.

'Tungipur is only a small town, Ben. There's a lot of bomb and shell damage, especially to the Victorian railway station, built in 1895. Much track and rolling stock was damaged during the fighting too. At least some engines have been repaired. All steam. I love travelling by steam train, don't you?'

'Couldn't agree more, Dr Rahman. They're machines, for sure, but more like living breathing beings huffing and puffing and spluttering. But in Britain now electric and diesels have more or less replaced steam.'

THREE

In Tungipur's people-packed litter-strewn streets, more mud, dust and dirt than tarmacadam, merchants stood behind small wooden stalls. Less successful traders, unable to afford a cart, squatted on the ground amidst their wares. Goats wandered around hoping to snatch a scrap of food. Traders had to constantly shoo them away. Hens, some with a string of chirping chicks in tow, pecked at spilt grain. Mange-infested sand-coloured feral dogs, not one without scars or seeping sores from fights, slept in the fusty air. Within an hour or two the gathering clouds will start dropping the daily dose of monsoon rain. Ben regretted not bringing an umbrella.

Most stallholders sold only a handful of items. One man displayed mangoes. Just mangoes. But wonderful varieties such as alfonsos, kesars and neelams. Across the Indian sub-continent, from west to east, Karachi to Chittagong, every grower claimed their mangoes were the world's tastiest. His neighbour sold lychees and breadfruit. Another, bananas. All kinds. Long, heavy bunches of green fingers freshly cut from the tree to over-ripe, brown, mottled specimens.

'*Kola manush?*' Ben eyed Dr Rahman for confirmation.

'Very good, Ben. Yes, he's the banana man. '*Apni Bangla bolte paren?*'

Ben replied hesitantly to the doctor's question. '*Ami kichu kichu jani. Ami ekhane nuton.*'

'Well done, Ben,' said Dr Rahman, 'You may speak a little Bengali. But that's not bad, considering you've only been in the country three months. Of course working with Biharis you'll need Urdu, although many of them speak Bengali too, certainly understand it.'

Sporting a colossal girth stretching his white vest to bursting point, one trader sat on a chair behind sacks of rice. To him his inflated belly was a symbol of success, displayed as proudly as his gold necklace and ring-festooned fat fingers. His Victorian-age seesaw scales, balancing two brass pans dangling on chains, had been placed on an upturned wooden box. Weights of various sizes shaped like chess pawns stood ready to measure the grain. A wizen old women dressed in a widow-white sari, bent low with arthritic bones, asked for a portion of wholegrain. Dr Rahman told Ben she was asking for one ounce. One ounce. Just enough to fill the palm of a hand. With her thin voice, she haggled over the price. More than yesterday, she complained. Fat man shrugged his shoulders and threatened to pour the portion back into the sack if she couldn't pay. But the widow, who appeared to have once known dignity, was compelled to accept the inflation. Or go hungry. Or buy a single banana. Scales of rice delivering an imbalance of justice, Ben thought. Her bony fingers, trembling, searched her small purse to find an extra coin.

As Abi had reported, several sacks were emblazoned with the unmistakable logo of America's humanitarian aid agency, USAID. Ben turned to Dr Rahman, and the doctor knew precisely what he was thinking. 'Yes, Ben, despite the efforts of many, I'm ashamed to say it is the way of things here. All the way through the distribution channels, the corrupt take their cut.'

'Same in Nigeria,' complained Ben. 'All over Africa. South America. Soviet Union. Asia. So many fraudulent leaders around the globe who allow this. It's outrageous.'

'You have the anger and fervour of youth, Ben,' Dr Rahman said kindly. 'I hope you can maintain that zeal throughout life to fight injustice. Alas, there's always someone who wants more than their fair share – land, gold, gems, silver, slaves. Hitler, Kaiser Wilhelm, the Romans, William of Normandy. So, so many. Likewise the empire builders – French, Spanish, Germans, Italians, Russians, Chinese. And, of course, the British.'

'The East India Company.'

'At first, yes, followed by the British state itself.'

As they ambled stall to stall, it seemed almost everyone in Tungipur knew Dr Rahman. Many offered the universal Muslim greeting of '*as-salamu alaykum*' and he echoed in kind, 'and peace be with you'.

Ben assumed some had been his patients in Tungipur's Salauddin Hospital or attended his general practice. Whatever Abi had said about some locals disliking the doctor working with Biharis in the camp, the resentment clearly wasn't widespread.

As expected, the gathering storm-clouds quickly and comprehensively blocked out the mid-afternoon sun. Everyone accepted this signalled the day's deluge. Even the sleepy street dogs roused themselves to find cover. Shopkeepers and street traders hurriedly gathered their goods under shelter as the first weighty drops struck the dusty ground. When the fresh rain fell, the musty smell of earth rose.

The dal woman speedily pulled a tarpaulin above her jute sacks of dried lentils, split peas and beans. The spice trader closed the flaps of his hut to stop any rain blowing in. His panch foran, the essential five spices of Bengali cooking – black mustard, cumin, fennel, fenugreek and nigella – alongside other herbs and spices were herded together, cosseted like tots at a nursery.

'Think I need to rush back to the camp, Dr Rahman,' said Ben, bending forward protecting his eyes from the increasingly heavy raindrops.

The doctor shook his head. 'I have a better idea. Come.'

FOUR

'Sorry, so sorry, Ben, please forgive me,' pleaded Dr Rahman. 'This damn leg of mine slows me down. As a result we are now soaked to the skin because of my tardiness. Come in. Come in.'

The doctor's spacious three-storey house stood on the southern edge of Tungipur. The house and grounds were encircled by a six-foot whitewashed wall, the top of which undulated like distant sea waves, gradually rising and falling. They entered through a heavy wrought iron gate, unlocked by one of the family's servants. He had rushed forward opening an umbrella to shelter them both. But it was too late to be of use.

Lime, lemon, mango and tall coconut trees filled the outer rim of the compound. Manicured lawns sported beds of roses, all tidy, sharp edged, weed free. Golden marigolds, cerise geraniums and cobalt blue lobelia burst from lines of clay pots on either side of the pathway leading to the house. A spectacular floral display, even under these dour, dark clouds. Sweet scents of jasmine, gardenia and honeysuckle merged to generate a heady atmosphere, enhanced by the fresh rainfall.

After mounting the few steps to the veranda, Ben and the doctor shook themselves like long-haired dogs after a swim. To little effect. Their soaked clothes remained clung to their skin. 'Let's get inside, Ben, and change. I'll find you something to wear while we dry your garments.'

'Abdur, my darling, you are absolutely soaked, quick, quick, come.' The woman's voice could be heard approaching along the hallway. She opened the mesh door, employed to keep insects at bay, but pulled up suddenly, surprised at seeing someone with her husband.

'Amma, this is Ben,' said Dr Rahman quelling her surprise, as they both removed their shoes at the threshold. 'He's come to work with Abi for Action Delta.'

Raina Rahman's smile instantly radiated warmth and friendliness, just like her husband's. Ben was immediately entranced. She was slim, elegant, breathtakingly beautiful and appeared to glide rather than walk in her multicoloured large-patterned sari. Ben also noted she was taller than most Bangladeshi women, a good five foot eight.

'Very pleased to meet you, Ben. You too must come inside quickly and dry yourself,' she stood aside gently waving him into the hallway. 'My darling husband should have known better than to keep you out when the rains were due. I rather suspect he spent too much time chatting with people in the marketplace. I call it his street surgery. He's too nice to shoo them off to the hospital or tell them to make an appointment.'

Mrs Rahman turned and called for Natcoo, the bearer. She whispered to him and he nodded his understanding. Within half a minute Natcoo reappeared carrying two large towels. After Dr Rahman and Ben dried their hair and faces, Dr Rahman led Ben upstairs into a bedroom. He opened a huge dark-wood wardrobe, ornately carved with scenes from rural life in Bengal: bullocks pulling two-wheeled carts; a family planting rice in paddy fields; fishermen casting nets from sampans and canoes; a tiger head peering through thick jungle at a river's edge.

Sliding hangers left and right along the rail, like a clothes shop assistant, Dr Rahman eventually selected a pair of trousers and a shirt for Ben. Spying several lungis folded neatly on a shelf, Ben said he'd be happy to wear one. But it was too late, Dr Rahman had found trousers and a shirt. Like most Bangladeshis, Abdur Rahman was shorter than Ben's six foot, and with a more expansive waistline. He described it as 'comfortable', although far from obese. It didn't bother Ben that the trousers were loose around the waist; the belt from his own pair secured them adequately. The shirt too was hanging loose. But in monsoon conditions, when clothes glued themselves to skin, tight fits were best avoided.

Leaving Dr Rahman to change, Ben returned downstairs and entered the spacious square living room. He was alone and, for a moment, at a loss of what to do. Each wall displayed tasteful artwork: some old and traditional, others in a modern, highly coloured style, mainly of country scenes, dancers and musical instruments. Tapestries adorned all around. One wall was devoted to what were clearly family photographs. Besides contemporary pictures in colour, one, in monochrome of Dr Rahman, dated 1931, showed him receiving a certificate, presumably his first medical qualification. Older sepia photographs, one of a married couple dated 1898 and taken in Calcutta, the man standing, the woman sitting, was perhaps Dr Rahman's parents, or those of Mrs Rahman.

Flip-flops patting the beige tiles announcing his approach, Natcoo arrived with a tray. He placed a pot of tea, cups and saucers on a large, square, low table in the centre of the room. He smiled at Ben and invited him to sit. Natcoo vanished but soon returned with an assortment of Bengali treats. Ben had already tasted rasgullas, languishing in sugary syrup, alongside other delights he couldn't name. Another servant entered, about the same age as Natcoo, Ben guessed both were aged about fifty. Ben was shocked when he later discovered this was Ali, the cook. How could he make all these delicious sweets and remain twig-thin? How could he resist dipping his spoon into a sugary syrup to taste the mix? Such self-control.

Mrs Rahman entered and Ben started to stand as a sign of respect. With the wave of a hand she signalled to Ben to remain seated. She had changed her bright patterned sari for deep purple with an embroidered red border. Relaxed day dress to formal evening attire, Ben wondered.

'Is this your first visit to our country?'

'Yes, Mrs Rahman.'

'Perhaps May is not the best time of year to arrive, with the monsoon and humidity and all,' Mrs Rahman said.

'I actually arrived in February – from an aid project in Nigeria. Since then I've been helping Action Aid's work near Chittagong. We drove up from there yesterday.'

'Yes, my husband tells me Abi does need extra help. More Biharis arrive every day, he says. They're flocking together from towns and villages because of the terrible harassment they are suffering. We all lived peacefully before, it's time we did so again.'

'Same in Nigeria after the civil war, Mrs Rahman. So much resentment and many revenge attacks after the Ibo in Biafra declared independence.'

'Bangladesh is a baby. We're only five months old and have not, as yet, learnt to walk. We're hardly crawling. It will take time for stability to arrive. Now, Ben, let's turn to a happy topic. Coffee? Tea? With or without milk and sugar?'

As if from nowhere, like rabbits from a magician's hat, Natcoo appeared to serve tea and Ali conjured up more plates of biscuits and confectionary.

'Excellent. Marvellous. Just the ticket,' enthused Dr Rahman returning to the room rubbing his hands. 'Refreshment. Much needed fluid and food after our tour of Tungipur, eh Ben?' Continuing in English, he thanked Natcoo and Ali for serving the refreshment. Looking at the cook, who stood wearing a broad smile, exposing a missing tooth, the doctor added, 'I swear we have in Ali the best cook in Tungipur for traditional sweetmeats. You'll love them. And unlike me, Ben, you clearly don't have to watch this.' He patted his stomach.

Mrs Rahman handed Ben a plate and fork and, with a sweep of her arm over the ever-growing number of dishes Natcoo and Ali presented, invited him to help himself. She and her husband sat directly opposite on one of the four four-seater settees surrounding the table of treats. Ben knew such a polite couple would not eat until he himself started.

'What would you like?' asked Mrs Rahman. She saw Ben eyeing one of the dishes. 'My favourite too,' she said. 'Cham-cham.' She placed two of the log-shaped desserts on his plate.

'Where are the girls, Amma?' Dr Rahman asked.

'They'll be here soon,' she replied. 'It's not quite five o'clock.'

Ben glanced at his watch to confirm it was five minutes to the hour.

'Have you told them we have a guest?'

'Of course not. Their studies should not be interrupted.'

'Amma, my dear, a few minutes won't make the difference between success and failure in life.'

'It might,' asserted Mrs Rahman, pleasantly. 'You never know.' She turned to Ben while setting her palm towards her husband. 'And he's the one who drafted their home-study timetable,' she said affectionately.

It was obvious to Ben that Dr and Mrs Rahman remained very much in love after perhaps thirty years of marriage. More tea was poured and Ben was constantly encouraged to eat. Try this. Taste that. You must have one of these. More tea?

Shortly after five, giggles and a good-humoured argument could be heard in the long hallway leading to the far end of the house. Ben believed the voices belonged to young girls, eleven or twelve year-olds. The animated debate was about the musical merits of the Rolling Stones compared with the Beatles. As they approached, the words became distinct.

'The Stones are not as melodic as the Beatles.'

'Nonsense. Just because it's heavy rock doesn't mean it's less tuneful.'

'Lennon and McCartney's harmonies are far richer than Jagger and Richard's.'

'That's not the case at all...oh!'

Ayesha and Bushra stopped statue still when they set eyes on Ben. And he swallowed hard to suppress a cough when one of the sweetmeats jammed in his throat. He was surprised when both young women entered the room. He later learnt one was twenty-two, a fourth-year medical student; the other was nineteen, studying philosophy, politics and economics at Dacca University and in her first year. Both wore printed cotton salwar kameez with a scarf draped loose around their shoulders.

'Come, sit down,' Dr Rahman instructed his daughters. 'This is Ben. Remember I mentioned he was coming to work alongside Abi at the camp. We became caught in the rain, which arrived a little earlier today than usual I believe.'

The sisters sat close together on the settee to the side, as if joined at the hip. 'This is Ayesha,' said Mrs Rahman, identifying the one nearer to Ben. 'And this is Bushra.' They nodded to Ben and, coyly, said hello almost simultaneously. Even though the doctor's family were clearly liberal-minded and completely aware of 'western' etiquette, Ben knew he should not offer a handshake. In any case, he was encumbered, carefully balancing a plate of Ali's delicacies on his knees.

The phone rang. Natcoo came in to answer. 'Okay. *Thik ache.* Okay Miss. For you Mr Ben.'

'It must be Abi,' said Dr Rahman. Ben looked surprised.

'*Ji,*' Natcoo confirmed.

Ben placed his plate on the table and took the call.

Dr Rahman and Mrs Rahman, Ayesha and Bushra, heard the urgency in Abi's voice, though the words were indistinct. They shot worried looks to each other. Their fears were confirmed.

'I'm sorry to be so rude, but I need to get back to the camp straight away,' Ben said. His face could not disguise his distress.

'I'll come too,' said Dr Rahman as he, his wife and daughters stood sharing Ben's concern. 'We'll go in the car.'

'That won't be necessary, Dr Rahman. Honestly. Thanks. But it's a personal matter.'

Dr Rahman raised his eyebrows seeking details.

'It's Abi's boyfriend. In Dacca. He's been admitted to hospital.'

The doctor wanted more.

'He's been…' Ben, looking at Ayesha, then Bushra, hesitated. 'In an accident. An incident really.'

After thanking the family for their generous hospitality, and again refusing to be driven, Ben rushed upstairs and quickly changed back into his damp, although no longer soaking wet, clothes. Dr Rahman worried that Ben might be unable to find his way back to Dak Cottage and offered to send someone with him. But Ben was certain of the direction. He remembered the post office, the *daak ghar,* was to his right and the road was straight thereafter.

Natcoo presented Ben with a large black umbrella for protection against the continuing downpour, and a torch. 'No light after this road,' he advised. Ben thanked him, *apnake dhonnobad*, for the brolly, torch, and for serving tea. Natcoo appreciated the curtesy with a shake of his head.

As Ben prepared to step into the heavy rain, Dr Rahman blocked the doorway before directing Ben along the veranda to avoid his family overhearing. 'Now, please tell the full story. And can I help? I know many very good physicians in Dacca.'

'Jonny's been stabbed,' Ben said. He had to repeat the news, raising his voice to counter the thunderous rain crashing down on the veranda roof. 'Attacked by some former freedom fighters for helping Biharis at the camp in Dacca.'

'Oh, poor Jonny. I met him a few times when he visited Abi. Nice fellow. Is he badly hurt?'

Ben hesitated. 'He's dead.'

FIVE

Abi's head was in her hands, slumped on the edge of her bed when Ben arrived. He was panting heavily, having ran most of the two miles from Dr Rahman's, constantly slipping on the muddy tracks and fighting against the driving rain. Stood at the living room door watching Abi, Ben hesitated, unsure of what to say, of what to do.

Abi, slowly, looked up, her face wet with tears, eyes raw with sadness. Ben rushed forward and knelt in front of her taking her hands in his. For a few minutes, nothing was said, nothing was done. Motionless in grief, time meaningless.

'I'm going into Dacca tonight,' Abi eventually said, breathing deeply, taking control of her emotions. 'Syed's bringing the Land Rover. He'll be here soon. He's topping up with petrol. He said the roads will be treacherous, flooded in parts, but he'll try and get through. I know it's only twelve miles, but in this weather, on these lousy roads, it could take hours.'

'I'll come with you.'

'No, thanks Benji,' Abi said firmly. 'I'll be okay. Richard and Bernice are at the office. They'll come with me to the hospital... or to wherever Jonny's body is.'

'If you're sure.'

'You're needed here. There's a delivery of two standpipes expected in the morning. The truck drivers won't accept a signature from our staff or volunteers. There's also a food delivery coming sometime. Then there's the drainage ditches in zone D to extend and don't forget about...'

'Hey, hey, come on Abi, don't worry about that stuff now. I'll muddle through until... well, until you're back.'

Immediately the thought struck him – and Abi – that she may not return for some time, if ever, recalling her despondency about aid work the previous night. She'd probably want to fly back to Britain with Jonny's body. If so, she would attend the funeral in Brighton, his home town. With a murder investigation under way, how long would the police retain the body for forensic examinations? Presumably the British High Commission would help arrange for Jonny's remains to be repatriated.

But since Action Delta first arrived in Bangladesh at the end of the war in December 1970, the newly-formed charity had found staff at the Foreign and Commonwealth Office pretty useless. AD's founder, Richard, described them as snobs more interested in garden parties than doing anything useful.

Syed sounded the Land Rover's horn. Abi rushed to pack a few things into her rucksack. At the door she suddenly stopped and turned to face Ben.

'I'm sorry, Ben,' she said slowly, quietly. When she addressed him as Ben not Benji, he knew she was being serious.

'What are you talking about? You've nothing to apologise for, Abi. I can manage here for a few days. Longer if need be. Forget about Mohpur. Hey, even forget about me!' he added, forcing a smile. 'Just sort out stuff for Jonny and his family back in Britain.'

'No, it's not that,' she said. 'I meant to tell you, as soon as you'd settled in. But you need to know before I go.'

The car horn sounded again, driver Syed expressing more urgency. Rain continued to hammer down. He knew many of the roads would be impassable, maybe all of them. At best he'd be driving at walking speed. They wouldn't reach central Dacca until dawn, Syed was certain of that.

'Whatever it is, Abi, I'm sure it can wait.'

'No, Ben, it can't. You have a right to know, and know now, especially after what's happened to Jonny.'

Ben looked puzzled.

Abi pointed towards the desk. 'Look in the buff folder in the bottom draw, the one to the right. You'll see what I mean.'

'Okay. Will do. You be off. Take care of yourself. See you when I see you.'

They hugged and kissed goodbye and Abi, head down against the storm, climbed in the Land Rover alongside Syed. Ben waved, but doubted Abi could see through the curtain of rain. He also shouted, suggesting Abi get some sleep during the journey. But the rain pounding the car roof made it impossible to hear. Syed had the wipers on full speed, although no match against the deluge. It would be a four-wheel low-gear crawl most of the way to Action Delta's office in central Dacca.

YOU GO OR YOU DIE. Written in red, it was the first toxic note Ben read. Blots of ink had been deliberately squeezed from the fountain pen to crudely represent drops of blood. 'You bad as Bihari pigs you help,' a different hand scrawled. The next poisonous letter Ben found in the folder was worse, far worse. It described in blood-curdling detail the appalling rape and sexual torture they would inflict on Abi '…then cut off head to throw in shit'.

Ben's stomach spun over and over mixing outrage with fear. He held back being sick, but bile stuck in his throat. The stifling hot room suddenly seemed bitterly cold. He shivered, and his senses heightened, aware of every noise and smell and movement.

He started reading another malicious missive when the lights went out. The ceiling fan shuddered to a stop. Ben felt a bolt of terror. But it was emotion overtaking logic. This was simply another routine power cut. An outage, to use the jargon. During the civil war Bangladesh's infrastructure was all but destroyed. Many generating stations and sub-stations suffered damage. At night torches were always kept to hand and matches at the ready to light lamps and candles. By a timely coincidence, the storm stopped pounding the ground outside, rattling the windows and bending the tall palms. It was as though the wind and clouds in the sky were powered by generators on earth and suffered the power cut too. All went still and silent. It wasn't long before the orchestra of cicadas and amphibians started to play.

With only the moon and stars casting their shadows and ghostly glow, Ben considered lighting a paraffin lamp and reading the remaining sickening notes. Abi had received about a dozen of them.

But it was approaching midnight. He'd been up since strong sunlight sliced through gaps in the broken venetian blinds. It was time to sleep. Or try to.

Dr Rahman had dismissed the threats he'd received as 'empty'. Jonny's murder proved otherwise. Ben couldn't clear his head of the menacing messages addressed to Abi. How amazingly brave of her to have stayed in the camp following these terror threats. The constant stress and fear she must have endured in recent months must have been immense – especially at night, here, alone in this room. Yet Abi put the care of Biharis before her personal safety, and while keeping the intimidation secret. Perhaps, Ben reasoned, it explains the unexpected despondency she expressed last night when the whisky oiled her tongue.

Before opening his bedroll and lowering the mosquito net, Ben checked he'd locked the door. Unlike last night, when Abi was with him and they relaxed after emptying the Bell's, he slid both black iron bolts across the door, top and bottom.

It was a restless night. Dreamless, but full of nightmarish thoughts.

SIX

It was Mrs Rahman's idea to invite Ben for dinner the following Saturday. He will need company in Abi's absence, she told her husband. Furthermore, he is almost as thin as many of our poor. Needs feeding up. He could not be eating properly, she scoffed. His mother would be distraught if she were to see him in this state. He cannot look after others if he cannot look after himself.

'Mrs Rahman,' Ben declared while stretching upright in his chair, 'thank you so much. I can honestly say that is the best meal I've had in months, if not years.'

'You are very welcome, young man. And there's more. Ali has made something special. He knows every Englishman likes…'

Bushra, wearing a pale pink silk sari, her sister in deep blue, interrupted excitedly. 'Make Ben guess, Ma.'

'Yes, good idea Bushra,' Ayesha chipped in. 'Have a guess what Ali's cooked up.'

Ben played the game, pretending to think deeply with a Rodin-like pose before answering. 'Rice pudding.'

'Since when was rice grown in England?' Bushra said with a touch of sarcasm.

'Well, never, I suppose. But it's probably our favourite pud.'

'Was rice another product appropriated from India by the British?' Bushra asked, this time with a sharper edge.

'Now, now, Bushra,' Dr Rahman said firmly. 'Let's not get into politics.'

'Abba, I was simply asking Ben a question to determine historical fact.'

'Yes, my dear. But I know where you are leading. I know the trees you like to bark at. Ben is a guest in our home and we do not make guests feel uncomfortable.'

Bushra, petulant, started speaking Bengali. Mrs Rahman cut her short immediately. 'English, Bushra. Only English.'

Fire remained in the younger sister's eyes. She fell silent, brooding, focussing on the remaining food on her plate.

Ayesha broke what seemed like minutes of tension, but really just a few seconds. 'Well, Ben,' she said, smiling, 'eliminating *rice* from the list of possible puddings, another guess?'

ON THEIR DRIVE to his home in Tungipur after the day's clinic, when thirty-four patients had been examined, Dr Rahman revealed that Ayesha wanted to specialise in neurosurgery after qualifying. He seemed in no doubt she'd pass all her exams.

'She has excellent spatial ability and delicate movement,' Dr Rahman said. 'Essential for brain and spinal cord work. Some doctors are quite ham-fisted, you know. I have advised Ayesha however to try several areas of medicine and surgery first before settling on one. But she is a very determined young woman and, like all you twenty-something-year-olds, you know better than us old fogies. Regarding our Bushra, she's a beautiful bright star too. But she doesn't yet know where to shine her light.'

Ben was not perturbed by Bushra's sideswipe. He was more than willing to talk about Britain's exploitation of India, from the East India Company to the British Raj. He agreed that Partition in 1947 was ill-conceived and mismanaged. He had many debates with his Action Delta friends about the politicians and administrators who stupidly thought that one country, Pakistan, in two parts, could possibly function. Be they Hindu or Muslim nationalists, or British politicians and administrators, they got it utterly wrong. Pakistan, East and West – with over twelve hundred miles between them – was doomed to fail. Ben also carried some guilt about Britain's colonial past, even that of France and Portugal, especially in India. But Ben took his cue from Dr and Mrs Rahman and chose not to 'bark up that tree' over dinner.

'BEN,' SAID AYESHA, looking directly at him with an intensity that distracted him from thinking about dessert, 'we're still waiting for your second guess.'

'Er, yes, sorry…'

It was too late. Natcoo arrived with a large bowl of sizzling and bubbling apple crumble. Ali followed with a tray offering homemade custard, thick cream, doi and runny honey. Natcoo served Ben with a generous portion and everyone waited for their guest to choose the accompaniment. With all eyes on him, including Natcoo and Ali, he said he couldn't decide. They're all delicious. Mrs Rahman rescued him: have a spoonful of everything! He declined that offer and decided on the doi, the delicious goats' milk yoghurt.

'A wise choice,' Dr Rahman said. 'It counteracts and so complements the crumble's sweetness.'

Natcoo proceeded to serve the family with crumble and their chosen accompaniment. Despite the doctor's comments, Ben noticed only Ayesha asked Natcoo to serve a spoonful of doi. Abdur chose custard. Ma, or Amma, as Abdur and the girls called her, took cream. Bushra, still silent and sullen, honey. None of the family was overweight, despite Mrs Rahman's comments about her husband's 'middle-age spread'. Ben wondered how they could remain so slim if they routinely ate meals like the one they had just finished.

Mrs Rahman said that Abdur had shared the sad news about Jonny. 'I'm afraid, Ben, we have a minority of people who continue to fight our war of liberation, even though, with India's help, the war was won last December. Have you heard from Abigail?'

'The phones were out all morning,' Ben replied. 'Very frustrating. But she managed to get through this afternoon. She's decided to fly back with Jonny's body and attend his funeral. Abi told me they'd planned to announce their engagement soon. But, obviously, that can't happen now.'

Everyone's head dropped, as if in prayer, and a moment of respectful silence ensued.

To Ben's surprise, if not to her family, Bushra broke the silence, her voice soft and slow. 'That is so, so sad.' Tears welled in her eyes. 'I'm so sorry.'

After a pause, Mrs Rahman asked, 'Have they apprehended the alleged assailant or assailants?' The formality of her question reminded Ben that Dr Rahman had revealed his wife had studied law. She was one of only three women in a class of nearly forty men at Calcutta University during the 1930s.

'I don't know, Mrs Rahman.'

'I doubt very much they will,' she said. 'The police might pull a couple of poor chaps off the street. But it will most likely be a token gesture. They will have little hard evidence, if any, nor the forensic ability to analyse what they do have. And I doubt anyone will admit to being an eyewitness. Any bystanders will have slipped into the shadows.'

'They would be too scared, Ben, fearful of reprisals,' Dr Rahman added.

'The sub-divisional police chief will wish to appease the district superintendent,' Mrs Rahman continued. 'He will want to take credit higher up the chain saying an arrest has been made. The government will also wish to calm fears amongst the foreign aid community. Eventually, when the dust settles, the charges will be dropped against those arrested and the fellows in custody released.'

Dr Rahman stood and suggested they all move into the living room for tea. Everyone followed his lead. It was his way of lightening the mood and enjoying the rest of the evening.

Ben couldn't believe his eyes on walking into the living room: the coffee table was full of yet more food. Banana cake, rosgolla, the cake-like balls in syrup, and as served on his previous visit, log-shaped cham-cham.

'I don't think I can eat another thing,' Ben declared.

'Of course you can,' smiled Dr Rahman. 'We Bangladeshis love our sweetmeats – but everything in moderation.'

'Well, if that's a doctor's advice...'

'Surely you can manage a cham-cham or two,' Mrs Rahman said. 'After you told Ali they were your favourite last time, it was inevitable he would serve a fresh batch when he heard Abba was to bring you home.'

'He'd be insulted if you failed to eat at least one, Ben,' smiled Ayesha. 'And it is never clever to insult your cook.'

'That, Ayesha, sounds like a threat,' he replied.

'To me, Ben, sounds like helpful advice.'

CONVERSATION COVERED MANY topics throughout the evening. Ayesha talked in a matter-of-fact way about her studies at Dacca's medical college. Bushra discussed Bangladeshi politics and governmental systems worldwide with breath-taking knowledge. Dr and Mrs Rahman recalled times under British Raj, the turmoil of Partition in 1947 and the bloodshed it created, particularly around Bengal and Punjab. With heavy hearts, the family reflected on the devastation the recent nine-month war had inflicted on Bangladesh, its people and infrastructure: Bushra reported that around three hundred road and railway bridges had been damaged; nearly nine out of ten of the country's trucks destroyed; its two major ports – crucial for food imports – rendered almost unusable.

'We can build new bridges and acquire more trucks,' Dr Rahman said. 'But we can't bring back our families and friends who died, nor repair the scars seared in our memories. Our recent war demonstrated that our love and blood of Bengal was thicker than the water of our Islamic faith.'

Listening carefully to the Rahman family openly discuss matters, Ben learnt a good deal about Islam and how, as in Christianity and Buddhism, there were many sects and divisions within the one faith with claims and counter-claims of who was right and who was wrong. Bangladeshis had what Dr Rahman described as a more 'benign and tolerant' interpretation of Islam than most people in West Pakistan.

Bushra jumped in. 'Abba thinks it's because we live in a wet soft green country and WP is largely dry desert of rock and sand. Soft-hearted people here and hard-hearted ones there, reflecting the respective geographies.'

'Thank you, Bushra,' her father said, chiding her gently while clearly admiring her intelligence. 'Believe it or not, my dear daughter, I am capable of expounding my own theories.'

'Of course, Abba.' She whipped around the table to hug him and deliver a beaming smile.

'Bushra always gets around Abba that way, Ben,' said Ayesha, grinning. 'She blows him up like a balloon – then bursts it.'

Amused, Mrs Rahman stepped in and addressed Ayesha. 'You also have your wily ways with your father, young lady.'

'My dear Ben, you can see why many men want sons when we poor chaps are surrounded by these pushy women,' laughed Dr Rahman.

'You wouldn't want it any other way, Abba, than to be surrounded by beautiful women, pushy or passive,' Bushra said.

'Abba, are you saying you wish Bushra and I had been boys?' asked Ayesha, widening her eyes anticipating his response. Abba rubbed his chin pretending to think carefully about his reply.

'Even if he did, he wouldn't dare say,' joked Mrs Rahman.

The whole family burst out laughing and both girls went to hug their father.

'I might have played more cricket with sons,' he said to Ben while being hugged and kissed.

'How insulting, Abba,' cried Bushra with mock sulkiness. 'Ben, we've played lots of cricket with him in the garden.'

'True, but your off-spin technique is terrible…'

SHOUTING OUTSIDE CAUSED the family's banter to stop suddenly. Voices became louder, aggressive, threatening. Natcoo rushed in shouting, 'Mukti Bahini, Mukti Bahini'.

They could hear the front gates being rattled, its metal bars banged with sticks and kicked. A gang of around ten young men tried forcing the lock and lifting one side of the gate off its hinges. Natcoo said something in Bengali. Ben looked at the family's faces. They were full of fear. And he became fearful himself.

'They're breaking in the garden,' Bushra cried.

'I shall go and talk to them,' Dr Rahman said calmly.

'No, Abdur,' Mrs Rahman said, gripping his arm with both hands.

'They're climbing over the gate,' Ayesha said, looking through the window.

'And the wall!' Bushra screamed.

'Get back from the windows,' Mrs Rahman said firmly. 'Quick, turn off the lights.'

Someone flicked the switch.

'This is my fault,' Ben said. 'I shouldn't have come here. They don't like Delta helping Biharis. Look what happened to Jonny. I've put you all in danger.'

'They're just frustrated young fellows,' said Dr Rahman, maintaining a calmness that impressed Ben. 'Freedom fighters with no freedom to fight for anymore – except from poverty.'

'Guys with guns, though.' Bushra sounded terrified. As Ben went to look she suddenly jumped back from the window.

The crash made everyone flinch. Glass fragments burst into the room and clinked and slid across the tile floor in all directions. The brick bounced off a settee before striking the wall.

'Get down!' Mrs Rahman screamed.

'Let go, Raina, please,' Dr Rahman pleaded. 'I must go.'

'No, Dr Rahman, it's my responsibility,' Ben said urgently. 'I'll tell them you'll no longer be coming to the clinic. Or have anything to do with Biharis in the camp. I can't let you and your family be harassed like this.'

Ben rushed towards the hallway.

'No, Ben, don't be stupid,' Ayesha cried. 'They'll kill you!'

Ali rushed in wielding a meat cleaver ready for a fight. Dr Rahman said something in Bengali to him and Ali's arm dropped slowly to his side.

Defying her mother's order, powered by curiosity, Ayesha looked through one of the four windows facing the front from the living room. 'Abba, Amma, they're approaching the house. One has a rifle. Others have sticks. Oh God – and a baseball bat!' She turned to see her father on the phone calling the police.

Ayesha suddenly leaped back falling flat on the floor as another brick smashed the glass.

'Ayesha! Are you all right?' Mrs Rahman cried rushing towards her. 'I told you. Keep away from the windows.'

'Yes, yes, I'm fine.' Ayesha carefully picked out several shards of glass from the folds in her headscarf and dark blue sari. Her mother plucked a fragment from her daughter's long black hair.

'You all need to go upstairs,' Dr Rahman said, still waiting for the operator to connect him to the police station. 'Lock yourselves in one of the rooms. Put something heavy behind the door.'

Mrs Rahman, Ayesha and Bushra didn't move.

'Go on. Go now.' Dr Rahman whispered, remaining calm and in control.

'Girls, go upstairs as your father says,' Mrs Rahman said with more urgency. 'I'm staying with you, Abdur. We'll face them together.'

The girls stood defiant, refused to move. Their message was clear: we're in this together. Dr and Mrs Rahman didn't know whether to be proud of their daughters' bravery or angry at their disobedience and stubbornness.

'Then at least keep down.' Dr Rahman's voice stayed calm even though the shouting outside intensified. 'Get behind the sofa.'

They huddled together, Mrs Rahman sat in the middle with an arm around her girls. Bushra started to sob and tremble. Ayesha left her mother's embrace and crawled around on her hands and knees to wrap her arms around her younger sister. 'It'll be all right, Bushra. The police will be here soon.'

'No... no... they won't be,' she cried. 'Abba hasn't even got through yet.'

Another brick smashed a window, this time upstairs. Pieces of glass in all shapes and sizes tumbled down into the bushes. Taunts and threats became louder as the gang approached.

'Operator. Please. Somehow get the police to come quickly.' Dr Rahman repeated the address. Slowly. Carefully.

Natcoo offered to sneak out the back and run to the police station. It was over a mile away at the top of Tungipur's main road. Dr Rahman thanked him for the offer. But he knew the fifty-five year-old's heart was not in the best of conditions – and Natcoo certainly couldn't run more than a few yards before becoming breathless.

A chilling shout went up from the assailants. Then sudden silence. Silence was scarier than shouting, the reason for it unknown. Everyone in the house trembled fearing what was to happen next. Even Dr Rahman dreaded the gang's next move. Gunfire? Petrol bomb? Grenade? Had the yobs broken through the back door? What would they do to his wife and daughters? Rape was rife throughout the recent nine-month war. Still is. No family was immune. Muslim, Bangladeshi, Bihari, West Pakistani, rich, poor, Hindu, Buddhist…

For the first time in his life, Dr Rahman wished he held a gun in his hands – and he realised, now, at this moment, he'd be willing to pull the trigger. A lifetime of life-saving only for it to end in a killing spree lasting seconds.

Then a voice, loud and clear through the broken windows.

'Hey, look who's here.' The guy with the gun shouted to his gangmates. 'It's the dude from Mohpur.'

'Yeah, he's the one who stays at the dak with that English whore who shags the doctor.'

'I bet he does too – three time a night!' He turned and made a rude gesture with his arm. The mob laughed mockingly. Mrs Rahman and her daughters squeezed tighter together behind the settee, disgusted at the gang's malice.

Ben approached with both palms raised shoulder high hoping to placate them. Strangely, although nervous, he didn't fear them. He assumed these were the same people who wrote the threatening letters to Abi. Right or wrong – gambling with his life – he surmised people who write threatening letters anonymously never carry out their threats. But it was too late to turn back, too late to find out if he was right or wrong.

He was surprised, reassured in a way, to hear them talk good English. That fact, and the trousers and shirts they wore, he took to mean they were from relatively well-off families. They were certainly not from impoverished hovels in the back streets of Tungipur, and all looked in their late teens or early twenties. Ben also recognised the signs he'd witnessed in Nigeria when the young soldiers had been using hash, cocaine, or something stronger: swagger, excitability, dilated pupils and a lot of sniffing, snorting, foot shuffling and hand shaking.

'Please, this isn't doing any good. What do you want?' Ben stepped forward to within six feet of the mob.

Their leader, wielding the battle-scarred AK-47 on a strap round his neck, turned his back on Ben and addressed his following.

'This fucking rich white dude asks us what we want.' He opened his arms and bowed slightly inviting his gang to respond. The automatic dangled below his chest.

'To stop helping dirty pig-eating Biharis…'

'We want him to fuck off out of our country…'

'To let us fuck his girlfriend in the camp…'

'We'll have her anyway…and those women in there.' He pointed towards the house.

A burst of raucous sneering laughter, primal gasps and grunts ensued. Mrs Rahman, Ayesha and Bushra froze at their declared intention and gripped each other tighter. Dr Rahman continued waiting for someone – the operator again or the police – to speak.

To the mob's surprise, Ben stepped two paces forward. The leader spun around quickly and his rifle's barrel pointed to Ben's belly, six inches away.

'Look,' Ben said, 'I'm here, our charity is here, to try and help everyone in your new country, not just Biharis. The more aid we bring in, even for Biharis, means there's more to go around for everyone…'

'Yeah, but the doc shouldn't treat those traitors down in Mohpur,' one of the mob shouted.

'Bangladeshis first…' yelled another.

'They should go back Bihar…'

'Or to Pakistan…'

'Let 'em starve…'

Inside the living room, with two broken windows, the Rahman family could hear every word the yobs said. But with his back towards them, they could only detect Ben's voice, not his exact words.

If they were going to attack, they would have already set about him. Ben grew in confidence. One lesson he'd learnt in Nigeria, the closer you get to someone with a machete, knife or gun and talk calmly, the less aggressive they'll become. And the longer you keep them talking, the less likely they are to harm you. He realised of course that being a foreigner in Nigeria at that time offered some protection. But if he had been an Igbo-speaking Biafran, even after the civil war ended, no amount of talking would have stopped the swing of the blade or the squeeze of the trigger.

'That's for your politicians, and those in New Delhi and Islamabad, to sort out,' Ben reasoned. 'Threatening your own people helps no one. What good does it do? Remember, Dr Rahman has helped thousands of Bangladeshis for years and years. He still does here at your local hospital, and down in Dacca. He will have treated you or your fathers, brothers and sisters. It wouldn't surprise me to learn he'd helped your mothers when you were being born…'

Ben smiled.

As in Nigeria, mentioning an aggressor's mother often quelled an angry man.

'Okay, okay,' the leader said. 'But I tell you, doc must spend more time with Bangladeshis, not shitty traitors in Mohpur. Right?'

'Right,' echoed Ben. It was a meaningless response. Dr Rahman would make his own decisions, especially in the light of this attack. But Ben's concession allowed the gang's gun-toting leader to retain some authority in front of his pals. The King should always be respected – especially when he's brandishing a gun.

Had the drugs started to lose their potency? Had the yobs lost their nerve? Perhaps Ben's words pacified them? He couldn't tell. It didn't matter. Their attack ceased and the yobs started to climb back over the gate.

'Hang on a minute,' Ben said to their surprise. 'I'll find the night guard and ask him to unlock it.'

Ben was amused when, as the lads walked out, gang members thanked him for having the gate opened – by a nervous-looking chowkidor.

MINUTES EARLIER, HAVING gone quiet, curious to know what was happening, Ayesha slithered across the floor towards one of the broken windows. Cautiously, she raised her head and rested her chin on the sill.

'Careful,' her father whispered. Dr Rahman was kneeling on the floor with the phone at his side waiting for someone at the police station to answer. 'Don't antagonise them by showing your face.'

With his back to the house, Ayesha struggled to hear what Ben said. Just the odd word, including their name, Rahman. But whatever it was, he seemed to be calming the mob. Although dark, moonlight filtered by heavy monsoon clouds casting only occasional light, Ayesha was pretty sure the gang leader was the son of the sub-divisional government officer. They had attended the same junior school and he was often seen hanging around town. She decided to keep that fact to herself. For now.

'They're going!' Ayesha whispered her announcement across the room. 'Pa, Ma, they're off down the road. They're leaving us alone.'

Dr Rahman handed Natcoo the receiver to keep listening for a response and joined his wife and daughters to look out. They watched the gang laughing and larking around swaggering out of town, appearing satisfied with their evening's drama.

'It looks to me they've been smoking something rather stronger than tobacco,' said Dr Rahman, confirming without conferring Ben's diagnosis.

Ben turned to stand facing the house. Until then, he hadn't realised he was shaking, his mouth as dry as Saharan sand. He felt the tight knot in his guts and fully aware of his rapid, shallow breathing, his heart drumming his ribs. Delayed shock. He'd suffered the condition before.

Danger over, someone switched on the living room lights. Long shadows were thrown across the garden. It caused Ben to look up towards the house, the sudden brightness temporarily blinding him. After his eyes adjusted, six silhouettes appeared. At one broken window the Rahman family. At the other stood Natcoo and Ali, still with his cleaver in hand. Ben stepped out of the limelight into the garden's darkness.

SEVEN

Natcoo, with Ali's help, had swept up most of the broken glass by the time Ben returned to the living room. He had deliberately strolled slowly around the back garden. He needed time to himself – to stop the shakes, untie the knot of nerves in his stomach, regulate his breathing. Slowly and deeply inhaling the exotic night-scents, released from stocks and other flowers, bestowed their therapeutic powers.

Bushra sobbed and sighed loudly, with sharp intakes of breath. They all recognised her tears of fear, and relief. Mrs Rahman wrapped a crocheted shawl around Bushra's shoulders and held her tight.

Ayesha looked hard at Ben when he returned to the room. It momentarily stopped him in his tracks. He couldn't tell what Ayesha's stare signalled: anger, hate, contempt. Perhaps all three. He had invited danger into their home, albeit unintentionally. He'd put the lives of her and her family in peril. It was perfectly understandable that she could no longer stand the sight of him.

Natcoo handed the phone to Dr Rahman. In a blend of Bengali and English he responded to questions. 'Nine or ten of them. *Thik ache. Ji.* Okay. Yes. Between eighteen and twenty-five I would say, no older. *Apnar nam ki?* Ah, thanks inspector Ahmad.'

More questions were asked. 'It was too dark. *Na.* No. I didn't recognise anyone. Too far back. In the house. Okay. *Thik ache. Dhonnobad.* Thanks. Thanks.'

'They are sending officers down now,' Dr Rahman announced.

'What's the point?' quizzed Ayesha angrily. 'They know the delinquents who have been beating up Biharis – and worse. But they don't lift a finger to…'

'Ayesha, enough,' Mrs Rahman said firmly but kindly. 'Your father has a duty to report the incident. You must respect that decision.'

It came as a surprise to Ben that Ayesha immediately backed down and offered an apology, a softly spoken *dukhito*. It was clear Mrs Rahman so rarely raised her voice that, when she did, it made a forceful impact.

'I'd better go,' Ben said quietly. He walked towards the door.

'No, please,' ordered Dr Rahman, stepping in front of Ben. 'You must definitely stay here tonight. We'll return to the camp in the morning. Together. If you go now you might meet up with those nasty fellows. And they're still as high as kites. There's no telling what they might do down a dark track. No, Ben, I insist.'

'My husband is absolutely right, Ben,' Mrs Rahman said. 'It would be a great worry for us if you went into the night by yourself.'

'In any case,' Dr Rahman continued, 'the police will wish to question you.'

'I can't tell them anything more than you,' Ben argued. 'And I'll be fine. Those lads will have gone home by now.'

Bushra gradually stopped crying and sat quietly next to her mother, hands in lap, shaking slightly, head down. Ayesha remained at the far end of the room peering into the garden and along the road; wary, on guard. She appeared more angry than afraid. When she glanced at Ben, he believed she was so furious she was holding back a tirade of abuse against him.

'They'll be on the hashish or cocaine again.' Ayesha spoke angrily, still rattled by the assault. 'It gives them courage they wouldn't otherwise have. Half the soldiers in the war were dosed up on it, whatever side they were fighting on.'

'You don't know that for certain, my dear,' said her mother.

'Well, if not half, certainly a lot of them,' Ayesha said.

Mrs Rahman turned to Ben. 'I don't know what you said to those thugs – we couldn't hear you – but whatever it was, it did the trick. Thank you. You saved us. It took a lot of courage to go and face them down.'

'Absolutely right, my dear,' endorsed Dr Rahman. 'Yes, thanks Ben. I dare not think of what would have happened had you not been here. We're forever grateful. You were exceedingly brave to confront them.'

'It was a stupid thing to do.' Ayesha spoke under her breath and was barely audible. Ben, closest to her, believed Dr nor Mrs Rahman heard her remark, and Bushra remained too upset to take much notice.

'But I'm so very sorry,' Ben sighed. 'It's my fault in the first place they were here.'

'No, Ben, I believe that not to be the case,' Dr Rahman said. 'They didn't know you were here. You may not know this, but I've received several threatening letters. We've also had our garden wall daubed with red paint saying nasty things. No, Ben, tonight's attack was not your fault.'

'Perhaps not personally,' Ben argued, 'but if Action Delta hadn't come here to help Biharis…'

'Some of us would have still helped these poor souls,' Dr Rahman insisted. 'No, Ben, you mustn't blame yourself nor Action Delta. These fellows who came here tonight need to help the country get back on its feet rather than hanging around blaming everyone and everything else for their situation. Violence achieves nothing, except provokes more violence.'

INSPECTOR AHMAD AND three constables arrived. They combed the garden, examining the perimeter wall and the broken windows, including the damage in the upstairs bedroom. Natcoo had collected the bricks that shattered them and handed them to a constable, pointing to where they had landed. The policeman's expression implied these were crucial facts, as if he could calculate the trajectory and establish sound forensic evidence. Ben believed the police were wasting time, putting on a show for the family. Ayesha's expression indicated the identical thought.

After interviewing Dr Rahman, the inspector asked for Ben's details. Ben had a visceral suspicion of officials, especially after his experiences in Nigeria. He knew corruption was endemic within the Bangladeshi police. But, maintaining politeness in front of the Rahman family, he responded albeit reluctantly. 'Ben – that's Benjamin – Altringham.'

'Date of birth?'

Again, Ben resisted, believing it had no relevance to this investigation. But he obliged. 'March twelfth, 1947.'

'Twenty-five and…' the inspector counted by tapping his thumb down his forefinger joints, 'and two months.' He seemed pleased at his speedy calculation.

'You work with Miss Abigale Benvin at the camp in Mohpur, yes? Please give her my regards.'

'You know her?' Ben failed to disguise his surprise at the inspector knowing Abi.

'Yes, Mr Altringham. Quite well. She has attended our station on several occasions. She reports to us transgressions – alleged transgressions – against people in the camp.' Ben wondered if Abi had reported the threatening notes to the police. But no, it was clear she hadn't, knowing nothing would or could be done to find the perpetrators. 'I'm afraid our inquiries have fallen on dry ground. We do however take all such matters seriously.'

Ben nor anyone else in the room appeared to believe him, if bland faces served as a sign. Even the inspector sounded as if he didn't quite believe himself. He told Dr Rahman that the police would thoroughly investigate tonight's incident. But without clear identification it would be very difficult to apprehend the miscreants. Ayesha decided not to reveal that the gang's ringleader was the sub-divisional officer's son: his father and family would doubtless provide an alibi, swearing he hadn't stepped out of the house all evening. The inspector departed. His three constables followed two paces behind, each carrying a glass-breaking brick in the palms of their hands, as if they were bars of gold. 'Important evidence,' said the inspector.

Mrs Rahman graciously thanked the police officers as they left, and Dr Rahman accompanied them to the front gate. The policemen talked briefly with the night guard. Ali had said the chowkidar had been inspecting the back of the property when the gang arrived. (It was common knowledge he'd been sleeping in his hut at the back of the garden. And, perhaps wisely, he would have wanted to avoid facing the gang anyway: being of lowly status, the yobs would have beaten him without fear of reprisals.) The chowkidar opened the gate for the officers and was quick to relock it as they stepped into their jeep. They drove away in the opposite direction to the 'miscreants'.

The longcase clock in the hallway struck eleven. It's bell must have rang every hour since Ben arrived at the Rahman household, around six o'clock. But this was the first time he registered it striking. He had been so engrossed in the warm hospitality of the Rahman family, engaged with their lively conversation, the grandfather clock's hourly announcement had eluded him. The antique dark wood timepiece stood like a sentry in the hallway, six foot six inches tall, and nearly as wide as a soldier's shoulders. The pendulum swung side to side counting each second.

'Buna has made up a bed for you,' announced Mrs Rahman, breaking his attention to time passing.

Ben looked inquiringly.

'Buna's our housemaid, Ben. It was her evening off. But she was disturbed by the commotion and came to see if she could be of assistance. She lives round the back. You'll see her sometime, I'm sure. She's a lovely girl. Only fifteen. Both her parents and all her close family were… were lost a few months ago.' Mrs Rahman did not need to explain they had been killed in the war.

Dr and Mrs Rahman said they had experienced enough excitement for one evening and retired to bed. Ben, Ayesha and Bushra were left in the living room. Natcoo had instructed them to avoid sitting in two of the four settees. He said pieces of glass needed to be removed in daylight, and this would be done first thing.

In Bengali, Ayesha spoke quietly to Natcoo. Ben knew that *lebu pani* meant lemon water, a popular cold drink. And, within a minute, Natcoo left a large jug on the table complete with a thick layer of ice cubes and sliced lemons. Ayesha indicated to Natcoo she would serve the drink and that he should go and sleep. He's normally in bed by nine, she told Ben later, and he'll be buzzing around soon after five in the morning.

'Good night, Mr Ben,' he said. 'I apologise for your disturbance this evening. These men not good.'

So surprised by Natcoo's words, Ben couldn't think of a reply fast enough before Natcoo turned and slipped away, the sound of his flip-flops fading into the distance. Why should he be apologising for those yobbos?

It is an insult to a visitor in our country, Ayesha explained. It is highly embarrassing to him that fellow Bangladeshis behave in such a manner. It is our custom, and a requirement of our religion, to be hospitable to guests in our home.

EIGHT

Ayesha filled three tumblers with lemon water. The large chunky jug was full to the brim and obviously heavy. Ben confirmed her father's observation: Ayesha had a steady hand and well-controlled movement, those of a neuro-surgeon.

'I'm sorry too,' said Bushra suddenly, addressing Ben.

Dr and Mrs Rahman. Natcoo. Now Bushra. Everyone's apologising to him, he thought.

'I was so scared when that... that thing crashed through the window,' said Bushra. 'Thought it was a bomb. Thought we'd die. That's how Abba's leg got smashed last year. Exploded when he was operating.'

'If anyone should apologise, Bushra, it's me. Your father is such a wonderful man. So kind to all the patients. Amazingly brave. Abi told me he'd had threats – your wall here daubed in red paint. That's horrible. I'm going to recommend to my Action Delta colleagues that we close the clinic – or find a Bihari doctor.'

'You can't,' Ayesha snapped.

Her sharpness surprised Ben. It took a few seconds for him to recover. 'While your father continues running the clinic, working for us, for which he doesn't even get paid, it's putting him – and you two – at risk. I can't live with that.'

'But Abba can,' Ayesha said, her voice steady and assertive. 'You're right. He's brave. A great doctor. Kind. He does what he believes is the right thing to do. Always has. Always will. It's his choice to work with Biharis, not yours.'

Stunned again for a moment, Ben said, 'But, Ayesha, I'd never forgive myself if something happened to you...'

49

Ayesha started to interrupt. But whatever she was about to say was never said. Her lips remained slightly parted, her eyes set static on his – and his on hers.

For several seconds Ayesha and Ben remained wary of each other, uncertain of the next move, the next words. Like two prize fighters at their weigh-in, who would blink first?

Bushra was baffled. What's happening between my sister and our guest? Do they hate each other that much? Was that an argument or what?

'Excuse me,' Ayesha said suddenly, standing quickly and rushing from the room. It felt as if all the air followed her.

IN THE VACUUM Bushra and Ben looked at each other, both puzzled, seeking an answer to Ayesha's unexpected departure. Was she angry? Upset? Tired? Is she coming back or has she gone to bed? Bushra had never known Ayesha to behave this way. Her sister was always in control, calm, never crabby. Nor could Ben calculate why Ayesha had walked off. Was she in a huff or simply in a hurry? Perhaps she's popped to the loo. Or to get an aspirin, or a handkerchief. Had he offended her? All Bushra could do was look at Ben with raised eyebrows, pursed lips and a shrug of her shoulders. He mirrored Bushra's expression.

'Maybe I should go back to the dak,' he said, rising from the settee.

'No, don't.'

'I think I've upset Ayesha. I don't know how. Despite what your father said, she must blame me for tonight's attack. She's certainly not very happy with me.'

'I don't think it's that. But I don't know what's wrong. I've never seen her moody like this before. She'll be fine, I'm sure. If you go Abba and Amma will be really upset. They'll be demanding to know what's gone on. We'll get a rocket from both of them.'

'But I don't know what's "gone on".'

'Neither do I. But I know you must stay. Anyway, it's nearly midnight.'

Ben and Bushra sat in silence, both listening hard in the hope of hearing Ayesha's return.

Breaking the silence, Bushra asked Ben if he'd like more *lebu pani*, before realising his glass was still full. She felt stupid. But it encouraged him to drink up allowing her to refill.

'I'm sorry about earlier,' Bushra said.

'Earlier?'

'Yes, when, as Abba said, I started barking up the wrong tree. You know, going on about rice and the Raj and stuff...'

'Oh that. No worries, Bushra. I completely agree with you that Britain has a lot to answer for regarding our empire-building. We went to places, such as Australia, stuck a flag in the ground and claimed it as ours for queen – or king – and country. Unbelievable arrogance. But that was a different time, different beliefs, different attitudes.'

'Britain wasn't the only country building empires,' Bushra said. 'Truth is, if your East India Company's army hadn't beaten the French here, they'd have continued to dominate Bengal and most of India. Hey, I'd be speaking French now!' Bushra declared happily. 'And if not the French, the Portuguese would have exploited India far more than just grabbing Goa and one or two other places. We had hundreds of maharajas, maharanis, princes, sultans and others fighting each other. One lot would invade another lot killing and enslaving people. Most of them as bad as each other. We didn't need the Brits to teach us how to do that.'

'I know, but...'

Bushra was on a roll, demonstrating her knowledge of history and politics.

'Around 1700 we had a guy who claimed himself emperor, Aurangzeb. He locked up his dad, Shah Jahan – you know him, Ben, he's the guy who started building the Taj Mahal. Then Aurangzeb went on to murder all his own brothers.

'Ben, we've been divided by religion and other stuff as much as anyone. Invaded from all sides. Even when you Brits were trading like crazy around here in Bengal, Nadir Shah, a guy from Persia, invaded Delhi. He slaughtered more than thirty thousand people in the old walled city before running off with a great big diamond – the Koh-i-noor.'

'The one now in Britain's crown jewels.'

'Absolutely correct, Mr Altringham,' Bushra said. 'Hey, Ben, next time you bump into the queen, ask her for it back.'

'Sure. I'll drop into Buckingham Palace the next time I'm in London. I'll get her to pop it in the post to you here – although it should really go back to Delhi, not Dacca.'

They laughed. Then stopped.

IT WAS THE patter of her sandals that signalled Ayesha's return. As she entered through the door's archway, Ben jumped up bolt upright. Then wondered why. He sat down slowly, trying to hide his unease.

The night's heat and humidity seemed to intensify. Awareness increased of the monsoon chorus of croaking frogs and guttural toads, heard louder than usual through the broken windows. Adding to the amphibian choir came the insect soundtrack of the tropics: the almost continual humming from buzzing and clicking cicadas. A wall lizard above the doorway was on the prowl, preparing to pounce on a resting mosquito.

Ben was on the brink of saying something, but held back. He didn't want to risk upsetting Ayesha, if indeed that's what he'd done earlier. Bushra was also reluctant to speak, unable to assess her sister's mood, a rare situation, which she found disconcerting. By default, Bushra and Ben gave the floor to Ayesha. She didn't take it. Neither could read Ayesha's thoughts.

Then they struck. Twelve bells of midnight. The longcase clock cracked the spell of silence. Ayesha, Bushra and Ben counted all dozen strikes… silently, to themselves.

As the twelfth chime faded, Ben broke the icy atmosphere, or what he perceived it to be. 'Don't they keep you awake?' he asked tentatively.

'We've grown up with that clock,' said Bushra. 'I probably wouldn't sleep if I didn't hear it. The ticking's sort of reassuring.'

'It was our grandfather's clock, Abba's dad.' Ayesha spoke softly, pleasantly, all anxiety after the yobs' attack absent. 'It's like the heartbeat of the house. For me, as the seconds tick away, in reminds me there's a past, a present, and a future.' She smiled. So did Ben.

'And you don't need your stethoscope to hear it,' quipped Bushra, back to her bubbly self.

They joked, talked, and talked more, sometimes seriously, into the night. Ayesha reported how, during last year's war, her studies were severely disrupted. Many of her lecturers and students were murdered by rampaging West Pakistani troops. Bushra also lost nearly a year's academic work. Both were determined to catch up. In fact, they said, they had studied even harder and over-compensated for the loss of formal education.

'When you've been pushed back one step you have to take two steps forward,' Ayesha said.

'Ben,' said Bushra, 'believe me. If my dear sister missed an hour's lecture – not that she ever has – she would read all the relevant notes, go over the subject for twice as long, and some more.'

'It's obvious you do a lot of studying too,' Ben said.

'Yes,' quipped Bushra, 'but I'm not a boring swot like she is.'

Ayesha tossed a cushion at Bushra – in sisterly love.

Ayesha went on to outline how Mrs Rahman, she and Bushra stayed with relatives in India throughout most of the conflict. Both Abba and Amma's families originated in West Bengal near Calcutta, before Partition in 1947 divided them. Not all Muslims went to Pakistan, nor all Hindus to India. Sikhs settled both sides of the border, particularly in Punjab.

Bushra talked animatedly of Dr Rahman's younger brother and sister who remained in India after Partition, as did Mrs Rahman's brother, despite being Muslims. The extended family remain close and visit as often as they can. Dr Rahman chose to stay in Bangladesh throughout the nine-month War of Liberation.

'He helped anyone – friend or foe, rich or poor – who needed medical attention,' Bushra said proudly.

'Told you he was brave,' Ayesha added.

Not that Ben needed reminding.

'And so are you,' she said softly to Ben, for his ears only.

But Ben knew that not to be true. Since reading the threatening letters sent to Abi and Jonny's murder, he had lived in a state of almost constant fear, perpetually vigilant, jumpy at any unidentified sound, especially in the still of night. Then this evening's attack, seeing the hate in the eyes of the gang, the dread he felt, Ben considered himself anything but brave. In fact, a coward.

NINE

At the ministry of foreign affairs in central Dacca, Farook Hussain signed several executive orders. After blowing the ink dry, he replaced his fountain pen in its holder and the documents in their folder. He tied the bundle with green ribbon in a neat bow, the same knot he used for his shoes. With his expanding waistline, bending to tie his laces was getting harder by the day. His wife suggested using slip-ons. But if it became too much of a struggle he would order one of his servants to do the deed.

Although Hussain had an out tray on his large leather-top desk, he dropped the file on the floor. His assistant knelt to pick it up, stood two paces back, and waited further instructions. The minister, with a flick of his hand, without looking up, dismissed the peon assistant to the outer office. Three months into his new post, it was imperative that Hussain stamped his authority on ministry minions. Show who's boss. Demonstrate power, like in his military days. His hard-line reputation would spread like a virulent virus throughout the ministry.

Another underling appeared at the door and waited. As was his duty, this peon stood with his hands clasped behind his back like a soldier 'at ease' waiting for orders.

Hussain drank the remainder of his tea, although it was cold. He shook a little bell resting to the right on his desk and, within seconds, the tea-wallah appeared. Mohammed knew his job. Minister Hussain routinely demanded further refreshment around ten o'clock. A fresh cup full of hot sweet milky tea was served without a word between them. He also placed a tumbler of water, pani, to his master's right: icy cold but never with ice. Mohammed also replenished the plate of biscuits. As the tea-wallah left, he bowed as always on exit. And, as always, Hussain declined to acknowledge the tea-wallah's service, even his presence.

Amongst the ministry tea-wallahs however Mohammed had prestige, a position to maintain: he served The Minister, the top man. Others could provide tea and coffee and pani to hundreds of the junior civil servants. But Mohammed wasn't going to lose his job by speaking to, or seeking recognition from, The Minister. He knew his place as much as Hussain knew his.

'I'll see that fellow from Aid International now,' Hussain ordered. The peon turned and rushed from the minister's office on the errand. It would be a few minutes before the charity's chief arrived at the fourth floor from reception; longer, if the lift had yet again broken down. So Hussain stretched his heavy legs and, with cup and saucer in hand, a biscuit in mouth, he went to look outside his window. After an hour of reading government proposals, most of which seemed unachievable, and signing at least five directives, he believed a short break was fully deserved. He also needed to think carefully how to handle this sensitive issue with his visitor.

Dacca's Bangabandhu Avenue below was packed with people criss-crossing at all angles. Everyone in a rush, except the beggars. He must remind the chief of police to move them on. Let them beg on the back streets. With their blindness or deformity, or their half-starved bodies and naked kids, they hoped to cash in on the charity of the believers leaving Baitul Mukarram mosque. Whatever the religion, wherever in the world, beggars always received more cash immediately after prayers. Hussain assumed this was due to the believers' renewed inner-glow of godliness. Or, more likely, for having their guilty consciences pricked by the preacher. Beggars, he smirked, are not as stupid as they look. On Fridays they crowd around the mosques, Sundays the churches. A taka was a taka, be it thrown with a Muslim right hand or a Christian left hand.

Hussain watched with amusement two policemen trying to control the traffic. What fun. Street cops always made things worse. Both signalled simultaneously for the traffic to proceed at the crossroads. It became like a slapstick scene from a Laurel and Hardy movie he enjoyed as a youngster in the 1930s. Inevitably, chaos ensued. Angry truck and car drivers honked horns and waved fists claiming they had the right of way. Some mounted pavements trying to get round the jam causing pedestrians to jump away from danger. Cycle rickshaw-wallahs weaved in and out of the stranded traffic, pumping their sinewy legs vigorously to escape the blockage.

Hussain looked down on hundreds of chaps in white shirts and black trousers, most carrying a cheap briefcase. Small-time business fellows and government workers, many of them his staff. Everyone thinking they were more important than the next man, their business more crucial, their time more precious. But I'm the minister now, he praised himself. My business is truly very important. And if the prime minister continues in his incompetency, one day perhaps my business will indeed be the most important of all.

THE ASSISTANT'S DELIBERATE cough drew attention to the arrival of Thomas Womach. His appointment had been arranged for nine o'clock. But having worked in the charity aid sector across the world for nearly thirty years, Thomas Womach expected to be kept waiting. He couldn't recall one occasion when a meeting started on time. Ministers, from Guatemala to Manila, always had to reinforce their egos and importance, exhibit their vast workload, demonstrate the balance of power in their favour – even when all parties knew their impoverished tin-pot countries were crying out for foreign aid. Cash, goods, aid workers and expertise all urgently needed.

'Mr Womach, it's so good to see you again,' said the minister, extending his hand. 'A thousand apologies for keeping you waiting. But, you know, with a new government in place, we have much to do to correct the errors of the previous administration. Please, please sit. You will take tea?'

'Yes, thank you, minister. We realise it's a huge challenge to get the country back on its feet. You must be exceptionally busy.' Womach lied and Hussain accepted the lie graciously.

Womach sat on the chair facing Hussain, who settled himself slowly in his dark-leather swing-chair behind his desk. Womach was fully aware of another ploy at play: at six-foot three-inches Womach towered over squat Hussain, but the low chair ensured the minister was positioned higher than all visitors. Politicians' power-play. Pathetic, Womach thought.

'Has Aid International considered the proposal?'

'We have, minister,' Womach said placing his papers on the desk. 'I consulted with my colleagues to see what was possible.'

'And?'

'In principle, minister, no problem with the arrangement. If it helps us establish and consolidate our valuable work here – for the greater good of the people in the long term – then all should be well.'

'Good, Mr Womach. Very good. But what's the "but" I detect in your voice?'

'Quantity. It's simply a matter of quantity, minister. We can only secure six.'

'We discussed ten.' Hussain frowned.

'We are confident the full consignment can be completed later this year. But I'm afraid the demand from Germany is currently too great. Production can't meet supply. Everyone, even we Americans, are being rationed.'

'Is it known the products are destined for Bangladesh? Is that the delay? Are we being treated as a second-class citizen of the world? If so…'

'No, definitely not minister. Actually, if we agree terms today, then by this time next week the goods will start rolling off the aircraft.'

Mohammed arrived with a trolly of tea, milk, sugar and another plate of biscuits. He knew Hussain would have scoffed the earlier packet. He served the minister's tea first, being far more important than his guest, and knowing his requirements. The cha-wallah, holding up the teapot in one hand and a jug of hot milk in the other, asked without a word spoken how the American liked his tea. Showing a narrow gap between his thumb and forefinger, Womach indicated to Mohammed to pour just a small amount of milk in his cup. Deviously, Mohammed thought of pretending to misunderstand and pour a majority of milk and a dash of tea in the cup. But he'd lose his job. Hussain would instantly realise his deliberate mischief. He could serve his own damn sugar though. Americans had supported the murderous West Pakistanis during the War of Liberation. If they hadn't, perhaps his wife and daughter would not have been raped and his two sons bayonetted to death. Mohammed wanted to spit in Womach's tea. Perhaps one day he would find the opportunity.

The minister of foreign affairs did not hold all the cards in the negotiations. Womach retained an ace to deploy. 'If you're not happy with the arrangements, minister, would it be better if I contacted the minister of trade and industry regarding this matter?'

Hussain saw the game Womach played, but disguised his annoyance and played a cool hand. 'Regarding the importation of these products, you're correct to assume my good friend, the minister of trade, may be helpful. But, Mr Womach, I have no doubt this would lead to long delays in your licensing and import permissions. Very long delays. And these permits do, you understand, fall under my exclusive remit.'

Touché. Stalemate.

'So, minister, if we can agree on an initial batch of six, we can arrange transport from Germany within a few days.'

'And the consignment note?'

'As agreed, it will clearly state a delivery of four.'

BOTH MEN FINISHED their cha. Thomas Womach declined the offer of a biscuit. The minister promised all the charity's permits would be completed within days – following delivery. He also had every confidence the additional aid consignments would be received without hindrance. Minister Farook Hussain reassured Womach that his charity's initial donation to the Republic of Bangladesh was significant. The products will help eradicate poverty and allow ministers to 'progress our work for the people' more efficiently.

Womach recognised the standard bullshit. But he nodded in agreement. For his charity to thrive and build its contingency funds, it needed aid work. And the shattered new war-torn nation of Bangladesh had become the biggest basket-case in the world. Following 1970's devastating flood and last year's self-destructive so-called War of Liberation, Aid International couldn't miss out on this opportunity to raise capital. Aid agencies – government and nongovernmental organisations – were flooding into Bangladesh. No organisation in the international aid industry wanted to miss out. Hotel Intercontinental on Minto Road was awash with relief professionals, all vying for a slice of the expanding aid cake. Womach's AI had to fight for its rightful share. Poverty means profit: a thought he kept exclusively to himself and closest associates.

Womach wanted funds. He didn't care where the cash came from. Handouts from governments, UN agencies, the Red Cross and humanitarian trusts were all welcome. AI's own network of fund-raisers across the US had developed slick methods of raising cash from donors. Pictures of poverty, especially emaciated babies, guilt-tripped fellow Americans into giving cash – providing the shots were not too shocking to look at.

AI's quantitative and qualitative research, the results always kept confidential, showed when making appeals that a starving baby raised at least three-times more money than a starving middle-aged man; a sad-looking kid always earned more than one smiling.

Some donors were however contemptable. Buttons, paperclips and other such worthless items had been dropped into his charity's collection boxes, even those left in the back of churches. As with many charities, Aid International's headquarters routinely received nasty notes condemning their work, most written anonymously. The worst nutters wished yet more death, disease and destruction on some of the world's most destitute. Some were blatantly racist. Others believed poverty was punishment from God. One wrote: 'These foreigners reap the consequences for not believing in Him, the one true Christian God.' Womach dismissed such people as naïve, even stupid: couldn't they see poverty was a man-made problem – and a wonderful business opportunity.

Thomas Womach's Aid International had grown into a multi-million dollar enterprise. He needed the poor more than the poor needed him – to maintain his lifestyle and ambitions. He'd built a great organisation. Worked hard. Deserved reward. Fulfilled the American Dream, although for most Americans it would remain a pipedream. And believing the old mantra 'delegation is the art of good management', in recent years he could take more time out. Around four months every year he enjoyed leisurely pursuits on his ranch in New Mexico, thirty miles east of Albuquerque. But he never had a day off. 'I'm constantly developing strategy to help the world's poorest people,' he'd tell staff on location and friends around his barbeque and pool overlooking the semi-arid desert and towering barren peaks. New Mexico was indeed the Land of Enchantment.

When working in the field, there was always someone extremely grateful for additional food, or accommodation, or employment. Or a handful of dollars. Young girls themselves, sometimes encouraged by their parents, would show their appreciation. From the slums of Haiti to Rio de Janeiro, from his aid programmes in Ethiopia to Thailand, Womach took advantage of their desperate situation. And the younger the girl, the better.

TEN

Exactly one week after the meeting at the ministry, the first batch of products landed at Dacca's war-damaged airport. Farook Hussain's son, Mazharul, at the tender age of twenty-two, was given authority to supervise the delivery. All had been arranged with the army colonel in charge of the airport, a trusted brother of the minister, and Mazharul's most-admired uncle.

The Mercedes slipped slowly down the tailgate of the US Air Force C-130 Hercules. An identical top-of-the-range model followed. Raven black, highly polished, elegant, upholstered in cream-coloured leather, Mazharul eagerly anticipated the drive to their compound.

Senior ministers would be delighted with what Farook had secured for them when their cars eventually arrived. He would rise further in their estimation, consolidating his position as the cabinet's crowned prince, the leader in waiting. The vehicles would, without doubt, aid their ministerial work rebuilding the devastated country. It was vitally important to show the people that their politicians had international influence, that rewards could be achieved through hard work. It was also essential to travel in air-conditioned comfort.

After off-loading two Mercs, a routine aid delivery commenced. Watched closely by the aircraft's crew and a company of armed Bangladeshi troops, skinny half-naked lungi-clad men commenced carrying off hundreds of thigh-high bags of CSM – powdered corn, soya and milk. Each life-saving bag stamped USAID and emblazoned with the Stars and Stripes. Five three-ton army trucks stood in a line on the runway to be loaded and despatched to a military warehouse.

While the labourers carried heavy bags on their sweat-drenched backs, Mazharul was presented with the shipment documentation by the USAF captain, accompanied by a salute. The young man wasn't sure how to respond. He went to salute, but switched to a handshake. His uncle once told him you never salute without a hat or helmet. In any case, civilians shouldn't salute, surely. Mazharul slipped the paperwork inside his leather briefcase. The captain asked for the delivery note to be signed, and Mazharul scrawled something. The bottom carbon copy was handed back 'for your records, Sir', with another salute.

The captain added, 'A colleague will be landing sometime tomorrow morning with two more ministerial vehicles. There's more CSM and, I understand, some engineering kit. Until over Indian airspace, it's difficult to give a precise ETA. But the weather looks a-okay overnight, so I expect JJ – that's fellow captain Jimmy Johnson – will be touching down around dawn.'

'Thank you, Captain.'

'See you're still patching up the runway,' said the airman, scanning the area.

'Yes, it got bombed very badly,' Mazharul said. 'They keep doing repairs. But we have a shortage of concrete, tarmacadam, in fact all building materials.'

Seemingly unconcerned about such difficulties, the captain, patting the turboprop's fuselage, said, 'That's one of the great things about these great lumps. They land and take off on most scraps of terrain. You should see some of the landing strips we use in Vietnam, even worse than this.'

'Well, thank you. I hope your return flight is pleasant,' Mazharul said, extending a hand to shake. He was anxious to get away. His father had stressed the two Mercedes should be kept out of sight as much as possible.

'You might see me back with another pair of Mercs later in the week.'

'Yes, perhaps.'

Mazharul's uncle had arranged for a young lieutenant and a sergeant to drive both Mercedes down Mymensingh Road towards the minister's four-acre residence in Dhanmandi. They would be escorted, front and back, by armed military vehicles. Miscreants had been known to throw stones and other objects at nice cars. Sometimes the trouble-makers were kids. But, old or young, male or female, such people must be stopped causing trouble for decent citizens.

Both Mercedes, sandwiched between the eight-wheeled armed personnel carriers with mounted machine guns, drove tentatively off the runway. Both drivers took time familiarising themselves with the controls. At first the lieutenant couldn't find where to release the hand-break: his sergeant showed him.

Mazharul plunged in the back of the front car enjoying the air-conditioned luxury. He stroked the leather. Breathed in the new, pristine car's aroma, sweeter than any fragrance. Admired the facia and controls. Quality. Sheer quality, he thought. So much better than the Nissans and Land Rovers and Toyotas he was familiar with. It even put the family's Volkswagens to shame.

Homeless road-dwellers watched the convey with curiosity. There was no envy in their sunken blood-shot eyes. Such things were beyond dreams. When your roof is a sheet of plastic, held up by twigs, even a rusty bicycle is unattainable. Their focus was on food. Always food. Many had not eaten for days, apart from a palmful of rice – rice from which the rat shit had to be removed, piece by piece.

Further down Mymensingh Road a gang of children, orphans, or children sold into bondage by desperate parents, sat at the roadside breaking stones and bricks to sell for concrete powder. They threw hostile looks at the two gleaming Mercs. How they'd love to smash those blacked-out windows or scratch the polished paintwork. Just for the fun of it. But two gun-turrets quickly turned on them averting any hostile action. Their gangmaster performed obsequious salaams to the convoy before striking two of the girls across their backs with his bamboo stick.

Ahead of the convoy was, as Abi and other members of Action Delta dubbed it, the district's BCV – the body collection vehicle. Only three bodies rested in the back of the truck. But it was the early morning run. With no means to dispose of dead relatives, friends or strangers, road-dwellers placed bodies on the kerb to be collected by the local authority. Action Delta and other aid workers had asked where bodies were taken. But district commissioners up and down the country refused to disclose the whereabouts of graves. They claimed every man, woman and child was treated with dignity and buried correctly. Few believed the district commissioners. When mass graves came to light, the authorities used them as 'evidence of wartime atrocities' perpetrated by the West Pakistanis.

Turning right onto Sher-E-Bangla Road, the convoy could move a little faster. The police had earlier cleared away the poor from their street-side slum. Both car drivers had also grown in confidence handling their highly valuable vehicles.

Refuelled, the C-130 roared into the sky. Taking off into the prevailing south-westerly, the pilot gradually turned true west. Below, in Dhanmandi, the minister and his son watched the plane pierce the dark grey monsoon clouds, already amassing in readiness for the day's downpour.

'Can I get off to college now?' Mazharul asked.

'Of course, my son. I can drop you off. I shall be leaving in a few minutes. The cabinet meeting starts at ten.'

ELEVEN

Driving from Tungipur to central Dacca usually took around forty minutes. No reason was given for the army roadblock near the airport. Dr Rahman asked a junior officer at the barrier for the cause of the delay, not really expecting an explanation. And he didn't get one. The soldiers were, as soldiers do, simply following orders.

Bushra complained. She would miss the first lecture. Until her sister's grumble, Ayesha had not noticed the holdup. Her head was stuck inside a textbook: *Macleod's Clinical Examination*. She needed to memorise the correct sequence when investigating the trigeminal nerve – sensory, motor, corneal reflex, jaw jerk. Next to her in the back seat, Ayesha's lifelong friend, Khalida, was also studying intently. A year ahead of Ayesha at Dacca Medical College and Hospital, she too was revising for the end-of-term exam.

'You might still make it on time,' Dr Rahman said, pulling up outside the university.

'Maybe, Abba,' said Bushra, stepping out of the car. 'But I don't want to rush into the lecture theatre all hot and bothered. The air-con is useless in there, even if it's working today.'

'Relax, my dear. It's only eight forty-five.'

'Yes, all right. Thanks, Pa. See you later. Remember Bibi's driver is bringing us home.' Bushra waved and joined a bunch of her friends, who immediately made her the centre of attention.

At Dacca Medical College and Hospital, Dr Rahman parked his car and walked with Ayesha and Khalida, both dressed in white blue-bordered saris, to the entrance hall. He planned to see the college's deputy principal, a good friend and colleague since their own student days. The DP hoped to persuade Abdur to come as a permanent lecturer. Only two days a week, he said on the phone. No marking. Well, not much. You would enjoy it. You adore talking medicine and surgery. We desperately need you.

In the cavernous high-ceilinged atrium, echoey from the ornate tiled floor and walls, Abdul Rahman left Ayesha and Khalida to climb the marble staircase to the administration offices. He remembered the days when he could easily stride two stairs simultaneously. Alas, with his damaged leg, it now took time and he needed support of the banister. Aware Ayesha was watching his ascent, he tried his best to disguise the pain. But Dr Rahman couldn't hide the discomfort from his daughter's acute eye.

'Was Bibi's driver picking us up too?' Khalida asked.

'Yes, a few minutes after four, if Bushra doesn't keep him waiting chatting with all her pals. He'll park at the usual place on Secretariat Road.'

Khalida hesitated, scrunched up her face, rocked her head from one side to the other.

'Khalida, come on, what's the problem?'

'Maz called. Asked if I'd like to visit the museum.'

'What? Alone?'

Although by Bangladeshi standards Khalida's widowed mother was considered modern and liberal – almost as easy-going as the Rahmans – it would be unacceptable for a young unmarried couple to go out together alone and be seen in public.

'No, of course not. I hoped you and perhaps a small group of us could go together.'

'Khalida, there's no way I can spare the time to ramble around museums. I've got so much studying to catch up on. I've an exam coming up too remember.'

'Ayesha, you always say you're behind. Ever since junior school. But you never are. Officially you're are a whole year behind me. But in truth you're already ahead of me. You're studying stuff that I've not even looked at yet…'

'That's not…'

'No, Ayesha, it's no use denying it. You know it's true. Okay. Look, I'll get some of the others to come along. Don't worry about me getting home, Maz will have his car, or his father's driver, or we'll get a cab and he'll drop me off. Must dash. Bye.'

TWELVE

For two weeks, since the attack on Dr Rahman's house, one face, one voice, had dominated Ben's thoughts.

He couldn't believe the overwhelming power of these feelings. He tried resisting, denial, distraction. He worked even harder. Longer. Faster. He dug ditches. Erected tents. Lugged sacks of rice. Repaired water pumps. But all attempts to forget her failed.

He seriously considered the obsession had become an illness, physical and mental. His body literally ached for her company. Much of the day and most of the night she was there, somewhere in his mind. Even sleep failed to provide respite, for she was in his dreams.

Guilt arrived. There were far more important matters to consider than self-obsessed thoughts and selfish desires. And what he wanted was beyond reach. She was... she was...

In Britain Abi was attending Jonny's funeral alongside his grieving family. (In his letter to Abi, Ben deliberately omitted to say the baby boy in tent D121 died and his young mother... Abi could do without more bad news.) Action Delta friends in Bihari camps across Bangladesh are afraid for their lives. Dr Rahman must be worrying about more bricks crashing through his windows. Or worse. Hundreds of thousands of grenades and guns remain in the hands of former guerrillas. Even small children learnt how to make petrol bombs during the conflict.

Instead of this selfish obsession over her, he should be working to do more for the thousands around Dak Cottage living in atrocious conditions, half starved, threatened and often assaulted by former freedom fighters, the Mukti Bahini. Ben was told of more incidents of Bihari women and girls being dragged from the camp and abused. But the camp community generally kept quiet, or spoke only in whispers. The victims silenced by trauma, their families by shame. Those attacked often believed they themselves were to blame. A ridiculous notion that Ben could not understand nor accept: a clash of cultural attitudes and beliefs. West is West, East is East.

But if a victim complained, they faced threats of yet more violence – worse than rape, if anything could be. Their family would suffer too. It was known suicide and so-called honour killing had followed sex attacks: death considered better than individual shame or family dishonour because of the defilement.

A Bihari worker told Ben that one girl had not returned to the camp after being abducted two days earlier. Her mother assumed she had been murdered after the gang finished with her. She asked if some men could go in search of her body, pointing to the area of jungle outside the camp they dragged her through in broad daylight. Armed with sticks – for searching in the dense fauna and for protection – Ben went with the search-party, but they failed to find her.

Ben called into the district police headquarters in Tungipur and asked to see the officer who visited Dr Rahman's house after the attack. He reported the abductions and assaults, as Abi had on several occasions previously.

'It is of such regret to me, me personally Mr Altringham, that so often we only have allegations against these perpetrators,' the inspector sighed, lighting a cigarette in his drab and untidy office. 'Nothing would give me greater satisfaction than to bring hooligans to book. But we police need sufficient grounds to arrest. Our courts demand substantial evidence to convict.'

As if sharing a secret with Ben, the inspector lowered his voice and bent over his desk. 'You know, Mr Altringham, some of these Bihari fellows exaggerate such events. Some have been known to make up stories. Not all are trustworthy.'

Keeping his growing frustration in check as best he could, Ben asked how the investigation into the attack on Dr Rahman's residence was progressing. The inspector explained that such matters take time. Things may come to light. There are complications. Procedures to follow.

Ben placed his shoulder bag on the inspector's desk. It landed with a thud, louder than he had intended. But it gained the inspector's immediate curiosity, even concern, about what was inside.

'This "vital evidence" was left behind outside Dr Rahman's garden,' Ben said. 'Thought you might like to check them for fingerprints.'

'Ah yes, thank you, Mr Altringham. It was negligent of my constables to leave them behind.'

'I bet you told them to drop them,' Ben was on the brink of saying. But it would be unwise to make an enemy of the inspector. Staying as polite as possible, taking a leaf out of Mrs Rahman's book of diplomacy, Ben thanked the inspector for his 'valuable time', gathered his bag and returned to the camp.

Three bricks remained on the inspector's desk.

They were porous, rough, contaminated by many hands, dropped in mud and washed by monsoon storms. Ben accepted that even in the extremely unlikely event fingerprints being gathered, it would be inadmissible as evidence. He simply wanted to make a point, although it was pointless.

MA AND PA play a Frank Sinatra record on the gramophone, '*In the wee small hours of the morning*'. He sings, '*What is this thing called love?*' Cole Porter wrote it. A later line asks, '*Why should it make a fool of me?*'

He will not, repeat not, make a fool of me. Infatuation, like some prepubescent teenager, that's my diagnosis. Abba insists self-diagnosis can be self-deception. Always get another opinion, he says. But I can't consult anyone, not even my sister. She's still young. We all need a safe space for our secrets – a locked drawer, a corner of one's mind, a part of our heart.

Study. Study harder. That's my remedy. I must not, repeat not, let him distract me. Yes, that's the cure. Study. Medicine will be my medicine. But many diseases remain incurable. Will this be one?

We are different. That's impossible to deny, and wrong to do so. He is English, not Bangladeshi. His history is different to mine.

I am a Muslim, he is... a Christian, presumably. He is one race, I am another. This is my home, he is a visitor, passing through, transient, ephemeral.

The biggest difference of all is that I am a woman, he is a man. Perhaps that's not the barrier, but the bridge.

THIRTEEN

Ben had become a regular visitor to the Rahman household. Once or twice a week over the past two months he would be invited to stay overnight. It saved the two-mile trek in the dark to Dak Cottage. The narrow pot-holed track leading to Mohpur camp was unlit and weaved through jungle and scrubland. In a downpour the path transformed into a river of sludge.

Only the brave or the foolish or the desperate would now take that route after dark. Lawlessness was on the rise. Bands of seemingly homeless men had set up camp nearby. Even the very poor had been made poorer by these gangs – robbed of their dirty shirts, threadbare lungis and well-worn wafer-thin sandals. If Bihari, they could also expect to receive a beating and consider themselves lucky to escape with their life.

Action Delta had a Land Rover at Mohpur camp. But the charity's policy was to use drivers with local knowledge. Staff were not insured to drive, the cost too prohibitive. And Ben could not expect Syed to hang around until late to transport him back to the dak. Local gangs allowed Syed unmolested passage: they knew he had friends who would exact revenge if harm came to him. Nor did Ben want to have Dr Rahman drive in the dark, although he had offered. Cars had occasionally been forced to stop – a tree trunk across the track foretold of what was to come. Occupants were robbed and the vehicle stripped of tyres and engine parts: there was a shortage across the whole country.

Dr and Mrs Rahman recognised that a bond had developed between Ayesha and Ben. It was subtle. Not overt. But prolonged eye contact, relaxed body language and a shared sense of humour gave the game away. Dr Rahman told his wife he had diagnosed the signs and symptoms of mutual affection before the couple themselves, although Mrs Rahman detected them earlier.

Bushra had gossiped with her mother. She described the 'goings on' after her parents had retired to bed the night of the brick attack. 'Ayesha went all funny with Ben, Ma. The look in her eyes, it was weird. At first I thought she was going to throw something at him. But then she looked confused and stormed off. Walked out without a word. She's besotted, Ma.'

Mrs Rahman feigned little interest in Bushra's story, keeping her eyes on the pages of her magazine. 'My dear, I'm sure that's not the case. Maybe she remembered something about her studies and went to make a note. You know she often does that.'

Bushra's enthusiasm for telling the tale was not derailed. 'Then Ben went weird. When Ayesha came back he leapt up from the sofa. He was trembling, Ma, honest. Just for a few seconds. He was more frightened of Ayesha than those hooligans with the guns and baseball bats.'

'My dear, I'm sure you're misinterpreting the meaning of those events,' Mrs Rahman said. She bent her head deeper into the magazine. It didn't stop Bushra.

'Ma, I'm telling you, Ben's star struck. And Ayesha's doe-eyed.'

Impatiently, sighing, Mrs Rahman lowered the magazine to her lap and addressed Bushra. 'Young lady, you've been reading too many soppy books and watching too many romantic films. Now, please allow me to finish this article.'

'Ma, when Ayesha knows Ben's coming for dinner, she puts on one of her good saris and spends twice as long doing her hair and make-up. You must have noticed, surely?'

'Not particularly, Bushra, no.'

'And you know the biggest give-away?'

'Tell me, and then please give me a little peace and quiet. You must you have some revision to get on with.'

'Varnish on her toes! Unless it's a wedding or festival, you know she never – never ever – bothers with her toes. She has always declared it was a waste of time.'

RAINA RAHMAN WAS restless. Impossible to sleep. She tossed and turned to find a comfortable position. It wasn't the heat, nor humidity, nor the buzz of mosquitoes that kept her awake. Even the frogs and toads and cicadas were having a quiet night. And the rain had stopped. It was her mind, not her body, that failed to find comfort.

After twenty-eight years of marriage, it was easy to detect that Abdur remained awake too.

'What are we to do?,' she asked. She whispered the question a second time.

After a long pause, Abdur sighed, 'Sleep.'

'We can't ignore what's going on.'

Abdur surrendered, stirred and sat up, pumping his pillow against the bedhead. 'Raina, my dear, I don't know what you are talking about.'

'Don't play that dumb card with me, Abdur Rahman. You know precisely what's on my mind – because it's also on yours.'

'Yes, yes, and I know you can read it. So I could just go back to sleep and, in the morning, you tell me what I've thought and said.'

'It's no laughing matter, Abdur.'

'No, my dear, you're right.'

'Well, do you think we should curtail Ben's visits? Even stop them completely. Should you have a word with him?'

'I've been asking myself those questions for the last few weeks. I don't know the answers. And what could I say?'

'Tell Ben that it's impossible for our daughter to have a... a relationship with him. She's a Muslim and he's a...'

'A Christian, I assume. I'm not at all sure. I rather have the impression he's not religious.'

Both paused for thought. Abdur broke the silence. 'But it's not *impossible* though, is it? I wouldn't have any objection to either of our daughters having a relationship with anyone, really. As long as he is a good man, a nice person. And, most important, our daughters are happy. We've always said so, haven't we? We've tried to bring them up without prejudices of race, religion, creed and so on.'

'I agree, Abdur. But have we been too – what's the word – liberal? Because now we face the consequences. Don't misunderstand me. He's a lovely young man. Polite. Intelligent. Quite handsome. His blond hair and blue eyes certainly stand out from the crowd around here. I can see why Ayesha's fallen for him. But… but… it's…'

Both of them stretched the seconds to think of the right word. Or they knew it, but neither wanted to say it.

'Dangerous.' But it didn't need saying aloud.

The couple could hear the ticking of the longcase clock in the hallway downstairs. Its pendulum must have swung a hundred times before Mrs Rahman spoke. 'Abdur, if we lived in London, America, even in Calcutta, it would be acceptable to most of our family. Although some would certainly object. But here, now, with so many nationalistic hotheads.'

'Raina, I think we're getting ahead of ourselves. It's just infatuation. On both sides. In a few months Ben will have probably moved on. And we know nothing will get in the way of Ayesha becoming a doctor.'

'Do we know that for sure? Do we know Ben will go and that Ayesha won't do something silly?'

'I can't guarantee Ben leaving Bangladesh. But I can guarantee Ayesha will become a doctor, and a fine one at that.'

Dr Rahman thrust his arm through the mosquito net and switched on the table lamp. 'Pani,' he asked his wife, and he poured a glass of water for her and handed it over before taking a glass for himself.

'We've raised both our girls to be good Muslims,' Dr Rahman said. 'But we allowed them choice. Gave them licence to make up the own minds in this modern world. None of us are dedicated followers. I go to the mosque most Fridays as much to meet old friends as to pray.'

With anxiety in her voice, Mrs Rahman asked the question that had also played on her husband's mind. 'Do you think anything, you know, something has happened between them? They've had time alone. Bushra has told me she's gone to bed on several occasions leaving them downstairs alone. I suppose they could have…'

'No, Raina. Both are far too sensible.'

'Abdur, come on, you know what young men get up to.'

The clock struck two.

EARLIER THAT NIGHT Bushra sat on Ayesha's bed, both dressed in pyjamas. As always before sleep, Ayesha had a textbook open and her notebook at the ready. She found that reading before sleeping helped her retain facts better than at any other study time. Her theory, her hypothesis for further study sometime in the future, was that a brain's neurons – just like a body's muscles – needed to rest after exercise. And because the nerve cells became relaxed after working hard, they retained facts more efficiently. How? She didn't know. But one day she hoped to find out. She once heard a famous Shakespearian actor on the BBC World Service say he learnt all his lines in bed before sleep, which reinforced her theory.

'I need to prepare for tomorrow's lecture, Bushra. Go away.'

'The point of a lecture is that you listen and learn. It's the lecturer who needs to prepare the lecture, not the student.'

'As I've told you before, if you read about the subject beforehand, you get more out of the lecture.'

'I'm not going to leave your bedroom until you tell me. Have you?'

'Bushra, I haven't the faintest idea what you are talking about.'

'Yes you do. Have you, you know, kissed him?'

'Mind your own business.'

'So, you have!' Bushra shot both hands to her open mouth.

'That is a totally illogical conclusion. I didn't say yes. I didn't say no. And just because I didn't say no, you can't assume I would say yes. Now buzz off. You're annoying me.'

'Okay, dear sister, I'll leave you in peace.' Bushra slipped off Ayesha's bed. 'But you know you'll have to tell me more one day.'

'There's nothing "more" to tell.'

'Oh yes there is. By the way, what's tomorrow's lecture on anyway? Boring anatomy? Learning loads of names of body bits no doctor ever remembers after qualifying?'

Ayesha had to force a smile. She exposed the pages she was reading in *Macleod's Clinical Examination* to show her sister.

Bushra sniggered. 'Chapter ten. Hmm, interesting. All about the reproductive system. How timely.'

FOURTEEN

Before dawn every Friday Farook Hussain heeded the azan, the call to prayer. It was delivered from the mosque's minaret by the muezzin. He recited the Takbir and the Kalimah, *There is no God but Allah, and Muhammad is his messenger.*

Alongside hundreds of early-rise worshipers, Farook Hussain, facing Mecca, completed the required rituals during fajr, the first of five daily prayers. As demanded, he asked Allah for forgiveness and mercy: he sincerely believed Allah would grant his supplication.

Most days Hussain did not attend mosque. But Friday is the day of congregation, Al-Jumuah, especially for the men. Often he missed prayers during the day, but he vowed to compensate at his next salat. Islam is a far more flexible faith than many non-Muslims think, he routinely told foreign politicians, diplomats and journalists.

Despite his early start, Hussain routinely worked late into the night. It was already after midnight, but he was determined to go over his business accounts before retiring. A desk lamp provided all the light he required for the paperwork in his office at home. With only his desk illuminated, it helped focus his mind on the matters to hand, what he would read, what he would write, what he would plan. The rest of the room remained dark, shadowy and indistinct.

Hussain prided himself on his capacity for hard work. It was an open secret that some of his cabinet colleagues were lazy fellows, appointed for sycophancy to the prime minister rather than ability. Hussain didn't mind: idle and fawning friends don't pose a political threat, to the PM or himself. He was canny enough to play that political balancing act necessary for high office – for the highest office. He maintained the leader's friendship without flattery; demonstrated collaboration while retaining individuality; kept his friends close and his enemies closer; projected power without posing an existential threat. In that, he was typical of a leading actor's understudy: one really wishes the show's star would break a leg on the day of opening night.

One week after 16 December 1971, at the birth of Bangladesh when the West Pakistan regime was finally ousted, Hussain resigned as a major-general in the army. He was hailed a hero. Now the military battle has been won, I wish to serve my people by building prosperity through peace, became his rally cry. Naturally, after thirty-one years in the army – recruited under British Raj in 1940 during the Second World War – Hussain retained close friendships with senior military figures. He was fully aware of the growing discontent in the ranks at the lack of firm leadership from the prime minister, the escalating lawlessness, the slowness of economic progress.

Hussain heard his guards in the compound outside being roused. The heavy iron gates opened and allowed the car to enter. He was annoyed that his son spent more time partying than studying. Then he remembered his own misspent youth: like father, like son. To his wife, Mazharul remained the apple of her eye: the favourite son, her only son, their only child. Mothers can only see good in their sons, Hussain mused. He could see more.

The minister told his servant on duty outside his door to instruct Mazharul to attend his father's office immediately.

'Still up, Abba? It's past midnight. And you attended fajr this morning. Did you nap this afternoon?' Mazharul remained standing. He was eager to get to his bedroom and enjoy sweet thoughts about Khalida.

'One doesn't become foreign minister by working office hours, Mazharul. If you are to make anything of your life, it is imperative you work twice as hard and twice as long – and especially twice as smart – as those around you.'

'Yes, Abba. I do. And I will. Promise.'

'When I get you to Harvard in Massachusetts, or London School of Economics, you will be up against the best brains. There will be no time for dilly-dallying.'

'No, Abba. Yes, Abba. But post-grad stuff isn't for another year or two.'

Hussain pointed to the chair in the corner. Mazharul pulled it over to face his father across the desk, resigned to another one of his fatherly lectures.

'Listen, son. It's not safe to be out late at night. You won't see it in the newspapers, obviously, but there are increasing numbers of assaults and robberies going on. Several cars every night in Dacca alone are stopped at gunpoint and people inside forced to give up their cash, watches, jewellery and whatnot. It's all these left-over freedom fighters and others with too much time on their hands and too much greed in their stomachs.'

'My driver's armed, isn't he? And I've the shotgun in the boot. Perhaps I should keep it closer to hand.'

'That would be wise, son. I doubt the dacoits will invite you to pop to the boot and let you aim your Beretta to blow their heads off.'

Hussain opened a desk drawer and rummaged around. Mazharul assumed he was reaching for a packet of sweets or a chocolate bar – until the handgun was slammed on the desk and pushed towards him.

'Keep that nearby, son. And a gun without these isn't much better than a water pistol.' Hussain again reached into the drawer before a box of 9mm bullets was slid towards Mazharul. 'Take it up to the range and practice using it. Know how to load and assemble it blindfolded until it becomes second nature. Always be as familiar with your gun as your dick.'

Surprised at his father's bluntness, Mazharul simply replied, 'Yes, yes I will.'

'There is something else you need to know, Mazharul,' Hussain said gravely. 'Another matter you will not see reported, for fear of copycats you understand. In the last month alone there have been at least three cases of kidnapping – kidnaps followed by ransom demands.'

'Really?'

'Yes, really,' Hussain said wearily. 'They stop cars at gunpoint, grab the driver or an occupant, and make off into the night. Before you can say Jack Robinson the telephone rings demanding a ridiculously high sum of money.'

'And if it's not paid?'

'What do you think? They threaten to start removing fingers. Some have been cut off and left on the doorstep. If a girl or woman… well, you know what they promise to do, the whole gang.'

'The police?'

'Haven't a clue, son. Useless. We need a firmer hand on the tiller before this gets out of hand. Now get to bed and leave me to complete some work.'

As Mazharul stood and replaced the chair his father asked, 'By the way, where were you tonight? Did you see Khalida? Where did you go?'

'The museum. It's opened again. But lots of stuff has been looted or damaged.'

'The museum closes at four or five. So where since?'

'With friends. You know, with Shamsul's family up in Gulshan. Talking about our studies and relaxing.'

'Trust you were discreet.'

'Of course, Abba, of course.'

'As my father always advised me, as I shall you, and you your sons, "If you can't be good, be careful".'

FIFTEEN

Ben always felt guilty eating at Lucky House, the Chinese restaurant in Tungipur. It was hard to leave the squalor of the camp and dine in such pleasant air-conditioned surroundings without a twinge of conscience. He could never finish a three-course meal without thinking of the half-starved souls at Camp Mohpur.

Action Delta had 'made a difference', to use the fashionable cliché of the emergency relief aid industry. More water pumps had been installed. Deeper and wider drainage ditches dug. Food deliveries and medical supplies had improved slightly. Still, the demand of need far outstripped the supply of essentials. Dysentery and other water-borne diseases had not declined. Smallpox remained rife. Several camp residents died daily, old and young, men and women. Death discriminates – against those with least.

Months ago Abi noticed whole sides of tents deliberately torn and removed. She discovered the material had been used to wrap around bodies for burial. Cremation is haram, forbidden, in Islam. To prevent further destruction, Abi begged two large rolls of white linen from a clothing manufacturer. Ben continued to maintain the service, routinely cutting a length of the cloth to give the bereaved in need.

The Rahman family had introduced Ben to Lucky House owner, Jimmy Ong. He had recently returned from Hong Kong to reopen his restaurant. Jimmy and his family fled from the country soon after the civil war started in March 1971.

'They took all my money, food, whisky, wine, beer, pots, pans, everything. I left with nothing, Mr Ben. But got flight out next day with gold. I had secret hiding place.' It was probably the third time Ben heard Jim Ong's story, always told with a beaming smile, as if he'd experienced no hardship whatsoever.

Tonight's visit to Lucky House was different: the absence of Bushra. Ayesha's sister had declared that she had university work to complete. Being Saturday night, Ben became suspicious of the reason she gave. Ayesha more so of her excuse. And the motive for Bushra's absence soon became clear.

Daisy, Jim's daughter, cleared away the bowls after the first course of chicken and corn soup. It was Dr Rahman's cue. The tables were well spaced, plenty of ambient talk and laughter, but he spoke gently as always. He leaned forward across the table.

'You both know we need to talk. It's clear you two have formed a special relationship.' Indeed, they had. Ayesha squeezed Ben's hand tighter beneath the table.

'Ben, you know we have raised Ayesha and her sister to be independent women with minds of their own. We wished them to respect our faith and rich Bengali culture, but not be constrained by either.

'Islam itself is very respectful of women, as we've discussed on many occasions. Sadly, some cultural practices, from North Africa to our subcontinent and beyond, have at best misinterpreted our beloved Qur'an or, at worse, selected quotes to reinforce inhumane deeds.' He stopped talking abruptly. And he waited.

Abdur had expected Ayesha or Ben to jump in and say something. But they remained silent. Having boundless patience and the experience of a physician, he too was comfortable with silence. Dr Rahman continued to let the silence speak.

Mrs Rahman forced a response. 'Tell us, where do you think your friendship is going?'

Ayesha and Ben turned to face each other and back again at Dr and Mrs Rahman, Abba and Amma.

'I... no, you first, Ben.'

'No, please go ahead.'

Ayesha took a slow deep breath before speaking and she turned to face Ben. 'I don't know. We haven't discussed anything, have we? Not really. We're just getting along with our lives and... and I don't know what more to say.'

'And you, Ben?' Mrs Rahman asked softly.

Ben maintained Ayesha's gaze. 'It's true. We're great friends and…
and I don't know what more to say either.'

'As you realise, Ben,' Dr Rahman said, after the seconds of silence
stretched to perhaps a minute, 'we have no objection whatsoever to
your friendship with Ayesha. We all think you are a fine young man.
We enjoy your company. We also appreciate that you have been
respectful of our customs and expectations. It hasn't gone unnoticed
that when we've been shopping together, walking outside, here in the
restaurant or had visitors at home, you have kept your distance from
Ayesha, and Bushra, as is the way here.'

He smiled and added, 'Nobody could mistake you for my son.
Or their brother. But you, more than most, know there are certain
elements in our society who, to put it bluntly, deeply resent
Bangladeshi Muslim girls having anything to do with foreign fellows.'

Ayesha intervened, angrily, although kept her voice under
control. 'I don't give a monkey's tooth what these ignorant…
prejudiced people think. If I want to… to have an English boyfriend,
it's nothing to do with them. Do they still think we live under
medieval sultanates?'

Dr Rahman reached out to hold Ayesha's hand – the one not still
squeezing Ben's ever tighter under the table. 'My dear, my lovely
Ayesha, unfortunately we don't live in a Utopia of the future. We live
here. Now. Today.'

As Ayesha started to speak, Daisy arrived with hot plates for each
of the four guests. Her mother, Wai, lit the candles in the hotplate and
replaced the grill. Jim arrived with 'extra specials' of rice, noodles,
wind-sand chicken and steamed shrimp dumplings. The service
delivered, as always, at efficient breakneck speed with smiles from the
Ong family.

'More drinks? Another coke? 7Up? Fanta?' asked Wai. 'Mr Ben,
you want beer, nice whisky?' The Rahman family did not drink
alcohol. Weeks earlier Dr and Mrs Rahman told Ben they had no
objections if he wanted a beer or wine. Again, out of respect, Ben
had always declined at Jim Ong's Lucky House. Seeing everyone's
hesitancy, Wai forced the decision. 'Okay. I bring more cokes.' No-one
declined.

Abdur and Raina Rahman, Ayesha and Ben, became busy serving and sharing food with one another. They joked that Bushra would be having a warm-up, it being Ali's day off. 'I bet she just eats a bowl of cornflakes,' quipped Ayesha. 'Three bowls,' Amma chipped in. 'And a chunk of banana cake,' said Abba. 'You can't blame her,' added Ben, 'Ali's cakes – all of them – are delicious. I still don't know how you all stay so slim.' Mrs Rahman told Ben she was pleased to see that he had added a few pounds over recent weeks. 'And all the better for it.'

The banter didn't detract from what remained uppermost on everyone's mind. What would each say when the discussion about 'the future' recommenced, for surely it would. Ayesha considered how she could grab a few minutes alone with Ben. He was in tune with precisely the same thought. Unknown to them, Dr and Mrs Rahman thought likewise. It would be easy for them. They could talk privately in their bedroom. But despite regular visits to their home, Ben, respectful of the family's culture, had never stepped inside Ayesha's bedroom. Even if the door had remained open – replicating the stereotypical decorum of a Victorian melodrama – Ben never crossed the threshold. Every time he walked by it to his bedroom, he felt drawn inside as a nail to a magnet. He felt the pull, the force, the attraction. Resistance became harder. But resist he must. And if Bushra was hovering around the living room when they returned home, which without doubt she would be, privacy would be hard to find. Perhaps they could grab a moment in a side room or on the veranda.

Bushra knew something was stirring, something in the air. Amma had asked her to stay at home and not dine with them at Lucky House. Say you need to catch up on a project or something, Amma suggested, perhaps develop a slight tummy upset. We need to 'talk seriously' with Ayesha and Ben 'on neutral ground', Amma had said. Bushra became excited. A wedding? Would Abba and Amma stop the romance? Had her parents discovered that Ben and Ayesha planned to elope? And then it crossed her mind. Oh no, surely not, Ayesha... pregnant? Whatever the spicy news, and Bushra realised her imagination was in overdrive, she couldn't wait to find out what it was.

THE CHOWKIDAR UNLOCKED the gate allowing Dr Rahman to steer the car into his drive and park up. While he was delayed, searching for something in the glove box, Mrs Rahman, Ayesha and Ben walked towards the front door. Mrs Rahman crossed the veranda into the hallway and changed her shoes for slippers. Ayesha however took the opportunity to grab Ben's hand and pull him to one side of the house. It was a pleasant evening and, in recent days, Tungipur had enjoyed a welcome break from the monsoon rains.

'So, Ben,' she whispered conspiratorially, 'what are we going to tell Ma and Pa?'

'Tell them the truth.'

'We can't. It will cause… oh, I don't know… panic. It'll send them into a tizzy. We can't say anything. Not yet.'

'Let's just say we have no plans.'

'But that's not true.'

'Then let's say we have no *firm* plans. That's true. We haven't, not really. We can say that for now we're taking things steady. A day at a time. Just good friends. See what the future brings. That sort of stuff.'

'Okay. Decisive in our vagueness.'

Bushra, eager to catch the news, had keenly anticipated the family's return from Lucky House. She'd spied Ayesha and Ben 'sneak' round the side of the house, as she later put it. After watching them for a while, heads together in deep discussion, Bushra banged on the window causing them both to jump out of their skins and set their hearts racing. Ayesha turned up to the window and shot daggers at her sister. If looks could kill…

'My sister! She's so nosey!'

'That's for sure,' said Ben, watching Bushra deliver a wry smile. 'We'd better go in.'

Bushra met them in the hall as they slipped into their flipflops. 'Well,' she said, hands on hips, 'spill the beans.' They were saved having to respond – and Bushra from a telling-off from Ayesha for spying on them – by Dr Rahman's entry, locking the door behind him.

'Ah, Bushra, my dear, did you catch up on your project?'

'Not quite, Abba.' Bushra immediately knew she'd delivered the wrong answer. It conveniently presented her father with his next line.

'Ah, I'm sure then with another half-hour's effort it will be completed to the satisfaction of your tutor on Monday.'

Dr Rahman's eyes glared towards the stairs. Bushra, taking the obvious hint, followed their direction. With a touch of phony petulance, she nevertheless said goodnight politely, kissed her father and sister, and stamped along the corridor past the grandfather clock.

Ben and Ayesha stuck to their core message when Dr and Mrs Rahman resumed the subject about their future: their plan was to maintain they had no plan. One firm and genuine conclusion was however reached and agreed by all: Ayesha would complete her medical studies. She had insisted. Her father and mother were 'delighted' to hear it.

Ben had the final word before they all went to bed. 'There is nothing I want more than for Ayesha to qualify as a doctor. Nothing. Anyway, I know nothing will stop her. I certainly couldn't,' he said firmly, truthfully.

'Dr Rahman, Mrs Rahman, you have welcomed me with open arms into your amazing family. I promise you, I will do anything and everything to support Ayesha in her ambition to qualify as a doctor. Medicine is her first love. And rightly so. It's a wonderful profession. More. It's a vocation.'

'That's good to hear,' Dr Rahman said, and Mrs Rahman agreed.

Indicating they were ready to retire, Abdur and Raisa raised themselves off the sofa. Without thinking, Ben and Ayesha mirrored them and stood too. Dr Rahman offered his hand to Ben then hugged and kissed his daughter. In a surprise move Mrs Rahman stepped forward, placed her hands on Ben's shoulders, and kissed him on both cheeks. Other than a cursory handshake, this was the first time Mrs Rahman had drawn physically close to Ben. He looked dumbfounded. Felt abashed. Froze stiff in shock. Unsure of what to do with his hands, whether to hold her or not, he simply left his arms dangling aimlessly, limp, sapped of strength. Amma's perfume, powerful, spicy, hypnotic, momentarily intoxicated him.

Behind her mother's back, Ayesha threw Ben a broad smile and gave a thumbs-up.

'Please be discreet. Be careful. Very careful,' Amma said, maintaining a firm grip on Ben's shoulders. 'Let's be honest, there are people here, as in Britain, that do not like mixed-race relationships.'

'The difference, Ben,' Dr Rahman continued on his wife's theme, 'is that here the level of tolerance is lower. And we have many young hotheads, as you have witnessed. You also stand out far more here than, say, Ayesha would in London, or any big city in Britain.'

Ayesha and Ben nodded in agreement.

Abba and Amma retired upstairs wishing the couple goodnight and leaving them lost for words. But happy.

'So, it's official,' Ayesha smiled.

'What is?'

'Ma's hug. Kisses. That definitely means you've become a fully paid-up member of our family.'

SIXTEEN

By October the monsoon downpours had almost ceased. It remained hot but dry for much of the day and night. The intense energy-sapping humidity of June to September, when clouds congregated menacingly before releasing their payload, had abated. It was easier to breathe, sleep, work. And think, as if monsoon moisture penetrated one's head as much as the air.

Disaster relief poured into Bangladesh. The army of aid workers continued to grow. Projects to help the poor became established across the land. Various UN agencies, the International Committee of the Red Cross, Christian Aid, Save the Children, Oxfam and others from around the world, particularly the USA, Britain, Canada and Scandinavian countries became involved. 'Food for work' schemes became commonplace. Sadly, for many hundreds of thousands, they didn't have the health or strength to work: lifting an empty bowl to receive a ladle of rice was beyond their power. Some politicians argued the Bangladeshis should pull themselves up with their bootstrings. But, as others quizzed, what do you do if you don't have boots?

Action Delta was a small two-year-old self-funded group, a tiny fraction the size of established aid charities. It was often accused of being amateur by the cash-rich global-reaching organisations. Nevertheless it didn't stop the big agencies poaching Action Delta's highly motivated workforce, foreign and local, with pay and conditions far better than Action Delta could afford.

Because Biharis were considered traitors to Bangladesh, the few organisations working to support them found life hard. Many local Bangladeshis didn't want to help, or were reluctant to do so. The government made import licences and supplies harder to get for those working with this ostracised minority. Officials denied such discrimination. But nobody believed them, largely because they themselves couldn't lie with any conviction. Politicians played the ploy used for millennia: rally the majority by scapegoating a minority.

At a meeting in Dacca of the eight remaining Action Delta workforce from Britain, it was decided to close their operations in Bangladesh. They hoped their projects, including the camp at Mohpur, would be taken over by one or more of the major aid charities.

Two weeks before the meeting Abi, a founder member of Action Delta, revealed she would not be returning. In her open letter to every member she argued the group had a choice. They needed to either expand rapidly to handle the massive demand, or hand the projects to better-resourced agencies and work with them. She applied the 'economies of scale' argument. It made sense. And Abi simply reflected what Ben and the others had increasingly considered for several weeks.

Despite the wholesale poverty, the appalling living conditions, the heat and humidity, the violence visited on Biharis – and the very poor generally – Ben had fallen in love with Bangladesh. He loved Ayesha even more.

Action Delta's decision to hand over its operations to established aid organisations, or close them down, posed a problem for Ben: he'd be unemployed and he had few savings.

A week after Action Delta's decision to close or hand over its operations, Ben received a phone call at Dak Cottage from Richard, the charity's key coordinator in Dacca. They both found themselves shouting down the phone because the line was bad.

'I've found a new job, Ben,' he said after the opening chitchat. 'It's with Aid International, you know, the big American outfit. Their big boss is a bit like Billy Graham, hot on God.'

'But you're an unbelieving socialist,' Ben said light-heartedly, although true.

'Needs must, Ben. I've only signed up for six months. And the guys I met, Robert and Pete, didn't seem like big Bible-bashers to me. One of the god-squad charities down here start with prayers every morning. All too pious. Couldn't stand that. If AI turn out crap, I'll move on. There's plenty of work going. Oxfam are looking for people too.'

'Wouldn't you prefer working for them? Closer to your political persuasion, I would say.'

'Maybe. Later. But AI are willing to take on our project in Mirpur straight away. And they're interested in Mohpur. They want to come up tomorrow to take a look. Is that okay?'

'Of course, what time?'

'Half-seven, eight.'

'That's fine, Richard. Remember the clinic isn't open Friday morning. But I can show them around, let them know what we've done and see our records.'

'By the way, Ben, these two guys have typically American stupid job titles. They're called "international aid consultants". Like most consultants, I bet they do all the smooth talk while the likes of us do all the rough work. Cheers.'

AYESHA AND FRIEND Khalida met in the cavernous echoey entrance hall at Dacca Medical College. Both had finished schooling and library work for the week. Dr Rahman was to drive them home, stopping on the way to collect Bushra and her friend, Bibi, outside the university.

'Why does my father always take ages after taking a lecture?' whinged Ayesha. 'It finished at four and it's already twenty-past. He's just up there in lecture theatre two.'

'He's one of the few lecturers that hangs about answering students' questions,' Khalida said. 'Remember last week, the one I attended on treating dysentery, he was fantastic. Really engaging. Practical advice too, not just book stuff. About ten students gathered round him afterwards like chicks with a mother-hen.'

'You didn't.'

'That's because I knew I could cross-examine him all by myself on the way home in your car.'

'Are you meeting Maz later?'

'No. Tomorrow. Maybe. Don't know. Anyway, I'm staying at yours tonight, remember? Or is Ben coming… again? I don't want to get in the way of you two love doves…'

'Enough of that, Khalida. Ben and I are just good friends.'

'Yes, yes, of course. You don't fool me. I know you better than anyone. Although perhaps not as intimately as Ben.' Khalida grinned and raised her eyebrows.

'You, Khalida Chowdhury, have a mind not worthy of an obedient modest Muslim girl.'

Dr Rahman approached with a brief case in one hand and dangling car keys with the other. Both young women switched seamlessly to another topic of conversation.

AID INTERNATIONAL'S TWELVE-SEATER air-conditioned Mercedes arrived over an hour late. But adherence to appointment times in the tropics is more relaxed than Swiss watch precision. Both 'aid consultants' stepped out and immediately started fanning their faces against the stifling heat.

Ben welcomed them warmly and invited them inside Dak Cottage. Robert Beck's obesity left him breathless after mounting just the handful of steps to the terrace and front door. Inside the living room, which Ben announced as the office, Pete Conan's eyes opened as wide as his gaping mouth.

'Jesus, Ben, is this it? No other rooms, apart from the john?'

'And a shower room,' Ben responded enthusiastically with a touch of irony. Their deadpan reaction told him neither appreciated sarcasm, nor possessed a rudimentary sense of humour.

'You telling me, Ben, you eat, sleep, hold meetings, do the admin – *everything* in this room?'

Ben was tempted but held back from saying, 'Not everything. I pee and shower elsewhere.'

'And it's a goddam storeroom, by the looks of all those boxes and sacks of rice. So you've lived in this bombed-out shit-heap for months. For heaven's sake, fella.'

'It's ten times better than the people have out there, Pete,' said Ben, already irritated by his and Robert's attitude. Not once had they demonstrated the slightest interest in or concern for the poor folk in the camp. And Ben had grown to like Dak Cottage. He once described it as 'romantic' to Ayesha. She retorted by quoting Noel Coward's 'Mad dogs and Englishmen go out in the midday sun'. But Ben had become used to the dak, its shabbiness, the tumbleweed surroundings, its proximity to the people he had come to help. Like many – probably most – foreign aid workers, seeing the poverty of others made him realise how enormously privileged his own life was, how lucky he had been.

'No aircon,' Robert wheezed, wiping the sweat from his forehead with a huge handkerchief, the size of a tea towel. 'Jesus bleedin' Christ! This would drive me crazy.'

'It's not as hot now as it was a few months ago,' said Ben. 'Far less humid.' Neither visitor looked as if they believed him.

'And you sleep on that?' Pete quizzed in horror, pointing. 'A motheaten bedroll on nothing more than a plank. How the hell do you survive?'

Ben stayed silent. He wanted to shout forget about me, this bungalow, the bed, the peeling plaster, the cracked walls. Take a look outside. See the conditions several thousand Biharis are suffering. Sleeping on bare earth, most of them. Not to mention millions of half-starved Bangladeshis throughout the country.

'Why didn't you rent a decent property nearby, Ben? Or stay at a hotel in Dacca and drive up?' wheezed Robert, who continued to breathe heavily and sweat profusely. 'Mind you, fella, apart from the Intercontinental, they're all fucking crap from what I've seen. Some of our guys got bitten by bleedin' bedbugs at one place.'

Ben was intrigued by their blasphemy. He had assumed both Americans would be, to use Richard's phrase, Bible bashers. But it appeared by their language and behaviour they shunned respect for heaven, Jesus Christ and even hell. Most staff with various Christian aid outfits he'd met in Bangladesh had been prissy, even puritanical. And, discreetly, evangelistic – contrary to the assurances they had given government officials not to try and convert Muslims to Christianity.

Aid International's consultants told Ben that their chief executive officer, Thomas Womach, was paying a brief visit to Bangladesh the following week.

'He'll be having meetings again with various ministers and officials,' Pete added. 'You know, to calm the waters, oil the wheels. Most of these new government ministers don't know their arse from their elbow. A few of them spent years in jail, thanks to the previous cowboys.'

Ben again held back. This time from reminding the Americans that their government supported those 'cowboys' – until it became clear that, thanks to the Indian army, East Pakistan would be free of West Pakistan's yoke.

Pete and Robert didn't stay long, an hour at most. They were clearly itching to get back into the cool aircon of their people carrier. They looked at the latest estimate of camp residents, the site map, the inventory of kit and equipment, the delivery logbook of corn, soya, milk powder, rice, dal, salt and, in a separate book, supplies for the clinic, including medicines.

On departure, Pete told Ben they were confident Aid International would take on the camp. 'But there's not a cat-in-hell's chance any of our guys would stay in this shack. We'll have to spend more than a few dollars doing it up, extending it, put some proper gear in. If the foundations will take the weight, although I doubt it, we'll see if we can build another floor. But it's probably best to flatten the place and start again. Staff welfare is very important to us, Ben.'

Robert said, 'Before we go, like with your Richard down in Dacca, we'd be happy to offer you a contract to continue working here, certainly for a few months. We'd appreciate some handover period at least. How does that sound?'

'Sounds as if I need to think about it.'

'You'd have to move out while building work goes on,' Pete said. 'I guess there's no hotel nearby. We swung through Tungipur on our way here. Looks like a one-horse town. Boring as hell. But we'll put you up at the Intercontinental. All your food and transport expenses will be on top of your compensation package.'

When Robert disclosed what the 'compensation' would be, Ben's jaw hit the floor. It was around five times more than he withdrew from Action Delta's meagre funds – more than some months when he didn't need to claim his full allowance.

SEVENTEEN

'Khalida, Khalida.' Ayesha called softly while tapping lightly on the bathroom door, not wishing to arouse anyone so early in the morning. 'What's wrong?'

In an hour the sun would rise rapidly. The Rahman household would begin to buzz, even on Saturday morning. Maid Buna, cook Ali and servant Natcoo would be busy before dawn.

Ayesha did not need Khalida's answer. She had already guessed that her best friend was pregnant. This meant trouble. Serious trouble for Khalida, her widowed mother and her family at large. Disgrace. Embarrassment. Exclusion. Insults. Perhaps jostled and spat at by zealots. When medical school found out, she would be instantly dismissed, banished for all time.

After the sickness was over, Khalida emerged ashen-faced onto the landing. Ayesha immediately grabbed Khalida's wrist and whisked her into her own bedroom.

Khalida cried. Sobbed yet more when Ayesha held her. It took a few minutes before Khalida found sufficient control to speak. Ayesha was a good listener. Her father often reminded his daughters of an ancient saying: you have two eyes and one mouth, they should be deployed in that proportion. Ayesha with her enquiring mind was naturally eager to ask her friend at least a hundred questions. But she bided her time. This was not the moment to interrogate her life-long friend who found herself in urgent and extreme trouble.

'It shouldn't have happened, Ayesha. I didn't want Maz to go that far. In a way, I don't know how it happened.'

Ayesha wondered how many millions of women over many millennia had described their experience using similar words. She

96

waited to hear more. But Khalida just stared at both hands clutching her headscarf, damp with tears of fear, regret and shame.

Gently, slowly, Ayesha asked, 'What do you mean when you say "I don't know how it happened"?'

The sobbing started again. But Khalida, hesitantly, incoherently at first, explained. 'We were with Shamsul, his friend's place in Gulshan. Next to the lake. You've been there once, remember? That massive house. His father runs the state bank, or something like that. There were about a dozen of us, Safa, Fatima, Dahab. You know, the lot from my year. And the guys, Kasim and co.

'The servants brought us sweets and stuff. Maz handed me a mango juice. After a while Shamsul and Kasim suggested walking down the garden to the lakeside. I felt funny when I stood up. Legs like jelly. Then…'

Khalida paused to gather her thoughts and dab her eyes. She heard Ayesha say something like take your time. No need to say more. It's all right. It's all so overwhelming. But Khalida had to tell someone. And who better than her closest confidant? She'd been bottling up what had happened for several weeks, even doubting what took place. But now there was no doubt about her condition.

Khalida continued. 'On the way to the lake, walking through the house, Dahab and Shamsul slipped into a side room. Well, we all know they've been doing it for months.' She squeezed a half-smile, the other half tinged with worry.

'Then Maz pulled me into a cloakroom or storeroom – anyway, it had cleaning stuff in it – next to the back door. We were behind all the others, so nobody noticed. I didn't mind, Ayesha, honest. Thought he just wanted a quick kiss and cuddle. But my head was spinning. Couldn't quite focus my eyes. Not sure if I fainted.'

Khalida broke into a fit of tears again. Ayesha was anxious someone would hear and think it was herself crying. She left Khalida briefly on the bed and slipped the bolt on the door: Bushra and Buna never knocked before barging in.

'When… when I came round… even then I wasn't sure if he'd… but then… then I could see and feel he had…'

Khalida took several deep breaths regaining control of her emotions. 'I've been meaning to tell you. Since it happened. Then when I realised... How unlucky can I be? Once! Just once, Ayesha. And now this.'

'Does Maz know?'

'Not yet.'

'You'll have to marry him, you know that don't you? And quick.'

'No, no Ayesha. That's not my plan. Not my plan at all. My dream, like yours, is to become a doctor.'

'After the baby, you can always go back and qualify. You'll only lose a year, perhaps two.'

'You know there is no way I'd be allowed to do that. Maz's family are, well, you know what they're like. His dad makes a big thing about attending mosque. You know he makes the media report him going every Friday. You've seen the photos in the newspapers. No, Ayesha, the Hussain family wouldn't allow me to study. After one baby they'll want me to have another, and another.'

'But if you...'

'But nothing, Ayesha. I've decided what I'm going to do.'

Ayesha saw the determination in Khalida's face. Further argument was futile. Ayesha worried.

'I want... I want an abortion. And I'm going to have one. By hook or crook. One way or another.'

Khalida's words turned Ayesha's stomach. 'How? Where? You can't. No Khalida, you can't find someone down a backstreet. They're butchers.'

Khalida turned her head to face her friend full on, her eyes burnt deep into Ayesha's: they spoke loud and clear.

'Oh no. Oh no, Khalida. No. You can't expect me to...'

'You have the skills. The knowledge. Your father's surgery has all the instruments. We could go there... tomorrow, the day after... tell him we want to practice stitching or some procedure or something. Anything.'

'No, Khalida, I'm sorry. But no. Even if I had the skill and knowledge which, by the way, I don't, it's wrong.'

'I'm not forty days gone, I know. Way under ensoulment. Most of our teachings allow abortion...'

'Stop right there, Khalida. You know that's only if your life was in danger or the foetus had really serious disease or deformities. Even so, you know almost everyone will condemn you. Life is sacred. A gift from Allah.'

'My life *is* in danger, Ayesha. Ruined. I don't think Maz would marry me. His family want someone from a wealthy family, a minister's daughter, someone with powerful connections. You know since father was murdered we can just keep our heads above water, even with my half-scholarship for college and...'

The door handle turned. The girls threw a worried glance at each other.

'Why's your door locked, Ayesha?' Mrs Rahman asked.

'It's okay, Amma,' answered Ayesha quickly. 'Khalida and I are having a private chat. I didn't want Bushra disturbing us.'

'Don't be too long. Remember we're driving into Dacca shopping for clothes. And your father is in desperate need of new shoes. Let's try and get there by eight-thirty, nine at the latest. We can drop Khalida home on the way, unless she wants to join us.'

'Thanks, Ma. We won't be long.'

Ayesha listened closely to make sure Amma had not set her ear against the door. In case she had, Ayesha whispered, 'So?'

'So?'

'What are you going to do? Are you going to tell Maz? Or are you not going to tell him?'

'Oh, Ayesha, I don't know. I just don't know.'

EIGHTEEN

'You're a damn fool,' Farook Hussain told his son. Mazharul had chosen a bad moment to tell his father that Khalida was pregnant. The minister had been engrossed in preparing a strategy paper in his study before an important meeting. 'If you needed to... to do that, you should have gone to one of the whores. There's plenty of them down... well, you know where.'

'I'm sorry.'

'So you keep saying. But saying sorry doesn't solve the problem.'

'Are you sure it's yours?'

'Of course.'

'Not necessarily. In my experience, if a girl lets one boy do it, she lets more.'

'Definitely not, not Khalida.'

'It's a good thing her father is dead. If he'd been alive, I'd need to arrange a round-the-clock squad of guards to protect you. Even then, he'd get you. He was a cunning fox. Smartest secret service boss we've had since forty-seven. British trained. Helped them beat the Japanese in Burma. Once worked alongside Mossad – the only Muslim Israelis trusted.'

'Not cunning enough to avoid Yahya Khan's henchmen.'

'That bastard betrayed him. Maruf Chowdhury was never going to reveal details of our plot, even under torture. Then to claim he'd sold secrets to the Chinese as a pretext to hang him, well... Pathetic. Nobody believed Khan.'

'So why did they string Khalida's father up?'

'Because Maruf had an encyclopaedic knowledge of West Pakistan's military and intelligence network. That information would have been invaluable to us during the independence struggle. Khan wanted him out of the way before it all kicked-off.'

'Then why...'

Farook Hussain raised both palms to stop his son from talking. In less than an hour he had to be in Minto Road at Gano Bhaban, the prime minister's office.

'Mazharul, shall we get back to the matter in hand rather than delve into history? I did not want Khalida for your wife. I thought she was a... a temporary measure. Very attractive, yes. I can see why you were tempted by her. But she's far too opinionated, head-strong.'

'She's very intelligent. That's good, isn't it?'

Farook Hussain shook his head slowly. 'Son, you know that I had your friend Shamsul's sister in mind for you. For a start, she's younger, sixteen or seventeen and...'

'Her father's very rich.'

'Well, that too. Our families would have enjoyed an indomitable alliance. Unlike Khalida, the girl has a father, a sound traditional family. Remind me of her name.'

'Farah. She's just turned sixteen.'

'Farah. That means beautiful. And I suppose she is. Perhaps more so than Khalida. I've not seen her for a while, but she was a cute little thing,' the minister said. 'So she's six or seven years younger than Khalida. It's good to have a wife younger than yourself, obviously. But do you wish to marry Khalida?'

'Yes, Abba, I rather think I do.'

'Then that's what must happen. Perhaps in a few years, if Khalida doesn't give us sons, Farah could become your second wife, although I doubt she'll be available then. There will be many dogs sniffing around her.'

Farook Hussain hurriedly pushed more folders into his briefcase. He could see the police escort waiting, their blue lights already flashing in front of and behind his black Mercedes.

'We'll talk more about this tonight when I'm back. Meanwhile, tell Khalida you'll marry her and it must be soon. We'll inform people we've had a secret arrangement for quite a while. Nobody will believe us, especially when the child is born in… how far gone is she?'

'Around two months.'

'When the time comes, we'll announce the baby was born prematurely. And, son, it's time to grow a beard.'

NINETEEN

Maz leapt out from an alcove to confront Khalida. She stepped back, surprised, alarmed by his aggressive stance. He had been watching to make sure none of her friends were around, Safa, Dahab, Fatima, Ayesha. He'd been told fifth-year students were in classroom G2 along the corridor.

'You haven't phoned,' he snapped. 'Did your mother not tell you I called? Several times. Yesterday. The day before. Early this morning.'

'I told you, Maz, I am not going to have this…' she lowered her voice as a group of first-years walked by between lecture rooms. 'Come, we can't talk here.'

In Dacca Medical College's garden, in the shade of palms, Khalida announced their 'problem' would soon be over. She'd heard of a woman who could help.

'You can't, Khalida. It's against our faith. Our Qur'an is clear. I've learnt it by heart. *"Do not kill your children for fear of want. We shall provide sustenance for them as well as for you. The killing of them is a great sin"*.'

'Look, Maz, I'm going to be a doctor. I want a life, to travel, to be free. I don't want to be a baby-making machine for you and your family and kept more or less in purdah. Why, Maz, can't you get that into your head?'

'That wouldn't happen. You'd be free to study and so on – after the baby's born. Promise.'

'Maz, I don't believe you. I regret telling you I was pregnant in the first place. I should've kept it secret, just gone and done what I'm going to do.'

'Then why the hell did you tell me?'

'Because I thought it right that you needed to know the consequences of your behaviour.' Khalida turned to go back into college, but Maz gripped her arm and forced her to face him.

'You have my son inside. He's mine. He's mine as much as yours. I have rights. I forbid you from killing him. I won't allow it. I will…'

'See!' Khalida stamped her foot on the ground reinforcing her anger. 'You've just provided irrevocable proof that you don't care about me, what I want! We're not even married and you're telling me what I can and can't do.'

Maz slapped her face. Hard. Khalida reeled back. She staggered to stay upright. The pens, notepad and textbooks she carried scattered across the grass.

To Maz's surprise Khalida stepped forward to face him. Close. Almost nose to nose. Daring him to strike again. Her father's face flashed before him. Maz saw the same grit and courage in her eyes. Khalida's boldness unsettled him. He lashed out.

'Marry me or, or… I'll get you kicked out of this place,' he blustered. 'I'll tell the principal what you've done. You'll never, never become a doctor. My father will get the police to make sure no harm comes to my son. And…'

'And I'll tell everyone what really happened.'

Maz looked puzzled.

'Yes, I know what you did Mazharul Hussain. I worked it all out. You dropped vodka or something in my mango juice – so much for your Islamic principles. You hypocrite! You drugged me and you… and you raped me.'

He paused, thought about a denial, but returned to the offensive. 'You didn't object,' he smirked.

'I couldn't, otherwise I would have done.'

'Do you think anyone will believe you? Nobody will, Khalida. They'll think you tempted me, wanted it, forced yourself on me. You wanted to entrap a minister's son because you and your mother are down on your heels now. Anyway, you can't prove a thing.'

'Some will believe me, some won't. They're free to choose. Yes, we're down on our heels, as you put it, because my father suffered and died for this country's freedom.'

Khalida's eyes moistened, her lips quivered, but she remained proud and defiant.

Mazharul softened, tried a different approach. 'Look, Khalida, you're beautiful and clever and I like you. I really do. We can solve this problem by getting married. I will forgive you for what you said about having an abortion and…'

'Ha! *You* forgive *me*! No, Maz, we're finished.' Khalida was aware she was on the verge of shouting. She took a deep breath, lowered her voice and said firmly, 'I won't marry a man I can't trust. I'm going to do what I said I was going to do. And do you think I want a man who only *likes* me and not *loves* me? Get out of my way.'

Khalida pushed Maz aside to pick up her pens and books littering the grass behind him. She gave him one last lingering hard look, eyes of hate, before turning back into college. She was both furious and frightened. But she was certain she wasn't going to show him her fear. The side of her face still stung after his strike and she pulled her scarf higher to hide any mark or swelling.

Maz watched Khalida walk away, head high, dignified, determined. Perhaps because of her refusal to marry, his craving for Khalida doubled… tripled… overwhelmed him. She had become more beautiful, desirable, needed. Forbidden fruit, that one at the top of the tree, is always the tastiest when plucked.

But there was another driver: part of him was now in her.

Perhaps I should have said 'love' instead of 'like', Maz thought. But he screamed towards Khalida, 'Bitch!'

MINISTER OF STATE Farook Hussain returned home from the prime minister's official residence in central Dacca. The PM was a nice enough man. Made inspiring speeches. Gave many promises to all who sought his help. Few were fulfilled. The revolutionary leader had outlived his usefulness: independence, from the economic exploitation by West Pakistan, had been achieved. The wonderfully rich traditional Bengali art, culture and, importantly, its language had been restored to their rightful owners, the Bangladeshis, the East Bengalis of old India.

People across the new nation loved the PM, genuinely revered him. But Farook Hussain knew most citizens were, at best, unaware of the PM's incompetence. At worst, people were simply too stupid to understand politics and economics. Several ministers, the astute ones, and a growing band of senior military figures, realised that eventually, perhaps in a year or two, a new leader would be required. For now, it was time to make hay while the sun shines. Time to wait. Time to watch. Time to prepare.

'BITCH!' HE SHOUTED to Mazharul across his desk at home. 'She can't. She cannot destroy our flesh and blood. Where is she now?'

'Home, I assume.'

'I'll have her arrested.'

'What for?'

'You said she's planning an abortion. That's murder. So this is clearly conspiracy to murder.'

'But, Abba, she'll just deny it. Say I'm making it up. She'll claim it's me telling her to arrange an abortion. And remember her family name is still highly respected up and down the country.'

'If nothing else, she will know the police are watching her every move. That will probably be sufficient to prevent her from carrying out the destruction of our child. We'll have her house watched. Day and night. In a week or two she'll surrender and agree to marry you.'

'She's very determined, father, very smart, like you say her father was.'

'Not as determined as me. And she can't be that smart if she let you get her pregnant. First thing tomorrow I'll call the principal or dean or whatever he's called at the medical school. She won't be allowed to step foot in the place again. She won't be allowed to study anything anywhere, regardless of her family name. I'll make sure of that. But you can tell her that after she's had our child, and if she looks after him well, she can resume her studies.'

'I tried that line. She didn't believe me.'

'Then I'll talk to her. She'll believe me.'

AN HOUR LATER that evening, around eleven o'clock, Dr Rahman answered the phone. The rest of the family had gone to bed and he'd turned off the ceiling fans and living room lights.

At this late hour, his first thought was that it was a medical emergency. A relative or friend wanting help. Perhaps a medical colleague seeking advice or assistance: patients were not privy to his home number.

It was Mrs Chowdhury, Khalida's mother. Tearful. Fearful. On the brink of hysterical.

Abdur confirmed her daughter was not staying with them tonight. Then he spent a minute trying to calm and console her. He'd dealt with thousands of worried mothers over the years. He said to Fazana Chowdhury that he was sure Khalida was absolutely all right. Although he wasn't sure at all and regretted using the word 'absolutely'. She's a sensible girl. Very intelligent. Not likely to do anything silly. Maybe the phone network is down in the area where she's staying. Sure you'll hear news soon, Fazana. No need to worry. He had, perhaps for a few minutes, calmed Mrs Chowdhury. Abdur said he would make one or two enquiries and call her back if he had any news, or no news.

Dr Rahman limped heavily along the hallway. His injury routinely became more painful as the day wore on. He climbed the stairs, one step at a time, and knocked quietly on Ayesha's door. At first she thought it was Bushra coming for a late-night gossip. But can't be, she never bothered knocking. Ayesha was, as her father expected, at her desk making notes from a textbook. The light creeping out from under her door was always a give-away.

'Abba?' It was unusual for him to disturb her. She saw his expression and was instantly anxious.

He pulled up a chair next to her. At first he said nothing, just looked into the depth of her eyes. 'Ayesha, my dear, how long have you known?'

She didn't answer, but asked who was on the phone. Once he revealed it was Khalida's mother, Ayesha knew what her answer to her father's question must be.

'About two weeks.'

'Do you know where Khalida is?'

'No, Abba.'

He paused and looked at her square in the eyes. Dark, deep, mysterious eyes, just like her mother's. Abdur had always trusted his daughters to tell the truth. But this was a matter of life and death: he needed to double-check. He had no need to worry. Before he could ask again Ayesha said, 'Honestly, Abba, I really wish I knew where Khalida is at this very moment. Because I... I think she's in danger.'

'From?'

'Herself. Mazharul Hussain. His father and... and the people who are to abort the foetus.'

TWENTY

Khalida's mother, Fazana, retained many influential friends. Husband Maruf was considered a hero, a martyr for Bangladesh. For that reason, the district superintendent of police decided not to search her house, despite pressure from the home affairs minister to do so.

When Mrs Chowdhury told him Khalida had gone missing, not at home, he believed her. After thirty-five years of questioning suspects, the officer had ample experience to differentiate between truth and lies. No actress in the world was good enough to fake the intense distress Fazana Chowdhury displayed.

Fazana told him she had telephoned all Khalida's close friends and spoke to their parents. She was convinced they were not hiding her daughter.

'We would like to help you find your daughter, Mrs Chowdhury,' the district superintendent said. 'It would be extremely useful if you could spare a photograph or two of her.'

THE DISTRICT SUPERINTENDENT of police deployed four squads to search for Miss Khalida Chowdhury, aged twenty-two, height five feet six inches, smooth skin. The squad leaders were told, off the record, of her condition and that she was seeking an abortion. This abhorrent behaviour was because of her state of mind, he briefed, possibly suffering paranoid schizophrenia.

'Abortion is illegal. Seeking one necessitates a charge of attempted murder,' the four senior policemen were told. 'But when found she must be handled with the utmost care. Make sure your men treat her with respect.'

Squad one was ordered to make their first search in Chouk Bazar in Dacca. It was a shabby ground-floor apartment in the crowded ramshackle road opposite the central jail. They didn't knock. Kicked open the door. One man, one woman, one girl occupied the room. The 'doctor' froze holding a long steel spatula mid-air. His 'nurse' assistant stood with a bloody rag in bloody hands. The girl, fifteen at most, was flat on her back on a bare wooden table, both legs raised and tethered with leather straps to a bamboo frame.

The inspector in charge of the squad stood over the girl. She coughed then groaned and pleaded for water. *Pani, pani...* He looked at her face and, double-checking, took a photograph from his top pocket. She was not Khalida Chowdhury. Khalida was a proper woman. This reedy flat-chested girl was some silly street urchin who hadn't followed her pimp's instructions. The inspector, confirming it was not their suspect, dismissed the sergeant and four constables. They stood outside and lit up their bidis.

The former doctor knew what to do. Raids were a regular occurrence. He placed the blood-stained spatula on his square stainless steel trolley, removed his latex gloves and opened the wall cabinet. From the wad he counted five ten-dollar bills. The inspector said nothing, just shook his head. Another ten-dollar bill was added. Another shake of the head, and another, and more.

'It's gone up a lot since last time.'

'So has the price of rice.'

Walking out, distracted while tucking one hundred dollars into his shirt pocket next to Khalida's photo, the inspector accidentally kicked over a plastic bucket. It bounced across the room spraying its gory contents everywhere. A fist-sized foetus slid through the pool of slippery blood before smacking the skirting. The officer remained undisturbed. He'd seen far worse during the war. But he was angry that his neatly-pressed khaki trousers had been splattered with blood and pieces of flesh.

He took out the photograph of Khalida again and summoned 'doctor' to cross the room to look.

'If she comes, you call central station and ask for me, Inspector Iqbal Subhan. Nobody else. Understand?'

'Yes, of course. Her name?'

'You need not know. Anyway, I'm sure your customers give false names.'

'That is true, inspector.'

'And you do not do this to her.' He swept his arm towards the trussed-up girl, now paler and losing consciousness.

'No, of course inspector.'

'If she comes in, I suggest you tie her up like this slut and call me straight away. Keep her down. Don't let her go. If I'm off duty, tell them to call my home. We use codewords to authorise such contact. Mine is Lalmatia. Do you need to write it down?'

'Lalmatia is easy to remember, inspector Subhan. I live there.'

The 'nurse' hadn't moved an inch since the police intrusion. Not to give the girl a sip of water, nor stem the blood seeping from her, nor stop the drips falling to the filthy floor.

One hundred dollars would be split in the standard proportion: ten each for the constables; twenty for the sergeant; forty for the inspector. If, later, his chief asked for a report on the raid, Subhan might need to relinquish twenty.

'I'm sure we will catch a dangerous driver going through a red light on our way back to the station,' he told his men. 'We shall all clearly witness it.'

'Even if the lights aren't working,' the sergeant quipped.

They sniggered and nodded agreement, stubbed out their bidis, folded their dollar notes and found a pocket to store their reward.

AYESHA SUGGESTED TO her father that she calls Khalida's friends to see if she was staying with them. Mrs Chowdhury had already called every one of them, he reported. Perhaps Khalida asked them not to say anything, suggested Ayesha, but she'll talk to me. Dr Rahman told his daughter that Khalida would have called if she wanted her to know where she was hiding. Ayesha accepted her father's reasoning and agreed that it appeared Khalida didn't want her whereabouts known, perhaps for their own safety as well as her own. They continued to discuss all the possible consequences for Khalida until the bedroom door opened slowly.

'What's going on?' asked Mrs Rahman through a yawn. 'Abdur, Ayesha, did you not hear? Great-grandfather's clock just chimed midnight.'

TWENTY-ONE

Ben, reluctantly, signed a contract with Aid International, for three months only. It would at least allow him to earn money while looking for a permanent role. Professionally, he remained committed to helping the oppressed minority group of Biharis; personally, he was bound to Bangladesh by Ayesha.

Ben had also developed affection for the country – the crowded chaos of downtown Dacca, the lush greens of the countryside, the pace of life, even its sticky stifling climate during the monsoon season. Most of the people too were warm and welcoming.

He couldn't put his finger on it, but he didn't feel comfortable working for AI. He told Ayesha he didn't like their 'style', for want of a better word. He thought the organisation was more business-oriented than humanity-driven. He had to admit however the agency operated very efficiently. Within days of taking over Action Delta's projects, supplies of food, tents, medicines and equipment arrived regularly and on time. This big agency clearly had resources and influence that Action Delta couldn't command. Regardless of AI's methods, Ben could not deny they were delivering more aid to more people. Perhaps he should cut them some slack.

Nevertheless, meanwhile, Ben would put out discreet feelers for a job with other agencies, including Oxfam and Save the Children.

'Thomas is looking forward to meeting you tomorrow,' Pete Conan said, calling from AI's office in Dacca for his daily report. (Ben laughed to himself: even the phone worked better since AI took over Mohpur Camp.) 'He's meeting with one of the ministers this afternoon and some of the other aid providers. He'll update you himself, Ben, when we see you. But, fella, heads up on that shit heap you live in – looks like our building work can start pretty soon.'

Dak Cottage remained Ben's main residence, apart from the occasional night in Tungipur with the Rahman family. None of the AI people could understand why he stayed there in, as Pete described it, 'that shit heap'. But the bungalow was part of the camp, at the heart of residents' lives, and Ben felt closer to them in the dak. Proximity built trust. Staying in the luxury of the Intercontinental Hotel in central Dacca would be too much of a distance – ethically, as well as geographically. AI's plans to construct a brand new property would highlight the difference between the haves and have-nots. The poor would feel poorer, if that were possible. Ben had argued that surely the money would be better spent on the camp's residents rather than on pristine air-conditioned premises. But he was told a new onsite office, with better accommodation, air conditioning, proper facilities, would deliver greater efficiencies.

'We have duty of care to our staff, Ben,' Pete Conan declared. 'It'll be better for these Biharis too in the longer term.'

Ben remained unconvinced. But accepted he may well be wrong.

THOMAS WOMACH WAS pleasantly surprised to have been kept waiting for only a few minutes. The minister's lackey arrived at reception out of breath. He had obviously rushed down the stairs from the fourth floor. This bothered Womach. Although he considered himself in great shape, thanks to his gym at home, daily workouts, fitness coach, pool and tennis court, he didn't relish having to climb four flights of steps in the heat of Bangladesh. The elevator was however working, albeit slowly. Hussain's peon kept apologising while frantically pressing the call button. Eventually it rattled up to the minister's floor and came to a juddering halt.

'Mr Womach, a pleasure to see you again.'

'Minister, please, call me Thomas.'

They both settled into their chairs at either side of the minister's desk.

'Cha, Mr... ah, yes, Thomas? I have an excellent second flush from Darjeeling. Best tea in the world. You know it's called the Champagne of tea.' Farook Hussain rang the handbell.

'Now I know you're a good Muslim, minister, but I'm sure this will be welcomed by your many Christian friends you mentioned on my last visit.' Womach produced two large cardboard cartons from his briefcase, each containing a litre bottle of vodka, and placed them on Hussain's desk.

'This is very generous of you Thomas. No need. No need at all. But, as you can imagine, I meet many fellows here from foreign embassies who would appreciate the offer of a small measure with tonic, or whatever they wish.'

Cha-wallah Mohammed arrived with his trolley and, as always, served his master with hot sweet milky tea. Mohammed poured Womach's fine Darjeeling into a delicate white china cup. He left the visitor to serve his own milk and sugar, although it should be imbibed without either. He drank it incorrectly, with milk: an insult to a fine tea. Womach also failed to detect the dribble of saliva Mohammed had deposited inside the cup before entering the minister's office. Infidels and transgressors deserve to be spat at for their sins, punished for disobeying the word of Allah.

Seeing the vodka on Hussain's desk, despising its iniquitous presence, Mohammed nevertheless would remember to top up the minister's fridge with tonic, lime and lemon. Mohammed bowed as he left. Neither man noticed. He closed the door, slowly, silently.

'Early next Friday, minister. Is that a suitable time?' Womach asked.

'Couldn't be better. I shall be at mosque, of course, but my son and brother will oversee operations at the airport as before. All four cars?'

'Yes, as agreed. And I'm told the manufacturer has upgraded this model, minister. Same beautiful shell. Look identical. But these have better air-conditioning units and tighter suspension.'

'I shall do a swap and give the health minister mine,' he laughed. 'I have somewhat more bulk to cool down than that stick-insect.'

Hussain and Womach indulged in small-talk while sipping their tea. They discussed Idi Amin's declaration that he planned to expel fifty-thousand Asians from Uganda. Would any be returning to Bangladesh? Womach wondered. The minister thought not. Most were Indian, not Pakistani or, now, Bangladeshi. Many will go to Britain, he believed. Both men admired the seven gold medals achieved by swimmer Mark Spitz at the Munich Olympic games. And Womach talked about that 'lovely little Russian waif', gymnast Olga Korbut.

While they chatted, Mohammed came in and placed bottles of tonic water, coke and 7-Up in the minister's fridge, plus a plate of sliced limes and lemons. He bowed on entry and exit. He doubted either man noticed, and he was pleased. He followed the advice of his father: servants should neither be seen nor heard.

Hussain asked Womach to predict the outcome of next week's American election, McGovern or Nixon? It will be no contest, Nixon all the way back to the White House.

'Thanks for putting a good word in too with the development minister,' Womach said. 'We received the planning permissions for the developments at Mirpur and Mohpur. At Mirpur after the people are, shall we say, rehomed, I have already contacted friends in New York who are willing to finance the project. They understand you and your colleague will redirect sufficient funds via Bermuda. Is that still correct?'

'Yes. My friend wondered if Switzerland would be better.'

'Your fellow minister is a little naïve, Farook. Swiss bankers are not always as discreet as they make out to be. Their PR is better than their practice. Fund holders can be disclosed – for the right price. In Bermuda we have complete control. We have only partial control in Zurich. The guys in New York will need to see an initial transfer. Just to show the channel is open and functioning properly. I'm sure you understand.'

'How much?'

'Five million. USD of course. Is that a problem?'

'No, not at all, Thomas. My other friend who will be arranging this diversion of funds is an experienced banker. Thanks to the generosity from around the world to help my country after suffering devastating floods and such a destructive war, I'm sure five will not present a problem. He'll need a few days to establish the accounts, adjust the paperwork, that sort of thing.'

'Of course. A few days, no problem.'

'And my land at Tungipur, the camp at Mohpur?'

'We shall build the property as per your architect's plan, subject to a site survey. My consultants will supervise the development. As we gradually clear the area south of Tungipur, you will enjoy sixty acres of lovely estate. Excellent alluvial soil. We'll also landscape the four acres around where the bungalow stands, as you requested, and construct proper drainage channels.'

'You know the British built that place. Daks once were rest houses, post collection points, overnight hunting lodges, that sort of thing. Civil servants, sometimes army chaps, used them for temporary accommodation.'

'Ah, Farook, the good ol' British Raj. Bet you're glad to be rid of them.'

'Actually, Thomas, I know it's trendy to bash the Brits. And of course they shouldn't have been here plundering our riches. But many here, especially the old timers, believe the whole subcontinent ran somewhat better under their rule.'

Hussain leaned over his desk and took hold of one of the vodka boxes. 'What about a little of this?'

Womach nodded. Minister Farook Hussain twisted the top off the bottle. The handbell was rung. Mohammed knew what was expected of him, instruction not needed. After bowing, he went immediately to the fridge and removed ice cubes, a bottle of tonic, a plate of sliced limes and lemons. He placed two tumblers on the minister's desk. Mohammed bowed and retreated, pleased he had not been noticed, in compliance with his father's advice.

Hussain poured generous portions of vodka, the USSR's finest.

AID INTERNATIONAL'S PEOPLE carrier arrived outside Dak Bungalow around eleven, two hours later than scheduled. The Bangladeshi driver in a light brown uniform trotted round to open the sliding side-door. He then stood to one side at soldier-style attention. Two men, unknown to Ben, came out carrying clipboards and what looked like a large round measuring tape. They were followed by a young blonde woman in a pale blue blouse and bright yellow thigh-high skirt. Her chunky suede leather desert boots somehow didn't match the rest of her chic style. She struggled with a heavy camera bag, its strap refusing to stay over her shoulder. A black Nikon F2 dangled around her neck with a telephoto lens attached. Pete Conan emerged next and waved up at Ben. He was stood on the veranda with around twenty camp staff and volunteers who had gathered to welcome the visitors.

Then he appeared. AI's founder and chief executive officer. Pete and the others formed what resembled a guard of honour. Ben almost expected the driver to salute. He didn't. But he did stretch taller and pushed his chest out.

Dressed in a pristine white linen suit, Thomas Womach dazzled and swaggered like an ageing rock-star. A generous head of bouncy silvery hair – Arctic blonde, he called it – made him appear even taller than his six-foot three-inches. Against his deep New Mexico tan, Womach's generous smile exposed his gleaming teeth, spaced perfectly, like ivory notes on a piano.

'At last I get to meet the hero of Mohpur.' Womach pointed to Ben and spoke loud enough for everyone around to hear. He presented all those gathered with a presidential-like wave, as if arriving on stage at an election rally. Womach marched onto the veranda and grasped Ben's hand with both of his. He shook vigorously, holding on far longer than Ben expected. Then Ben realised this was what Womach called a photo-op. His photographer was snapping away.

'I hear, Ben, you've done marvellous work here over recent months. Fantastic achievement. I'm delighted you're helping us for a couple of months to smooth the transition from your outfit to Aid International's. Maybe you'll stay with us longer. What you say?' Ben was about to reply when Womach continued without pausing. 'But my team can't understand why you've stayed in this tumbledown shed.' He turned to investigate the bungalow and pulled a sour face. 'There's a room at the Intercontinental just waiting for you. We've taken almost a whole floor for our guys. Just say the word.'

Ben hadn't said a word. Not had chance. Womach wasn't playing the star; he was the star. After welcoming Thomas to the camp, Ben asked about the others.

'They're building guys looking to see what's needed to upgrade this place. They're taking a few measurements, checking the ground, strength of foundations, lie of the land, all that stuff. Did you know these dak places were built by your people, the Brits?'

'Yes.'

'Hundreds of them all over the place.'

'That's right. And the photographer?' She was changing lenses and taking pictures of the bungalow from several angles.

'Yeah, she's one of my PR team. Ben, my boy, it's important to show the great work we do when raising money for projects. Photos are needed for our press releases and publicity campaigns. We also publish a glossy monthly magazine. It's sent to senators, our sponsors and our membership. You not seen a copy? Hey, Pete,' Womach shouted down to him stood next to the photographer, 'you ain't given Ben here a copy of *InterAid*?'

'No. Sorry Thomas. Next time I'm up, Ben. I'll bring you a couple of back-copies too.'

'Okay, Ben,' Womach said, 'let's take a quick look inside this place of yours. Then I'll have a look around. We've got to be back in Dacca for lunch, so I can't stay too long.'

Ben introduced Womach to some of the key workers and volunteers. He found it strange Womach just raised a hand and said 'Hi', even when the men offered a handshake. Ben explained that Dr Rahman regrettably couldn't make the clinic today: an urgent unexpected family matter had arisen. Ben however presented Syed, his driver, Masaad, the medical assistant to Dr Rahman, and Faiyaz, who also helped in the clinic and was vital for dispensing.

'Yeah, Pete's told me about you guys,' Womach said, but looking only at Faiyaz.

After a polite hello, Syed, Masaad and Faiyaz turned and went about their work.

Ben explained to Thomas and Pete that Faiyaz desperately wanted to qualify as a pharmacist. Her studies had been cut short by last year's war. But that wasn't the worst impact: her parents, brother and younger sister died in a bombing raid. Faiyaz was saving hard for the college fees to complete her degree. But Ben said it would take her three or four years to save enough to complete her final year.

After a brief meeting inside the bungalow, Womach announced he was going to have a look around. Alone. Ben was surprised. He had naturally assumed he would accompany Womach, but Pete interrupted and said he needed to go over the delivery records. Ben was sure they'd covered these figures before, but Pete was surprisingly insistent.

IN THE CLINIC Faiyaz was stacking fresh batches of creams, lotions and medicines. Since Aid International had taken over, they had far more supplies, including antibiotics and painkillers.

She heard the door close firmly. Faiyaz turned expecting to see Masaad carrying more stock. She was shocked to see someone else.

'Hi there,' he said. 'What was your name again?'

'Faiyaz, Mr Womach.'

'That's a pretty name. You've been doing a great job I hear helping that doctor, right?'

'Dr Rahman is an excellent physician, Mr Womach. He gives us so much of his time, all for free.'

'And you want to be a chemist?'

'A pharmacist.'

'Ah, right.'

'Oh yes. Very much would like to be pharmacist. My studies were interrupted by… by the events of last year.' Faces of her lost family crossed her mind's eye.

Womach walked towards Faiyaz. She stepped back, respecting traditional distance with a man not her husband, father or brother. He reached out for a box of medicine on the shelf behind her. She dodged his arm and stepped aside.

Holding the box, he attempted to pronounce the drug's name. 'Gri… seo… fulvin. Is that right? What's it for?'

'It's an antifungal, Mr Womach. It binds polymerised microtubules and inhibits fungal mitosis. That's the splitting of cells. So it stops fungal spread. In high humidity of my country and poor conditions in camp, we have many cases of ringworm, for which it is primarily used.'

'Very impressive. Very good.' Womach paused while he looked along the shelves before turning towards Faiyaz. 'If I got you into college, or wherever you study your stuff, I'm sure you would be… grateful. I could probably get you started in a week or two. I know people in Dacca. You're a bright girl, so I'm sure you wouldn't have a problem catching up.'

Faiyaz was indeed a clever woman, far more astute than Womach took her for. She knew exactly what game Womach played. Since the death of her family, she had to go out alone far more often. With no father or brother nearby, she had been 'Eve teased' regularly, even by cycle rickshaw-wallahs, teenage boys and, to her greater disgust, old men. To get their kicks, many whispered indecent suggestions as she walked by. Some deliberately brushed against her, using crowded streets or markets as their excuse. Bolder men pinched her behind or, on two occasions, grabbed a breast.

Faiyaz edged towards the door. It was too late. Womach lunged. She stepped back but became pinned in the corner. He gripped both arms and tried to kiss her. She shook her head rapidly so he couldn't fix on her lips. But his mouth slithered down her neck to find her throat.

Womach bent both Faiyaz's arms behind her back, locking them in by pushing her hard against the wall. His hands were free to roam. One grasped her breast, the other searched between her legs.

But Faiyaz was stronger than her delicate build would suggest. She kicked Womach's shins and wriggled free.

'I'll scream,' she threatened.

'You silly…' he growled and stepped back to the middle of the room. Faiyaz had triumphed, stopped his assault.

In a speedy switch of personality, he tried a different tack.

'Look, look, I'm sorry. Really sorry. I shouldn't have done that.'

Womach's became sorrowful, his voice mournful, his shoulders slumped, almost pleading. 'Please, please forgive me. I'll never do that again. Most out of character. I don't know what came over me.'

'You are very bad man,' Faiyaz said simply, softly, reassembling her sari and headscarf. Seeing such a rapid change of character, she seriously considered whether Womach suffered a mental illness, possibly a schizoid personality disorder. She remained vigilant. And frightened, in case his evil side returned.

'It's… it's just that you are such a beautiful, intelligent girl. It would be such a pity if you couldn't fulfil your dream. And I can do that for you, make your dream come true. You could become my special friend here, here in Bangladesh. I could find you a nice place to live in downtown Dacca and…'

'Mr Womach,' she interrupted. 'What you did just now, what you suggest, is wrong.'

'No, not if you agree to… to return the favour. No one needs to know. It can be our little secret. I can see you when I come to Dacca, stay with you.'

Faiyaz refused to be taken in by his false promises. Maintaining her dignity, standing upright, head high, she said proudly, 'Mr Womach, I must finish my duties here in readiness for tomorrow's clinic and Masaad will be here any moment.'

WOMACH RETURNED TO the office, anxious to leave swiftly and get back for his lunch appointment in Dacca. Just as suddenly, Pete lost interest in the figures they were covering, as if the data no longer mattered.

'Before we go we'd better do the usual, Tom,' his PR said as he left the bungalow. 'Over here by the tents and the water pump will be a good spot.'

Walking across the dusty scrubland, Ben noticed Womach put an arm around her waist and pulled her into him. She pushed him away, playfully, giggling. Watching from the veranda, Ben asked Pete the photographer's name. Maeve, he replied, adding the 'a' came before the 'e', as if Ben was about to write it down.

'Is Maeve his girlfriend?' asked Ben. 'They seem to get on well together.'

'Nah,' Pete said. 'Thomas is just a touchy-feely sort of guy.'

The first line of tents at Mohpur started fifty yards from the dak. Dozens of camp residents had been watching the party from Aid International since their arrival. Maeve summoned the crowd of curious Biharis forward. She positioned about thirty of them in an arc behind Womach. Children to the front, then women, men at the back. She changes lenses from telephoto to wide angle. And before Maeve's Nikon snapped shots from various viewpoints, Womach finger-combed his hair, slapped the dust off the bottom of his trousers, checked his shirt was fully tucked in and levelled his collar. He displayed an impressive array of expressions: happy, sad, worried, caring, each turned on and off as easy as a light switch. Maeve then dismissed all the adults and, after another change of lens, went in for a close-up of Womach and the children. She indicated to the kids to look up at Mr Womach and smile. They did. Then he crouched down and looked lovingly into their faces. One girl, pock-marked after recovering from smallpox, was singled out for several pictures alone with Womach. At fifty yards away, Ben couldn't swear to it, but it looked as if Womach was wiping a tear away from an eye.

Ben hoped Womach or Maeve would hand out some taka for their modelling efforts, at least to the children. They could have bought peanuts or mangoes or coconuts from traders who passed by on the edge of the camp most days. But both turned their backs and walked to the people carrier, where the driver opened the sliding door as they approached. The children waved goodbye, but their efforts were not seen. Pete and the surveyors had already taken their seats by the time Maeve and Womach reached the car.

'Many thanks, Ben,' Womach called and waved as he bent into the car. He flashed a smile for a split second when Ben signalled back and mouthed, 'See you'.

As the driver closed the door, Ben heard Womach hiss, 'Okay, let's get the hell out of this dump.'

IF BEN HARBOURED doubts about Aid International before, his instinctual dislike of Womach and his team made him feel that even three months working with them would be three months too long. For now, however, he needed the job. He'd stick it out.

'Have you seen Faiyaz?' Masaad asked, joining Ben on the veranda. 'She was putting new supplies in clinic. But door locked. Did she say goodbye?'

'No, Masaad. She probably didn't want to disturb us while Womach and his crew were here.'

Masaad stood square in front of Ben looking agitated, in contrast to his usual confident, smiling self. He clearly had something on his mind.

'You okay?' Ben was compelled to ask.

'Can I ask question?'

'Of course. Anything you like.'

'People say they hear rumour clinic is closing. Will I have no job as medical assistant?'

'People are getting mixed up, Masaad. Aid International plan to open a clinic nearby while the building work goes on. That's all. AI will want to keep you, I'm sure. And Faiyaz. I've told them how indispensable you both are. And Dr Rahman couldn't manage without you.'

'But when you leave, these new men take over. I don't like them.'

'It won't be Womach. It won't be Pete Conan or that fat guy, Bob Beck, working here. They'll be appointing experienced aid workers. I don't think you have much to worry about.'

'People say camp to move.'

'No, Masaad. I've heard nothing about moving the camp. They just want to build a better administration building and facilities, that's all. The clinic will be much bigger and better.'

'Will you stay?'

'No, Masaad. Sorry. I can't work for AI after my handover period.'

'Why?'

Ben hesitated. He didn't wish to taint Masaad's opinion towards his new employers. It would be unfair to him and AI. But before he could reply, Masaad said simply, 'I think you don't like them. And you don't like them because you don't trust them.'

Ben's breath was taken away by Masaad's pin-point analysis. He couldn't have described his feelings any better. But he replied, 'Let's just say, Masaad, Aid International and I don't see eye to eye on how things should be done.'

TWENTY-TWO

Natcoo placed Saturday's edition of *Bangladesh Times* next to Dr Rahman's chair at the breakfast table on the front veranda.

While waiting for her husband and daughters to come downstairs, Mrs Rahman strolled around the garden reflecting on this sombre day.

Lemons and limes, breadfruit, mango and coconuts grew well in Bangladesh's rich alluvial soil and humid climate. Gardenia and jasmine blossom combined to make an intoxicating scent in the still morning air. Sparrows flitted between the ground and bushes, squabbling and chattering. Crows and magpies competed for the best perches, squawking between their mechanical chak-ak-ak-ak rattles. Raina quietly sang to herself a lovely hymn recalling her happy days at Calcutta Girls' School in the 1920s, *All Things Bright and Beautiful*.

In this tranquil moment, it was hard to believe that exactly a year ago on this day, outside their house, the road was a river of blood. Mukti Bahini, the freedom fighters, had tried to repel West Pakistani forces. They failed. The victors wreaked revenge on dozens of injured local fighters unable to flee. No prisoners taken. No pity shown. They ransacked houses which the Mukti had used as firing positions. Where residents were found hiding, cowering, terrified – men, women, children, babies – they were murdered without mercy.

It was also on this day that, while treating casualties at the town's school, Dr Rahman became a casualty. A mortar shell shot shards of shrapnel into his leg. He was found just in time to staunch the bleeding. Mercifully, Raina and her girls were safe in Calcutta with her brother's family. Thankfully, the family home was not damaged, apart from a dotted line of bullet holes across the side of the house caused by the sweep of a machinegun. Following a family discussion, they agreed not to have the holes repaired. 'The damage will act as a reminder that our country's liberation came at a high price,' Raina said.

Before midday, citizens of Tungipur planned a remembrance ceremony in the garden outside the main mosque. It had been organised by the sub-divisional officer, who had lost one of his two sons that day. Raina, Abdur, Ayesha and Bushra would attend. They would bow their heads, remember the dead.

After midday, the muezzin would lead dhuhr prayers. Allah would be honoured and asked for guidance. Many in the town lost relatives and friends. Everyone knew someone who had suffered. The Rahman family's neighbour lost both sons fighting for their country's freedom. In the house opposite, their only child, a daughter, was one of 'the disappeared', her fate unknown. Distraught, mother and father secretly abandoned the house during the night. Nobody knows where they went. It was as if they had voluntarily joined 'the disappeared'. Three houses along from Dr and Mrs Rahman, the home was ruined by tank shells. It remains a wreck, uninhabitable, and the family remain with relatives in Dacca, unable to afford a rebuild.

Nobody knows how many died across Bangladesh during the nine months of fighting. Some say quarter of a million, others half, the government continued to claim three million. Today, in Tungipur, they will remember the known dead and known disappeared. And the unknown.

DR RAHMAN ANNOUNCED as he sat and read the headlines, 'See Nixon won the election, Raina. Landslide majority over McGovern, it says here. Forty-seven million to twenty-nine million of the popular vote.'

'I suppose that allows him to keep bombing North Vietnam into submission,' Raina said. 'They'll never win the war on the ground by dropping bombs from the sky.'

'Hiroshima and Nagasaki forced the Japanese to surrender.'

'True, although I'm not sure the situations are comparable.'

Bushra arrived. 'What situations don't you think are comparable, Amma?'

'America's bombing of North Vietnam with the atom bombs being dropped on Japan in 1945.'

'I think…'

Dr Rahman interrupted. 'My dears, today I feel we should turn our attention to our own people who suffered on this day. Are you and Ayesha to join us in the mosque garden?'

'Yes, of course, Abba.' Bushra's inclination was to continue debating the comparison of North Vietnam today with Japan in 1945. But she saw the sadness and pain on Abba's face. Her sudden silence, her immediate compliance, showed the respect she held for her much-loved father.

Natcoo returned with a rack of toast and a pot of coffee. Ali followed with a jug of fresh coconut milk, extracted from the garden's fallen palm drupes. Ayesha completed the gathering. Although not silently, they ate with little conversation, respecting the significance of the day. As breakfast drew to a close, Natcoo arrived with the post, presented as always on a round silver tray to Dr Rahman's left. He shuffled through the pack. Amongst the letters, including one from Raina's brother in Calcutta, there was an air-mail from Bushra's pen pal in England, Sarah Goodwin. For over seven years they had corresponded to each other, but still hadn't met. *'One day we shall meet,'* they mutually promised in every missive, *'in England or Bangladesh.'*

'And one for you, Ayesha.'

She didn't recognise the writing. Nor did she know the name of the sender, Mrs Aahana Haq. The postmark was smudged, making it difficult to decipher. Ayesha hesitated in opening it.

'Sarah says, Abba,' said Bushra eagerly, 'the National Health Service in Britain is terribly short of doctors. She says if you came to work over there we'd be able to meet up at long last.'

Dr Rahman smiled. 'She always says that. But she forgets we have patients who need doctors here too.'

'Well, then, when Ayesha goes to study further in England, I think I should go with her,' Bushra said.

'My dear, there's no guarantee she'll be accepted by a university in Britain for post-graduate studies.'

'Of course she will, Abba. My sister is a medical genius. Scholar of the year – every year! And you completed your post-qualification studies in London.'

'I was very lucky, Bushra, and remember India was still under British Raj in those days.'

Ayesha had opened the letter. It shocked her. She was deaf to the family's conversation.

'Ayesha?' quizzed Mrs Rahman, noticing her daughter's inattention. 'Ayesha? What's the matter?'

'Oh, nothing, Ma. Nothing at all. Excuse me, I must get ready for our prayers. Thank you, Natcoo,' Ayesha said, as he started clearing the breakfast things.

Dr and Mrs Rahman glanced at each other, puzzled by Ayesha's sudden departure. Bushra was too engaged with her pen pal's letter to notice her sister's sudden departure.

'More toast?' Natcoo asked.

'Thank you, no, Natcoo,' said Mrs Rahman. 'Ali's kitchuri is always filling for the rest of the day. Will you and Ali be coming to mosque? Buna is.'

His head indicated a firm yes, as she knew he would. Natcoo and Ali planned to meet cousins and squeeze into what would be a crowded mosque on this special day in Tungipur. After wudhu, cleansed from head to toe before Allah, they would unroll their prayer rugs, face Mecca, and pray alongside their fellow worshippers. Before leaving the mosque, they will turn right and left to their brothers and offer the salutation, 'Peace be upon you, and the mercy and blessings of Allah'.

TWENTY-THREE

Only once before had Ayesha visited the Bihari camp. It was with her father, months earlier, when Abi ran Action Delta's operation alone. She wanted to see the clinic where her father had volunteered to help. Because of the threats from disgruntled Bangladeshis towards anyone showing sympathy to Biharis, it was, to use her father's word, 'unwise' for her to visit. He meant 'dangerous'.

Even the cycle-rickshaw wallah expressed surprise, if not alarm, when she told him her destination. A young Bangladeshi woman going by herself to Mohpur Camp – full of traitors and collaborators – was a one-off request. He would drop her on the track behind the bungalow and hurry away. And charge her an extra taka, or try to. He discovered Ayesha would not be bullied into paying over the going rate for two miles.

It was late afternoon, following the special prayers at Tungipur's main mosque, when Ayesha arrived. Tension was higher than usual: rumours were rampant that former freedom fighters would launch an attack on the Bihari camp, in revenge for the events this day a year earlier.

Residents watched with increasing disbelief this well-dressed Bangladeshi woman walking towards the bungalow – alone. No father, no brother, no husband, no one accompanying her. The news spread as fast as floodwater, whispers on the wind.

Ben was out at the far end of the camp. Masaad, unsettled by her presence, asked her to wait in the office while he fetched him. Masaad, a Bihari, initially spoke Urdu to Ayesha, momentarily forgetting she was Bangladeshi. But Ayesha, like her father and sister, spoke Urdu fluently, and she took no offence. Only her mother refused to speak Urdu, although she could, perfectly. It was her personal protest against the imposition of the language by West Pakistan's politicians.

Ayesha sat on the edge of one of the office's two beds and waited. She was not impressed with the cracked concrete walls, the peeling paint, the broken blinds, the decrepit furniture and general mess. How can he stay here? He doesn't need to. He should stay at our home. He knows he can.

Ben was helping erect a batch of new tents delivered that morning by the International Red Cross. Monsoon gales had ripped many of them. And those which survived the storms succumbed to humidity-loving moulds or small red rubber-munching 'weepokas' – termites. Although fewer displaced Biharis arrived daily, usually between ten and twenty, materials for solid shelters were increasingly hard to find. Bricks, breezeblocks, timber and corrugated sheeting were in short supply with prices rocketing week by week.

Ben rushed in. He'd ran all through the camp after Massad had told him of Ayesha's arrival at the bungalow. Something shocking must have happened. Bad news about… Khalida?

'What the…'

Ayesha stood quickly interrupting him. 'You can say "hell" if you want, Ben, we Muslims believe it exists too.'

'You shouldn't be here. Not alone. You know that.'

'I need you to do something.'

She stepped forward taking both his hands. They kissed. Then held each other closer, tighter. They had snatched embraces together before at Ayesha's home, but they were always tense moments and aware parents, sister and servants were nearby.

Here, now, at Dak Cottage, presented their first opportunity. Both knew their liaison was dangerous: local woman, foreign man, conservative society, nationalistic fervour. But love overwhelmed logic. Desire dominated judgement.

Without a word, with shared understanding, both scanned the room confirming the blinds were fully down, although gaps remained where slats had broken. Ben bolted the door, top and bottom. Ayesha loosened her sari and it fell to the floor, all six yards of cotton. She lowered her petticoat and unbuttoned her blouse. Their eyes locked into each other, smiled, and slowly, tenderly, fulfilled with their bodies what they'd desired in their minds for months.

STEPPING INTO HIS trousers before buttoning his shirt, Ben said quietly, 'I'm so sorry, Ayesha, we shouldn't have done that. It's my fault.'

'It's not your fault, Ben. Nor mine. It's not a question of fault. We're both grown-ups, not children. I wanted what happened to happen. And you may have noticed I played as much a part as you.'

'So why do I feel terrible? Guilty? It's as if I've let you down, abused your trust, your family's trust.'

He sat on the edge of the bed with his head between his hands.

'Hey, hey, Ben, don't get upset. We've done what we've done. And what's done can't be undone. I'm pleased. Happy. And I want you to feel the same, not guilty.'

Having completed pleating her sari and throwing the loose end of it, the pallu, over her left shoulder, she went to kneel next to Ben and put her arm around him.

'Ben, being together like that was lovely.' Then, lightening the mood, she added flippantly, 'Although I must say it was a bit, shall I say, uncomfortable in this dreadful room. The décor is not exactly conducive to love-making, is it?'

'Is that why you came here this afternoon, so we could…'

'No, Ben. No. That just happened. Unplanned. The opportunity presented itself… and we took it.'

'But you said you wanted me to do something.'

'Yes. I need you for another task. But it won't be as pleasant as the one we've just completed.'

AYESHA AND BEN'S universe, populated exclusively by the two of them, for a length of time they could not calculate, crashed to a close.

Suddenly, shockingly, they became aware once more of the real world outside. Their privacy was public. Their intimacy exposed. Everyone surrounding Dak Cottage knew they had been together, alone, unmarried, unchaperoned. There would be consequences, repercussions. The zealots would not forgive. Others would not forget.

Some of the camp helpers and Biharis might excuse Ben as an *Ingrez*, an Englishman, ignorant of custom and practice. Although after many months in the country he should know better. He was also liked and respected by all who knew him. But this young unmarried Bangladeshi woman, especially Dr Rahman's daughter, must realise her behaviour is unacceptable. It was a disgrace for her to be deliberately alone with a man who was not her father, brother or uncle.

After checking her sari was neatly tucked in the waistband, pleated evenly and arranged correctly, they snatched a kiss before stepping out to sit on the veranda. They tried – perhaps too hard – to appear formal and business-like. But they sensed the eyes of hawks, the ears of bats, the tongues of snakes.

Syed had his head inside the Land Rover's engine. He looked up and waved. Was that a knowing, sarcastic smile? Had he been recording their time together? Then Masaad appeared from the direction of the clinic. Had he been there all the time, or listening some of the time at the office door? Be it imagined paranoia or clinical observation, Ben and Ayesha felt they had been scrutinised by everyone around the bungalow.

'May I say, Miss Rahman,' said Ben with a serious face, certain that no-one nearby could hear but many could see, 'that you are the most beautiful woman in the whole wide world.'

'May I say, Mr Altringham,' Ayesha replied mirroring Ben's fake formality, 'that you are quite handsome. However, as you have not travelled the whole wide world, I fail to see how your observation about me can be justified.'

Both suppressed a smile behind serious faces.

'You need to go, Ayesha. People will talk.'

'They already are.'

'I'll get Syed to drive us back home. I'm assuming your family don't know you've come here.'

'Correct. They think I've gone to visit a friend – a girlfriend, obviously. Oddly enough I don't have many boyfriends.'

'We'll drop you off close to your place but round the corner so no one will see the Land Rover. 'Incidentally, what was the task – the other one – you wanted me to do?'

Ayesha handed over the letter received at breakfast.

My dearest Ayesha,

Help! The Hussains are after me. Safa overheard Kasim's father say he would ask around to learn where I was hiding. She thinks they plan to make me marry Maz. They will keep me in purdah, I am sure of it. I will be a prisoner, Ayesha. That is why I had to get away.

The Hussains have medieval minds. I need to get out of Bangladesh. I have my passport, but the old Pakistani one. In any case, Maz's father will have alerted all the border posts and airports.

Amma does not know where I am. Somehow, please get a message to her and tell her I am all right. But do not use the phone. I am sure they are bugging it and they might be bugging yours. They will know from Maz and from college who my friends are. I know what they can do: Abba, remember, was in charge of all those covert operations and that spying stuff.

I am at my uncle's house in Jessore. But he says I must go soon because I am putting his family in danger. What to do? Oh, Ayesha, what a mess! I must get out of the country. It's my only hope. Please, please, please write soon to:

Mrs Aahana Haq, PO Box 296, Jessore.

My cousin will collect the post.

BEN RETURNED THE letter to Ayesha.

'Well, any ideas?' she asked.

'My first thought, seek political asylum. Go to the US Embassy or the British High Commission. Tell them what's going on.'

'I doubt they'd believe her. She has no proof that Maz and his dad are planning to abduct her and force her into marriage. They'd deny it, claim she's mentally ill, and if the rumours are true...'

'What rumours?'

'That Farook Hussain will become the next prime minister. So there is no way, no way at all that a foreign government will want to upset the cosy diplomatic apple-cart.'

'But I thought Khalida's family, because of her father being a war hero, was highly respected.'

'Yes, but her dad's dead. And the dead of Bangladesh have no influence whatsoever, even as martyrs.'

Unexpectedly, without being asked, Masaad arrived with two glasses of lebu pani. It was an especially hot afternoon, he said, and he thought they would like some refreshment. Ayesha, Ben too, wondered whether Masaad was being sarcastic, making a reference to what he – correctly – suspected had gone on in the office when they were alone. Ben thanked him for being so thoughtful. Ayesha also respectfully thanked Masaad, a Bihari, in Urdu, *apka shukria*.

'I have an idea,' Ayesha said, sipping the lemon drink, waiting for Masaad to remove himself. 'But think before you agree to it.'

'Go on. You have my attention.'

'Marry.'

Ben nearly choked on his juice.

'How does that help Khalida?'

'Not me, you idiot… well, not until after I qualify, as we agreed.'

'You mean Khalida? Marry Khalida?'

'You could arrange a marriage in one of the churches here. In Dacca there's the Church of England, there's Baptists, all sorts. Presumably, not being a Catholic, they won't marry you. Can the British high commissioner perform the ceremony? Or on board a ship you can get the captain to marry you. Isn't there an old law of the sea which allows that?'

'Ayesha, slow down.' Ben tried to remain restrained, in voice and body language, aware people around the cottage continued their vigilance. To them, the veranda became a theatre stage, they the actors on it. Their performance was being judged by a highly critical audience. Ben would tell Masaad, Syed and other camp workers that he was 'interviewing' Miss Rahman, a medical student, with a view to her helping in the clinic. It might, at least for those willing to be tolerant, provide a reason for her visit to Mohpur. Even so the critics would say she should have been accompanied by her father or mother.

'You read the letter,' Ayesha said. 'You can see how desperate she is. She needs help. Fast. Now.'

'Let's get you back home. I'll call in later and we can talk this through without prying eyes, perhaps in the garden. And if Bushra comes nosing around, you can tell her to buzz off.'

'Or you could,' Ayesha said with a touch of humour.

'Certainly not,' Ben said. 'Your sister is far too scary for me.'

'She'll know we're cooking up something. Her emotional antennae are more sensitive than any radar.'

'Yes. But she won't know what.'

Ben signalled to Syed they were ready to drive Miss Rahman home. They emptied their glasses of lemon juice and approached the Land Rover. It had already been emblazoned with the crest of Aid International, on the bonnet, tailgate and both doors. Stepping off the veranda, Ben whispered to Ayesha, 'We have to be very, very careful.'

'Ben, you don't need to tell me. This is Bangladesh, not Britain. We still have jungle with scorpions, snakes and tigers roaming around – and it's the law of the jungle that rules.'

TWENTY-FOUR

Ben arrived at the Rahman household late afternoon. He and Ayesha somehow had to secure time alone to plan Khalida's rescue. Even if a marriage of convenience could be arranged, any plan to help Khalida would be packed with danger with the Hussains in pursuit.

The chowkidar unlocked the garden gate and greeted Ben as usual with a one-finger salute.

'*As-salamu alaykum,*' said Ben, giving the traditional greeting among Muslims.

'*Wa 'alaykumu s-salam, sahib,*' came the response. The added 'sahib' embarrassed Ben. It seemed a throwback to the days of British Raj, which ended twenty-five years previously in 1947. He'd asked the chowkidar and others not to use the term, but most persisted. Dr Rahman explained it was simply used as a term of respect, not of subservience.

'Just in time for tea, Ben,' greeted Mrs Rahman.

'Mrs Rahman, whatever time of day I arrive, it's always "just in time for tea".' Bushra had recently said flippantly to Ben that he should start using Amma or Ma 'now you're almost part of the family'. But Ben believed that to be a step too far. He would only call her Amma at Mrs Rahman's invitation. Even then, he would be extremely careful when and where used. Perhaps in a year or two…

When not too hot, the family routinely used the veranda at the rear of the house in the evening. It faced west, the setting sun. And Mecca. Dr Rahman claimed he was a bad Muslim. Nobody believed him. To his family, friends, thousands of patients over the years, he was the epitome of a good man, far better than just a good man. Often he would pray only once a day, he said, as if that defined his sinfulness. On certain days, however, Dr Rahman took his prayer rug and completed salat, the five prayers. Today, Saturday, November 11, being the first anniversary of the Tungipur massacre, Dr Rahman wished to observe salat. He had completed Asr, the afternoon prayer, shortly before Ben arrived. Later, as the sun melts into the horizon, he will perform Maghrib, the day's penultimate prayer.

When the haunting, beautiful, intoxicating sound of the muezzin calling worshippers to prayer in the nearby mosque, talking and tea drinking ceased momentarily. Dr Abdur Rahman quietly limped away with his prayer rug, a gift from his father when he became a man. When Abdur returned to the table, Ben mentioned this day was also special in Britain, Remembrance Day. And tomorrow, Sunday, at the Cenotaph in London's Whitehall, the dead of both world wars and other conflicts would be honoured.

The day was marked throughout the Commonwealth, Dr Rahman said. Mrs Rahman added that in India particularly, many, including the Indian Army, would take part in tributes and ceremonies. At Kohima and Imphal, in the remote hills of north east India, services of remembrance will be conducted. It was in these places the Allies reversed the fortunes of the Japanese in the Second World War. Dr and Mrs Rahman knew the details well: both lost cousins or friends among nearly eighteen thousand Indian and British troops killed, wounded or missing on that front.

'Raina and I have been to the monument at Kohima, Ben,' Dr Rahman said. 'The Commonwealth War Graves Commission maintain the cemetery beautifully. You should visit sometime.'

'Yes, I'd like that.'

'You may remember it is at Kohima, below the monument, that bears the sombre epitaph, "*When you go home, tell them of us, and say: For your tomorrow, we gave our today*".'

There was a moment of reflection before Natcoo replenished the tea and a bowl of spicy peanuts.

BECAUSE IT WAS a special day in Tungipur, and a year since Dr Rahman nearly died, Ali prepared a feast of everyone's favourites.

Sour lentil soup, creamy lamb curry, chota chingri – using tiny shrimps from Bangladesh's south-east coast – and several other dishes before a choice of three desserts, including paesh, spicy rice pudding.

Despite the delicious food, the mood over dinner was subdued. Ayesha wondered if her parents, both highly observant, had detected a subtle change in her behaviour, her feelings, her thoughts since the afternoon's love-making.

Or had they correctly surmised the letter she received at breakfast was from, or about, Khalida? Ayesha thought it strange that they had made no enquiry about who sent it. Perhaps they were distracted by their prayers and memories of the tragedy a year ago. She knew her father thought a great deal about young Dr Abu Hasan, who died at his side in the mortar blast. She wondered if he felt guilty because Abu had taken the full force of the shell and thereby saved him: survivor's guilt. She had read an article about the condition in *The Lancet*. And mother had been an inch away of becoming a widow.

Ever since childhood, Ayesha knew how perceptive her mother was, as if Amma could read her mind – even better than she could assess Bushra's more temperamental nature. Was it possible, by intuition, almost by magic, her mother sensed that she'd had sex with Ben? That her eldest daughter was no longer a virgin?

Although not deeply religious – modern in most ways – Ayesha knew her mother naturally retained several traditional views. 'Saving yourself' for your husband was one of them: her mother had expressed that view to both daughters. Ma would be sad, but not angry, to discover she had not 'saved herself' for her husband. But Ma would also understand. Her love would remain undiminished, perhaps enhanced by her empathy for her daughter.

Since returning home in the afternoon, Ayesha had consciously tried to 'act normal'. But trying to do so often exposed things that appeared not so. 'Acting normally' hadn't prevented Ma from perceiving things in the past. Ayesha did feel, in some way, different. She was, in one way, different.

She couldn't quite describe it, but I'm… I'm… now more… more mature, whole, I've undergone a *rite de passage*. And she couldn't stop replaying over and over again in her mind the love-making with Ben. Ayesha was confident too that she would not experience the same 'problem' as Khalida: her cycle was regular and she had already started to feel the symptoms of her next period.

Ben too had noticed a different atmosphere throughout the evening. Not sombre. Just not as upbeat as usual. Even chatty bouncy Bushra appeared pensive. Like Ayesha, he too repeatedly replayed what happened between them in the afternoon. Step by step, scene by scene, with questions about how it started so spontaneously. It was a wonderful moment in his life. The first time he had experienced such emotion beyond the physical. But immediately afterwards he felt guilty, although he recognised guilt was a futile, perhaps destructive, emotion. The trust which Dr and Mrs Rahman expected of him had been betrayed. He had crossed a cultural expectation and perhaps a religious doctrine.

In England, thanks to the Swinging Sixties, most parents would not expect their daughter to 'save herself' until marriage. Indeed, many would be surprised if she did. But here in a long-established predominately Islamic culture, expectations and social attitudes were different. Whether right or wrong, Ben could not judge. But he accepted that his values clashed with those of Ayesha's homeland. Respect must be paid to different cultural standards. And he'd broken one upheld by the vast majority of people he was now living amongst. He knew his – their – act of love, if discovered, could generate difficulties, even danger. If discovered...

Ayesha said she had no regrets. And that was true. She had not lied to Ben. But that did not dispel other feelings churning her stomach and confounding her thoughts – of fear. Nobody, absolutely nobody must learn of their intimacy.

AYESHA HAD WAITED long enough. She had to make a move. Khalida needed help urgently. This was no time to dilly-dally. When dinner ended she stood up and declared, 'Before coffee, Ben and I are going for a walk around the garden.'

Her move took Ben by surprise. 'Oh, are we?'

'I'll come too,' Bushra chipped in and jumped up.

'No you won't. Ben and I have things to discuss.'

'Don't worry, I'll keep quiet.'

'Sister, dear, haven't you heard of *privacy*?'

'Yes, Bushra,' Mrs Rahman offered Ayesha support. 'Let them chat together without your comments.'

Bushra pretended to sulk. 'Well, if that's the case, I'll finish off the cham-cham. And I don't think Ali has any more tonight. So, Ben, you'll have to do without.'

Light leaking from the house and a full moon cast more than sufficient glow for them to saunter through the garden. Ben walked by her side, close but not touching: they remained in sight of the family and Natcoo serving drinks on the veranda. At a thicket of shoulder-height camellia bushes, Ayesha wistfully held a small white flower between her fingers and asked, 'Well?'

'Well, what?' Ben looked into her eyes asking the same question.

'Don't act thick, Ben,' she said, producing a loving half-smile. 'Do you think marrying Khalida will rescue her from the hands of the Hussains? And are you willing to do it?'

He was taken aback. 'Ayesha, forget about that for a second, I need to know how you are?'

She looked puzzled, tipped her head and raised her eyebrows.

'Now who's being thick?' Ben sighed. 'After this afternoon. You know. You do remember what we did. Are you okay? How do you feel? No regrets?'

'I'm fine. It was… lovely. Really lovely, Ben. And definitely no regrets. But my life isn't in peril. Khalida's is.'

Unbelievable, Ben thought. Was that the reason why he was utterly in love with her? How many people would be so selfless, so caring to put others before themselves?

'I'll do anything for you, Ayesha, you know that. But will it be possible?'

'Of course. There's no law stopping you from marrying a Bangladeshi girl.'

'Are you sure? I can't imagine it will be as easy or as simple as you think.'

'No-one said it would be easy, Ben. Or Simple. I'm sure it won't be, especially with the Hussains after her. I'll write tonight and post the letter tomorrow to the box number in Jessore and tell her our plan.'

'Khalida might not agree to marry me.'

'She'll agree. She's desperate to get out of the country. You, Ben, are her ticket to freedom. You could save her life. Literally.'

Ayesha moved slowly away from the tea bushes towards a trio of lemon trees, all dripping with an abundance of fruit. Ben noticed she'd changed her sari. The white, light cotton red-bordered one she wore at Dak Cottage had been replaced with one of rich, smooth, purple silk with a crimson blouse. She was breathtakingly beautiful, elegant, intelligent, and it was her he wished to marry, not Khalida. But Ayesha's wish was his command.

'First thing Monday I'll go to the British High Commission on Topkhana Road. I'll ask about the legal requirements for marrying a Bangladeshi woman and what's needed to get her a British passport and so on.'

'Make out it's me.'

'What?'

'They'll want to know a name. Give them mine. Don't say it's Khalida Chowdhury. We can't trust them, Ben. We have to be careful. Very careful. You don't understand what it's like in this country. There is so much corruption. So much collusion. So much bribery. Unless it's close family, we have to assume everyone snitches on everyone else.'

'Have you told your folks yet about Khalida's letter?'

'No. And I'm not going to. Not because I don't trust them, obviously. But I don't want to worry them any more than they are already. Remember, besides worrying about Khalida, who is virtually another sister to me, Ma and Pa are lifelong friends of Khalida's mother. They are as worried as Mrs Chowdhury.'

'What if Khalida doesn't have an abortion, has the baby, but refuses to marry Maz?' Ben asked. 'Surely the Hussain family would drop all interest in her.'

'It doesn't work like that here amongst people like the Hussains.'

Ben looked puzzled. He needed an explanation.

'Married or not, Maz's child is the family's child, not exclusively Khalida's, not even an equal share with Maz. As we've discussed before, here – across the whole subcontinent – a marriage is a bond between two families almost as much as two people. To the likes of Farook Hussain Khalida's body, her child, is *his* body, *his* child, or at least now part of it is. The foetus in Khalida's womb is like a gem inside a protective pouch, a diamond in velvet. Understand?'

'But if she's aborted? No longer pregnant?'

'Then the Hussains will seek revenge. They'll see it as Khalida murdering their own child. And I suspect they'll already be calling it a son because of their... their male chauvinism. Even among the middle classes, many men see sons as an asset and daughters as a liability. And still, today, in the twentieth century, many girls are not registered after birth. They don't exist, officially, certainly in remote areas of West Pakistan.'

'But if nobody knows about Khalida's pregnancy, there's no reputation to lose so...'

'The Hussains know. That's all that matters. The father must avenge on behalf of his son... and his grandchild, alive or dead. A strong signal must be sent throughout the family so everyone, certainly every girl, every woman, knows what to expect if they transgress. Do wrong – in Hussain's eyes, that is.'

'In what way "avenge"?'

'Ben, they'll kill her!'

'Seriously?'

'Yes, seriously. That's what the likes of the Hussains think like. And it won't be a quick death. They'll torture her first. A gang of cruel filthy men will abuse her in ways you can't imagine. I feel sick at the thought. That's why we have to do something. And something quick.'

Ben wanted to hold Ayesha close. As close as two people could be. Reading his mind, she turned to face him. She wanted his arms around her again and their two bodies to be one. Noticing her parents and sister had gone inside, Ayesha took a risk and kissed Ben.

'That was nice,' he said. 'A bit quick. But thank you.'

'Sadly, Ben, no more kisses for a while.'

As they strolled towards the house Dr Rahman returned to the veranda carrying his prayer mat.

'He'll have just completed Isha,' Ayesha said. 'The last prayer of the day. Anyway, quick, come on. Despite what my dear sister said,

I'm sure she'll have left at least one cham-cham for you. And you must be hungry after all your... shall I say extra activities today?' Ayesha delivered a mischievous smile.

'You must be kidding. Tonight's meal was unbelievably good. But the mosquitoes are hungry, they're feeding on me.' Ben slapped one piercing his neck.

Ayesha suddenly stepped directly in front of Ben and stopped his stride. 'If this marriage scheme works, you do know that you will not be allowed to consummate your marriage to Khalida, don't you?'

He laughed. 'I was thinking it was my reward. She's almost as beautiful as you.'

'No, Ben. I'm your reward.'

TWENTY-FIVE

'Did the exchange go well, son?'

'Yes, smoothly. Only an interfering customs officer at the dockside delayed us for a minute – until uncle's men made sure he could say nothing more.'

Mazharul Hussain, alongside a squad of twelve soldiers from his uncle's airport unit, had driven to the port at Narayanganj with two Mercedes, escorted front and rear by armoured vehicles. Both black cars boarded the ferry where, in the captain's cabin, Maz met Saw Maung.

'Ne Win has asked me to convey his personal greetings to your father,' Saw Maung said. 'The Revolutionary Council of Burma is most grateful. These sanctions are so ridiculous and harmful to our people.' He placed a small suitcase on the table.

Maz was accompanied by a currency expert from Bangladesh's state bank. It was important the dollars were genuine. The Burmese had excellent counterfeiters, despite their limited access to the correct inks, paper and specialist printing equipment. The serial numbers also needed to align with US Federal Reserve issue. Methodically, the specialist took random notes from the bundles to scrutinize. During the examination, his poker-face gave nothing away. Maz and Saw Maung stood watching anxiously for the outcome of his meticulous deliberations. After several minutes the banker removed his magnifying glasses. He placed his ultra-violet torch carefully to one side, next to the list of the Fed's serial numbers. He turned to Maz and Saw Maung and, with not a smile nor frown nor word, flicked his head. Maz closed the case, shook hands with Maung, the deal done.

Uncle would pay a handsome bonus to the fiercely loyal officers and men in his elite squad. Each one had been hand-picked and served him during the War of Liberation. Even the ranking soldiers as well as the officers earned enough from special duties to live handsomely. Already they owned property and land, their sons attended or would attend good schools, their daughters would marry well.

MAZ ASKED HIS father if there had been any news of Khalida. Had they managed to track her down?

Farook Hussain paced his study at home before heading to the ministry. He had plenty on his mind. He was pleased he had offloaded the two cars to the Burmese for personal gain. But they constituted chickenfeed compared with the scheme to siphon aid funds to Bermuda. He and his four partners would be set up for life. Through a string of shell companies, he planned to buy property in New York, London and Switzerland.

When an army officer, in East Pakistan days and under military rule, he'd attended a conference on 'Third World development' in Lausanne. One day, he promised himself, looking over Lake Leman from his hotel balcony at the Beau-Rivage Palace, I will buy a house here. Switzerland seemed a pleasant, clean, safe, calm country, devoid of monsoons, corruption and political danger. And, thanks to specialist notaries and bankers, easy to conduct business with, although for outrageous fees.

Khalida Chowdhury was an irritant. But family came first. It was important to show his son that once a strategy had been set, it must be achieved. He wanted the girl found, so found she must be. She has my grandson within her womb. She has no right, no right whatsoever, to dispose of my flesh, my blood. And why would any woman not want to give birth.

'Our police, son, as you know, are inept. It is time we chivvied them along or made our own enquiries, give them a helping hand. Make me a list of the girl's closest friends. One of them, at least, must know the whereabouts of the bitch. I'll ensure they each receive a visit and are questioned closely. If necessary, other methods may need to be employed.'

'Other methods?'

'Phone taps. Mail interception. Surveillance. Financial inducements: everyone has their price. I'll also have enquiries made at the medical college to see who her close friends are.'

TWENTY-SIX

Syed had not expected to drive into central Dacca on Monday morning. At first he assumed Ben had been called to a meeting at the Intercontinental Hotel with his new Aid International colleagues. When Ben asked him to drive on to the British High Commission in Topkhana Road, Syed asked 'the nature of your visit'. Ben found this very odd. Not once before had Syed taken the slightest interest in where he was going, or for what reason. Ben waved his passport and explained he needed to alter his registration now he worked for AI not Action Delta.

In the phone call, second secretary Nowel Cribb said he could spare around fifteen minutes at eleven forty-five. Ben was early, eager to get information about the British citizenship status of a Bangladeshi bride. One of the secretarial staff showed Ben to Mr Cribb's first floor office. There was nothing on the diplomat's desktop other than a pen holder. Not even a tray for incoming and outgoing papers. Did this guy do any work? Or was he, Ben wondered, obsessionally tidy? Cribb's office overlooked the commission's spacious grounds to the rear of the building with a well-manicured lawn and sharp-edged rose borders. A marquee had been erected and, inside, people were busy setting up tables and chairs in readiness for what looked like a presentation, perhaps alongside a reception party. A team of Bangladeshi men were stringing up lines of bunting: half union jacks, half the new flag of Bangladesh, a red disc on a green background. The red represented the sun rising on the new nation – and the blood shed fighting for its independence. The green, the fertile lush land of Bangladesh.

Nowel Cribb marched in. Tall, athletic, square jawed, delivering a firm, brisk handshake. Ben immediately recognised public school deportment. He'd met many at university, although they generally gravitated towards their own kind. Grammar school didn't quite cut it for most of them, even if you excelled at rugby or cricket. Cribb sat briskly and leaned over with his hands clasped under his chin and elbows resting on the desktop.

'You're the third British man I've seen this year, Mr Altringham,' he said, implying three were three too many. He lowered his voice, as if talking confidentially in a crowded restaurant. 'As you will appreciate, even expressing the wish to marry a local girl is an extremely delicate matter. You've been here, what, nine, ten months? You must know the vast majority of people here are against interfaith and interracial marriage, particularly a white man with a local woman. Frankly, it's not much easier if a Bangladeshi Muslim chap wanted to marry a white Christian woman, even if she converted to Islam.'

It was not the encouraging start Ben hoped for. 'A friend told me it could be done through the equivalent of our civil ceremony, through the court, using a kazi, a civil judge.'

'I'm afraid that's also a misunderstanding the two previous applicants held. Let me explain. In short, the new government here are rewriting many of the laws. At present, in theory, the Special Marriage Act of 1872 remains in force and allows a Muslim man to marry a Christian or Jewish woman…'

'A religion belonging to the Abrahamic faith.' Ben interrupted to illustrate he had some awareness of the legal and Islamic position. He had hours of discussion with Ayesha and especially her mother, Raina, on the legal aspects.

'Quite,' Cribb said, although it didn't curb his ready-made script. 'But a Muslim woman cannot marry a Christian or Jewish man – unless she declares herself an atheist or converts to a non-Muslim faith.'

'Yes, I understand that.'

'Unfortunately, Mr Altringham, amongst some hard-liners here, that's a dangerous declaration to make. And many of these hard-liners believe a Muslim cannot renounce their faith.' Nowel Cribb paused and, this time, Ben had no response. 'Can I assume that…' Cribb checked his notes, '… Miss Ayesha Rahman is Muslim?'

'Yes.'

'And that she is not willing to renounced her faith?'

'Yes. Well, I think so. I've not asked. We've not discussed it.'

Nowel Cribb disguised his reaction well. But a split-second scowl shouted, 'What – you've not talked about that fundamental matter?' But he continued calmly, 'And presumably you're not willing to convert to Islam?'

'No.'

Ben tried another approach. 'Could one of the British vicars or American reverends or preachers here marry us?'

'Mr Altringham,' Cribb exhaled impatiently, 'I can guarantee that you will not find any church leader here willing to marry you, even if they could legally. In the highly unlikely – and possibly dangerous – event that Miss Rahman renounced her faith, any Christian minister marrying you would have their whole church kicked out of the country. All their aid efforts closed in retaliation. It could even cause a riot. No, Mr Altringham, give up the idea of marrying Miss Rahman... well, here in Bangladesh.'

Ben didn't give up. 'I understood this new constitution Bangladesh just introduced declared the country a secular republic with no legal status for Sharia.'

'I don't wish to sound contemptuous, Mr Altringham,' although Cribb's expression indicated contempt, 'but there is theory and there is fact. Sure, Bangladesh is certainly more tolerant of other religions than some of the zealots in West Pakistan and the Middle East. But that doesn't mean they're as open-minded as we are. And certainly when it comes to you marrying one of theirs, well...'

Ben felt defeated. It seemed marrying Khalida, to enable him to get her on a flight fleeing Bangladesh, was out of the question. 'So, in short, you're telling me there's no way I can marry K... marry Ayesha here.'

'Look, I must go in a few minutes. But let me give you an off-the-record tip. Can she get to India?'

'Yes, she has a lot of family in Calcutta. She and her mother and sister stayed there during the war.'

'Then travel separately. Meet in Calcutta. Get married there. Easier for all her family and friends too to attend the ceremony.

It won't be easy swimming through India's Byzantine bureaucracy, but at least it's possible. I can put you in touch with our chaps at the commission there.'

'Once married, would she then be entitled to British citizenship, as my wife?'

'Of course, as long as your marriage is one of love and not one of convenience.'

'Oh, it's definitely love.'

'I can see that.'

'And if a wedding was arranged in Britain?'

'Same principle applies. But presumably all her family and friends are here. And Bangladeshis love big weddings. Off the record again, marrying in Britain would be the easiest option.'

Nowel Cribb stood indicating the interview was at an end. If Ben had any doubt, Cribb looked at and put a finger on his watch.

'By the way, Mr Altringham, I believe you told Jane – our secretary who brought you upstairs – that you now work for Aid International.'

'Yes, we closed Action Delta. But I doubt I'll stay with them for long, once the handover period is over.'

'Oh, why's that?'

'It's hard to put my finger on it. I suppose I don't like the way they work. Maybe it's their pushy American style. Something like that. If you hear of any jobs going in the aid sector, I'd appreciate a call.'

'They'll be plenty of them, I'm sure. Aid is pouring in like monsoon rain.'

'Thanks for the information, especially the tips about sneaking off to Calcutta or marrying in Britain.'

'Oh, Mr Altringham,' Cribb said while grinning and tapping his nose, 'you must have misheard or misunderstood me. I couldn't possibly give such advice.'

'Ah, yes, thanks for the advice you definitely didn't provide.'

Taking an instant like to Ben, while shaking hands, Cribb invited him to the commission's reception, starting at four o'clock. 'HC, our high commissioner, is introducing our visiting minister to members of the government. No need for a tie. Smart casual will be just the ticket. I'll have Jane issue you an invitation card. Several of the British aid agency people will be there. Perhaps you can have a few cosy chats and find yourself a new job.'

BEN REGRETTED ATTENDING. It seemed everyone knew everybody else, except him. He was Billy No-Mates, stood alone with a glass of salty lassi. Red Cross and UN agency people had their badges displayed and, after the speeches, he would approach them. He would push in, politely of course, and engage in conversation. It was the only way in these situations. When the guests were called to take a seat in the marquee, Ben sat at the back on an empty row.

At the lectern, set on a small flower-adorned stage, the high commissioner welcomed Britain's under-secretary of state for the Foreign and Commonwealth Office, responsible for overseas aid and development. The minister presumably had to present the usual guff: new country, new government, new opportunities for cooperation. He claimed he was absolutely delighted to visit Bangladesh. He hoped it would be the first of many happy visits to this beautiful verdant land. With Edward Heath's Conservative government back in Britain in turmoil, a few faces looked doubtful whether the minister's party would remain in power long enough for another visit.

When the high commissioner introduced Farook Hussain, Ben was utterly stunned. Until that moment, it hadn't occurred to him that the minister of foreign affairs would be at the event. But of course he would be. It was obvious. He felt stupid for not realising. Here, twenty yards in front of him, stood the man whose son had made Khalida pregnant.

Hussain approached the lectern and thanked the minister for his kind words.

'Citizens of Bangladesh greatly appreciate the generous support that the United Kingdom has bestowed upon our new nation on this ancient land… our shared history… together we will…'

Whatever else Hussain said, Ben heard through a thick haze of anger. He wanted to stand up. Shout. Scream. Tell everyone this man and his son were persecuting a young woman. Wanted to capture her. Force her to marry. Keep her in purdah. And, if what Khalida told Ayesha was true – and he had no cause to doubt it – this man's son

Mazharul Hussain had spiked her drink with vodka to make her dozy enough to rape her.

'... *and minister, commissioner and distinguished guests, on behalf of the government of Bangladesh, I can say with both hands on my heart, our two countries can look forward with hope and optimism to a long and mutually beneficial relationship...*'

'Mr Altringham, are you all right?' whispered Nowel Cribb close to his ear. Ben jumped, taken by surprise. Cribb appeared seemingly from nowhere.

'No. Yes. Err... thanks. I'm fine.'

'I must say, old boy, you don't look it. You've gone white, as if you've seen a ghost.'

'It's just...'

'Come.'

Nowel whisked Ben through the back of the marquee to the commission and unlocked a door to a room resembling a doctor's waiting room. Six rows of ten chairs faced a counter hatch. It was where Bangladeshis applied for a British visa. Nowel served Ben with a paper cup of ice-cold water from a dispenser in the corner.

'Thanks, I'm fine now. I should go...'

'No. Take a minute. You know you were shaking, positively seething when Hussain started his speech.'

'Were you watching me?'

Cribb laughed a little. 'I was watching everyone. I'm responsible for security. And I'm especially responsible for you. You're my guest, Benjamin, remember?'

'Ben, please. Only my mother calls me Benjamin nowadays.'

'What, all the time, or just when she's telling you off?'

Ben emptied the cup.

'More?'

'Yes, thanks.' Ben noticed the gun in a holster under Cribb's jacket when he bent forward to take the cup.

Cribb returned with Ben's water.

'Can I ask, Ben, when you said this morning you didn't like the way Aid International worked, can you elaborate on that?'

Ayesha's words echoed around Ben's head: in Bangladesh, you can't trust anyone — apart from your close family. But Cribb was British. A diplomat. A civil servant. Surely he could be trusted.

Cribb, accurately reading Ben's mind, took the initiative.

'Let me level with you, Ben. It is rumoured — and I must stress rumoured — that one or more aid agencies are being forced to... shall I say... pay over the odds, some might say pay bribes, to be allowed to operate here. Aid International might — and again I stress might — be one of those involved. So, a straight question, Ben: have you detected something not quite right with AI? Perhaps the way they go about things? Is that why you feel, shall I say, uncomfortable working for them?'

'A straight answer? Yes. But I've no proof of anything dodgy. It's just that the people I've met, so far at least, don't really seem to care about the people they're supposed to care about. It's as if they're running a straight commercial business. Having said that though, they seem to get supplies of things, medicines for example, in days when we took weeks. If we got supplies at all. And in quantities we at Action Delta could only dream about. But I put that down to their scale of operations, their buying power, their experience around the world. AI have millions of dollars and we... well, Action Delta... scraped by on a few thousand pounds. We always struggled to keep afloat.'

'Can I ask a favour?'

'Sure.'

'If you see or hear of anything, anything unusual, give me a call.'

Cribb plucked a card from his jacket's top pocket and, after writing something on the back, presented it to Ben.

Nowel Cribb
Second Secretary
British High Commission
Topkhana Road
Dacca
Bangladesh
Tel: 24 63 46 / 24 63 47
Fax: 24 63 48

'The number on the back is my residence. Call anytime.'

TWENTY-SEVEN

Khalida complied with Ayesha's instruction and replied 'care of' Dacca Medical College and Hospital. The type-written envelope, from Mrs A Haq, PO Box 249, Jessore, was in her pigeon hole alongside notes from friends, lecturers and a letter from DMCH Administration. The latter was a note requesting next year's fees. It announced a fifteen percent rise 'to cover inflationary costs'. Not good news for Abba. But he never complained. We'll manage, he'll say. Bushra's university fees will doubtless be increasing too.

Khalida's letter gave a phone number. She suggested ringing from the college, or a friend's house not known to Khalida. 'Just in case they are monitoring,' she wrote.

The vice-principal's personal assistant had long admired Ayesha. He knew, of course, she was an exceptional student. A prize-winner. She was also the most beautiful of all the attractive female students. When Ayesha asked if she could make a quick urgent call to her father, he was delighted to let her use his office phone. It was the first time she had cause to talk to him for months. Her dark deep mysterious eyes, soft silky voice, slightly shy but coquettish manner, turned Mostafa's stomach all a-flutter, his legs to jelly, his fingers to clumsy thumbs. Tonight, on his charpoy, he would drift to sleep with her face on his mind and, he hoped, her body in his dreams. He had even considered the possibility that his family could approach hers with a proposal of marriage. After all, they were of the same social class. And our fathers both doctors...

He stood watching, imagining the possibilities, as Ayesha sat at his desk and picked up the receiver. Her perfume transformed his small room into heaven and he hoped it would linger long, long after she'd gone.

'Sorry, Mostafa,' she said softly, her scarf covering half her face so enhancing her eyes, 'it is a call I must make in private. But it will only take a minute. Thank you so much. I'm very grateful.'

'Oh. Of course. Apologies.' He left the room feeling awkward, embarrassed. *He should have realised she would need her privacy. And now she'll think I'm stupid.*

It rang. And rang. Ayesha was aware that her minute had already expired. As she started to replace the phone she heard…

'Yes.' The voice was distant, cautious.

'Is that Mrs Haq? Mrs A Haq?'

'Oh,' Khalida cried, 'it's so good to hear from you and...'

'Khalida,' Ayesha cut in and whispered quickly. 'I've only got a minute. Ben has agreed. But we need to get you both to Calcutta…'

'But I told you, I've only got my old Pakistan passport.'

'Doesn't matter. He's going to pick you up in the Land Rover and smuggle you across the border. You'll have to hide…'

'Where?'

'I don't know, do I? Behind the seats, maybe, under some boxes. Anyway, that's for him to sort out. When and where can he collect you?'

'But Ben doesn't usually drive the car.'

'He's making an exception. He arranged paperwork allowing him to import aid supplies from Calcutta. So he should be able to cross the border without any problems.'

'Okay. Let's say noon on Thursday. That's the fourteenth. I'll be at the far end of the bridge over the Bhairab river on the left. It's Dacca Road, the one approaching Satkamair Railway Station. I'll wear my burqa. But I'll have a large blue bag. My cousin will be with me. He's tall and skinny. Sweet sixteen.'

'Remember, Khalida, the Land Rover now has Aid International on its front doors and bonnet, not Action Delta. Okay?'

'Okay.'

'If I can, I'll call again tomorrow. But if not… all my love and good luck. God be with you.'

'And with you, my life-saving friend. And… and thank Ben.'

'Oh, Khalida, how could I forget? Are you still… you know… pregnant?'

'Yes. Yes, I am.'

TWENTY-EIGHT

Faiyaz had not turned up for work in the clinic at Mohpur since Aid International's delegation visited the camp a week earlier. She was normally as reliable as clockwork, and always said hello and goodbye. Ben, worried, had written a note to her and asked driver Syed to deliver it. He wanted to check she was all right. That was four days ago. There had been no reply. Faiyaz shared a small apartment in central Tungipur with her cousin, her husband and four children. She slept on the cramped living room floor, helped look after the kids, shared household chores and took her turn shopping.

All Faiyaz's close family had been killed in the war. She was already vulnerable, her status in the community uncertain: her mother Bangladeshi, her father Bihari. Faiyaz had a foot in both camps, but belonged to neither. She had loyalties to both, but neither had loyalty to her. Her hopes and dreams of becoming a pharmacist fading into fantasy.

Before the conflict most Bangladeshis and Biharis lived side by side peacefully. But the nine month War of Liberation drove a deep wedge between them. As Faiyaz's parents demonstrated, in some areas both communities had integrated well. But no longer. Faiyaz was one of thousands caught in the crossfire. Just like many Anglo-Indians in colonial India and still, today, prejudice remained.

It would be unwise for Ben to visit Faiyaz. It would remind Bangladeshi residents she worked in the Bihari camp. Tongues would wag. At best a visit would embarrass her and, at worse, endanger her, especially in those poor crowded rat-infested back streets of Tungipur. He considered asking Ayesha or Dr Rahman to call to ask how she was. But Ayesha had end of year exams approaching and Dr Rahman his private surgeries, hospital work and lectures, in addition to his voluntary work at Mohpur. It would be an unfair imposition – because they would without rancour find time to visit.

The main person affected by Faiyaz's absence, as well as Dr Rahman, was medical assistant Masaad. He had to work harder and longer helping Dr Rahman, and on the days between his clinics. Ben, too, spent more time administering medicines prescribed by Dr Rahman. Masaad had some knowledge about common conditions. But Ben observed Masaad exaggerating his abilities and diagnostic skills. Faiyaz was far more careful, less cavalier, worked within her abilities quietly and competently. Dr Rahman had full confidence in her capabilities too. In fact he planned to encourage Faiyaz to become a doctor and, secretly, had applied for a scholarship on her behalf to cover all her fees. He hadn't, to date, heard the outcome of his application.

At the desk in Dak Cottage Ben completed a timesheet for the previous week's work. This additional paperwork had been imposed by Aid International, much to his annoyance, to account for each hour of his working day. Pete Conan, now his 'line manager', claimed it helped 'drive efficiency'. Ben almost resigned immediately when asked to complete this task. He failed to see how such bureaucracy helped Biharis. But he hid his anger. He would bide his time. In a few weeks his handover contract would end and he'd be away from Womach and his cronies.

With the ceiling and desk fans whirring, Ben barely heard the light tap on the door.

'May we come in?'

'Faiyaz! Of course. Good to see you. Have you been unwell?'

It was then Ben noticed another woman behind her fully veiled in a black burqa.

'This is my cousin, Mr Ben, Sana.'

'Pleased meet you, Mr Ben,' Sana said. He nodded his head in acknowledgement.

'Come, please, take a seat. Would you like some tea, coffee? Instant, I'm afraid.'

'No. We're fine. We won't keep you long,' Faiyaz said.

'Don't worry about that. Take as long as you like. I was only doing boring paperwork.'

The two women sat close together on what Ben continued to describe as Abi's bed. Faiyaz immediately looked on the brink of tears, clearly very upset. Ben, not knowing what was bothering her, gave her time and stayed silent.

Sana spoke first. Her English was not good, but perfectly understandable. And certainly better than what Ben could have achieved speaking Bengali or Urdu. 'This serious matter, Mr Ben. My cousin feel disgrace. She think her fault. But I told her not her fault. And she must tell. But she think her not believed. Man will say nothing happened.' She turned to look at Faiyaz, gripped her arm and nudged her to speak.

Faiyaz took a handkerchief from her sleeve and dabbed her eyes, but said nothing. Ben encouraged her. 'Faiyaz, I know you to be completely honest and trustworthy. I will believe what you tell me. Everyone who knows you will, including Dr Rahman. Now, what is it?'

'It was that man. The tall one with the white hair...'

'Womach? Thomas Womach?'

Faiyaz nodded. 'He came in the clinic. Alone. He... he... tried to touch me. He did. He... he... said if he...' She cried and it took a minute to regain her composure. Ben went to the new fridge and poured two long glasses of water for Faiyaz and her cousin.

Sana spoke for Faiyaz. 'He told Faiyaz if she did things with him, bad things, he would get her place at college and pay fees. I think once he did bad things he would go back America and do nothing.'

'But I told him "No!"' Faiyaz spoke up with fire in her belly. 'I said I would scream if he touched me again.'

'And then what did he do?' asked Ben.

'He called me bad things. Used dirty words and rushed away. I thought he was going to hit me.'

'Oh, no. That's terrible, Faiyaz. I am so, so sorry.'

'He's a bad man. Very bad.' Faiyaz closed back into her shell, covered half her face with her headscarf and put the handkerchief to her watery eyes.

Sana asked, 'What can be done, Mr Ben?'

Ben paused to think. 'That's the right question, Sana, but I don't know the right answer. I can't see what action to take right now.

But I promise you this, Faiyaz, I will do something. I am really, really sorry this happened to you. And you definitely should not feel ashamed. You did absolutely nothing wrong, Faiyaz. Womach was totally to blame, not you.'

In the conversation that followed, Faiyaz thought that following the incident – nay, the assault – it was best not to return to work at the clinic in case Womach returned. Ben promised that if he heard about anyone visiting from Aid International, he'd let her know. Although he didn't expect to see Womach again before he left Aid International. In any case, she'd never be left alone again with any of them, not while he remained at Mohpur.

Ben asked Faiyaz if she felt ready to return to work. 'The place is falling apart without you,' he said, trying to lighten the mood. Faiyaz believed that she may have lost her job, that Womach would stop paying her, and she wouldn't be paid for her absent days.

'Faiyaz, as long as I'm in charge of running Mohpur and the clinic, you have a job. And I'll pay you in full for the days you've been off. Have no worries about that.'

'Thank you, Mr Ben,' Sana said. 'My husband has little work and my cousin helps us. You very kind.'

'It's the least I can do,' he said. 'But in a few weeks I won't be working for Aid International. They say they'll keep running the clinic and improve conditions. So, Faiyaz, you'll have to see who is coming to replace me and see how you feel working for the new team. They may be okay. Proper aid workers. I just don't know.'

'Okay.'

'Dr Rahman and Masaad will also be delighted to hear you're coming back. And I apologise in advance – I think we've messed up your well-organised cupboards and shelves a bit. We need you to sort us out.'

She half-smiled.

'On the other matter, Faiyaz, I'll let you know what I'm going to do when I work out myself what I'm going to do. But I promise, I will do something.'

'Thank you. I will see you tomorrow.'

FURIOUS WITH WOMACH, frustrated with Aid International, Ben ripped his time sheet into bits and threw the pieces in the bin. They can sing for them. He picked up the phone and dialled the direct line number on the card he always now carried.

'Hello.'

'Nowel? It's Ben Altringham.'

'Yes, I recognise your voice.'

'I have some information regarding...'

'Let me stop you there. I'll come and see you. Will you be at Mohpur later this afternoon?'

'Yes.'

'See you then.'

TWENTY-NINE

Ayesha and Ben agreed they wouldn't meet for two weeks. It was a hard decision to make, but they believed it to be the right one. Ben would miss her, and the Rahman family. He would definitely miss Ali's meals. But Ayesha needed to focus on her end of year exams. And Ben had to execute Khalida's evacuation to India: it was safer to put 'distance' between himself and the Rahmans.

Bangladesh's December weather was pleasantly warm. More significant for the running of Mohpur camp was that it was mostly dry. Days of endless sunshine and blue skies made life a little easier for those in the camp. Far better than monsoon storms. Good weather reduced but didn't stop the daily toll of death and disease. Ben's figures recorded that, on average over the past month, seven adults and five children died daily from amongst the eight thousand residents now in the camp. Smallpox, cholera, typhoid, tuberculosis and other infections continued to run riot and cause distress.

Ben had asked Aid International for more rolls of white linen to give those who had none to shroud their deceased kinfolk. Pete Conan questioned whether this was 'an appropriate use of resources'. Ben pointed out that if AI didn't provide the material, tents would be torn to be used as shrouds.

'Why can't they just put the bodies in a coffin?' Conan asked.

'Muslims don't use coffins, Pete,' said Ben, surprised he didn't know that basic fact. 'A man's body is wrapped three times in white sheets, a woman five times. They place the body in the ground with their feet facing towards the Ka'bah.'

'What?'

'The Ka'bah. The house of Allah. In Mecca.'

Pete Conan said they would need to discuss this 'issue' at their next management meeting. Impatient for action, Ben phoned Abi's contact at the clothes manufacturer and sweet-talked him into donating a couple of rolls. Syed would drive into Dacca and collect.

Ben woke up Tuesday morning to find a dead man, probably aged around seventy, outside Dak Bungalow. It wasn't the first time a body had been left on the doorstep; it wouldn't be the last. When someone without close relatives perished, it was left to Action Delta or, now, Aid International to arrange the burial.

At the Bihari burial ground, towards the western end of the camp, volunteers and camp workers ritually washed the body and shrouded it to bury before sunset. Several men in Mohpur were Islamic clerics and performed the relatively short and simple burial ceremony over the grave. Ben had stopped attending burials months earlier; there were just too many.

After arranging for the old man's skeleton-thin body to be taken away, Ben returned to the office for breakfast. The phone rang.

'Mr Altringham, have you been out?' quizzed Ayesha impatiently. 'I've been ringing for the past half hour.' Ben explained that he'd been undertaking what he called his undertaker's duties: disposing of another corpse. 'Oh, sorry,' she said, regretting her tetchiness. 'We need to meet, Mr Altringham. I've heard from Mrs Huq. You remember Mrs Huq, don't you?'

Ayesha had put him on guard. 'Yes, that old lady we met.'

'That's right. She wondered if you could help her granddaughter improve her English. But I need to talk with you first.'

'How urgent is it?'

'As soon as possible, if you can, Mr Altringham. She faces her English exam very soon.'

With Syed away collecting cloth in Dacca, Ben walked quickly the two miles into Tungipur without delay, eating a banana along the way.

AYESHA HAD TAKEN Khalida's advice and, as a precaution, assumed their telephone had been tapped. Last night, calling a college friend to borrow a textbook, her own voice kept reverberating. She also heard an unusual click several seconds after her friend had replaced the receiver. It aroused her suspicion even more, hence calling Khalida by her pseudonym, Mrs Haq.

It had been an early start that morning and Ben was surprised it was only eight-thirty when he arrived at the Rahman household.

'*As-salamu alaykum, sahib*,' the chowkidor said accompanied by his one-finger salute before unlocking the iron gate.

'*Wa 'alaykumu s-salam*,' Ben replied. '*Kemon achen?*'

'*Ami okay*, Mr Ben, *dhonnobad*.'

Ayesha, on the front veranda, lifted her head from the textbook as Ben approached. As always in public, respecting convention, no physical contact was made and a dutiful distance maintained. Ayesha's smile was sufficient for Ben, and his for her. Natcoo, clearing the breakfast things, asked Ben if he would like tea or coffee. Coffee, please, for it was clearly going to be a caffeine-fuelled day. Breakfast? Ali hasn't gone to market yet. Omelette? Ben settled for scrambled egg on toast.

'Have you got that?' she asked after giving Ben details of where to collect Khalida.

'My brain might not be as capacious as yours, Ayesha, but I think I can remember your instructions.'

She teased, although it was vitally important he had grasped them. 'Prove it. Repeat them.'

Ben sighed. 'Okay. If I must. Day after tomorrow, Thursday, drive to Jessore. Approaching the railway station on the main road from here, conveniently named Dacca Road, I cross the bridge over the river...'

'Name of river?'

'Is that absolutely necessary?'

'As Abba would say, details make the difference between life and death.'

'In medicine, maybe, but...'

'And in saving Khalida.'

'It's the... the... the River Bhairab.'

'So far, so good.' She waited for him to complete his exam.

'At the station end of the bridge, on the left, at noon, Khalida will be waiting in a burqa with a large blue bag and her skinny sixteen year-old cousin.'

'And he's tall. Well, tall for a Bengali.'

'May I eat breakfast now?'

Ayesha released Ben's hand, held conspiratorially under the table. (In fact, they had done this so often, everyone had noticed one hand often 'went missing', as Bushra later put it, when they were both at the table.) He tucked into his egg on toast and a few minutes of silence ensued. Ayesha, making every spare second count before her end of year exam, returned her head to the textbook.

Suddenly, Ben announced, 'You know we can't marry, don't you?'

'What? You've not even asked…'

'Hey, calm down, Ayesha. It's Khalida I'm talking about.' He smiled. She faked a frown. 'And now we're getting her to India we won't need to marry. So no consummation I'm afraid.' He pulled a sad face.

Ayesha kicked Ben.

'Ouch! That hurt.'

'It meant to.'

While rubbing his shin, exaggerating the pain, Ben said, 'The high commission guy, Nowel Cribb, told me there was little chance of marrying a Muslim woman here in Bangladesh. No Christian vicar or parson or priest would touch us with a barge pole. I'd have to become a Muslim, or Khalida would need to renounce Islam. Even then, it would be a legal as well as moral minefield.

'So, Ayesha, that means when it comes to us…'

'Let's cross that bridge when we come to it.'

DR RAHMAN DROVE Ben back to Mohpur and was pleased to hear that Faiyaz had returned to work at the clinic. Had she been unwell? he asked. In confidence, Ben shared with Dr Rahman the disturbing news of Womach's assault on Faiyaz, which explained her week's absence. Ben had not known what to do for the best. Going to the police was a waste of time. And he was certain any complaint to Aid International would be brushed under the carpet. None of Womach's underlings would challenge him. He also shared Faiyaz's judgement that Womach would deny everything. Ben told Dr Rahman he had however informed a representative at the British High

Commission. And, it seemed, they were already aware of unusual activities within Aid International.

'I'd like to leave AI right now,' Ben disclosed to Dr Rahman. 'But Biharis need support here. It's wrong, I know, but no-one will deliver supplies to the camp unless a representative of AI is here. Even our reliable staff are not allowed to sign a chit for anything, food, kit, medicines.'

'It is another way, alas, the government keeps Biharis in their place,' said Dr Rahman. 'It reminds them that they remain the enemy. Collaborators. Traitors. Not welcome. It will take time, Ben, a long time to heal the scars of war. If ever.'

'AI haven't said who is going to replace me or what their intentions are for improving the camp. We know they plan to build up Dak Cottage and make it much bigger with better facilities. Pete Conan says they are in negotiations with the government to re-site the camp too.'

'Really? Where?'

'Don't know exactly, Dr Rahman. Two or three miles further out from Tungipur I expect.'

'Why would they do that?'

'Your guess is as good as mine. But to isolate Biharis further is going to put them in yet more danger. Attacks and abuses around the camp perimeter are still going on by gangs. I don't know if they're former freedom fighters or just disaffected lads. Two nights ago a group came in and smashed a water pump beyond repair.'

Having parked the car, Ben and Dr Rahman walked towards Dak Cottage. Faiyaz, back to her reliable efficient self, had already tidied the clinic. Masaad was setting up the table and chair in readiness for Dr Rahman's surgery. Around fifty people had formed the queue to see him.

As they approached, slowly because of Dr Rahman's injured leg, he spoke more despondently than Ben had ever heard him speak before.

'Ben, my dear chap, we have to face facts. There are too many frustrated young men who thought that, after the war, riches would fall from heaven. Politicians promised a bright future for Bangladesh. Perhaps one day the light will shine through.'

'But this is a poor country. Perhaps the poorest. Corruption and incompetency is as endemic as the terrible diseases we see before us.

'These young people are just as poor as before the war. Poorer, in most cases, because of the broken economy and infrastructure. Bangladesh is on its knees and, apart from prayer, I cannot see how we can extricate ourselves from this poverty.'

Dr Rahman maintained his routine of walking from the back of the queue casting an eye on his patients. Those in greatest need, particularly mothers with sick babies, he escorted to the front. Today there was an exception. He spied a man sat on the steps of the cottage with a black foot and ankle oozing stinking pus. No examination was needed. Even Ben made the correct diagnosis.

'Ben, please take this man immediately to Salauddin Hospital.'

'I'm afraid Syed is picking up rolls of cloth in Dacca. He won't be back for at least another hour.'

Without hesitation, Dr Rahman reached into his pocket and handed his keys over. 'Here, use my car.' He called Masaad to bring the largest dressing he could find to wrap loosely around the man's wound. 'Ask for surgeon Dipu Razzak, Ben,' Dr Rahman said calmly. 'Tell him I sent you and that the patient has wet gangrene. Dipu will determine its spread. With luck his life will be saved, but not the leg.'

'What if he's not there?'

'He definitely is, Ben, I spoke to him just before we left home.'

THIRTY

Ben calculated around one hundred and seventy miles from Tungipur to Calcutta. In Britain, even driving a sluggish Series III Land Rover, the journey would take about four hours. But here, much longer, even in the dry season. He needed to allow at least twenty-four hours, leaving tomorrow lunchtime latest. He'd sleep in the wagon Wednesday night within striking distance of Jessore. This would let him time Thursday's noon rendezvous precisely.

Most roads in Bangladesh, even on main routes, were nothing more than pot-holed dirt tracks. Even where they had been tarmacadamed, most had deteriorated. And, understandably, during the war maintenance had been neglected.

Roadside villages would be packed with people. Street traders, goats, poultry and feral dogs littering the roads. Children, carelessly, will dash in front of the car. Ambling water buffalo, stubborn mules and scrawny horses hauling carts will cause further delays.

Many bridges remained war-damaged. Crossing some seemingly dry riverbeds, or where water flow was sluggish, the weighty Land Rover might sink. It would need hauling out with his tow ropes. Helping hands would expect a taka or two.

Then there is the mighty Ganges river to cross, although Bangladeshis call it Padma. Ben could be waiting three or four hours for one of the notoriously unreliable ferries. Like trains and trucks, many vessels were destroyed in the war. Others had been hastily patched up. Overcrowded ferries sank regularly with up to three hundred victims. But such routine tragedies no longer made news headlines.

AFTER RETURNING FROM the hospital in Dr Rahman's car, rank with the acrid sticky smell of gangrene pus, despite all the windows being open, Ben started to collect what he'd need for the journey to India.

Passport. Importation licence. Order forms from companies in Calcutta. Lots of taka in coins and low-value notes. Pounds sterling. US dollars. Four half-bottles of Bell's: not to drink, but to bribe border and customs officials should they become 'difficult'. Two blankets, to drape over Khalida crossing the border, and several large empty cardboard boxes for her to hide behind. Drinking water. Food for two. A change of clothes.

To confirm the arrangements, Ben called Ayesha in the evening. Natcoo answered. 'Yes, Mr Ben, she here.'

'Is everything still the same?' Ben asked quickly.

'Sorry?' It was Dr Rahman who had taken the receiver from Natcoo. He was naturally curious. 'What needs to be the same, Ben?'

'Oh, oh,' thinking fast, 'just that I should stay away while she's preparing for her exam, that's all.' Ben hoped he'd doused Dr Rahman's curiosity.

'Well, Ben, you may ask her yourself in a minute. I wanted to tell you the man you drove to Salauddin Hospital did have the leg amputated. Inevitable, I'm afraid. There is no alternative treatment. Dead flesh cannot be returned to life. But Mr Razzak is confident our patient will live.'

'That's good news.'

'Unfortunately, Ben, the man doesn't think so. He's constantly crying saying he wished he'd died. Hopefully, in a few days when he's over the shock, he'll be pleased he lived. Here's Ayesha.' He handed over the phone.

Ben didn't delay. 'About Mrs Haq, is the first lesson still on for her granddaughter at noon on Thursday?'

'Yes, Mr Altringham. I confirmed the arrangements this afternoon.'

'Good, I'll be there in ample time. I've everything prepared. You know, for her first lesson.'

'Yes, thank you again, Mr Altringham. I believe with your help she'll pass the English exam with flying colours. Goodbye.'

Dr and Mrs Rahman and Bushra turned to face Ayesha with openmouthed puzzlement.

'Mr Altringham. Mr Altringham. Where's Ben gone?' Bushra mocked.

'That was very mysterious, Ayesha,' Amma said. 'What arrangements have you confirmed? Who's facing an English exam?'

'It's just a little private joke, Ma.'

Amma wasn't convinced. Nor was her father. Ayesha could tell from their expression that they didn't buy it. Neither was anybody's fool. They knew something was in the wind, be it a cotton wool cloud or a whirling tornado.

THE NEAREST MOSQUE to Dak Cottage stood half a mile away. From the minaret the muezzin's amplified azan, the call to prayer, awakened Ben. It often did, and he had come to welcome the elegiac chanting. Ayesha told him the call is compiled from a group of Arabic phrases devised by the Prophet Muhammad, peace be upon him, she would always add after naming him.

Ben had learnt the opening phrases, beginning with Allah akbar. This is repeated four times. After 'Allah is the greatest', the phrases following, also repeated, declare there is no god but Allah; Muhammad is Allah's messenger; followers should go to pray.

Ben smiled when Ayesha told him that for fajr, the first prayer of the day before sunrise, included the sentence, 'Prayer is better than sleep'.

'If you lived close to the mosque,' he quipped, 'it's so loud you wouldn't be able to sleep through the azan anyway.'

Ben lied to Masaad and Faiyaz: the truth too dangerous for them to know. He said he would be away most of Wednesday and Thursday at meetings in Dacca. But he knew it would be Saturday at the earliest before he could return to Tungipur. And after delivering Khalida to an aunt in Calcutta, Ben had no plan other than to collect the medical supplies and return. In India Khalida would be safe. At least safer. Hopefully.

Awakened by the muezzin's call, Ben decided to leave immediately. There was no point in delaying. If he waited till lunchtime, he would get drawn into camp work and his departure would be noticed. Syed would also question why he wasn't driving. It was thirty-six hours before he was due to collect Khalida at noon Thursday. But better to be early than late. He showered, scattering the frogs as usual, scooped down breakfast of warmed-up rice and dal, and made a large flask of instant coffee. He loaded the Land Rover and set off. To his annoyance, the tank was nearly empty. But he couldn't have asked Syed to make sure the wagon was full of fuel. Having never checked before, the question would have aroused his curiosity. Strangely, Ben thought, Syed had over recent weeks taken more interest in where he was going and what he was doing.

He drove north to Tungipur past Ayesha's home on the left, regretting that he couldn't stop to see her. He blew a kiss and imagined she could feel his breath on her face. The rising sun bathed the breakfast veranda in a golden glow through the tall palms. He glimpsed Dr Rahman at the table, presumably having just prayed. Natcoo would be serving breakfast soon.

Few cars used the roads – cars still a luxury for all but the well-off – but the streets buzzed with motor and cycle rickshaws. Hundreds of people went about their business. Shops and stalls started opening, shutters raised, doorways washed and swept. As in all tropical countries, it was best to get on with tasks before the energy-sapping sleep-inducing heat of the day arrived.

At the top of town Ben turned left and headed west. With Tungipur still visible in his mirror, the road had already turned into little better than a dusty rut-filled two-lane track. Trucks coming towards Ben swerved along the road seemingly without a care in the world. Trucks behind tailgated Ben hoping he'd get a move on. Occasionally he pulled over to let a convoy of impatient drivers pass. With all the Land Rover's vents and widows open, after a few miles his face had grown a second skin of dust glued on with sweat.

Ben tapped the fuel gauge. The dial remained stubbornly in the red. Of course it would. The heavy Land Rover with its 2.25-litre engine was a gas-guzzler. Fifteen miles to the gallon, if lucky. He'd need to stop soon and top up from one of the two green ex-military jerry cans the wagon carried. But within five miles it was too late. It stuttered to a stop. Ben unbolted the bracket holding one of the cans. It was empty. Damn it. He released the second can, shook it, also empty. He swore at Syed for his negligence. Now, at around eight o'clock, Ben realised Syed would soon be arriving at the bungalow and wonder where the Land Rover had gone.

Ben tried waving down passing trucks travelling in both directions. But they trundled past leaving him choking in a cloud of dust and fumes. Almost every lorry coughed out a cloud of dirty exhaust: they 'ran rich' with oil mixed with petrol or diesel in the belief the engine lasted longer.

Eventually a small flatback truck, with around a dozen goats tethered in the back, pulled up. Ben, holding the fuel cap in one hand and pointing to a jerry can with the other, left the farmer in no doubt what was needed.

'Gas *na* diesel,' Ben said. The farmer, toothless and unshaven with a torn dirty white shirt, nodded his understanding. He pulled out a five-gallon can from behind the passenger seat which his wife, nursing a baby – and three children – occupied. 'Gas *na* diesel,' he reassured Ben his fuel was indeed petrol.

Holding the can to Ben's face, the man smiled. He demanded money. An outrageous amount. From Syed's receipts, Ben realised it was at least four times the normal price. The haggling started. After several minutes Ben paid half that first demanded. He had been well and truly stung. But Ben's need to buy far exceeded the farmer's need to sell.

Ben kept pleading he had no more cash, *amar ar nai* money. The farmer knew he lied: foreigners, especially Americans, always have more money. After he emptied the can, they shook hands, the deal done. By pointing with his chin towards his cargo of goats, and drawing a finger down his neck, the farmer told Ben they were off to be slaughtered. With his gummy grin, delighted at his highly profitable deal, he jumped in his crowded cab, elbowed his family back to their side, waved at Ben and drove away.

Even if the farmer's petrol can contained a full five gallons, Ben realised within fifty miles, sixty at a stretch, he'd need to find fuel. But he relaxed, confident he'd reach the large ferry town of Harirampur on the banks of River Padma. On its outskirts, Ben pulled into a garage. Since the war many pumps had remained unrepaired. Fuel was routinely discharged direct from tankers into barrels before being siphoned into watering cans, the type typically used for gardens. Despite rusty No Smoking notices – in English, Bengali and Urdu – both mechanics, who had put down their tools to serve Ben, continued to smoke their short rough-tobacco bidis while filling up the Land Rover and both jerry cans. It was a good time to stand back. Ben went for a pee in a pile of rubbish at the side of the workshop. Not unexpectedly two rats shot out almost between his legs: where there's rubbish there's rats.

Queuing for the ferry was chaotic. Like jockeys on the starting line, trucks, cars and carts jostled to be at the front. Motorbikes weaved between the bumpers, squeezing through the slightest space. Everyone's cargo was more important than anyone else's, every car driver's journey more urgent. It was as if they forgot they were all catching the same ferry. Arms waved and hands pointed in all directions. Drivers, passengers, ferry and quayside employees, even local stallholders, tried in vain to organise the traffic. At one point Ben noticed several people instructing three vehicles to park – in the same space!

When buying his ticket at the counter of Bangladesh River Steamers, Ben was told the ferry would arrive in two hours: that could mean four. He was pleased he'd allowed ample time. No need to worry. For now. So far, so good.

A pair of policemen walked down the shambolic line of lorries, cars and carts waiting to board the ferry. They asked for papers from some of the drivers and made cursory checks on the condition of their vehicles. They would extract cash fines should a violation be found: infringements could always be found. Suddenly one officer pointed at Ben's Land Rover. The senior officer reprimanded his junior who quickly dropped his arm. It looked like the inspector didn't want Ben to know he'd been spotted. They turned and walked quickly away. Strange, Ben thought, but he shrugged off the incident. Not many foreigners crossed this ferry. Perhaps they didn't want him to see how they extracted bribes from trumped-up offences.

FORTY YEAR-OLD Syed cycled from his hut in the village along the dense jungle path to Mohpur. His father and grandfather had told him tales of tigers once roaming freely across most of Bengal. A man-eater lived in this very jungle, they said, firing his boyhood imagination. Golam's wife was taken in its broad jaws. Carried away like a rag doll. And Imran, grandfather's friend, fell victim to the man-eater's appetite. Not a bone was left, only Imran's ripped lungi remained in a cluster of areca palms.

Today, there was no danger of a tiger attack. The sultans, maharajas, nawabs and the British – especially the British with their powerful rifles – killed them all. The only place wild tigers in Bangladesh could now be found were south in the Sunderbans, the Chittagong Hill Tracts to the east, and perhaps a few in the forests near Modhupur.

'Leopards too,' grandfather growled, with his eyes wide, hands raised and fingers curved like a cat's claws. 'Stronger than tigers, leopards are. But they don't like the taste of our flesh.' He'd growl and chase little Syed, who'd run to his mother screaming pretending to be terrified; when younger, he wasn't pretending.

When he arrived at Dak Cottage, Syed planned to fill up the Land Rover and jerry cans with petrol. He must ask Mr Ben for more cash because the price of fuel had once again risen. Syed's cousin as always would make the receipt out for more than the actual cost. Their fifty-fifty share of the surcharge helped pay for little extras.

'Masaad, where's the wagon?' Syed shouted angrily in Bengali as he propped his bike against the wall. 'It's not in the lock-up where I left it. It should be.'

Masaad always resented Syed's attitude. The feeling was mutual. Both born and raised in near Tungipur, Masaad to once well-off Bihari parents, Syed to farm labourers. The war had flipped the coin. Bangladeshis, being the victors, and their Bengali language now dominated. But Masaad's superior education, good English and skilled work grated with Syed, who could hardly read and whose English was poor. Masaad's work at the clinic was also considered more important than the phrase he once overheard Masaad use against him: 'Syed's *only* the driver.'

'Ben's gone to Dacca,' Masaad replied sharply in English which, to Syed, served to reinforce his arrogant Bihari attitude. 'For a meeting.'

172

'He never drive. I take him. All time.' Syed was offended.

'This time he's driven himself,' Masaad shrugged. 'He's not back until Friday. Consider yourself lucky, Syed. Two day's pay for not one day's work.'

Syed angrily mounted his bike and peddled furiously to the post office in Tungipur. Following instructions, given in confidence weeks before, he called the number on the card.

'Mr Conan?'

'Yes.'

'It Syed, Mr Ben driver at Mohpur. You asked to tell you where he go.'

'Yes, I remember. And?'

'He coming you for meeting, Masaad say. He driving, not me. Mr Ben back Friday, Masaad say.'

'No, he's not here and we have no meetings scheduled. So where's Mr Altringham gone?'

'Not know, Mr Conan. Land Rover gone. Not at Dr Rahman house where he go lots. I looked.'

'Good work, Syed. If you get any more news about him, call again straight away. As we agreed, when I see you next time, I'll compensate your efforts, okay?'

'Okay, Mr Conan.'

PANDEMONIUM BROKE OUT as the ferry approached. Cars, carts, cycles, motorbikes, trucks and foot passengers surged forward. Inch by inch, bumper to bumper, everybody wanted to board the ferry first. But traffic couldn't get on the ferry because traffic couldn't get off. Gridlock. And the more ferry workers, police and dockside officials tried establishing order, more chaos was created. No-one wanted to concede ground, reverse an inch, pull over a centimetre, resulting in everyone being delayed. Ben watched with both frustration and amusement. Eventually, after everyone blamed everyone else for the commotion, Ben drove up the ferry's ramp for the hour-long crossing. 'This scramble happens every trip,' a fellow passenger complained, shaking his head slowly. 'They never learn... never learn...'

It was mid-afternoon when the Land Rover bounced down the rusty ramp off the ferry. Traffic control at this side of the Padma seemed little better organised than at embarkation. But Ben was relieved to be back on firm land. There were times sailing across when the mighty river's current seemed stronger than the ship's struggling propeller driven by its unhealthy-sounding coughing engine.

With around seventy miles remaining to Jessore, Ben was pleased he'd left early morning. He hoped to reach the small town of Arpara before dark. With time in hand he decided to find a guest house or small hotel for the night. But if suitable accommodation couldn't be found, the Land Rover's back cabin had ample space. Arpara, only twenty miles from Jessore, would allow Ben to have a reconnaissance run soon after sunrise. He would familiarise himself with Khalida's pick-up point and be able to time his midday arrival precisely. He didn't want any last-minute hitches.

Night arrived the same time Ben entered Arpara. He was halfway across a long iron-girder bridge when the police roadblock came into view at the far end. There was no turning back. The bridge was barely wide enough for two vehicles side by side. Slow traffic slowed further, to walking speed. Everyone was waved on, including horse-drawn wagons and bullock carts. But as Ben approached, the barrier was hurriedly dragged across and he was waved to the side.

'Passport,' the senior officer demanded.

Ben said nothing, turned to his rucksack and retrieved the document. Ben couldn't tell if the officer was inspecting the passport or looking at him: mirror-fronted aviator sunglasses hid his eyes.

'Where you come from?'

Ben was in no doubt he knew, but answered. 'Tungipur.'

'And where going?'

'Calcutta.'

'Purpose of journey?'

'To collect medical equipment. We, that's Action... sorry, Aid International... run a clinic near Tungipur. Here, these are the purchase orders and import permits.' Ben took several papers from the folder and handed them over.

'Wait.'

Ben smiled to himself. What else could he do? His passport and papers had been taken, a barrier blocked the road – and about twelve armed police officers stood watching his every move. The officer walked away and took a military-style walkie-talkie two-way radio from one of his men. It became clear the inspector was taking orders from someone senior. *Ji. Na.* Yes and no were almost all he said for two minutes. And the way he stood, almost to attention, gave Ben the impression he was listening to someone very senior indeed. He marched back.

'We check inside cab.'

Ben was tempted to argue, ask why, but he had nothing to hide. He unlocked the cabin door.

'You have empty boxes.' His gruff observation implied empty boxes posed the same danger as a cargo of grenades.

'To put the medical equipment in. For extra protection on all these bumpy roads.'

'You have blankets.'

'If I can't find a hotel, I'll need to sleep in the cab. There's my bedroll too, see?'

'We have hotels in Arpara.' He sounded offended. 'No need to sleep in car.'

'Can you recommend one?'

Ben wasn't being facetious, although it looked like the inspector thought he was flippant. The walkie-talkie was called for and another conversation with the inspector's superior took place.

It was obvious this was a targeted stop and search. It was also clear the authorities wished him to know it wasn't random. Otherwise, unless they were completely incompetent, they would have stopped several vehicles to mask the true focus of their operation. More likely, the police expected to find Khalida hiding in the cabin. The inspector appeared disappointed she wasn't there. And whoever was on the other end of the radio, Ben, ten yards away, could hear the shouts of anger and frustration.

Hussain's hand had been exposed. It meant Ben's rescue mission was thwarted. There was now no chance, no chance whatsoever, of smuggling Khalida across into India: the Land Rover would be searched inch by inch at the crossing point.

The inspector thrust the walkie-talkie back into the chest of one of his constables and returned to Ben in the driver's seat.

'Thank you, Mr Benjamin Altringham,' the inspector said with a distinct change of tone, from overbearing to conciliatory. As Ben started the engine, the officer returned Ben's passport and said, 'May I recommend Hotel Jasmine. It is very comfortable. Turn next left down Salikha Road and it is a mile on the left.' He pointed to the turning, not fifty yards away. The inspector removed his aviators, although seeing his eyes didn't make him any more trustworthy.

Ben followed the inspector's directions. But the policeman's recommendation guaranteed Hotel Jasmine would be the one hotel in Arpara he would not stay at. After parking for several minutes, allowing time for the police to dismantle their roadblock and disperse, Ben doubled back and crossed the road in search of another hotel.

The twenty-two bedroom Hotel Shuktara boasted four stars, despite the low-wattage single lightbulb, the bed lamp having no bulb at all and a slow-turning ceiling fan. Without the horde of cockroaches squeezing under the skirting as he entered the 'luxury suite', perhaps the Hotel Shuktara would, he thought sarcastically, have qualified for five stars. At least the sheets looked clean. Ben had however decided to use his bedroll. He hoped this would provide enough of a barrier to stop any bedbugs biting, for they doubtless lurked in the bed's crevices.

Hotel Shuktara provided two benefits more important than the bed. The Land Rover was locked into a high-fenced compound with a nightguard. Post war, with desperate shortages, any vehicle left outside unattended would be stolen or stripped. Nothing was safe. Wheels, mirrors, wipers, seats, steering wheels, radios would vanish. The manager also assured Ben the telephone in his room was connected.

Recalling what Nowel Cribb said about investigations into Aid International, Ben wondered if he had been stopped because of his 'cover-story' mission: to collect medicines and medical equipment in India. Was it Aid International the police were targeting? Maybe he was wrong, it wasn't the Hussains chasing Khalida.

Although it was evening, Cribb had said Ben could phone anytime. Taking him at his word, Ben called Cribb's residence, the number he'd written on the back of his card.

'Cribb.'

'Nowel. Ben Altringham. I have a problem.'

'Sorry to hear that. How can I help?'

'I'm in a town called Arpara, on my way to India via Jessore. I got stopped by the police in Aid International's Land Rover. They didn't stop anyone else. Would you have an explanation for that?'

'No.'

'What I need to know is, was it me personally or AI they were targeting?'

'I can't say, Ben, because I don't know. If your journey is in connection with the reason you first came to see me…'

'No. I'm alone. This trip has nothing to do with our discussion. I'm off to get medical supplies in Calcutta.' Ben was compelled to lie because it was likely the diplomat's home was bugged and Ayesha had warned him to trust no-one.

'Then I doubt you have anything to worry about,' Nowel said.

BEN HAD PLENTY to worry about, many doubts and impossible questions to answer. Should he pick up Khalida and risk her capture? Was he being followed? Should he abandon the whole venture and leave her to her fate? But wouldn't that be cowardly? What would Ayesha think of him if he were to turn back now?

First things first. He needed to let Ayesha know that the police were onto him. Before making the call, Ben considered how he could tell Ayesha about the roadblock using coded language. He needed to stress that the chances of smuggling Khalida into India with the current plan were now zero. It was guaranteed the Land Rover would be thoroughly searched before crossing the border. And if Hussain had ordered the action, even a full barrel of Bell's wouldn't secure a blind eye turned by border officers.

AYESHA ANSWERED THE phone. Ben liked to think it was telepathy, a sign of their special relationship. But it was coincidence; she was on her way to her bedroom after dinner.

'Hello, Miss Rahman.' Ben didn't pause for breath and continued quickly. 'Regarding Mrs Huq's granddaughter, there was an interruption on my way to deliver the English lesson.'

'Oh, that's unfortunate.'

'I got stopped. Interrupted by a puncture. Searched all over my vehicle... but couldn't find the jack. It would be hard to pick up the... you know... to pick up the axil to fix the problem. I have a temporary repair. But my tyres are thin and I might get stopped again... you know, by another puncture. Is it worth continuing to Mrs Huq's?'

Ayesha understood. 'Could you still make it on time?'

'Yes, I'm quite close. But if I get another puncture after I meet the granddaughter, that would be double the problem. Do you get it?'

Ayesha took a few seconds to reply, slowly. 'Yes, I understand. It must be your decision, Mr Altringham. You're there. I'm not. But whatever you do, I'm sure it will be the right decision and I'll square that with Mrs Huq.'

'Look, Miss Rahman. I'll keep the midday appointment. I'll discuss the requirements with the granddaughter when we meet. But if I can't deliver... deliver the full lesson, I'll return to Tungipur. Can you let Mrs Huq know of the puncture and the search, you know, the search I had for my jack?'

'Yes, Mr Altringham. I'm sorry to put you to so much trouble.'

BEN ORDERED A spicy goat biryani in Hotel Shuktara's dreary restaurant, its drab yellow walls stained with a layer of tobacco tar. The biryani was not up to Ali's standard – swamped in ghee and too much red colouring.

'Sorry, Mr Altringham, that not working,' the receptionist told Ben as he walked towards the lift. 'It break down too much. No part to mend properly, mechanic say.'

'Don't worry, climbing three flights of steps is good exercise and it will help me sleep.'

'What time you like morning call and breakfast?'

THIRTY-ONE

Ben timed his drive over the bridge at Jessore to perfection, precisely midday. His early morning rehearsal run and parking just minutes away had paid dividends. Many women wore black burqa near the rendezvous point, but all were busy burdened with bags of shopping and boisterous children. Only one stood still. She was holding a bright blue bag. Next to her, a lanky teenage lad wearing a lemon-coloured grid-check shirt. Ben flashed his headlights. Khalida turned to the boy, said something, and he walked away looking dejected. She stepped to the kerb. Ben stopped and Khalida climbed quickly inside and slammed the door, squeezing her bag into the footwell.

'I can't thank you enough, Ben,' she said breathlessly.

'It's too early for thanks, Khalida. We have to decide what to do. I presume Ayesha told you I was stopped by the police yesterday.'

'Yes, she called last night.'

'The authorities are on to us. Presumably they've been listening to our calls, perhaps worked out what we were talking about.'

'They've been listening, Ben, without a shadow of doubt. Farook Hussain has tentacles everywhere.'

'You realise it will be impossible to get across to India. Before I was stopped, I thought there was a chance. Now there's not a cat in hell's chance of getting out of Bangladesh without this Land Rover been thoroughly searched. I've been really naïve, if not downright stupid. So what do you want to do?'

Khalida removed her head-covering revealing her face, drawn pale by weeks of distress. 'You're right. It's hopeless. Absolutely hopeless. I don't know what to do. To keep the baby or not. Try and escape Bangladesh or not. Go home or not.'

'Stay in Jessore?'

'That's out of the question. My uncle doesn't want me back. Can't blame him. He has a district government job. If Hussain found out he'd harboured me, he would lose it. Or worse could happen. And I don't want to put his family at risk. At least at home in Tungipur with Amma I'd have some protection – she still has a few friends in high places. But no longer high enough. They can't stand up to Farook Hussain. He's getting more powerful by the day and has the army's backing. One thing I do know, know for sure, is that I don't want to see Maz ever again.'

'I'm sorry,' was all Ben could say.

'I assume Ayesha told you what Maz did, why I'm in this predicament.'

'Yes. Terrible. Unforgivable.'

'Abuse, harassment, it happens here more than people think – or want to think about. We are often mistreated. Even us, educated, upper class girls, not just the poor and the village women. But it's absolutely not talked about. Swept under the rug. It's like that other misconception many of you have in Europe and America.'

'What's that?'

'You assume almost nobody in the Middle East or Asia has sex outside of marriage. It's not true. It may not be as common as in the west, obviously. There are fewer opportunities with the restrictions our societies impose. But of course couples find a way. Always have, always will. And always very, very discreet. Only the closest of closest friends you might tell. It's just too risky to talk about.'

'I'm sorry, Khalida, sorry about what's happened.'

For a few minutes nothing more was said. Ben steered around the humps and potholes in the road as best he could to smooth the ride for Khalida. He was on the lookout for a convenient turning point to head back to Tungipur.

'So, Khalida, back home?'

'I have no choice.'

THE SOUND WAS faint at first. Distant. Commonplace. Expected in a busy town. Unrelated to them. As it grew louder, their anxiety matched it. There was no mistake, the screaming sirens came from behind. Ben's eyes flashed to the mirror. Khalida turned rapidly and looked out the back window. Blue lights flashed a hundred yards behind from three police cars.

'Shit!' Khalida hissed. Her swearing shocked Ben. She'd always been so calm, always so polite. 'Shit! Shit! Shit!'

'Maybe they're off to an accident or something. Let's see if they overtake us or turn off.' Ben knew he was hoping for the best but feared the worst.

'I don't think so. They must have been trailing you. Did you see anyone following?'

'No. I thought they might. I kept a lookout. But I never saw anything suspicious.'

'They'll have monitored the road. Positioned observers along it. There's no alternative route to the border from Arpara.'

On the traffic-packed road, Ben was boxed in. He had no choice but to go at snail-speed. There was no turning off, left or right. No chance of a get-away. No dramatic movie-style car chase. And heavy Land Rovers are not Aston Martins. The posse of police cars gained ground, weaving between trucks, cars, carts and rickshaws, the sound of sirens increasingly sinister.

Ben gripped the steering wheel tighter, his knuckles whiter. Khalida kept whipping her head around watching the police getting closer, their blue lights brighter, their sirens louder.

Khalida suddenly smashed the dashboard with both hands. 'Stop!' she shouted. 'Let me out. They can't have me. They can't…'

'It's no use, Khalida, you'll never get away,' Ben pleaded. 'If they're after you, better face them together. And you can't run wearing those clothes.'

'I'll take my chances. Stop. Stop nowww!'

Shocked by her scream, Ben slammed on the breaks.

Skidding tyres kicked up a dust cloud engulfing the car. The string of tail-gaiting vehicles juddered to a halt. A cacophony of angry horns rattled the air.

Khalida tumbled out, tripped and rolled down the steep side of a drainage ditch. She splashed across a paddy field, her gown gathered across one arm, water up to her knees. The farmer and his son planting rice froze, open mouthed in shock at this extraordinary sight.

'Out.'

Ben wasn't going to argue with a gun aimed at his head.

Three policemen dashed after Khalida. One with his pistol drawn. She scrambled up a narrow embankment enclosing the square paddy and ran along it. Two of the three cops gained on her fast.

A shot rang out. Khalida didn't know it, but Ben saw the shot fired skywards. A warning volley. Nothing more. This time. But Khalida was waiting for the bullet's pain. Or the death it delivered.

Surprised to be still alive, Khalida kept running. But another two cops had climbed down from the road onto the embankment and stood not fifty yards ahead. With two officers in front, two behind, one to her right wielding his gun, Khalida leapt into another paddy to her left. But she misjudged the depth of the mud, lost balance, and splashed face down into the mire.

She struggled to stand, her legs stuck in the sludge, captured as if set in concrete. The chase ended. Khalida's fight for freedom hadn't. She wriggled and kicked as the two officers grabbed her, one on each arm. They dragged her out of the swamp and frogmarched her back to the road.

Water dripped from her long black hair which had closed like curtains drawn across her face. Her mud-splattered waterlogged burqa clung tightly to Khalida's body outlining her shape, but with no hint of pregnancy. She had lost both sandals in the paddy.

Ben was forced over the Land Rover's bonnet, his arms yanked behind and wrists handcuffed. As they clipped tight they caught a fold of skin causing him to wince.

'What's all this about? There's no need to do this.' His protest was ignored.

As Khalida approached, sandwiched between the two officers, Ben spoke loud enough for her to hear. 'I've just come to pick up a friend to take her back to Tungipur. What's wrong with that?'

They needed to coordinate their story. She nodded making it clear she understood the line to take.

The officer in charge issued orders in Bengali to his men. Ben was pushed into the back of one of the three police cars, an officer on either side. Khalida, also handcuffed behind her back, was bundled inside the Land Rover's cabin with the two officers who caught her. The third, having re-holstered his gun, drove Ben's wagon in the convoy.

Ben worried about what they might do to Khalida out of sight. It was common knowledge that people in police custody were routinely abused. He had the ridiculous notion that perhaps, because she was soaking wet, as were the three policemen, they decided to use his wagon to avoid their police cars getting wet and stained with paddy mud. Perhaps he was being naïve.

In Britain, when the emergency services have blues and twos flashing and sounding, vehicles make way. Even caught in this trouble, Ben was bemused to see that few vehicles moved aside. Someone in an ambulance could be fighting for their life. A fire could be raging through a factory. It seemed to matter not a jot to anyone on the road in front. Like at the ferry, no-one wanted to move aside, as if it would be a loss of face, a lowering of one's self-importance. Everyone else should give way, not me.

Ben repeated his question about why he'd been arrested claiming he had committed no offence. But the senior officer in the front passenger seat remained as silent as stone.

In the Land Rover's cabin both officers ogled Khalida. They wanted to touch her. Gratify themselves. She was so beautiful. Much more desirable than their scrawny wives. This one was classy, too. Aloof. Proud. Superior. She needed to be pulled down a peg or two. She needed to learn she was just a woman, nothing more.

As always they would deny any accusations of assault. No forensic evidence would be found, because none would be gathered. If she had been a common girl, a nobody, a woman from a slum, they would be having their fun.

But they had been given her name: Khalida Chowdhury. The daughter of Maruf Chowdhury, the famous Bangladesh war hero, a martyr in the country's liberation struggle.

More important, they had been told she belonged to a minister, another man's property. They hadn't been told which minister, but their chief inspector warned them to keep their hands off. No harm must come her way when arrested. She was the minister's woman, not theirs. If you touch her when arrested alongside the Englishman, you will be lucky if only your hands are cut off – alongside your manhood.

And they saw the fire in Khalida's eyes, felt the heat.

They became more fearful of her than she was of them.

If she said one word against us…

THIRTY-TWO

It was the smell of stale urine she noticed first. The same unmistakable stink that polluted doorways, nooks and crannies in the back streets. Then the echoey indistinct sound of voices; murmuring, talking and, further away, shouting. Her eyes half-opened, slowly. She faced, inches away, a grey concrete wall. Rough. Unplastered. Cracked. She stayed still on the floor, calculating who may be stood behind her in the low-lit cell.

Once Khalida's eyes fully opened and focussed, spots and streaks of dried blood splattered on the wall made her jerk away involuntarily, repulsed, nauseated. As she turned, she faced worse – a mound of rotting faeces in the corner forced her to retch uncontrollably.

Khalida staggered towards the heavy iron door, drummed it with both fists, screaming for someone, anyone, to release her from this hell hole. But the small observation trapdoor behind three thick vertical bars remained shut. Somebody heard. Nobody responded.

Shouting would make her mouth dryer, her thirst greater, her temper rise. They want me to shout. To hammer the door. Get angry. So I won't. I'll stop.

What would father do? What did he do when incarcerated? Keep calm. Be brave. Endure. Control what you can control: your mind, your emotions. Think of a glade of green grass, a blue sea as far as the eye can see, a snow-capped Himalayan mountain.

Khalida slumped to the floor hugging her legs close to her chest. Almost the foetal position. She checked, just in case it had been lost. Her child remained. Three months it would be now. Distinctly human. One and a half inches long. Tiny fingers and toes already forming on little arms and legs. Still in the breech position. End of the first trimester. Her breasts swollen, tender.

Someone had removed all her clothes and replaced them with a threadbare cream-coloured cotton salwar kameez. Who had done this? Men? Had they seen her naked? Touched her? She knew these clothes had not been washed since the last occupant, if ever. They stank, rank, foetid. Whatever drugs they used to chemically cosh her, to knock her out, they had left Khalida with a thumping headache. Her arms hurt too. Both bruised blue-black with finger prints left by the grip of policemen.

Must stay calm. Breathe slowly, deeply. Ignore the stink of shit. Take control. Think of luxury perfume, the aroma of gardenia... Abba, oh Abba.

Khalida closed her eyes. Darkness was better than anything the single lightbulb, encased beyond reach in the ceiling, illuminated. A night light for all day light. No chair. No bed. No table. No toilet. Just a corner that prisoners before her had chosen for bodily waste. A concrete cube of incarceration. Length, width, height, eight foot, perhaps nine.

The scream made her leap to attention. It was so loud she thought someone had entered ghost-like into her cell. Again a pain-induced shriek. Louder than before. This time followed by wails and weeping and cries of 'no' and 'mercy'. But the torturers took no heed of her appeals. The screams went on and on, intercepted only by weeping and whimpers. Ten minutes? Twenty? Eternity? Khalida couldn't work out how long, her watch had been removed. Her jailors were telling her time itself was no longer relevant to you, none of your concern. Your time is now our time.

Khalida started to vigorously rub her ears hoping to swamp the sound of suffering. She hummed as loud as she could, any old tune, any old rhythm. But, like the piercing frequency of a new-born baby, cries of pain bypass the ears and penetrate the skull.

The gunshot rocked Khalida. Left her terrified.

Then the silence became more terrifying than the screams.

'Sorry, Abba,' she cried quietly, both body and voice trembling, 'I am not my father's daughter. I'm not as brave as you.'

Her back to the cell door, Khalida slid down to the floor, knowing before long she would need to approach the toilet in the corner.

SUPERINTENDENT ABDUL HAFIZ was the most senior police officer for the Jessore district, one of only nineteen administrative areas in Bangladesh. He considered himself important, powerful, a big man, ambitious. Perhaps the country's next chief of police, if he played his cards right with ministers in Dacca.

He smoked Marlboro. Plenty of them. One after another. The heavy glass ashtray overflowed with butts, most only half-consumed. Ben could see the packs had been purchased, or acquired one way or another, duty free.

'Mr Altringham, you keep insisting that you have done nothing wrong.' He sucked in another lungful of nicotine and tar, as if it fuelled his speech. 'But I must correct that notion.' He coughed until another intake of toxins cleared his throat.

'For the tenth time, I was simply asked to pick up Miss Chowdhury from Jessore and return her to her home in Tungipur. Please tell me, in doing that, what offence have I supposedly committed?'

'You told officers in Arpara yesterday that you were going to India for medical supplies. We found the orders in your rucksack.'

'After a call I made from the hotel to a friend in Tungipur, I changed my plan. That's all. Miss Chowdhury's need to return home became greater than my need to go to India. I can go to Calcutta later.'

'But the evidence points otherwise, Mr Altringham. You were stopped heading in the direction of India?'

'I was looking for a place to turn around. The road was crowded, narrow. Land Rovers can't turn on a sixpence.'

Superintendent Hafiz stubbed out another cigarette and rubbed his chin, slowly, carefully, thinking.

'Why? Why did Miss Chowdhury need to get back so urgently?'

'You need to ask her.'

'Are you aware she's with child?'

Ben was temporarily distracted by the quaint almost Biblical term 'with child'. But he didn't know how to answer the question. What were the pros and cons of saying either yes or no? He couldn't decide the right answer for himself or Khalida.

'It is interesting, Mr Altringham, you hesitate. All your other responses have been by immediate return. I'm sure you know she's with child. Are you the father?'

'No!'

'Thank you for confirming your knowledge of her condition.'

Jessore airport's police station, the size of a small bungalow, was a dreary single-storey concrete block, adjacent to the small passengers' lounge. The single-strip runway only handled a handful of daily domestic flights. Outside a Bangladesh Biman Fokker F27 twin-engine turboprop cruised to a halt. It broke their conversation for a minute until the pilot cut the engines and the propellors stuttered to a stop.

The inspector, whose office Hafiz had commandeered for Ben's interview, stood beside him, ready to serve his every need. His two constables remained at either side of Ben, privileged that the district superintendent of police had honoured their humble untidy office to deal with this international criminal.

'Superintendent Hafiz, do you think these handcuffs could be removed? Please. I'm hardly going to run off.'

Hafiz waved his hand without looking at either constable. Eager to oblige, both policemen clumsily got in each other's way fumbling with their keys trying to be first to follow the order. They embarrassed the inspector, who wanted to impresses the big cheese. Their incompetency, like two circus clowns, reflected on his competency: badly.

'Thank you.' Ben rubbed his wrists but opened the cut inflicted by the cuffs. 'Would you have plaster, you know, in a first aid box?' He showed Hafiz the cut. As no-one moved, Ben decided to wrap his own handkerchief around the wound. After the terrible injuries the policemen would have witnessed during the war, and in their routine work, a small bleed on Ben's wrist was considered not worthy of attention.

Robotically, in one smooth operation without looking, Hafiz reached for a fresh pack of Marlboro, detached the cellophane, flipped the lid, removed the silver wrapping, placed a cigarette in his mouth, struck a match and lit it. Ben wondered if Hafiz was consciously aware of what he had just done.

'As things stand, Mr Altringham, unless I hear to the contrary, I could charge you with several extremely serious offences.'

'But I haven't done anything wrong.'

'Let's start with conspiracy to pervert the course of justice.'

'Ridiculous.'

'You are also an accessory in planning a very serious crime.'

'I'm sorry, I haven't the faintest idea what you're talking about.'

'Abortion. Abortion is illegal here. It may not be in your country, where moral standards have degenerated.'

'Really?'

'Yes, really. Your men grow their hair long. Some have curls put in, especially your footballers, even the cricketers. You've done away with the law that prevents men having relations with other men.'

'I don't think any laws stopped that, anyway, just kept it in the dark.'

'But worse,' Hafiz continued, ignoring Ben's assertion. 'You allow your women and teenage girls to wear tight blouses and short skirts, almost up to their backsides. Our religion demands women behave with modesty. But, Mr Altringham, let's get back to the matter in hand: abortion. Here, abortion is illegal. And as you were taking Miss Chowdhury for an abortion, that makes you an accessory, an accessory to murder. Murder, Mr Altringham. Let me quote you the precise letter of the law: *"Whosoever shall aid, abet, counsel or procure the commission of any indictable offence shall be liable to be tried, indicted and punished as the principal offender".'*

'I was doing no such thing. This is nonsense. I need to phone the British High Commission.'

'I haven't finished, Mr Altringham, not by a long chalk. Although clearly not as serious as planning murder, you stole a vehicle and used it without authorisation.'

'Well, you're wrong there. It's Aid International's Land Rover. At Mohpur. For my use.'

'Except you no longer work for Aid International.'

'What? Of course I do.'

'We have it on good authority, in writing from a Mr...' Hafiz looked at a notepad 'a Mr Pete Conan that on Tuesday morning you were dismissed from Aid International's employment.'

189

'First I've heard of it.'

'Perhaps. But that doesn't change the fact. Therefore, you took a vehicle not belonging to you and, I'll wager, that also means you were driving without insurance. But that's a relatively minor offence. However, your dangerous driving and resisting arrest…'

'What? Rubbish! Lies!' Ben told himself to calm down. Don't let him rile you anymore.

'You caused chaos on the main road out of Jessore – in the direction of India. Nearly caused a major accident involving many vehicles. And, inspector, how many police officers witnessed this man attempting to flee?'

'*Dosh*, Sir,' the inspector, caught off guard not expecting the superintendent's question, blurted his answer.

'Ten. Ten officers witnessed your aggressive resistance, Mr Altringham. I'm sure some bystanders too observed your attempt at escape. Good, respectable, honest citizens of Bangladesh.'

FOOTSTEPS. KEYS RATTLING. Someone's coming.

Khalida stood up and took three steps backwards to the middle of her cell.

A key turned. A guard opened the door. Farook Hussain's huge frame filled the doorway.

He took one step in before immediately taking several steps back holding his sleeve against his nose, offended by the stench.

'Get her out of there. *Ekhun!* Now! It stinks worse than shit. Bring her to the office. *Ekhon!* Right now! Tie her hands. *Joldi!* Quick! No. Stop. Make her shower and put on fresh clothes, then come. *Joldi!*'

HANDCUFFED TO ONE policeman and accompanied by the inspector, Ben boarded the Fokker F27 before the forty or so passengers. They sat at the back, Ben next to the window. Within an hour the turboprop had landed in Dacca. Passengers alighted first. Two police cars crammed with officers waited on the runway, blue lights flashing.

Despite the seriousness of his situation, Ben found light relief watching the policemen having a serious argument amongst themselves. There was not enough room for them all in the two cars:

three constables were left standing on the tarmac complaining about being ousted, pride hurt.

The route south from the airport down Mymensingh Road and along Racecourse Road, passing by Hotel Intercontinental and the High Court, was familiar. The cell in Central Jail was not.

Superintendent Abdul Hafiz had reassured Ben the British High Commission would be informed of his arrest.

THE SALWAR KAMEEZ was too small, too tight. And the female guards gave Khalida no scarf to wrap around her body or cover her face. To them she was a woman with no dignity to hide, a tart, little better than a prostitute. Unmarried – and pregnant.

They wanted to hold her naked in front of this important man. Shave her head. Teach her to be humble and how a good woman should behave. Had they not had strict orders to the contrary, they would have invited the male guards to violate her, rip away her arrogance.

Hussain sat at the prison governor's desk. Khalida stood, in chains to her wrists and ankles, with guards either side. The taller broad-shouldered woman, their senior, stood behind holding a lathi, her yard-long inch-thick bamboo stick of authority.

'Well, Khalida, you have led us a merry dance,' he sighed, as if he had personally chased her all the way to Jessore. 'What have you to say for yourself?'

She held her head high, her hair wet, the dampness seeping slowly into her top and turning it dark. She stayed silent.

The guard cracked her stick against the wall. Khalida flinched, raised her shoulders and tucked in her head expecting to be hit.

Hussain signalled to the guard with his hand to lower her lathi. As a former army general, he was fully aware that electric probes, truncheons, sticks and fists provided means of persuasion. Ultimately, the noose around the neck. Now, as a politician, his words should be persuasive enough – especially when accompanied with benefits, in kind or cash.

'This could all end, Khalida. End now. Happiness could return to your life. You don't want to stay here, do you? In that cell. In that cesspit. Of course not. And you must have loved my son, otherwise you would not have allowed him to…'

'I didn't allow him.' Her voice croaked, her throat as gritty as gravel. She eyed the governor's water jug.

Hussain thought carefully. Should I allow her to quench her thirst or keep her dry? What is best with this girl, carrot or stick? He signalled they should let her drink. Kindness… first. The guard on her right poured and handed her the glass. With hands chained, she took it with both.

Khalida remembered that rehydration should be slow and steady and refrained from gulping down the whole glass. He would expect her to sink the whole amount in one go. Show gratitude. But she denied him any satisfaction. A small triumph. Steady sips. No 'thank you'. All within her control.

'I suppose your son didn't tell you what really happened.'

Hussain showed interest, his bulk bent forward and he turned an ear. Khalida, uncertain how much English the guards understood, whispered. 'He spiked my juice. Vodka. Perhaps some sleeping pills. Crushed into powder between two spoons. Then he…'

'No! Absolutely not!' Both palms slammed the desk to silence her. The guards locked her arms and the stick whipped up in front of her face demanding silence. Like dogs straining chains desperate to bite, all three prison officers had to be told to heel by Hussain, to back off.

Khalida Chowdhury, like her father, had guts, a rare inner strength. She's her father's daughter, he had no doubt.

'Be that as it may,' Hussain continued when everyone calmed down, 'you are carrying my son's s… my son's child. There can only be one sensible outcome. Best all round, for you, for Mazharul, for the child.'

He waited for Khalida to respond. But she remained defiant, showed strength through silence.

'By this time tomorrow, or in a few days, you could be a happily married woman living in our family home. Perhaps enjoy a honeymoon. Up in the tea gardens in Sylhet, maybe. Or what about Cox's Bazar? Beautiful soft sand. Miles and miles of it. My brother has a lovely villa. Eight or nine bedrooms. What could be better?'

Khalida was aware of her own stubbornness, even belligerence. At school and at college, with several teachers and lecturers, she often insisted she was right, argued her case. It landed her in trouble. Pupils publicly questioning teachers: not expected. Girls openly challenging men: not acceptable. Youth challenging age: not polite.

As the vice-principal at medical school told her after one incident: 'Yes, research as reported in *The Lancet* did indicate new findings about diabetes. But as a pupil – and just a first year – it was not your role to contradict the professor in a lecture theatre packed to the rafters. Scientifically, perhaps you were correct; behaviourally, you were distinctly incorrect.'

Khalida's instinct was to throw the remaining half-glass of water at Hussain. No! More! She'd like to smash the glass and stab a shard in his face. She'd like to wrap these chains around his neck and strangle the life out of him. But she bit her lip, squeezed her toes, dug her nails deep into her palms.

Father told her self-inflicted pain reduces that inflicted by others. If things got worse, she was ready to bite her tongue in half, smash her head on the nearest wall, gouge her own eyes out.

She had to analyse the situation. Fast. Consider the alternatives. Quickly. Take decisions. Immediately. She also had to disguise her true feelings of loathing and contempt for the Hussains, father and son.

Hussain seemed genuine. But he was utterly untrustworthy. Khalida knew most successful politicians fake sincerity. He possessed the patter of a politician but with a mouth full of tiger teeth. She'd been kidnapped, drugged, transported, thrown in this awful hellhole to soften her up. In his terms, to bring her to her senses.

She wondered, only for a second, if the sounds of torture from the adjoining cell were fake. The gunshot, a bullet fired at the wall. A show to scare, to terrify, to gain compliance. But torture was endemic and routine in the country's prisons and police stations. Why act brutality and murder when you can do so for real with impunity? And how can you trust a man who can treat someone the way she's been treated?

Hussain was making Khalida a clear offer: a choice of life, death, or living hell. Khalida also strongly suspected it would be death after birth. Once 'our son' had been ripped from her in some prison clinic, she'd be left to bleed to death. So sad mother died during childbirth, Hussain would say, and Maz would marry another.

Face facts, Abba always said. Facts remain after all your opinions. And the truth was that she was imprisoned in the inner sanctum in a maze of concrete corridors. There were bars and barbed wire, high walls and electrified fences, and dozens of locked doors and armed guards between this room and freedom. She thought herself bound like a proton within an atom within an element within a compound.

What, her thoughts continued, are the facts in my favour? Not many. But there was one: Hussain wants my child. He wants 'his grandson', seemingly more than the child's father. Maz had his way, had his fun with my body, didn't think of the consequences. If I refuse to marry, I'd be kept incarcerated until my child is born and then I'll 'disappear' as many thousands have. My son will be wet-nursed. My daughter...

Khalida decided the route of least resistance: play Hussain's game, live for another day.

Father often said, implement long term strategy to win the war rather than short term tactics to win a battle.

THIRTY-THREE

Ayesha faced her end of year exams next week. She would normally experience no problem retaining information required to pass with flying colours. She never studied to pass an exam, only to excel in it. Like a marathon runner running the course twice – to insure against any miscalculation of the mileage, apply a margin of error.

Before the nine-month war, Ayesha had won Dacca Medical College and Hospital's prestigious outstanding student award in her year – thrice. The certificates, framed, were hung in the hallway by her father. Everyone in the family was extremely proud of her achievements. But Ayesha deflected praise, prioritising what she must achieve in the future rather than basking in what she had achieved in the past.

But for three days, since the phone call from Ben in Jessore on Thursday night, Ayesha had heard no news. Surely he or Khalida could have called, let her know where they are, how they are. Her worries about them made it impossible to focus on revision. Ayesha thought the adage 'no news is good news' silly, definitely illogical: it's always better to know than not know, even if hope is lost.

She heard the phone ring in the living room and dashed to the top of the stairs listening acutely, hoping to be called to talk with Ben or Khalida. Abba answered. It's always frustrating hearing one side of a phone conversation.

'Really? No. No, I simply do not believe it. Most peculiar. Surely not. What, you and Masaad? No, Faiyaz, I have not been informed. That's terrible. I'll ask Ayesha, but no, I don't think he's been in touch for a day or two. Yes, of course, if I hear anything I'll get a message to you. Thanks for calling. Good night.'

Ayesha had rushed down the stairs into the living room. Mrs Rahman and Bushra had already stood, for Dr Rahman's face foretold bad news. They waited uneasily for his announcement.

'That was Faiyaz. You know, the clinical assistant at Mohpur. She says Aid International have dismissed Ben. AI people say he's stolen the Land Rover. They say he was driving to India to sell it for cash and then fly home to England.'

'That's utterly ridiculous,' hissed Ayesha.

'Agree,' Mrs Rahman said. 'There's more to this than meets the eye.'

'He'd get a lot of money for that Land Rover,' Bushra quipped. 'It's almost new.'

'This is not a joking matter,' Ayesha snapped.

'Correct,' said Mrs Rahman. 'This is very serious indeed.'

'Sorry, yes, you're right.' Bushra told herself again to engage brain before mouth. She accepted it was a bad habit to speak out of turn, not quite correctly assessing the mood of the situation.

Dr Rahman, still stood with one hand on the replaced receiver, said more. 'Faiyaz says AI have proof that he arranged for false papers to be sent from medical suppliers in Calcutta to justify the journey.'

Ayesha was about to tell all about Ben's rescue mission when her father continued. 'There's more.' Dr Rahman limped to the sofa and the family gathered around waiting to hear it. Natcoo, sharing the family's upset, stood in the doorway for the news and if he could help, perhaps with a tray of tea.

'A bulldozer has demolished Dak Bungalow. And our clinic. Both totally levelled. They've dismissed Masaad, the nurse, and Faiyaz. They've retained the other staff for now, including Syed, the driver. Apparently Aid International people will come up from Dacca every day to run the camp's aid programmes.'

'Have they moved the clinic to a different building?' asked Mrs Rahman. 'Do they still want your voluntary work?'

'As I told Faiyaz, I've heard not a word. But if there's no clinic...' He shrugged his shoulders.

'How will they care for the sick?' asked Bushra.

'I suppose they'll have to attend clinics and hospitals here in Tungipur.'

'What about Ben?' Mrs Rahman looked hard at Ayesha. She sensed her daughter had something important to say.

AYESHA REVEALED EVERYTHING. Khalida's pregnancy. How Maz drugged and raped her. The letter and codename Mrs Huq. Khalida's dash to Jessore to escape the Hussains. Ben's rescue mission to collect her and drive on to Calcutta.

'But since that call, three days ago now, I've not heard a word from him or Khalida. I'm worried sick. Oh, Amma, Abba, what's happened to them?'

Ayesha sobbed uncontrollably, wrapped in the arms of her mother, father and sister.

Natcoo slipped away to bring a tray of tea.

THIRTY-FOUR

To the Hussains, the ten-bedroom house in Dacca's elite Dhanmandi district was their lavish home. To Khalida, it was prison. Still, it was preferable to that subterranean cell in Dacca's central jail in Bakshi Bazar. Only hell's sewer could be worse.

As a minister of state, Farook Hussain was entitled to armed guards at the gate. All politicians have enemies. Razor wire looped over the eight-foot wall provided extra protection from potential intruders – and escapees.

Mazharul has been sent away to stay with an uncle until the wedding, Mrs Hussain informed her future daughter-in-law. It is correct you do not meet him until the wedding ceremony. Khalida thanked her for letting her know, and for providing such a lovely room on the top floor, and the maid. Very kind of you, she added respectfully. Khalida was fully aware the maid was also her minder and Hussain's round-the-clock spy. She slept in the corridor connecting Khalida's rooms with the rest of the house.

The 'situation' is far from ideal, sighed Mrs Hussain, but the best had to be made of it. She had, naturally, wished for the traditional big Bangladeshi wedding for her only son. A grand affair with hundreds of guests, even the prime minister would have made a guest appearance. But, despite the circumstances, she and her husband will do their best for him.

'As you can see, Khalida, we have nearly four acres of garden,' Mrs Hussain said, stood on the second-floor balcony of Khalida's room overlooking the back lawn. 'A marquee will be erected tomorrow and we shall decorate all around and make the occasion special. Strings of bunting and fairy lights, plenty of flowers, ample food, as you'd expect.'

'It will look lovely,' Khalida said demurely.

'The chief kazi has agreed to complete the legal formalities of marriage and you will both sign the *nikah-nāmah*.'

'Yes, of course,' Khalida said quietly. 'Thank you.'

'In a day or two, before the *biye* ceremony itself next Saturday, we will apply the *gaye holud*, as our Bengal custom with turmeric dictates. You will look beautiful for your husband, our son, our family and our guests. It is fortunate your condition doesn't show. Are you quite sure you're three months?'

'Yes, Mrs Hussain. A little over actually.'

'Oh. Well, we shall delay the announcement of the birth and say it was a little premature. Some will gossip. Some will guess you were careless. One can never stop wagging tongues.' Mrs Hussain paused and eyed Khalida directly. 'I believe my husband instructed there should be no mention whatsoever of the pregnancy.'

'Yes, of course, Mrs Hussain. Understood.' Khalida lowered her head.

'And you may, from now, address me as Amma.'

'That is very kind of you… Amma, and an honour.'

'I see you have not been taking good care of yourself recently.' Mrs Hussain stood back and inspected Khalida head to toe, then toe to head. She slid off Khalida's scarf and finger-combed her hair through its full length. 'The maid will wash your hair and we need to oil it well. It's looking a little thin and far too dry. Do you normally use coconut oil? I find it better than caster or olive.'

'Yes, Mrs… Amma.'

Continuing her examination, Mrs Hussain stepped to the side and, starting at the throat, slowly slid her chubby right hand down the front of Khalida's body, over her breasts, lower, pausing and resting it over the position of her grandchild, her first, cosseted in the womb.

Khalida breathed in deeply, set her jaw and thought this damn woman thinks I'm a bloody racehorse. It took all her will-power not to thump Beno Hussain's fat face.

'You are too thin,' Mrs Hussain declared. 'Remember you must eat for two from now on.'

'At medical…' Khalida quickly faded her voice. 'Yes, Amma, of course. It is true, I haven't eaten too well over recent weeks.'

Khalida refrained from reminding Mrs Hussain that she had studied medicine for four years. She was – or had been – about to enter the fifth and final year of her Bachelor of Medicine, Bachelor of Surgery qualification.

She also held back from screaming that she'd been on the run from her heartless husband for the last month. Then captured and locked up by him in an underground cell worse than a cess pit.

But the long game had to be played, carefully. Sometimes you have to give ground to gain it, Abba's wise words echoing again. Consolidate your position. Dig in. Freedom could not come fast. Long term strategy not short term tactics…

'Your skin is somewhat sallow too. Goodness knows what you've been up to.'

Oh, if you only knew…

Khalida, compliantly, quietly, modestly – lowering her eyes, almost as a plea – asked her prospective mother-in-law if, kindly, her mother could attend the wedding. Perhaps a friend or two as well?

'I shall ask my husband.'

THIRTY-FIVE

Mohammed served the minister's tea on time at nine. He didn't disturb the lively discussion with the tall silver-haired American. How could he? They didn't notice him, even when he slid a plate of butter toasted biscuits in front of them. As before, the Yank accepted the minister's invitation to drink a fine flush Darjeeling. But Mohammed served him watered-down low-grade black Bangladeshi tea. For anyone who adulterates best Darjeeling with milk, as he had on previous occasions, Womach wouldn't be able to tell the difference. Mohammed, small, thin, undistinguished, bowed from the hip and left the office closing the door slowly, imperceptibly.

It was time for his own tea-break. He would brew the best Darjeeling leaves from the Singbulli estate, near his birth village of Mirik. Its aroma, clarity, colour and taste took him back to his childhood. From the age of five Mohammed had worked long days alongside his mother, dragging her basket to the weighing bench. She was one of the best tea pickers and could harvest one hundred and seventy pounds of fine leaves a day. Even at that tender age, Mohammed calculated that the manager cheated his mother. He claimed she had only picked about one hundred pounds. But any picker who complained would lose their job and their hut. They would be branded a troublemaker and barred from working on neighbouring estates. 'Don't say a word,' she often told him when he wanted to complain. He stayed silent, harnessing his anger.

'I must thank you again Thomas for the information about this fellow at Mohpur,' Hussain said while his hand automatically reached for another biscuit. 'Coupled with other snippets that came to my attention, it was clear he was up to no good. I trust the police have returned your vehicle?'

'Actually, no, Farook,' Womach said. 'I told my people to let the police in Jessore keep it. We've a consignment of Jeeps coming in from the US next week. They're arriving by sea in, er, what's that port down south?'

'Narayanganj?'

'No. Er...'

'Chittagong?'

'That's the place. Chittagong.'

'Oh, really?' Hussain's eyes widened with interest.

'Hey, Farook. They are not like those Mercs. No air con. Rough and ready. Great up country in mud and potholes. And my guys prefer driving nippy Jeeps to those heavy British things.'

'Yes, I know very well from my army days...'

'Of course you do. Look, I'm sure there'll be one to spare – maybe your son would like it.'

'That would be very kind, especially as Mazharul is to be married this weekend.'

'There you are, a wedding gift,' Womach said, sitting back in his chair and clapping his hands. 'Congratulations to him and you. I bet he's marrying a beauty...'

'Oh, yes. Yes she is...'

'And it won't be long before I'll be congratulating you again – as a grandfather!'

Farook Hussain, without showing it, became suspicious of Womach. Did he know the real reason why this aid worker chap at Mohpur went to Jessore? Womach was, after all, informed almost immediately that the Land Rover had been unexpectedly driven from the camp. This British fellow knew Khalida Chowdhury was pregnant, superintendent Abdul Hafiz in Jessore had confirmed that. But did the aid worker – and Womach – know Mazharul was the father?

Hussain changed the subject to more important matters than the consequences of his son's foolishness.

'On the substantive matters, Thomas, it is good the channel to Bermuda is fully functioning. My colleagues in the two ministries we discussed, in addition to our banking associate, will ensure a steady flow. We've agreed the allocation of funds to each party and to where the money will be deposited. Zurich is still my preference, at least for some of my share. I take it that you will square matters at the highest level in Washington and there will be, shall we say, no political interference?'

'The man in DC is aware of the agreement in general terms. It would not be wise for him to know details, obviously. If political opponents or the media came sniffing around, it is essential he can claim ignorance of such activity.'

'That I understand. Agents and intermediaries and off-shore companies have their uses.'

'I'll also ensure Bangladesh is mentioned specifically in his keynote speeches about America's generous humanitarian aid programmes.'

'Most welcome, Thomas. Most welcome. I'm sure his public support will generate extra contributions.'

After his tea break, Mohammed had slipped back into the minister's room. The American had again arrived with vodka and, although only mid-morning, the bottle was open. Tonic, ice, lemon and lime slices needed to be placed within easy reach of the minister's desk. Mohammed departed the room as unobtrusively as he had entered.

'I must tell you, Thomas, about another project. It will arouse much international interest. And I have every confidence it will stimulate sympathy and provide additional charitable donations?'

'What, in addition to the terrible plight of these Bihari guys?' Womach feigned a sad face.

'Yes. Better. I've been in touch with associates in Rangoon.' Hussain paused and, on cue, Womach responded.

'I'm intrigued, Farook.'

'My country will soon have a new terrible humanitarian problem to face.' Hussain smiled wryly. 'It will require yet more international aid, perhaps even from your friends in Washington DC.'

'And Aid International?'

'Of course.' Hussain leaned across his desk. Womach mirrored the minister, bringing their heads closer together.

'It will work like this,' Hussain said. 'The Burmese army will soon make moves in and around the Arakan Hills, to the southeast of our border. They will oust many, let's call them "illegal immigrants" and "terrorists". This will result in many thousands of Burmese refugees flooding into our already overstretched, overburdened nation.'

'That's awful, but welcome,' Womach grinned. 'Compassion fatigue about these Biharis has set in. Well-off folks in the US and Europe need a new tragedy, more misfortune of others in pitiful countries to prick their consciences, arouse their guilt. So another humanitarian crisis to re-stimulate the aid economy sounds like a very good idea.'

'You realise my Burmese friends will require a reward for their efforts, a slice from our Bermuda account. But the increase in income will doubtless outweigh the additional expenditure.'

Womach and Hussain took another slug of vodka and sat back in their chairs, at ease, satisfied with their morning's business, delighted that more international aid will boost their personal fortunes.

After a minute or so, Womach said, 'I have more good news, Farook.'

'Really?'

'Building work at Mohpur has begun. That shitty bungalow has been flattened and the foundations for your fine new property are being laid as we speak.'

'I believe you meant to say for Aid International's new Mohpur office, Thomas?'

'Quite right, minister. Quite right.'

'That deserves an extra peg, Thomas.' Hussain lifted the vodka bottle and tipped it towards Womach's glass.

'Peg?'

'Ah, it's a term the British used in their inglorious days of empire. It's a measure of a drink, especially their fondness for brandy and soda.'

'Then let's have two pegs – of vodka and tonic.'

AFTER HIS MINISTER and the American departed for a meeting elsewhere, Mohammed gathered the used glasses and the empty vodka bottle. He kept the glasses and bottle at arm's length and held his breath to avoid inhaling the fumes of alcohol. All the biscuits had gone, and crumbs littered the top of Hussain's desk. But it was not his job to clean the room.

He felt ashamed of Hussain for alcohol is forbidden, harām, to Muslims. It prevents pure thoughts of Allah. But what could he do? If he complained, he'd lose his job. Perhaps he'd suffer a beating for disloyalty, if he were allowed to live at all. He couldn't live again in a rat-infested roadside ditch. Not now. Not at this age.

Hussain would argue the Qur'an only refers to wine. But alcohol from any source muddles the mind. Allah will punish him.

But I am Allah's servant and must do His will.

THIRTY-SIX

It was Nowel Cribb's third visit to Dacca's central jail representing British citizens.

His first involved a Scottish woman. She claimed her Bangladeshi husband forcibly kidnapped their two young daughters from home in Glasgow. She had mounted a protest outside the husband's house in Sylhet. It caused a commotion, upset the neighbours, windows broken, doors damaged, traffic congestion. She was subsequently arrested for causing civil unrest. Back in Scotland, she continues fighting for custody and her daughters' return to Britain. She told *The Herald* that she feared they are to become 'child brides'. Her estranged husband, she claimed, was 'only interest in the money he'll get by selling them to a rich old man'.

The British High Commission also assisted a nineteen-year-old student who attempted to smuggle hashish, opium and other illegal drugs into the country from India. Nowel managed to negotiate the student's release. His task was made easier because, thanks to lucky timing, Britain was on the brink of agreeing a substantial aid package for Bangladesh. The student was the son of a cabinet minister. Should the news leak out, the Foreign and Commonwealth Office had already drafted a press release firmly denying any connection between the student's release and the aid package. The words 'purely coincidental' appeared in the text.

Ben Altringham's case posed a different problem for second secretary Cribb. Before visiting the prison, Nowel's diplomatic counterpart in Bangladesh's ministry of foreign affairs assured him that Altringham would be released late next Saturday, or early Sunday.

'Then why not now?'

'Nowel, my friend,' Nafis Ahmad purred down the line, 'I simply do not know, and neither can I find a satisfactory explanation.

But that's what I've been told to tell you. If I, or you I believe, persist in enquiring further, it may upset the apple cart. Let's both leave well alone.'

'Strange,' Nowel said. 'Very peculiar.'

'I agree,' said Nafis, before lowering his voice to increase Nowel's attention. 'Off the record, my friend, and this is only my opinion, this order must have come from the very top, or jolly close to it.'

DEPUTY PRISON GOVERNOR Ali Ghaffar met the British diplomat and escorted him to the air-conditioned VIP guest suite. It was important to portray to the outside world, especially at this time when foreign aid was pouring into the country, that Dacca's top prison maintained prisoners' human rights as defined by the United Nations. Official visitors from the UN and the International Committee of the Red Cross had been persuaded that, although standards of prisoner care and facilities could improve, the prison met international standards. Ali Ghaffar's charm and eloquence doubtless helped persuade visitors that all prisoners were treated well. There had been a few bad apples and incidences of poor practice in the old days but, thankfully, no longer. Prisoners were now treated with dignity and respect. What Ghaffar failed to mention was that VIP visits excluded the subterranean cells, their existence denied, the heavy iron door to the deep dungeon labelled, in English, STORE ROOM.

Nowel was aware UN and ICRC officials were either naïve or deliberately observed only what they wished to observe, report only what they needed to report. After all, they had to dance to politicians' tunes for access to a country and for most of their funding.

Nowel also maintained the neutral expression of a well-trained diplomat listening to Ghaffar's blatant lies. Reports of torture and maltreatment were too numerous to ignore. But the dead and the disappeared had no voice to speak; their family no body to bury, no evidence to present. And the poor have no power, no chips in the roulette of life.

Ben, in his own clothes and not restrained in any way, was brought into the visitors' room. It was about the size of a tennis court with an exceptionally high roof. A row of narrow windows encircled the walls immediately under the ceiling. Because it was outside routine visiting times, Ben and Nowel were alone, apart from the escort guard who remained sitting casually near the door. They faced each other across one of about thirty laminated tables and sat on plank benches. Both items of furniture were bolted into the concrete floor, presumably so prisoners, should they be tempted to riot, couldn't use them as weapons.

'Hello, Ben.' Against prison rules, they shook hands. But the guard appeared as uninterested as he was unobservant. He preferred staring at the ceiling.

'Am I pleased to see you, Nowel. Thanks for coming. When did you hear about my arrest?'

'Yesterday evening. A call from the police in Jessore. They said you were being flown to Dacca and driven here. Are you being treated well?'

'Surprisingly good, in fact. Guards have been really polite. Far better than I expected. I've a cell to myself. It's not the Savoy – not that I know what the Savoy's like. Even the food isn't bad. Although I keep asking for no sugar in my tea, it comes like syrup. The main problem is the constant echoey noise and, you know, the smell.'

'Ah, yes, reminds me of our school changing room after a rough game of rugger. It's that heady combination of stale sweat and undiluted teenage testosterone.'

'You got it in one.'

'Well, to business. First, excellent news. You are going to be released.'

Ben's reaction was cautious, with a hint of humour, 'And the not-so-excellent news… not for twenty-five years?'

'No, no, nothing so bad as that. Next Saturday afternoon, I'm told by a contact at the ministry. Sunday morning latest.'

'Then why not now?'

'That's precisely the question I've asked, Ben. I've tried my hardest to get an explanation of what's going on. The best reason I've been given is that the police in Jessore are considering charging you for an offence. But that offence would only amount to a fine, not imprisonment. So, we await Mr Plod in Jessore.'

208

'They have my passport. I can't leave the country. Delaying my release doesn't make sense.'

'You're right. It doesn't. And I can't work out why they're keeping you here until the weekend either. It seems an arbitrary date. But that's the situation.'

Ben recounted to Nowel what happened in Jessore. The abandoned plan to smuggle Khalida to India. The reasons for it. Stopped by three police cars. Khalida chased through paddy fields. The fabricated story against him about resisting arrest. Discovering he'd been sacked by Aid International so they could claim he'd stolen the Land Rover – and the rest of it.

'Do you know what's happened to Khalida?' Ben asked.

'No.'

'Can you find out?'

'Unfortunately, Ben, I'm not allowed to ask. She's a Bangladeshi citizen and it would be against protocol to ask questions.'

'I'm really worried for her, Nowel. She thinks she's going to be drugged, forced into marriage to a man she loathes – and you know what that means. She could be kept in purdah, even after the baby is born. It's a horrible situation. Can't you do anything at all to help?'

Cribb grimaced and shook his head slowly.

'Can you at least phone Ayesha and let her know what's happened?'

'I could, but better you talk to her. There are phones for prisoners to use,' Cribb said. 'But remember somebody will be listening and the number you call logged. They also automatically cut off after three minutes. Apparently it stops arguments and fights breaking out over someone hogging the phone. Redialling is allowed though if nobody's waiting to use it.'

Nowel reached into his pocket and took out a handful of coins. 'Here, you'll need these.'

'Thanks, Nowel, I'll pay you back when they give my things back.'

'No need, Ben. I won't miss a few taka.'

'I'll call Ayesha. But if I can't give details, I'll ask her to ring you, if that's all right.'

'Yes, fine. Regarding your sugary tea. I'll ask the deputy governor on my way out to ask the tea-wallah to serve *chini*-less tea. But I can't guarantee it will arrive in a delicate bone-china teacup.'

Nowel stood ready to leave, picked up his briefcase and rummaged inside. 'Almost forgot. Here, Ben, a copy of *The Times*. A few days old, I'm afraid, but I'm sure something to read is better than nothing.'

Ben looked at the headline: APOLLO 17 ASTONAUTS WALK ON MOON.

'Don't you find it annoying, Nowel, that we spend billions on space projects while we have people around the world starving to death? Dying because they don't have basic medicines. We have all the brilliant technical and scientific skills to get people to the moon, but can't supply enough food to hungry people not fifty yards from here. And I bet in another fifty years we'll still have stupid wars, people suffering and starving primarily because of power-crazy politicians. What do you think?'

Nowel pulled a wry smile. 'I'm a diplomat, Ben. That means I must be diplomatic.'

THE PAYPHONE HUNG in the long drab concrete corridor of his prison wing. Built when Britain ruled East Bengal, the jail replicated the austere Victorian architecture of those in Manchester, Leeds and London. With inmates and guards wandering around, some aimlessly, others seemingly with purpose, a handful clearly mentally ill, there was no privacy for Ben. As the only foreigner, an oddity in their midst, all eyes were on him: curious, bemused, and one or two threatening eyes. But from his few attempts at conversation, most if not all his fellow captives had little or no understanding of English. He could talk freely, remembering however that calls might be monitored.

Natcoo answered. On hearing Ben's voice, Ayesha, uncharacteristically and to Natcoo's surprise, snatched the phone. (She apologised later for being so rude. But Natcoo, cook Ali and housemaid Buna knew she was in love and therefore, as Ali put it, 'not of right mind'.)

'Mr Altringham! For heaven's sake, where have you been?'

'We can drop the formalities, Ayesha. Forget about using Mrs Huq and all that stuff. Look, I don't have long.'

After quickly recounting what happened in Jessore and his current predicament in prison, Ayesha asked, 'So where's Khalida, what's happened to her?'

'I assume she's in prison too. Or held captive somewhere. But where? I don't know. Nor did Nowel Cribb from the commission. But you know who – best not mention his name on the phone – must have a hand in it. Let's hope we hear from her soon before I see you at the weekend – well, hopefully, if Nowel's information is correct.'

'I'll phone her mother straight away, see if she's heard anything. She'll be worried even more now with what happened in Jessore. But she needs to know. Can't keep it from her.'

'Agree. It would be wrong to withhold that news, however unpalatable. Bad news doesn't get better waiting to be delivered.'

'I've also some surprising news for you.' Ayesha paused, suddenly wondering if this was the right time to tell him. But it was too late to hold back.

'Well, don't keep me in suspense,' Ben said. 'Remember this phone will cut off any second.'

'Dak Cottage has been demolished.'

'What? Already? So that's another reason why Aid International wanted me out of the way.'

'Abba is astonished they managed to get the building permissions so quickly and all the construction materials that have appeared on site.'

'The clinic?'

'Gone as well. As flat as a chapati.'

'In England we'd normally say pancake,' Ben teased, lightening the mood.

'I know, Ben, of course. As you also know, we do pancakes here in Bangladesh...'

'And they're delicious.'

'But as you also know, I like to be original.'

'So, from now on Ayesha, you and I will always say "as flat as a chapati". Forget pancakes. Right?'

You don't need to see someone smile – when you can hear it.

THIRTY-SEVEN

'She seems pleasant enough and content to remain upstairs in those quarters,' Beno Hussain told her husband over dinner, dabbing her mouth with her napkin. She sat at the end of a long heavy ebony table facing him. Two servants cleared away dishes from their first course.

'Don't be fooled. Remember her father. He was extremely intelligent and charming – but utterly devious. If she has inherited only half those qualities, that makes her brighter than most. Khalida knows while she carries our grandson she is protected. After the birth... well, we'll have to see how things are. She may come round to our way of thinking and realise what's best for us is best for her. How are the wedding arrangements going?'

'Remarkably well, considering the rush. But because it's all so last-minute some of the suppliers want paying extra.'

'Grasping vultures,' gasped Hussain. 'If they become greedy, tell them I will have the tax department pay a visit, if not the police for breaking regulations. They're bound to be cutting corners somewhere. If anything, these fellows should be offering us a discount for the privilege of working for a minister.'

The bearer served Farook Hussain's favourite dish, magur kalia, catfish curry, surrounded by kitchuri, spicy rice with lentils. At least once a month for the past twenty-five years of their marriage, Hussain told his wife the same story of how, as a boy, he was the best catfish catcher in his village. She always listened attentively, or gave the appearance of doing so, as if hearing the tale for the very first time. Over the years she had noted the estimated size of the catfish he caught had grown. His 'fame' also become exaggerated, gradually extending beyond his village to 'many villages' in the area. Beno amused herself by speculating that, in another twenty-five years, her husband would be claiming his catfish catching fame had spread to the whole of East Bengal, if not all Bengal. And doubtless the specimens he caught would have grown to the size of a whale.

After praising her husband's fishing prowess, Beno Hussain returned to the matter of Khalida. 'The girl has asked if her mother could attend the wedding, perhaps even a few friends too.' With her husband's mouth full of food, she knew he couldn't reply immediately. 'To keep up appearances of normality,' she continued, 'it would be good to have Fazana present. I could have a word with her beforehand to make sure she understands the... the delicate position.'

With his mouth still half-full of catfish, Hussain agreed. 'That would be a good idea. Ah yes, I forgot, you've known her a long time.'

'Since primary school. Fazana is also very smart. She'll understand. She'll play the game and cause no problems.'

'But I'm not sure if any of her friends should attend. They could cause trouble.' Hussain paused to think, suspending a piece of catfish near his lips in his right hand. Like most Bengalis, he preferred the traditional way of eating, only resorting to a knife and fork when necessary. 'However, it would be interesting to discover who her closest associates are. So, yes, Beno, ask who she would like to invite. Get their names and addresses – for their invitations. If you ask Khalida immediately after telling her that her mother is welcome, her guard will be down in the glow of the good tidings.'

Beno acknowledged her husband's idea was a clever ploy.

KAHLIDA WAS DELIGHTED her mother would be at the wedding on Saturday. She named her friends Safa, Fatima, Dahab and 'perhaps Ayesha Rahman' as the girlfriends she would like to attend. Khalida deliberately played down the importance of her closest friend to her future mother-in-law. She suspected Farook Hussain would use such knowledge of her friendships to exert even more control over her, to keep a closer watch. And Khalida couldn't rule out the possibility that Hussain knew of the relationship between Ayesha with Ben Altringham, the man arrested in Jessore with her: Hussain had informants everywhere, as pervasive as blood in the body.

If this had been a 'normal' wedding, as Khalida thought of it, many family members and dozens of friends would have been in attendance. Aunts, uncles and cousins would have flown in from America, Australia, Canada, Great Britain and India. But this was a wedding on the sly, a covert operation, a forced marriage in all but name.

Watching from her second-floor balcony, Khalida had to admit the Hussains had not spared any costs in preparing for the ceremony. A traditional wedding would normally involve months of planning, certainly many weeks. But the Hussains had pulled out all the stops.

All day and much of the night around fifty men and women, boys and girls, worked hard unloading, carrying, cutting wood, sawing and hammering nails – activities of all kinds preparing the grounds for the event. There seemed to be as many bosses as workers issuing orders and instructions. One saying this, another pointing there, someone contradicting someone else, arms waving and heads shaking everywhere. It seemed chaos. Yet the Hussain's open lawn had transformed into something resembling a colourful circus fairground. With the marquee's side-flaps open, Khalida could see the ceremonial stage gradually taking shape. Gold, silver and colourful bunting and elaborate decorations filled the grounds. Strings of lights spread like a giant spider's web from the marquee to the garden perimeter. Although power cuts in Dacca were less frequent than elsewhere in the country, especially in the prestigious area of Dhanmandi – it was known the state-run electricity organisation prioritised the area in which many politicians and business leaders lived – the Hussains left nothing to chance: a generator had been installed on standby.

Khalida gained a clue as to how many guests would turn up. She had thought it would be a small gathering, perhaps twenty or thirty, but she counted nearly three hundred chairs being taken into the main marquee.

Terracotta pots arrived, large and small, packed with sunshine yellow and orange marigolds, pelargoniums, vivid scarlet spikes of cannas and other flowers she couldn't name. On Wednesday, three days before the ceremony, five waist-high steel cooking pots arrived and placed on top of portable gas burners in the catering tent.

Pots and pans of all shapes and sizes arrived too. Outside, four half-barrel barbeques were bolted onto metal frames and hessian sacks of charcoal stacked nearby. Preparing and cooking the food started: the meat would be well-marinated and tender, succulent and flavoursome. As with most traditional weddings, there would be more than sufficient food. A feast of spicy, savoury and sweet dishes to satisfy all the guests, the ample leftovers distributed amongst the local poor.

Corners in the customary marriage procedures had however been cut. There would be no paka dekhi, a meeting between both families to formalise the couple's engagement. Nor would there be the full gaee holud, where the bride and groom are decorated with turmeric paste. But Beno Hussain arranged amongst her trusted married friends to have her future daughter-in-law 'stained yellow'. Khalida's hands, arms and feet would also be dyed with henna, but not by her own close friends, such as Ayesha.

After her release from the hell-hole of prison and brought to the Hussain house, Khalida had believed she wouldn't be allowed to attend her own wedding. The Hussains were devious enough to arrange for two witnesses to claim she had approved the marriage. This would be acceptable in Islam, despite being haram – forbidden – for parents or others to trick or coerce someone into marriage. It could be worse, she told herself. Far worse. If she had resisted Hussain's 'offer' she could still be in that underground toilet in Dacca's jail. Or joined one of those they call 'the disappeared'.

AFTER KHALIDA'S FRIENDS received their hand-delivered invitations to the wedding, Safa, Fatima and Dahab agreed to meet at Ayesha's house in Tungipur. They were variously shocked, surprised – and worried – at the news of Khalida's marriage. Knowing Ayesha was Khalida's closest friend, they pressed her for answers.

'Why the rush?' quizzed Dahab.

'Don't understand,' Safa frowned. 'Khalida was so set on completing her medical studies.'

'She wasn't *that* smitten on Maz. He's too...' Fatima searched for the right word, 'too flighty for husband material.'

'Not flighty,' Dahab added, 'untrustworthy. And his fat dad – Urgh!'

'So, come on, what's gone on?' Safa, Dahab and Fatima all eyeballed Ayesha.

Suspecting her daughter might come under such pressure for answers, Mrs Rahman stayed in the living room and responded. It had been pre-arranged that Dr Rahman would absent himself. Mrs Rahman had stipulated that a frank 'women only' discussion would need to take place. Bushra was allowed to stay. But she had been firmly advised to keep her knowledge of what had happened to Khalida and Ben to herself.

Mrs Rahman had agreed with Ayesha they had no alternative but to reveal Khalida's pregnancy. They are very intelligent girls; denial would be ridiculous. They would know, or strongly suspect, the answer to the key question of why the marriage had been hastily arranged. Mrs Rahman, Ayesha – and Bushra – determined they would not however disclose information about Khalida's failed flight to Calcutta with Ben, nor that she had wanted an abortion, initially at least.

'Even pregnant with Maz's baby, does she really want to marry him?' Safa asked. It was the question Ayesha – and Amma and Bushra – knew the true answer to.

Mrs Rahman replied to save her daughter from deceiving her friends. 'As you know very well, Safa, in our culture it is extremely difficult to be an unmarried mother.'

'We wouldn't condemn her,' Safa said.

'We could even help her,' Fatima chipped in.

'That's true, I'm sure,' said Mrs Rahman. 'Sadly, the reality is that many people would condemn her, and anyone seen to support her, and not just the zealots. Both Khalida and her mother would be ostracised, even by some so-called friends and neighbours. They certainly would not lift a finger to help.'

'Khalida will do what she needs to do,' Ayesha said calmly. 'And we'll remain her friends.'

'Where is she?'

'At Hussain's house,' Mrs Rahman said. 'Mrs Chowdhury telephoned me last night and told me about the wedding on Saturday.'

'Why is she not at home with her mother?' Safa asked. 'Then we could go and help get her prepared for the ceremony.'

Mrs Rahman improvised an answer. 'Convenience. Because all the preparations are going on at the Hussains. They have all the servants, a personal maid for Khalida and so on. It was easier to prepare her on site. Mazharul has been sent to stay with an uncle until the ceremony, Mrs Chowdhury told me.'

'Has Khalida phoned you, Ayesha?' Safa asked.

'No'

'Why not?'

'Don't know.'

'I suspect the Hussains are not letting her use the phone.'

'I wouldn't put it past them,' snapped Fatima.

'That's speculation,' Mrs Rahman said, trying to keep the conversation calm. 'We simply don't know.'

Natcoo's flip-flops could be heard coming towards the living room and they all turned to look at him. He announced that Dahab's father had arrived to pick up his daughter. He was also going to drop off Fatima at home.

Safa's driver would be another hour, so she and Ayesha retreated to her bedroom.

'Now, Ayesha,' Safa quizzed impatiently, squatting on the bed, 'spill the beans. The truth. You might have fooled Dahab and Fatima, but you haven't bamboozled me. There's more to this than meets the eye. What's really gone on? But before you tell me, I have something to tell you.'

'Really?'

'I know what happened at Shamsul's house.'

Ayesha put her face into neutral. It would be the face she would use as a doctor in front of patients – until the diagnosis was determined or the prognosis became as certain as it could be, be it good news or bad.

'And I have no doubt Khalida told you what happened.'

Ayesha remained expressionless.

'When we went to Shamsul's house, you know, after we'd visited the museum about three months ago. Remember, you didn't come

217

because, as the college's chief swot, you claimed you had to catch up on study.' Safa grinned. 'I came back into the house to use the bathroom after we'd walked down the garden to the lakeside. Well, apart from Shamsul and Dahab. And we all knew what they were up to. Then, in the cloakroom next to the bathroom, I heard Maz with Khalida. It was obvious what they were doing. I didn't think anything of it at the time. That was their business, not mine.'

Ayesha's cool ended suddenly. 'Then why didn't you do something? Help her? Go and drag him off her?'

Safa winced. 'Because... because I thought she'd agreed. Wanted to do it. For all I knew they'd been together before. It wasn't until later I realised her drink had been spiked with vodka.'

'And how did you discover that?' Ayesha asked, still seething.

'Because mine was laced with vodka too,' Safa said. 'But I hadn't touched my drink until I joined the others back in the garden. Halfway through my juice I started to feel woozy and figured out what happened.'

'And then?'

'I argued with Kasim. Challenged him. In front of the others. Fatima and all of us were furious when we realised our drinks had been laced with alcohol. We all poured what was left of our drinks on the grass. The boys just laughed. We realised afterwards those guys had plotted to get us girls plastered so they could have their way with us. It was only Maz who succeeded. But I was the only one – well, of us girls – who knew about Maz and Khalida.'

'What a pig!'

'I'm not sure, Ayesha, but I think Maz told his mates afterwards what he'd done to Khalida. You know, to show off, as lads do about their sexual conquests. Later in the house he was full of swagger. Khalida just seemed, well, dazed, spaced out. And the guys were looking at her. You know, as if they knew.'

'Disgusting,' Ayesha growled. 'Damn disgusting. Filthy swine. All of them.'

'I totally agree. That's why I have nothing to do with those fellows anymore. You already know Dahab has broken off seeing Shamsul. Did Khalida... you know... did she want to get rid of the baby?'

'Look, Safa,' Ayesha said softly, 'you mustn't tell the others because Khalida doesn't want anyone to know. But, yes, at first, she did think of having a termination.'

'And now?'

'I think, but don't know for sure, she's accepted the situation. She will realise that, inside, it's a baby, a human being, not a fertilised zygote and implanted blastocyst.'

'Typical!'

'What?'

'Ayesha Rahman, you're the only person I know who would describe the early stages of pregnancy as, you know, an "implanted blastocyst". But seriously, do you really think she's being held against her will at Hussain's place? I can't believe she wants to marry that... that rat-bag!'

'I haven't the faintest idea because I've not talked with her for a couple of weeks.'

'Is there anything, anything at all we can do to help her escape Maz's clutches? If the rumours about his dad are true, that family is capable of anything. They could be drugging her! Keeping her under lock and key! Maybe that's why she not phoned you, or any of us.'

'You might be right, Safa,' Ayesha sighed. 'I simply don't know. But I really can't see what we can do. If we interfere, we could make the situation even more dangerous for her. And, for all I know, she might have agreed – freely but reluctantly – to marry Maz.'

'But if she hasn't, perhaps we could...'

A gentle knock on Ayesha's bedroom door interrupted their conversation.

'Miss Safa, your driver here,' Natcoo announced.

THIRTY-EIGHT

Despite the circumstances, Farook and Beno Hussain wished to observe as many Bangladeshi wedding customs as possible. Although predominantly a Muslim country, weddings in Bangladesh are more in keeping with traditional Bengali customs than Islamic ones. On the face of it, apart from the brief religious aspects, you could be attending a Hindu wedding in India's West Bengal, the difference between them negligible.

Wedding celebrations would normally take place over three joyful days, families and friends mingling freely, coming and going at will. But this could not happen. Too risky. The possible disclosure and embarrassment. Who knows what that silly girl might do or say, or her mother, or her friends? They must be monitored – closely, discreetly.

And servants' eyes see, their tongues wag. They pretend not to watch, hurriedly averting their eyes if we turn towards them. But we see their glances. They feign deafness but hear every word. They press their ears to our doors. Ha! They think we don't know. That's how stupid they are. We see their shadows in the gap under doors and hear floorboards creak outside our bedrooms.

Our servants know what's happened with Mazharul and Chowdhury's daughter. They are not *so* stupid. Khalida's maid will know of the pregnancy, see her in the shower, watched her body change, aware the girl is confined to her quarters.

Servants gossip with servants elsewhere. They tell their masters and mistresses the secrets of other households. Servants are spies, some are even rewarded for their information.

Hussain needed the marriage deal done and dusted. Fast. Adversity must always be turned to advantage; personal misfortune used for political gain. To this end, to officially announce the wedding, Hussain ordered his chief press officer to call a press conference for Thursday morning.

Behind the lectern on the stage in the ministry's main meeting room, Hussain declared to the TV cameras, radio microphones, newspaper reporters and their photographers:

'My wife Beno and I are delighted to announce our dutiful son's forthcoming marriage. Mazharul's beautiful bride, Khalida, is the daughter of one of our nation's greatest martyrs, general Maruf Chowdhury. God rest his soul. It was my privilege to know him and, at times, serve alongside him.

'At this moment in our history, when our great prime minister and my hardworking cabinet colleagues are extremely busy serving our new nation, our families have agreed to a short and simple wedding ceremony. Now, while rebuilding our country, is not a time for nonessential extravagance. We must all tighten our belts, economise for the economy.

'I am therefore pleased and proud to say that son Mazharul and daughter-to-be Khalida generously agreed to holding a humble and modest marriage ceremony on Saturday. However, let me assure you all, it will not diminish our enjoyment with family and friends, nor devalue the significance before Allah of this match.

'Thank you all for your devoted prayers and good wishes.

'In the name of God, merciful to all, compassionate to each. God is greatest.'

Questions were not allowed. But the minister posed, smiled and waved for the cameras before leaving the stage. The acquiescent domestic media obediently reported verbatim the minister's statement. Several embellished his devotion to serving the nation by foregoing protracted wedding celebrations to return to work. The handful of foreign correspondents in the country were not invited, and probably would not have attended. It was hardly a story to excite editors in Washington, New York, London, Paris, Bonn or elsewhere. The only story in which they had some interest – even then it wasn't 'hold the front page' material – was the plight of refugees fleeing the brutal Burmese army into the south-east of Bangladesh and the UN secretary general's call for additional emergency funding.

Hussain hoped his press statement would quell gossip and explain the speedily arranged and shortened wedding ceremony. But he was astute enough to accept it would not silence some scandalmongers, nor justify the scaled-back celebrations.

ON SATURDAY MORNING guests, dressed in their best, displaying their finest jewellery, started arriving in the manicured grounds of the Hussains.

Being the property of a senior government minister, with many distinguished visitors expected, guests understood the need for extra security at the gate when presenting their invitation cards. It was also rumoured that even the Father of the Nation, the prime minister, would make an appearance. Those wearing hand-crafted Swiss watches and generously adorned with gold jewellery studded with large diamonds and emeralds, welcomed the show of force. Lawlessness was on the rise. The streets were not as safe as when East Pakistan had martial law. Dacoits need far tougher penalties. Special forces from the airport, under the command of the minister's brother, had been deployed to guard the perimeter and strengthen the contingent of around one hundred police officers.

Everyone entering the grounds praised the beautiful setting, the lush garden, the lavish decorations, the magnificent marquee. Such opulence was the least they could expect from a government minister, possibly the next prime minister. Guests, stood with glasses of sherbet, were equally generous in praising the array of delightful food. Lamb biryani, curries, kebabs and bowls of fruit salad filled the main dining tent. Many appreciated the additional area serving Chinese cuisine, operated by Jim and Wai Ong from their highly regarded Lucky House restaurant in Tungipur. Guests could tell no expense had been spared. And why should it? As several whispered to their closest friends in quiet corners, the Hussains had only one son to support. And no daughters.

Groom Mazharul would arrive mid-morning in a procession of family and friends. Traditionally, he would be greeted by the bride's father or a brother. But Khalida, having neither, would be received by her uncle from Jessore, accompanied by his teenage son.

Bride Khalida Chowdhury would make her appearance for the main ceremony. She would be impeccably adorned in the finest red silk sari in the whole of Bangladesh. Hand-woven, it would be heavily embroidered in dark green and bright yellow – all colours in precisely the same shades as the nation's first 'liberation' flag.

'Sadly, our lovely daughter-to-be has been ill with a tummy bug,' the Hussains whispered to selected family members and friends. 'We're afraid she'll only be capable of attending the brief marriage ceremony on the podium itself. But please keep it under your hat,' they added. This guaranteed the news would spread like seeds in a storm.

Ayesha, Safa, Fatima and Dahab arrived together and presented their invitations at the gate. They giggled and laughed as they walked around the grounds. Nobody would guess they were camouflaging their nervousness. Ayesha and Safa remained especially vigilant, their eyes constantly but discreetly scanning the crowd to find Khalida. They had conspired to whisk her away to a quiet corner and discover the truth behind this 'sham wedding', as Safa dubbed it. But after twice circling the grounds, Khalida could not be found. In the distance they did see Shamsul with his father, the banker, and Dahab's former boyfriend, Kasim. They were in animated conversation with an exceptionally tall man dressed in a white suit. He spoke so loudly his American accent spread far beyond his circle. Although no alcohol was being served, the fellow appeared intoxicated. But, with the benefit of doubt, perhaps that was his routine exuberant behaviour. The four girls kept their distance.

Fatima and Dahab wanted to approach the house and ask to see Khalida. But Ayesha and Safa, understanding the situation better than their companions, knew it was too risky. Even if the two surly security guards allowed them entry – which was doubtful without seeking permission from the minister – the chances of finding Khalida alone were zero. She'd be surrounded by a clutch of Mrs Hussain's women friends and family, fussing over every detail of Khalida's dress, hair and make-up. Some, with giggles and innuendo, would be offering titbits of advice for a new wife. Two or three of the more daring might suggest what to do or expect on her wedding night, as if

Khalida was an innocent. Some might forget that Khalida's knowledge of anatomy and physiology and human reproduction was far superior to their own.

THE ARMY HQ band struck up playing a cheerful march. It signalled to the guests to head towards the main gate, decorated with a gigantic arch of flowers and flags. As they pressed together, guests cheerfully clapped in time with the music. They were helped by the booming bass drum, the drummer's uniform complete with a Bengal tiger pelt, a remnant of British military apparel.

Maz and his entourage must be approaching. Ayesha and her friends shot worried glances to each other. Time was running out. If they couldn't rescue Khalida, get her away from this parody, this forced marriage, within the hour she would be Maz's wife.

But how could they extract Khalida from the clutches of the Hussains? They were powerless. Unless Khalida shouted and screamed during the ceremony in front of all the guests, there was no escape. If she saw her friends in the crowd, would that give her the courage to protest and put a stop to this charade? Perhaps, Ayesha considered, they have dosed her with an optimum dose of tranquillisers – enough for her to appear normal but mentally coshed, emotionally dead. And nobody knows what threats hang over her if she fails to marry Maz.

When Khalida appears, even if they could squeeze through the crowd to within talking distance – certainly if they attempted to pull her away – the soldiers and police, some in mufti, would surely intervene. At best they'd be kicked out on to the street. At worst they'd be taken away, beaten, abused and 'disappeared'. Hussain would be outraged. He'd order full force against them. No mercy shown. Without doubt, even if they survived with black and blue bruises and scarred skin, they would be expelled from college for bringing their establishments into disrepute. Their families would be made to suffer too.

Fear helped doubts creep in. Dahab, Fatima and Safa expressed them quietly to themselves and each other. Ayesha didn't know what to think; she knew even less what to say, so maintained her silence.

What if Khalida's changed her mind and wants to get married? Perhaps she's come to an agreement with the Hussains and is happy now? Maybe she's forgiven Maz? Some women forgive their husbands who mistreat them, don't they? Maybe she believes she's to blame for what happened? Perhaps she encouraged him. We don't know, do we? If only she'd behaved more modestly. She'll grow to love him, even if she's angry with him now. Isn't it better to have a husband, a father to her child, than to be an unmarried mother?

'There is nothing, nothing we can do,' Dahab concluded.

Fatima agreed. 'We're utterly powerless.' Her arms dropped lifeless to her side.

'We must accept whatever happens,' Safa sighed, defeated.

They waited for Ayesha's opinion.

But suddenly the crowd engulfed them. As a ship splits the sea, the girls were swept to one side as a wave of guests made way for Mazharul's procession. He walked alongside Khalida's uncle and nephew and several cousins towards the marquee, followed by the marching band – some players out of tune as well as out of step. Maz waved and smiled to relatives and friends, and they applauded him. To welcome him formally to the ceremony were Maz's proud parents. Father and son embraced before turning towards the marquee.

THEN EVERYONE NOTICED. It was truly a breath-taking sight, almost spectral. On the podium beneath the pergola, on a gilt and purple-satin throne, sat Khalida. With a magician's sleight-of-hand, as eyes were distracted by Maz's entrance, Khalida had somehow slipped onto the stage. She sat serenely as still as a statue, head bowed, eyes down – guests momentarily spellbound. From high on her head to the rings on her toes, Khalida was dripping in ornate gold jewellery.

Ayesha tried to look beyond her friend's striking beauty, bedazzling jewellery and perfect make-up. But it was impossible to assess Khalida's health, physical or emotional. If anything, perhaps a little thinner, despite approaching the fourth month of pregnancy. But with Khalida's midriff wrapped in multiple yards of silk sari, nobody could detect her condition. Nor could Ayesha or her three companions determine if Khalida's traditional expressionless demeanour signalled compulsion, compliance or consent.

Minister Hussain led his son, relatives and guests, including Thomas Womach, into the marquee towards the pergola, Khalida its spectacular centrepiece. Although Islam doesn't require a religious figure to officiate at the ceremony, Imam Mustafa, from Dacca's main mosque, agreed to read from the Qur'an and deliver a short sermon, perhaps a few words of wisdom for newlyweds.

The solemn moment of marriage, the nikah, was approaching. Mazharul walked steadily towards his bride on 'the throne' to present his mahr, the dowry pledge to secure his wife's financial future. His promise was sealed inside a small square ebony casket inlaid with ivory motifs of daisy-like flowers. Farook and Beno Hussain had already gifted gold bangles, pearl earrings and gem-studded rings to Khalida, alongside a collection of traditional and fashionable saris, salwars and kurtas in Tussar and Kantha silks and cotton. Later the couple would graciously receive gifts from guests filing past who will add their best wishes. Old men might whisper in Mazharul's ear while embracing him that they hoped, God willing, he would be blessed with many sons.

SECONDS OF SILENCE followed the gunshots. Two cracks in quick succession. Ear-piercing screams came once the stunning impact of the horror ceased. People scattered in all directions like shrapnel from a grenade.

His revolver jammed. Before the assassin's trembling hands could unblock it, a soldier's AK-47 sprayed bullets across his chest. The murderer's body slumped over that of his victim, their blood flowing together onto the grass and seeping into the soil.

But others fell dead or injured. Shouts and screams of anguish filled the air. Some stood still in shock. Some fled in fear. Some spread-eagled themselves on the ground. In the soldier's haste to kill the killer, his automatic rifle sprayed bullets into guests stood behind the assassin. 'Collateral damage,' the subsequent report described their deaths and injuries. Policemen and soldiers brandishing weapons rushed to the scene of carnage.

Confused, panicking, some thought the soldier was the assassin. Guns aimed at him. *'Na, na, na!'* he screamed, nervously pointing to the small thin body on top of Minister Hussain's. 'Him. It's him,' he cried. 'He killer.'

Mazharul rushed forward and dragged the murderer's scrawny body off his father. Others helped the wounded bystanders, including children – accidental victims of a rapid-fire rifle. Joy had turned to tragedy in the blink of an eye.

'Get a doctor. Quick! Now!' Maz knelt over the bleeding body of his father. In shock, fearful, he seemed incapable of action and collapsed sobbing over his father's chest haemorrhaging arterial blood. Dozens of others were also screaming for help for their injured relatives or friends.

Looking up in desperation as people rushed around, Maz noticed Ayesha thirty or so yards away. He screamed pleadingly towards her. 'Please, please help!'

As she rushed towards Maz as fast as her tight-wrapped sari would allow, a panicking policeman crashed into Ayesha bundling her to the ground. Unconcerned, he ran on leaving her sprawled on the ground. But she gathered her dishevelled self and stumbled towards Maz. Ayesha dropped to her knees alongside Hussain's body.

'Here, use this.' She ripped half her headscarf to make a compress for the arterial bleed from Hussain's chest. 'Maz! Come on. Pull yourself together. Help.' She needed to shout to break Maz's shock-induced paralysis. 'Press hard. Harder. Just keep the pressure on. Don't let up for a second. Don't look to see if you've stopped the flow – you won't have done.'

Ayesha felt Hussain's carotid artery for a pulse, more in hope than expectation. She detected a weak, rapid flow. Ayesha knew severe blood loss would soon cause hypovolemic shock. It posed the biggest threat to Hussain's life. She was not hopeful.

'You! Yes, you. Come and press on this wound.' The soldier, still confused after shooting the assassin – and, in error, several guests – jumped to it as if Ayesha was his commanding officer. She unravelled what remained of her headscarf and formed another wad. 'Press hard until help comes.' He nodded, understanding her instructions.

'Oh, no. No!' Beno Hussain stood behind Ayesha wailing, her hands clamping her head. 'Farook, Farook, please, please don't die.' Relatives and friends surrounding Mrs Hussain wrapped their arms around her. They tried pulling her away from the carnage, but she kept shrugging them off and insisted on staying.

'I'll be back,' Ayesha, standing, told Maz. 'I must help the others.'

'No, stay, please. You're the best. Khalida always praised you...'

'GO, AYESHA, I will help my husband and father.'

Ayesha was stunned to hear Khalida, who knelt and placed her hands on top of Maz's to apply extra pressure. Blood, slowly, oozed between her gold-ringed fingers and across her turmeric-patterned hands.

'Maz – Khalida – you're doing all you can. Restricting the bleeding is the best you can do for now. It's the only thing you can do. Make sure this guy keeps the pressure up. Your father's airway is clear. The shoulder wound isn't critical. But this shot to his chest... at least the bullet's missed his heart. He might live if we can stop him bleeding out – and get him transfused and into surgery quickly.'

Where there is life, there is hope, Abba often said. But Ayesha, despite her father's eternal optimism, secretly believed Farook Hussain would die within minutes.

Ayesha didn't need to check the assassin's pulse: his chest was slashed wide open with a string of bullet holes. She rushed to help others lying bleeding, prioritising those most likely to live. She ripped the hem off her blood-soaked sari to form a tourniquet. The little girl's arm had been virtually severed at the elbow.

General Hussain, Farook's brother, took charge of the situation. He quickly issued a volley of orders to his senior officers. They ran in all directions shouting instructions to their underlings.

'DID YOU SEE that? Did you see that?' Thomas Womach screamed in shock. 'That fucker was aiming at me!'

'You're okay though...'

'His gun jammed...'

'You're in shock. That's all...'

'That's all? That's fucking all? That madman nearly killed me,' Womach shouted.

'Here, drink some water.'

Womach's hands trembled as he grasped the glass, water spilling over the sides and down his chin as he sipped.

General Hussain and two senior police officers approached and stood over the body of the killer. It was lying just yards away from where the general's nephew and Khalida still applied pressure to his brother's chest.

'I... I...I recognise him from somewhere,' Womach told the general looking at the assassin's body, already covered with blood-thirsty flies.

'Get a better look at him,' said Hussain. His big black boot turned the assassin's face upwards.

Womach studied the man's face. 'It's the tea and biscuit guy from his office. That's it. The tea and biscuit guy.'

'Do you know his name?'

'Fuck, no.'

'I'll get on to the ministry for his details,' the senior police officer said. He stood away and shouted orders into his walkie-talkie.

'Why would he shoot Farook?' his brother quizzed. 'Doesn't make sense. He had a nice easy job. What could be easier than serving cups of tea? And why should he try killing you?'

Womach shook his head, unable to answer, unwilling to speculate. For the first time he noticed his blood-splattered suit – and his eyes set on a slice of flesh stuck to his sleeve: the tea guy's flesh and blood, dangling, dripping. Womach turned, dropped to his knees and vomited.

'Perhaps someone put him up to it,' the policeman offered.

'This is not the time nor place to speculate,' Hussain said firmly in Bengali, making it clear to say no more, especially in front of the American, not that he was paying any attention other than to his own distress.

'Where... where did he get that from?' asked Womach, still on his knees, coughing and recovering, panting and pointing with a trembling finger at the gun in the general's hand.

Hussain had already cleared the revolver of the remaining four cartridges and started inspecting the weapon.

'Regrettably, there's too many of these old handguns around. I used one in Burma. It's a Webley mark four, dates from the nineteen twenties or thirties. It hasn't been maintained properly. Look, see the rust. The barrel didn't roll. You should be thankful, Mr Womach – otherwise these would be in you.'

General Hussain opened the palm of his hand displaying four cartridges in front of Womach's face. Womach turned and vomited again.

TWO .38 CALIBRE bullets were extracted from Hussain's flesh at Dacca's PG Hospital, fortunately just over a mile away from his home and wedding venue in Dhanmandi.

Hussain's brother shared with Ayesha the credit of saving the minister's life, and that of other guests sprayed with bullets.

General Hussain, the special forces commander, had the foresight to have a military ambulance on standby at the back of Hussain's house. Two minutes after Ayesha left Khalida and Maz to help others, the military medic had plasma pumped into Hussain's veins. Two minutes later would have been too late, resuscitation impossible: bodies need blood. And had not Ayesha stanched the flow of blood within seconds of the shooting, even the transfusion would have been too late.

Ayesha and Khalida – both with blood-stained hands and saris – found a corner to speak freely in the packed reception at PG Hospital. The police had cleared everyone apart from Hussain's family and relatives of the four unlucky wedding guests who'd been shot, including one seven year-old child. They were being consoled while anxiously waiting for news about their loved ones under the surgeon's knife.

'Why did you call Maz your husband?' Ayesha asked.

'Because he is.'

'But the ceremony hadn't – hasn't – taken place. And this… this situation provides an opportunity for you to get away. The Qur'an, the law, is clear, you know that – you cannot be forced into marriage. You can be free.'

'You don't understand, Ayesha. I'm already married. I've already signed our marriage certificate, our nikah-nāmah. Today's ceremony was just a show.'

The revelation stumped Ayesha for a moment. She regathered her argument. 'But that was under duress, so it doesn't count.'

'Ayesha, my dear lovely friend, you still don't get it. Listen.' Khalida gathered both Ayesha's hands in her own. 'I want a father for my child. Our child. Look, I know Maz is far from perfect. And he shouldn't have done what he did...'

'You can say that again...'

'But after weighing up all the pros and cons, even after what I was put through by his father – which I'll tell you about one day – I still believe I've made the right decision.'

'Khalida, Maz...' Ayesha dropped her voice and checked no one was nearby, 'raped you. You've been brain-washed. You can't...'

'Stop. Stop right there. I know. I've played back in my mind what happened a thousand times. More. But what you don't know is that if Maz had asked, gone about making love in a nice way, I'd have consented. I was ready. I wanted him. He didn't need to ply me with vodka.'

'Even so...'

'And, as part of my dowry, I have three signed copies of a contract which guarantees that, within a year of our baby's birth, I can – if I still wish – return to complete my medical studies. I have my copy, so too my mother, and the third is with Imam Mustafa. So, Ayesha, "All's well that ends well," as Shakespeare said.'

Ayesha concealed her immediate thought: but it's only just begun.

Mrs Hussain and Maz approached and broke up the conversation.

'Miss Rahman, Ayesha, thank you so very much for your quick action today. You saved my husband's life.' Beno Hussain spoke sincerely, softly. 'I cannot thank you enough.'

'Thank you, Mrs Hussain. But it was Mazharul and Khalida who carried out the first aid. And thankfully the army ambulance was on hand with the plasma.'

'No, Ayesha,' Maz shook his head. 'I didn't know what to do. Couldn't think straight until you came over and told me what to do with the pad – oh, your lovely headscarf. And your sari got soaked in…'. He couldn't bring himself to use the word blood.

'Yes, we must replace them,' interrupted Mrs Hussain.

'Oh, please, there's really no need.'

'What's the latest news of Abba?' Khalida asked.

Mrs Hussain answered. 'He'll live. That's the key thing. But the doctors think it will be at least three months before he'll be able to resume his ministerial duties.'

Doctors may have provided an accurate prognosis of his physical state: they grossly underestimated Hussain's ambition.

THIRTY-NINE

'Goodbye, Sir.'

The steel door slammed shut.

Outside jail, in people-packed traffic-choked Bakshi Bazar, Ben inhaled deeply as if the air was pure Alpine. Real or imagined, he didn't care. Fume-filled air outside prison was better than the stale atmosphere inside. The sky seemed bluer, the light brighter. Even a patch of dry grass seemed as green as an Irish meadow. Oranges on a cart at the roadside became balls of sunshine, each one radiating warmth, joy and promise.

Street sounds became music, reaffirming life being lived. Even street smells were more agreeable than the perpetual odour in prison of man-sweat and stale piss.

Colour had returned to Ben's life. Everything was no longer prison grey and prison drab and prison hollow. He thought of the men he'd met over recent days. Some had been incarcerated for years. If he felt so liberated after just nine nights in jail, what would freedom mean to them? For those inside for life, their remaining time will be as perma-grey as those who faced the noose will be perma-black.

'I COULDN'T BELIEVE my ears,' Ben told Ayesha at the Rahman's home in Tungipur. 'The deputy prison governor apologised to me for the "inconvenience" of being stuck inside.'

'Was it ghastly? Did they treat you well?'

'Sure, it was grim. The place needs more than a lick of paint. But not as bad as I imagined and, honestly, they treated me very well.'

'That's because they knew you were to be released soon. They didn't want you kicking up a fuss and bad-mouthing Bangladesh back in Britain.'

'Probably. But I suspect there's part of that prison where a lot of nasty stuff happens.'

Ayesha tried to avoid thinking about what that 'nasty stuff' might be.

'I couldn't get the full picture,' Ben said. 'Most of the prisoners couldn't speak English. But one inmate mentioned narak. That is the word for "hell", I think. And he pointed downwards.'

'Yes, that's hell,' Ayesha confirmed and, from the brief description Khalida had since given of her detention, Ben's informant was correct.

'This inmate told me very few come back from narak after they've been dragged there kicking and screaming and...'

Ben stopped. He could see Ayesha's anguish and decided to change the subject. Everyone knew torture was routine throughout the country. She was ashamed by its widespread practice, the wholesale abuse of human rights.

'But, more important, how are you feeling, Ayesha, you know, after yesterday's shooting? Must have been a terrible shock for you, for everyone.'

'Once it became clear it was just that guy, a lone-wolf attack, I felt okay. The danger was over. I just knew I had to help the wounded. I did what I did without thinking really.'

'But afterwards? Did the shock kick-in?'

'Ben, you might think I'm callous, heartless...'

'Never.'

'But no. I felt okay. I feel okay. I was just pleased to help some casualties and... and...' Ayesha paused and reflected.

'And?' Ben eventually asked.

'It confirmed everything in my heart and soul – that I want to be the best possible doctor I can possibly be. Just like Abba.'

'It scares me, though,' Ben said. 'To think you could have been one of those innocent bystanders shot.'

'But I wasn't.'

With a sudden surge of affection, Ben, sat opposite Ayesha, rushed over and grasped her hands. As their lips moved closer Natcoo's flip-flops prevented the embrace. Ben retreated to his seat. They threw each other a disappointed smile. (Both were convinced that, when alone, Natcoo deliberately slapped his soles harder to announce his entrance. 'What does he think we'll be up to?' Ayesha once quipped.)

'Good you here again, Mr Ben,' Natcoo's smiled his happiest of smiles. 'We all worried for you.' He placed a jug of lemon juice on the coffee table and a bowl of warm salted pistachios.

'Thanks, Natcoo. I'm very pleased to be back too,' Ben said.

When Natcoo departed – his flip-flops distinctly quieter – Ben said, 'It's good news all the charges against me have been dropped.'

'Sure, but we still have a big problem.'

On leaving Dacca's Central Jail, deputy governor Ali Ghaffar, smiling broadly, had handed Ben an envelope. Inside, on flimsy paper, was a two-sentence typed letter from the ministry of home affairs.

EXPULSION ORDER

By Order of the Minister of Home Affairs, you, Mr Benjamin Altringham, date of birth 12th March 1947, passport ref GBR 60701933, are hereby instructed to depart from the Republic of Bangladesh within ten days of this notice. Failure to adhere to this Expulsion Order will result in your arrest.

'What can I do? I don't want to leave Bangladesh. More important – much more important – I don't want to leave you, Ayesha. I can't leave you.'

'There is one possibility. I don't really want to, but I'm willing to give up…'

'No! Ayesha, no. You must finish medical school above everything else. We promised. And think what you've just said about helping all those people. You can't leave the country and come with me to… I don't know… to wherever.'

'You interrupted me, Ben.'

'Sorry, but…'

Ayesha quickly raised the palm of her hand to stop Ben saying more.

'I was about to say that I could give up my self-respect, or perhaps it's stubbornness, and contact Mrs Hussain. I could ask her to contact her husband's deputy at the ministry to see if the expulsion notice could be rescinded.'

'I can't ask you to do that. You – we – hate the Hussain's for what they've done to Khalida. We can't go asking favours of them.'

'It's against my instincts too. But if I swallow my pride. Forget the past. If Mrs Hussain credits me with saving her husband's life…'

'You did.'

'I helped. But that doesn't make it any easier to ask her for a favour. But if you agree, I'll do it.'

Ben thought long and hard. He didn't want, for himself and Ayesha, any involvement with the Hussains. They were poison. Well, Farook and his son, if not the wife and mother.

While he thought, Ayesha said, 'It's possible, Ben, she may not be able to have the decision reversed.'

'Come on, Ayesha, I've been in Bangladesh long enough to know how things work here. The minister of foreign affairs – even from his hospital bed – could have my expulsion order revoked instantly in one quick phone call. Once he knows the request is from you – his life-saving angel – how can he refuse?

'You agree then?'

'How can I disagree with you?' Ben laughed. 'Hussain will be so grateful to you, your wish will be his command.'

Ben's approach to kiss Ayesha was thwarted again – Natcoo's flip-flops and, perhaps as an extra precaution, a deliberate cough outside the living room door.

'Mr Ben, will you be eating with us tonight? And staying?'

'Thanks, Natcoo. Yes and yes. As you know, they've demolished my lovely bungalow. I've nowhere else to go.'

'Ha! "Lovely"? That's a joke. Natcoo, that dak was a garbage can,' Bushra chirped, bouncing into the room and flopping onto a sofa with a sigh. 'Ben came to rescue homeless displaced persons and he's become one himself.'

'Dr Rahman and Mrs say Mr Ben always welcome. Buna already prepared bed and Ali making favourite sweets.'

'Thanks, Natcoo,' Ayesha said. 'He needs fattening up again after his travels and time in… well, you know where. Tell Ali we know his meals will be much better than those in jail.'

'I tell him "Maybe a little bit better" than jail kitchen – so gomangse bhoona will be extra special.' Natcoo beamed a mischievous smile as he left the room, eager to tease Ali, his life-long friend.

'I know bhoona is a dry curry, but gomangse?'

'Dear Ben, if you are allowed to stay here, you must improve your Bengali.'

'I know. You can teach me.'

'Definitely not.'

'Why not?'

'First, because it will create such friction we'll fall out during your first lesson. Second, where do you think I'll find the time – and the patience – to teach you? Grammar is not so important speaking Bengali. But your pronunciation is terrible.'

'Hang on a minute, Ayesha, that's not quite fair,' Ben faked his protest. 'I've noticed people from Sylhet, Saidpur, and even in Jessore, pronounced some words differently to you.'

'Yes, for a small country, we have some different ways of speaking, just as in Britain. Your northern clans sound different to your southern tribes, although they're speaking English. But there, as here, most of the words are the same.'

Ben turned to Bushra. As he was about to speak…

'Don't look at me, Ben, I don't have the time to teach you Bengali either. Perhaps Amma will. Her pronunciation is perfect, classical, old style, and the patience of… oh, I don't know, whatever has lots of patience. A tortoise?'

'Okay, I give in for now, please tell me what gomangse bhoona is?' pleaded Ben.

'It is simply the best slow-fried beef curry. Ali will have started making it hours ago. You can't rush good food.'

FORTY

Hussain's room at PG Hospital stank of disinfectant. It reminded Thomas Womach of the smell at that clinic in Tungipur – and that very pretty girl. *Why didn't the silly cow let me fuck her? If she'd played ball, she could be back studying pharmacy, chemistry, or whatever it was. She'd be in a nice little room in Dacca, on hand during my visits to this god-forsaken country. Far better than the hovel she lives in. Bet she regrets her decision, now she's out of a job. Bob will have to arrange another.*

'How are you, Farook?'

'Much better, Thomas, thank you.' But Hussain winced as he struggled to sit upright in bed. The nurse, a nun seconded from St Xavier's, helped lift him while pumping up his pillows.

Womach placed a large basket of fruit on the bedside table. 'You can't eat flowers,' he said. 'Is there anything else you need?'

'Yes, a miracle, to get me out of this bed and back on my feet. But you're not God.'

'Not today,' Womach grinned.

Hussain enjoyed the quip. But the nurse shot a disapproving glance towards Womach: God nor His name should be used in jest.

'I shall be back for your TPR and BP in half an hour, Mr Hussain,' Sister Agatha said, tidying the bedsheet and shooting a stern glance at Womach. 'Doctor will see you shortly afterwards. I pray we will find your blood pressure remains stable.'

'Why don't you just tell me to fuck off in under thirty minutes and don't upset your patient,' Womach thought, but presented the nurse a Hollywood smile of perfect sparkling white teeth. She left the room thinking precisely what Womach thought – although thinking it far more politely.

'Do you think she's a virgin?' Womach asked, smirking. He watched the door closing and considered that she may have heard his question. Not that he cared.

'I thought Christian nuns were supposed to be.'

'Oh no, my friend. I'm sure half of them are having it away with priests. Even the ugly ones – with the ugly priests, which most of them are.' Womach laughed.

Hussain grimaced. 'Now, now, Thomas. Remember what nurse said. You're not to raise my blood pressure. Anyway, it hurts when I laugh.'

'Okay, Farook, I get what the nunny-nurse meant by BP. Blood pressure, obviously. But what the hell is TPR that she's coming back to do before "Doctor" arrives?'

'Hospital jargon, Thomas: temperature, pulse and respiration.'

'Well, I have just the thing to help your TPR and BP.' Womach removed a small bottle of vodka from his briefcase. 'Fancy a… what's that word you taught me your terrible British overlords used? Ah, yes, a "peg".'

'I shouldn't.'

'Go on. For medicinal reasons. Remember, Farook, alcohol kills germs, it's a great disinfectant. It's a preservative too. You'll live longer. And you told me it was allowed in your religion if it benefits your health.'

'Make it a small peg. Then I'd better eat a banana or something to disguise the smell. Otherwise, we'll be getting reprimanded by that dragon. She's very, shall we say, observant. A speck of dust isn't allowed to land in this room before she has the cleaners in.'

'No problem, Farook. Smell will vanish. We Americans always carry a supply of this.' Womach produced a packet of chewing gum from his shirt pocket.

As Womach poured the drink, Hussain adopted a stern face. 'You do know, Thomas Womach, you were responsible for the attempt on my life. I should get one of the guards outside to arrest you.'

Womach looked worried. 'I…I don't…'

'Ha! Don't fret, my friend. Keep your marvellous head of hair on. I'm pulling your leg. I discovered my tea-wallah had the audacity to claim I was a bad Muslim because of this.' Hussain held up his peg of vodka before taking a mouthful. 'He went crazy. Told another tea-wallah he'd been instructed by Allah to punish me. This chap then told my staff secretary, who fired the madman and thought nothing more of it. Who would have believed this ignorant peasant would have access to a gun?'

'But how the hell did he get inside your grounds at the wedding reception?'

'It's a mystery. All the guards claimed they checked everyone, including the well-known celebrity guests. It's as if this tea-wallah had the ability to walk in and around the place like the Invisible Man.'

'And you heard that little wiry bastard tried to shoot me too?'

'Yes, Thomas, I've received a full briefing. Heard you were sick at the sight of blood.'

'Oh yes, it was terrible. I'm not good with blood.' Womach scrunched up his face at the flashback.

Hussain had been told by his brother that Womach turned into a quivering wreck. Compared to the sights witnessed in the war, a handful of gunshot casualties was nothing to be squeamish about. Hussain wondered how Womach would react to the far worse sights after machetes and mortars, grenades and artillery shells had completed their grizzly deeds.

'Shall we concentrate on the business in hand? It won't be long before it's BP and TPR time and the doctors come fussing around.'

Womach updated Hussain about the substantial funds raised to help the plight of refugees fleeing for their lives across the River Teknaf from Burmese military aggression. Over two hundred villages had been torched. Men murdered. Women raped. Children orphaned. Following extensive heart-breaking news coverage, Americans had been particularly generous, Womach reported: the agreed percentage of incoming funds had been redirected to the off-shore accounts.

Hussain's dream of owning a house with a lawn stretching down to Lac Léman in Lausanne was becoming a step closer. A pleasant place to live after, say, five or ten years as president. Especially deserved now after suffering a would-be assassin's bullets. He told his brother, General Hussain, that he should let it be known that perhaps, just possibly, the attack had been ordered to destabilise the country. The army should perhaps, just possibly, prepare for a military coup. A firm not a friendly hand was needed to combat the growing lawlessness and corruption. It's what the people wanted. And if they didn't want it, they needed it.

One consequence of the assassination attempt had, according to media reports, increased Hussain's popularity: it seems taking a couple of bullets is good for personal PR.

Womach's yet undisclosed ambition of standing as state governor next year came a step closer too. His fighting fund was close to target. With his growing reputation for caring for the poor, the under-privileged, women's rights and minorities – at home and abroad – support for his candidacy would snowball. Sure, former film star Ronald Reagan was popular, but a Republican. And there's more dirt to come out on Nixon's bugging of the Democrat's office in Washington DC's Watergate complex. Everybody wants out of Vietnam too. Our brave boys are dying needlessly and getting nowhere against the Viet Cong. That recent photo of a little naked Vietnamese girl running out of her napalmed village – splashed on every front page and TV news show worldwide – has really turned public opinion. That'll mean more anti-war votes for me, Womach thought. And the aid we could pour into Nam post war…

'You can tell your friends in Rangoon, Farook, they've done a great job sending us these refugees. All those pictures and stories of suffering raised millions is a few days. And I hear the UN agencies will be chipping in extra.'

'If those Burmese generals were smarter and opened up a bit, they could join in the aid gravy train,' Hussain said. 'But for some reason they think it's better to cut themselves off from the rest of the world. Oh well, more for us, Thomas, eh?'

'As the astronauts say, Farook, "Affirmative".'

Womach offered Hussain another peg of vodka before topping up his own glass. Hussain refused but accepted a stick of gum.

FORTY-ONE

Ben's failed bid to smuggle Khalida to India, his subsequent arrest and incarceration, had both distracted and prevented him from fulfilling a promise. With the threat of expulsion from the country, he had only days to keep his word. He had assured Faiyaz and Sana, her cousin, that he would 'do something' about Womach's assault in Mohpur's clinic. But what he would do, what he could do, remained unanswered.

Ayesha asked Khalida's mother if she had the telephone number of the Hussain's house in Dhanmandi. Despite her reluctance, and after talking through the situation with her parents, Ayesha had decided to ask a favour of Mrs Hussain: could she help have Ben's expulsion order rescinded. She must know her husband's deputy and other ministers.

Four days after the assassination attempt, the newspapers however reported Farook Hussain was already sitting up in bed. The *Bangladesh Times* claimed he was 'directing ministerial affairs from the hospital'. Obsequious reporting across the media said he would be returning to work full time '…far earlier than expected owing to his remarkable resilience and eagerness to serve the new nation'.

If true, thought Ayesha, he could surely instruct an aide or make a simple call ordering Ben's ban be reversed. But the number Fazana Chowdhury had been given by Beno Hussain was never answered. Frustratingly, it just rang and rang. Perhaps it was the wrong number, she told Ayesha. Perhaps I wrote it down wrong.

Despite Khalida's reassuring words that she was resigned to marry Maz, Mrs Chowdhury harboured the belief that the Hussains were keeping her daughter in purdah against her will. Her view was shared by Ayesha. Khalida had not called her mother nor her best friend. Mrs Chowdhury had shared the secret that the marriage had already happened, the nikah-nāmah signed, the reception a sham show. And Fazana Chowdhury cried herself to sleep every night, fearful for her daughter in the grip of the Hussains. Oh, if only my husband were alive...

After calling the number several times with no response from the Hussain household, Ayesha suddenly declared over dinner, 'I'll go to the house. I'll call on the way to college in the morning.'

'I'll come too,' Bushra said. 'I'd love to look around that place. Someone said they have real gold taps in the bathrooms. And see Khalida again, of course.'

'There'll be no time for that,' Ayesha snapped. 'Remember I have the first of my end of year exams at ten. It will be a quick word on the doorstep.'

'I'm still not sure it's the right way to go about it,' Ben said hesitantly. 'It links you all with me.'

'The authorities already know the connection. After all, you gave them this address as your residence. So, I can't see any alternative but to ask directly. You've phoned the ministry. They said they can't help. As things currently stand, by midnight on the sixteenth of December, a week on Saturday, you must be off Bangladeshi soil.'

'Or you'll be in the slammer again.' Everyone gave Bushra a stern look. She returned her attention to the sour lentil soup.

'Ben, Ayesha is correct,' Dr Rahman said. 'The order to have you expelled clearly came from someone quite senior.'

'Probably from the police chief who interrogated you in Jessore,' Mrs Rahman added. 'Or from the prison authorities. Alternatively, it could simply be an automatic procedure following your arrest.'

'Therefore, Ben,' Dr Rahman said, 'the only way that order can be rescinded is by someone more senior.'

'As Ayesha is Hussain's life-saving angel of mercy, he can't refuse,' Bushra added enthusiastically.

'He can refuse,' Mrs Rahman said.

'He might refuse,' Dr Rahman said.

'But he shouldn't,' Bushra said. Her family agreed.

'One fact is for certain,' Ayesha asserted. 'If we don't ask, Hussain won't have the opportunity to say "Yes".'

Natcoo and Ali arrived and served the main course, the gomange bhoona, accompanied by simple atap chaul, rosewater-fragranced rice and a stack of chapati. Knives, forks and spoons were always laid out on the long hardwood table. But the family, including Ben, depending on what had been served, generally maintained the tradition of eating with the right hand. Natcoo and Ali stood back watching the family to see if they required anything else.

'Mr Ben, you like?' Ali asked, stood with his hands behind his back. 'Better than prison meal?'

It continued to amaze Ben that Ali remained so thin. He made dish after dish of delicious food with ghee and yoghurt and sugar, but a spare ounce of fat could not be seen on him. Most chefs, surely, would be nibbling away putting on the pounds – checking, of course, for the right balance of herbs, spices, salt and pepper.

Ben pretended to think carefully about his answer. He turned as if consulting with the family: their faces remained uncommitted. He was on his own. He then glanced at Natcoo, stood slightly behind Ali smiling. Natcoo shook his head, indicating that Ben should continue the charade that Ali's cooking was only marginally better than prison fare.

'Ali,' Ben paused for maximum attention. 'This is the...' He paused again. '...the best meal I've ever had. It's the best of your best.'

Ali's face beamed with joy. 'Thank you, Mr Ben.' He turned to his old friend Natcoo with an expression of pride and satisfaction. Natcoo feigned a frown.

'If I'm forced to leave your country, Ali, can I take you with me? Because wherever I go, I will never find food as delicious as the meals you make.'

Natcoo and Ali left the dining room speaking what Ayesha called 'street Bengali' so fast and enthusiastically Ben could hardly recognise a word.

Everyone smiled and enjoyed the slow-fried beef curry.

After dabbing her lips with her napkin, Mrs Rahman said, 'I'm sure you know, Ben, Saturday the sixteenth of December is very significant for us all in Bangladesh.'

'Yes, it's the country's first birthday. I noticed a lot of preparations are underway to celebrate.'

MRS BENO HUSSAIN entered the elegant hallway to greet Ayesha.

'Well, this is a pleasant surprise.'

'This is my younger sister, Bushra.'

'Yes, I can see you're very much alike.'

Ayesha, aware her father was waiting in the car with Ben, and thinking of her impending examination, cut to the chase. 'Mrs Hussain, I know this is probably the wrong thing to do, but I need your help. If you can, possibly.'

Beno Hussain raised an eyebrow.

'My…' Ayesha hesitated before starting afresh. 'A friend of our family, an Englishman, has been told to quit the country by midnight next Saturday.'

'Ah, yes,' Mrs Hussain said, her tone turning less friendly. 'That would be the chap who tried to take Khalida to India.'

'Yes,' Ayesha sighed, embarrassed.

'I understand he conducted himself very badly: resisted arrest, deceived the police, stole the charity's car…'

'That's not true, Mrs Hussain,' interrupted Bushra. 'That was all made up…'

Mrs Hussain jolted at Bushra's outburst.

'Please, Bushra,' said Ayesha, turning and shooting a warning stare at her sister, 'this not the time nor place to get into what exactly happened and why.'

Bushra pursed her lips but retained a determined stance.

'Agreed,' Mrs Hussain said firmly. 'That's all in the past and, thankfully, Khalida saw sense and decided that marriage to Mazharul was the sensible option.'

'Yes.' Ayesha accepted Mrs Hussain's statement softly.

'So, Ayesha, I suppose you want me to ask my husband if he can cancel the expulsion order for this young man. Am I right?'

'Yes, Mrs Hussain. I would be most grateful.' Ayesha realised immediately she should have used 'we' not 'I'. But to correct it would compound, perhaps highlight, her error.

'Is he, shall we say, a special friend?' Mrs Hussain placed a discreet emphasis on "special" and presented an expressionless face. But her eyes burned into Ayesha.

Ayesha knew exactly what the question implied. She could have equally asked outright if they were having sex. But Ayesha faced a problem. She didn't know if Khalida had mentioned their relationship. And if she had, did she indicate how close they were? Perhaps Khalida simply said that Ben was known because he worked alongside Dr Rahman with Biharis. Ben was merely an acquaintance. But then, surely, it would be her father here now making the request for Ben to be allowed to stay. And knowing how minister Hussain professed his devotion to Islam, but not knowing Mrs Hussain's attitude to a possible intimate relationship with a non-Muslim man, made it difficult for Ayesha to pitch the right response.

'Our father, Dr Rahman, thinks very highly of him. He saw how he improved the lives of many in the camp at Mohpur.'

Bushra, never one to keep out of any discussion for long, chipped in. 'And he's looking to work with one of the big aid charities here...'

'Yes,' Ayesha latched onto Bushra's cue, 'he knows a great deal about delivering aid programmes, accessing clean water, public hygiene and so on. He genuinely wants to help many of the poorer people in our country.'

Mrs Hussain did not seem overly impressed, but said, 'Of course I'll ask my husband. It's the least I can do considering your action saved his life.'

'Oh, thank you,' Ayesha said, perhaps too enthusiastically for a mere aid worker known to the family.

'Yes, thanks so much,' gushed Bushra.

'Before you young ladies get carried away, however, I must say I can ask. But it will be my husband and perhaps others to decide. They may have other details, legal reasons, why, er...?'

'Ben. Benjamin Altringham.'

'...why this young man has been asked to leave the country.'

'Yes, of course, Mrs Rahman, I understand.'

'And husbands don't always take notice of their wives,' Mrs Rahman smiled. 'As one day you may both discover. Would you like to see Khalida?'

The question took Ayesha and Bushra by surprise. They, like Mrs Chowdhury, had the feeling that Khalida had been hidden away.

Mrs Hussain waved her hand at the manservant hovering near the steps. 'Pawa Khalida,' she ordered, and he scurried down the long hallway. Ayesha, conscious of the time, anxious about her exam, wanted to get away. But she wasn't going to relinquish this opportunity to see her best friend. Eventually Khalida came into view walking gracefully towards Ayesha and Bushra. She appeared every inch a mature, married, contented woman, not the carefree medical student of earlier days. They embraced and exchanged small-talk for a minute – fully aware of Mrs Hussain's sharp eyes and sensitive ears in the background.

'Khalida, I'm so sorry, but we've really got to go.'

'Yes,' Bushra piped up. 'She has her first year-end exam… in about an hour!'

Mrs Hussain stepped forward. 'You must call in again, Ayesha. And Bushra. Perhaps a little more notice next time.'

'Yes, sorry for the intrusion,' Ayesha said. 'Before we go, I must ask, how is Mr Hussain? The news reports say he's making good progress, healing faster than expected.'

'Thank you for asking. Yes, he's doing remarkable well. And thank you again for… well, you know…'

Ayesha and Bushra hugged their goodbyes with Khalida and shook hands with Mrs Hussain.

The sisters returned down the long gravel path to the front gate. The marquee and all the wedding decorations had been removed. A chill ran down Ayesha's spine when she looked to the spot where the shooting took place. Ben was right: I could so easily have been a victim. Luck was on my side. The lawn looked as lush as ever, the pools of bright red blood absorbed through the blades of bright green grass.

'Hey, Ayesha, Mrs Hussain isn't the horrible ogre you'd painted her.'

'Maybe. But let's not be hoodwinked. She's as tough as old boots,' Ayesha said. 'I wonder if Khalida is playing for time, being acquiescent until the right moment to get away.'

'I didn't get that impression,' said Bushra.

'But notice how Mrs Hussain watched her like a hawk. Khalida wouldn't be silly enough to give us any sign other than that she was completely content while being observed so closely.'

Halfway to the gate, Bushra asked, 'Is it possible, Ayesha, that you can still have feelings for someone who raped you? Could Khalida still like Maz, love him, even after what he did to her?'

'Wow, that's quite a question to handle from my baby sister.'

'Well, my wise old wrinkly sis, what's the answer?'

'I don't know. Perhaps some women do forgive, although they shouldn't. And others don't. Can't. Khalida will never forget what Maz did, even if she does forgive.'

One of the two armed policemen on guard at the Hussains' front entrance opened the gate. Dr Rahman had parked about twenty-five yards away. Ayesha could see Ben in the front passenger seat fingering his watch. He was reminding her she had about forty-five minutes to be at college: an unnecessary prompt. Dr Rahman was also due at Dacca Medical College, invigilating at the final year students' exam in the main hall.

'Mrs Hussain's agreed to ask her husband if he'll rescind your expulsion order,' Ayesha said as her father drove off. 'But she stressed the decision would be his and perhaps others to make.'

TENSION WAS PALPABLE as Dr Rahman, Ayesha, Bushra and Ben entered the college's cavernous atrium, alive with the buzz of hundreds of students. Many faced a tough day. Some appeared supremely confident. Over-confident, or simply concealing their anxiety? Others stood to the side soaking up last-minute information from textbooks, perhaps hoping it would push them to a pass grade.

'Good luck, Ayesha,' Ben said, desperate to hug her but had to maintain a respectable distance.

'You'll walk it, you always do,' Bushra added before hugging her sister without any such inhibitions.

'Er, doubt it. You may have noticed I've had a few distractions recently.' Her eyes widened towards Ben.

Ayesha wanted to kiss Ben, hold him tight. But this was Dacca, not New York, not London. Certainly not Paris. She'd read novels. She knew lovers in America and Britain and France kissed openly in the street. But perhaps displays of affection in public are wrong. Maybe my culture is correct, my religion right. Intimate moments should be conducted behind closed doors. Privacy makes them special, more precious.

In public, to all outside the Rahman household, Ayesha's close relationship with Ben remained a secret, distance and decorum strictly observed. But body language linguists would easily interpret the signs of affection, even intimacy.

People had watched the Rahman family walking together down the road or in the market with the white man in tow – the foreigner, a *videshi*, the Englishman, an *Ingrejra*. Most were mildly curious or totally unconcerned. But a few fired glares of unequivocal hostility, mainly huddles of unoccupied young men stood on the street.

Ayesha said these frustrated fellows think they own us women, as if we have no choice, and they have exclusive rights. The Rahmans were angered by this chauvinism and racism. Ayesha told Ben she was ashamed of these people, their taunts and snide remarks as they passed by. But it's not just about skin colour, she had argued. See how some Bangladeshis display blind prejudice towards Biharis right here on our doorstep.

But this was no time to linger. An exam loomed. Ayesha turned on her heels and joined a group of fellow students who walked to their classroom. Her father limped towards the main hall to help supervise the fifth-year students' finals.

THE MOTOR-RICKSHAW stopped to drop off Bushra at Dacca University. She bounced out displaying her usual bubbly carefree self, delighted it was for her a day without exams. Ben remained seated: he had another destination in mind. It was the perfect December day in Dacca, warm without the humidity, a cloudless cobalt-blue sky, a whispering breeze to help the palms wave gently.

'You know, Ben, this place was founded in 1921 by the British.' Bushra pointed to the university's imposing red-brick frontage. 'I think the Brits were trying to buy off the East Bengalis with it. Gandhi had come back from South Africa and started agitating against the 1919 Rowlatt Act.' Bushra stopped suddenly. She looked boldly at Ben, challenging him to respond.

'And you're going to tell me what that was, Bushra, because you know I don't know.'

'Correct.' Bushra looked pleased with herself. She took a deep breath and continued. 'After the First World War the Brits wanted to maintain special wartime powers.' She stopped abruptly again.

'Go on,' Ben sighed and adopted a weary face.

'Yes, thank you, I shall. This act aimed to repress what they claimed was terrorist activity across India.' She paused again for Ben to react. He didn't. She continued. 'But all the act achieved was to arouse even greater opposition among Indian nationalists that wanted the Brits out. Some bright spark in London thought, ah, if we build a nice university in East Bengal, it will keep that lot quiet.'

'But it didn't. Look, Bushra, you can educate me further, this evening perhaps. But now I've an appointment.'

'With?'

'Aid International. I've an outstanding matter that needs resolving.'

'And that is?'

'Sometimes, Bushra, you're a bit too nosey.'

'But that's why I know so much. If you ask questions, you get answers. Well, when people cooperate.' She smiled cheekily. 'Oh, by the way, I've been meaning to say, as you're clearly going to become my brother-in-law and I'm going to be the best aunt to your six if not more kids, you may call me sister. Cheerio!'

Ben's breath was taken away by her audacity. Before he had chance to respond, Bushra had spun around, waved to a gang of friends and jauntily walked off towards them.

Ben, bemused, enjoyed his light-hearted spats with Bushra. He was both daunted and impressed by her knowledge of geopolitics and history, particular in one so young. But politics in Bangladesh is raw. It has a direct and immediate influence on daily life. Often a matter of life and death, as the War of Liberation so recently demonstrated. That's why, Ben thought, far more people, young and old, are more politically aware here than back in Britain with its stable democracy.

But it was now time for more serious matters. He told the motor rickshaw-wallah where he'd like to go. '*Doya kore, chalok, ami jete chai Hotel Intercontinental*', Ben said, pleased he remembered the Bengali for driver, chalok. The rickshaw-wallah made a sharp turn back down Fuller Road towards Racecourse Road before bearing left northwards to the Intercontinental, about a mile further on.

FORTY-TWO

Aid International consultant Pete Conan stood at the long bar. It wasn't quite 10 o'clock, but if you want a beer, have a beer. It was one of the few places in Dacca where you could buy a decent drink, despite the exorbitant price. Being a regular over recent weeks, the barman didn't need to ask which room the American's drink should be charged to. Before raising his arm, Conan watched the condensation form on the outside of the tall glass. He closely studied the tiny bubbles racing to the frothy top. He played a little game in his mind: the longer I wait for the first sip, the better it will taste. But he never waited for long, his resistance was weak, the temptation too strong.

Conan's contemplation ended the moment he saw Ben Altringham striding towards him. But there was no back door. No get-away. Conan braced himself.

'You lied!'

'Hang on there, fella.'

'You told the police in Jessore I'd stolen the Land Rover.'

'Thomas said you'd been dismissed. That's all I told the cops. And if you were no longer employed by us, the truck wasn't yours. I was just following orders.'

'That's what Hitler's cronies claimed at their trial in Nuremberg.'

'Have a beer, Ben, calm down.'

'Calm down? Are you joking? I spent a over a week in prison because of you — well, Womach — and I've been told to quit the country.'

'Yeah, well I'm sorry about that. But we heard you were using our vehicle to smuggle some girl you made pregnant out of the country.'

'There you go again, another lie. I didn't get her pregnant. That was… well, someone else.'

'If it wasn't your kid she was pregnant with, then it was even more crazy of you to get involved.'

As things turned out, Ben agreed with Conan, but didn't give him the satisfaction of saying so. He had acted impetuously. That was undeniable. And the outcome could have been far worse than a few days in jail and an expulsion order. What drove him to be so hot-headed? Feeling sorry for Khalida's plight played a part. But after endless hours of reflection in his prison cell, he had to accept his action was more to impress Ayesha. His heart ruled his head. Love turned out to be land he didn't know until he stepped on it.

Ben changed the subject. 'I see you have a new driver. He was out there stood smoking next to your car.'

'Yeah, your guy from up Mohpur. He's not quite as reckless as most of the drivers here. Most of 'em drive like idiots and shout "Inshallah" – it's God's will or something like that – as if the goddam steering wheel isn't in their hands.'

'Let me give you two facts about Syed. First, he'll be ripping you off every time he fills the car with petrol. Excuse me, gas, you Americans call it. He certainly did when he used his cousin's garage in Tungipur. I didn't realise the true price of fuel until I drove to Jessore and had to fill up myself.'

'Thanks, Ben, I'll keep an eye on him. And the second fact?'

'He's a lousy spy. It was blatantly obvious after your visits to the camp how more – shall we say curious? – he became about where I was going, who I was seeing and why.'

Pete Conan flashed a knowing smile before swallowing a mouthful of beer.

'And I'll tell you a fact, Ben.' Conan turned to his glass on the bar again and gulped another mouthful. Without turning to face Ben, talking to his beer, he said mockingly, 'Syed was observant enough to know that you screwed that doctor's girl in that shitty hovel of a bungalow you lived in.'

Ben clenched both fists, tightened his jaw, but somehow – somehow – refrained from striking Conan. The American had

253

touched a raw nerve. Insulted his genuine love of Ayesha. Turned their first meaningful love-making, something beautiful, into trivial sleazy sex.

'Is Womach upstairs in the office?' Ben hissed. It was a test question because he knew the answer.

'No. He's out with important people doing things that you and your crummy outfit Action Delta couldn't do.'

'Guess what? I don't believe you. Can't help noticing that big black shiny Mercedes parked over there.'

'So?'

'The guy on reception assures me it's Womach's. He also mentioned that five minutes before I arrived Womach caught the lift – excuse me again, elevator – to your office.'

WOMACH HEARD THE raised voices in the reception area outside his office. He knew the cause of the confrontation: Pete Conan had phoned from the bar to alert him that Ben Altringham was on his way up. 'And, Thomas, he ain't happy.'

'I've told him, Mr Womach, that you're extremely busy and he must make an appointment and…'

'It's okay, Susie, let him through. I can spare two minutes.'

Ben stepped inside Womach's spacious air-conditioned office. It was furnished with a suite of Scandinavian-style sofas and chairs, all shining chrome and cream leather. A six-foot long tank of tropical fish stood behind his desk. A shoal of leopard danios, which Ben had seen in Bangladesh's rivers, dashed between the aquatic greenery. A pair of dwarf gourami, also a local fish, hovered cautiously in the undergrowth of hairgrass. Womach's huge desk was devoid of papers or files, as if no work was conducted thereon. A heavy onyx penholder, complete with Montblanc fountainpen and ballpoint, stood to one side, seemingly more for show than for use. Only one other item adorned the desk, a so-called executive toy, a Newton's cradle. The pendulum of five round stainless steel balls apparently demonstrates a theory in physics.

'Yes,' Womach said, noticing Ben eyeing it, 'it's remarkable how that works, isn't it?'

Ben was not to be distracted. 'Have you any idea why I've come to see you?'

'I guess, Ben, you're pissed off about being fired. But we paid you up to your last day. You shouldn't have abused our trust and headed off to India with our truck. But that wasn't the half of it, was it? Trying to smuggle a local girl out to get an abortion, that was dumb, real dumb.'

Ben was itching to say Khalida was drugged and raped and faced a life of subjugation under the Hussains. But he couldn't share that information given in confidence with anyone, certainly not Womach. He said flatly, 'There was more to it than that.'

'Sure, there's always more,' Womach said, thinking he'd got the better of Ben. 'For example, I'm told under Bangladeshi law what you did was conspiracy to aid and abet murder. And you know how possessive most of these Muslim guys are over their womenfolk.'

Ben bounced back. 'Where does Bangladeshi law stand with regards to sexual assault?'

Womach's face froze. But only for a split-second before he regained his urbane composure.

'I haven't the faintest idea what you're talking about.'

'You're asking me to believe you can't remember attacking Faiyaz in the pharmacy at Mohpur. You pinned her up against the wall and groped her. Told her you'd pay for her to return to college if she'd be your resident whore here in this hotel.'

'Hey, Ben, Ben, Ben. Slow down. You've been duped. Fay… Fraz – whatever she's called – is taking you for a ride. She's making up this story in the hope of getting a fistful of dollars.'

'No, she isn't.'

'Oh yes, and she's fooled you into coming along to negotiate the price of her silence. Well, let me tell you, she's not getting a dollar, even a dime.'

'Faiyaz – her name's Faiyaz – is decent, honest, hardworking, and she's not asked for any money, nor would she.'

'If she doesn't want money, what the hell does she want? An apology?'

'No. Not even that. She never wants to see you again. It's not Faiyaz who's asking for money from you. I am. To give to her!'

Womach sniggered. 'Look, I run a highly successful multi-million dollar business worldwide. Do you really think I'm stupid enough to give money to this girl, even via you? That's an admission of guilt. And I'm not guilty. I never touched her.'

'We can keep the transaction confidential. I won't even tell Faiyaz where the money's come from – she wouldn't want anything of yours. I'll say it's come from a charity in Britain or something.'

'Sorry, no can do. You've already proved to be untrustworthy. And now your time's up.' He looked at his diamond-studded gold watch.

Ben made one last desperate plea. 'You sacked her. You assaulted her. She's destitute. She feels absolutely abused and ashamed. And that's down to you. The very least you can do Mr Womach is pay for Faiyaz to complete her pharmacy degree. Help return her confidence, pride, dignity…'

Womach stood suddenly, outraged. His face turned instantly ugly, eyes narrowed, head jutted forward, teeth bared like a pouncing pit bull. His chair on castors shot backwards crashing into the aquarium cabinet.

'Get the fuck out of here!' he shouted. 'You're not getting a cent. Neither is that bitch! And if I hear you've been spreading malicious lies about me, I'll sue the pants off you for defamation. You've probably only got two bucks in the bank, but I'll drag you through the courts and put you in debt for the rest of your miserable life. Get it? Now get out!'

Ben stood his ground, raised his voice. 'Just do the right thing, Womach. Help her get her life back together. Your attack has really disturbed her…'

'Jesus Christ! Altringham, I hardly… Look just get the hell out of here!'

The door sprung open. 'Shall I call hotel security?' Secretary Susie had heard the raised voices. She glared at Ben as if he were a bad smell.

'Don't bother, I'm going.' Ben turned back at the doorway. 'You won't get away with this, Womach.'

Womach scoffed. 'I already have.'

Ben immediately realised he'd been extremely stupid – again. Certainly impetuous. Just as the madcap scheme to liberate Khalida from the clutches of the Hussain family. Womach was right. He had got away with the assault on Faiyaz. Ben was powerless, in no position whatsoever to bring Womach to justice. Perhaps he had also made things worse for himself. Learning from Ayesha that he attended Khalida's wedding, in addition to the aid worth millions of dollars his charity was bringing into Bangladesh, it was obvious Womach had considerable political influence.

Had it been worth trying to get compensation for Faiyaz from Womach? No. He'd failed. Trying to 'do something', as he'd promised Faiyaz, was worse than doing nothing.

Why didn't I think through the situation? There were so many reasons why it was destined to fail. For starters, Faiyaz wouldn't want the police involved. Even in the unlikely event Womach's offence came to court, it would be her word against his. There's not a shred of evidence. No witnesses. And the very last thing Faiyaz would want to experience is to stand in court and recall what Womach did. She'd face fierce cross-examination on every explicit embarrassing detail. Her shame, compounded by the salacious publicity detailing the case, would be too much to endure. Her life would be in tatters, more so than now. Womach would employ the best lawyers and doubtless drop generous bribes to dodgy judges. And Faiyaz? Well, who would want to represent her? Established lawyers would not act for someone who couldn't pay; young lawyers would be told helping her would be career limiting.

FORTY-THREE

Nowel Cribb was in a meeting at the British High Commission in Dacca's central Purana Paltan district. If Ben was willing to wait, or return around midday, Mr Cribb said he could spare a few minutes.

'I'll call back at twelve,' Ben told the receptionist, then went for a walk to kill time. He also hoped to clear his head of the constant negative replays of recent weeks: the aborted mission to Jessore, his arrest, imprisonment, the expulsion order, the encounter with Conan and Womach less than an hour ago. Unlike debt, regrets can't be redeemed. Time may diminish Ben's sense of failure and foolishness, but never wipe his conscience clean.

He ambled along Topkhana Road towards Dacca Medical College and Hospital. With each step he was moving towards Ayesha. The closer he was to her, the better he would feel. For now. But if she failed to achieve her usual high marks in this exam – if not the highest – he'd blame himself. Worse, she and her family might blame him too. Another regret to add to his list of regrets.

Khalida's rape, pregnancy, disappearance, aborted rescue and the expulsion order had distracted Ayesha from her studies. Their own ever-closer relationship and his imprisonment caused her stress too. Even their love-making must have played on her mind. Perhaps the shooting at the wedding reception proved to be the last straw: how could she possibly focus on her studies after witnessing that horror and administering first aid to several bullet-torn casualties?

Ben remained confident that Ayesha would pass the exam. There was no danger of her failing to reach a pass mark. She was always ahead of the game. But she would consider anything but the highest marks disappointing. Second-best to Ayesha constituted failure.

As always in central Dacca, crowded streets bustled with food sellers and street vendors. Even in the relatively prosperous thoroughfares bullock carts – used on the Indian subcontinent for millennia – lumbered on alongside rickshaws, cyclists, cars, trucks and buses, invariably grossly overloaded with goods and people. Two, sometimes three people on one bicycle, passengers clinging to the side of a bus or sat on its roof, were not unusual sights.

Goats, hens, crows and vultures shared searching mounds of litter with street-dwellers. Some of the women, carrying a child on their hip, rummaged with their one free arm. Others carried a baby cocooned on their back. And if their child could walk, they could work. Dangerous work. The rat-infested mountains of waste were covered in broken glass and scraps of sharp-edged metal, besides rotting food and plastic sheeting, bags and bottles. On a good day, tip-wallahs may gather enough scrap metal to secure the price of a bowl of rice. On a lucky day, they might salvage a discarded item, such as an electric fan or an old suitcase. They'd receive an extra scoop of rice or dal if their gangmaster deemed the item repairable.

Twig-thin sinewy cycle rickshaw-wallahs, sweat trickling down their faces and dripping from their armpits, came alongside Ben asking if he wanted their services. Not many foreigners walked the roads in Dacca. He'd be a good fare. Rich pickings. They'd charge twice the price and get a bigger tip than any locals would pay. He turned them away and kept walking.

Thirsty, he stopped to buy a sugarcane drink. '*Koto dam?*' Ben asked. Although the standard price was twenty-five pice – one-quarter of a taka – the cane-wallah asked for two taka. Ben protested and threatened to walk away. The price was halved. Ben complained again, asking the street-vendor why he overcharged foreigners. He shrugged his shoulders. Ben of course knew the answer: because even at eight times the price, it was, for foreigners, dirt cheap.

On the black market the going rate was around seventy taka to the pound. Ben and the cane-wallah agreed on fifty pice, twice the standard price. Delighted with the deal, the seller grabbed three or four sticks and fed them into his old black wrought-iron mangle. It reminded Ben of the Victorian mangle his grandmother used in the cellar of her back-to-back terraced house in Newcastle upon Tyne: two wooden rollers squeezed excess water from clothes every Monday, washing day. The cane juice oozed into a glass which he handed to Ben, flies already buzzing around its rim to suck the nectar.

Beggars always made a beeline for foreigners. They know even the poorest is rich in comparison. Several flocked around Ben, all with an upturned hand in front of his face. He found it harder not to give than to share a few coins. But everyone, including Abi, Ayesha, Bushra, even Dr Rahman, advised against giving to street beggars. 'Their pimps will be watching, and it will be taken off them,' Mrs Rahman once said. Dr Rahman added, 'It is required of every Muslim to give charity, and we do, but rarely in the street.' Ben also found that, as in Nigeria, if he gave to one, more beggars would suddenly appear seemingly from nowhere and become even more demanding, occasionally aggressive.

Ben reached the well-kept gardens surrounding the front of Ayesha's college. The quadrangle felt tranquil, despite the rumble of traffic in the background. Palm trees acted like Praetorian guards around the grounds. Tall, firm and imposing, protecting the inner borders of delicate hedges and colourful flowers. Ben stood gazing at the imposing brick building. He tried to sense which room Ayesha was in, as if his mind's eye were a divining rod, a forked stick of willow or witch hazel twitching towards her. He couldn't of course detect where she was in the building. Fully aware his behaviour was irrational, telepathy illogical, he nevertheless whispered, 'Good luck, my love'.

He glanced at his watch, a cheap Timex, unreliable after water had penetrated the mechanism. But if correct, he needed to rush the mile-long journey back to the British High Commission. Time had passed quickly while deep in his thoughts. Conveniently plenty of motor and cycle rickshaw-wallahs waylaid him on Secretariat Road eager for his custom. He took the auto-rickshaw, a tuk-tuk, belching smoke from the two-stroke engine, as the majority did. Ben could never shed the guilt he felt sat behind a cycle rickshaw-wallah sweating and straining every sinew and muscle pedalling him. He knew it was their job, they wanted the work, but still… at least his tuk-tuk driver had engine-power.

BEN TOLD NOWEL Cribb he had confronted Thomas Womach over the assault on Faiyaz. But it had achieved nothing, apart from getting Womach angry and making him aware others knew of his assault.

Nowel agreed that it was unwise to upset Womach. 'Like so many Americans,' Nowel responded, 'he'll drag people to court at the drop of a hat. And, in total confidence, Ben, there are rumours he's used strongarm methods in the past to get what he wants.'

'Not a nice man,' Ben said. 'I saw that. A quick temper, too.'

'Regarding the assault on Faiyaz, also in confidence, that matches other reports we've received about Womach's behaviour.'

'What? Here?'

'No. In some of the places where AI has aid projects, such as Haiti, Kenya and the Philippines.'

'Why hasn't he been arrested, or banned, or someone do something to stop him?'

'Because they've hit the same brick wall as you – no hard evidence. If a complaint was made it came down to his word against theirs. The reports also usually come through third parties, like you on behalf of Faiyaz, not the victims themselves. He always targets people who are too vulnerable or frightened to say anything to the authorities. They can't trust the corrupt police, anyway. The girls or their families know police officers or officials will be paid off. Some of the girls do what he asks so they or their kids or family can get food or a roof over their head. His closest staff also appear to form a protective ring around him when he's with the girls…'

'Come to think of it, Nowel,' Ben cut in, 'that's what happened with me. One of his sidekicks, Pete Conan, kept me in the office going over some pointless paperwork when Womach went walkies.' Ben paused, thinking. 'So they knew he was going to try it on with Faiyaz?'

'That's his modus operandi, yes.'

'What a bunch of bastards!'

'There's another piece of bad news. Womach has been issued with US diplomatic papers.'

'What does that mean?'

'It means, Ben, short of murdering someone important in broad daylight in front of loads of witnesses, he's more or less untouchable. He has diplomatic immunity. And I can tell you now, despite what you hear about anti-American sentiment following their support of Pakistan in the war, America is the one country the Bangladesh government does not want to upset. Without US dollars and aid, Bangladesh will sink even deeper down the economic sewer.'

Ben turned to the main reason he came to see Nowel, could the commission help him stay in the country?

Nowel shook his head slowly.

From his report of visiting Ben in prison, the high commissioner himself was aware of the reason for Ben's arrest, imprisonment and subsequent expulsion order.

'I'm afraid, Ben, HC said your attempt to smuggle a local girl into India was, I'll use his words, "bloody foolhardy". I tried, Ben, really, to put your action into context. But HC was adamant. He will not support any appeal to rescind the expulsion order. Sorry, Ben, but it's best you know now. You need to leave before the sixteenth. That's next Saturday.'

'Thanks for confirming what I already suspected. But there is hope.'

'Really?'

'Ayesha went to see Mrs Hussain this morning, who said she would ask her husband if he would have the expulsion order overturned.'

'And because Ayesha helped save the minister's life, you're hopeful he'll return the favour by letting you stay.'

'Exactly.'

'WHAT, NO BASKET of fruit this time, Thomas? Good. If it's true you are what you eat, I've turned into a grape over the past few days.'

Hussain sat up cheerfully in his hospital bed, this time unaided by Sister Agatha. She was returning the stethoscope and sphygmomanometer to their rightful spot on the stainless steel trolley after taking Hussain's blood pressure. He asked, but she did not tell him the exact reading. That was for Doctor to know, not the patient, but said it was in the normal to high normal range. Hussain wasn't sure if 'high normal' was good or bad, but he didn't pursue the matter. With her ballpoint, the nurse placed the dots on his BP chart and recorded his temperature, which was normal. Hussain's pulse ran a little fast, matching his raised breathing rate. Understandable, considering the chest injury he sustained. And his obesity.

If it were up to her, Sister Agatha would ensure a diet with more fruit and vegetables and far less rice, fatty meat and sugary sweets. Perhaps more vigorous walking and less door-to-door chauffeur-driven limousine usage would also be beneficial to his health. Unfortunately, she concluded, the doctors at PG Hospital were too sycophantic towards the minister to tell him the necessary truth. And it was not her place to interfere.

'I shall bring tea at four o'clock, Mr Hussain,' Sister Agatha said walking briskly across the room.

'And a few biscuits, Sister?' He knew the question made her bristle.

'Doctor said one or two would be sufficient, Mr Hussain.'

At the door, about to leave, she explicitly eyeballed Womach's briefcase. She was making it crystal clear that she knew where he concealed the alcohol. Their arrogance to think she wouldn't notice her patient had consumed liquor during his last visit annoyed her. Sister Agatha assumed it was vodka: always hard to detect, especially after chewing gum. It was definitely not whiskey, mercifully.

The smell of that would evoke nightmare memories of her father in Cork, Ireland. It was usually Saturday afternoon. Pay day at the docks. He'd stagger in the terrace cottage reeking of the evil fumes. Yet again he'd squandered most of his meagre wages on whiskey in the pubs. Mother complained, always, knowing she'd face his leather belt while he screamed the devil's language. All seven hungry kids would cry or scream, 'Stop it, da!' But he'd turn and growl, 'Shut yer bleedin' little mouths! Or you'll get some of this too.'

He'd hold out his belt towards us, terrifying my six younger siblings.

She had often thought of driving a knife into his heart while he slept off the liquor. She'd swing for it. But it would save ma and the kids. But Mary, her name then, could never rid her mind of God's commandment: Thou shalt not kill. To atone for her sinful thought of patricide, entering The Good Shepherd convent became her pathway to redemption.

Sister Agatha, remembering her childhood, closed the door leaving Hussain and Womach alone. She would pray for them and their souls. And take penance for thinking ill of them.

'You're looking much better, Farook,' Womach said. 'Ready for some more of this magic medicine?'

Farook Hussain grabbed his glass from the bedside table and held it out to be filled with vodka. Womach scanned the room but couldn't find what he was looking for.'

'That cow has deliberately left only one glass,' declared Womach. 'Yours!'

Hussain sniggered. 'Now you see what I have to put up with. But she is very competent. The night nurses are more accommodating. If it wasn't for them, I'd starve. They bring me a few extras. We don't tell Sister.'

'I'll go and get another glass,' Womach said, turning.

'No need, Thomas,' Hussain said and he pointed. 'Look in that cupboard. You'll find some small plastic pots she puts my tablets in. Use one of them. Mind you, they hardly contain a mouthful.'

The two sat in silence for a minute or so, appreciating the rush of alcohol in their veins.

'Ah, I needed that,' gasped Womach after two or three mouthfuls.

'Yes, Thomas, you seem a little harassed today.'

'I had that English guy in my office just before I came here, the one we sacked at Mohpur – by the way, the building work is going well and we've managed to move out many of those Bihari guys.'

'Why did he come to see you?'

Womach lied. 'He claimed we hadn't paid him enough or settled his out-of-pockets. Which we had, right up to the day he set off to pick up your now daughter-in-law. He got very aggressive. Scared my staff to death. Thought he was going to attack me. My secretary called security to remove him from my office. She was really frightened.'

'That's a coincidence, Thomas. An hour ago my wife phoned. She said the daughters of that doctor in Tungipur called at our residence this morning. They appealed on that fellow's behalf for me to have his expulsion order rescinded.'

'I wouldn't do that, Farook. He's a trouble-maker. Mark my words.'

Hussain hesitated. Womach's description of the British fellow didn't match the intelligence reports about him he'd received from both the security services, the police in Jessore, and the prison governor. Even under duress and when provoked, he had kept a cool head, remained patient, and was polite at all times.

Hussain's face gave nothing away. 'One of the girls, the friend of Khalida, apparently told Mazharul and that stupid soldier how to stop me bleeding out. Her headscarf plugged the bleeding hole in my chest. She saved my life, Thomas. My brother, the army medic, all the doctors said. I owe her.'

'Yeah, but that's her, not the crazy Brit. Send her a bunch of flowers and a box of chocolates – and send him on his way.'

BETWEEN THE MORNING'S two examination papers, the medical students had a thirty minute refreshment break. Returning to the exam room, Ayesha casually glanced out of the corridor window. She was alarmed to see – although had to double-check it was him – Ben walking into the college grounds. *What on earth is he doing here? Is he the bearer of bad news? Has something happened to Bushra?*

But soon she could tell he wasn't rushed or concerned, just ambling around, seemingly aimless. Then he looked up towards her, almost as if he could see her through the window. But at that distance, and with her standing back from the window, that was impossible. He couldn't have known she was there, nor at that specific moment. Then he turned and walked briskly towards Secretariat Road. *Strange,* she thought.

By now everyone was rushing back to the exam room. There was no time whatsoever to go and quiz him. She'd find out later what he was doing in the college grounds. Ayesha must focus on facing the morning's second paper.

When she turned it over, she smiled: the nervous system was her strongest subject. And she knew the examination sequence of the twelve cranial nerves off by heart, starting with the olfactory. For her, it was a far more favourable set of questions than the earlier paper.

FORTY-FOUR

That evening at the Rahman family dining table, Bushra conducted an animated discussion with her mother about the proposed new constitution for Bangladesh. Knowledgeable about drafting legislation with her background in law, Raina Rahman informed her daughter how the changes could affect the country. Dr Rahman, Ayesha and Ben seemed to have other matters on their minds and completed eating their sour lentil soup in silence.

Raina and Bushra agreed a secular, socialist and non-aligned People's Republic – with no legal status for Sharia – would be better than the former status of an Islamic Republic. Islam in East Pakistan, now Bangladesh, although as sincere, seemed practised in a milder way than in West Pakistan. Bangladeshi Muslims, about eighty-five per cent of the population, were more tolerant of other religions, including the large Hindu minority of nine million, twelve per cent of the population. Christians, Buddhists and Parsees also generally enjoyed trouble-free worship in churches, monasteries and fire temples.

'Not always plain sailing though, my dear,' Mrs Rahman said. 'It was only nine years ago, in sixty-three, when our Hindus and Parsees were persecuted for a while by many hot-heads.'

'Yes, Amma, I remember. Our school was closed for a couple of days. But it was all a mistake, wasn't it?'

'Correct. It had been reported, wrongly as it turned out, that a hair said to be from Muhammad – peace be upon him – disappeared from a shrine in Srinagar. Quite a few Hindus and Buddhists were killed or beaten, many of their businesses damaged.'

'But on the whole it's good that most Bangladeshis show tolerance towards other religions, isn't it, Amma? Even Christians.' Bushra repeated, slowly, 'Even Christians.'

Bushra playfully exaggerated her smile across the table at Ben. He grinned back. He wasn't going to play this ballgame with Bushra. Well, not tonight. He wanted to declare he didn't believe in God or any gods. Ben thought such beliefs fantasies, and religions artificial constructs by egotists such as Abraham, Jesus, Muhammad and Hubbard, and their duped followers. Ben was acutely aware the Rahman family were curious about his beliefs. And they deserved his honesty, particular as he grew closer to Ayesha. But he would choose the time and place to discuss the matter. He wouldn't be goaded by Bushra, well, not this night.

Having emptied his soup bowl, Dr Rahman agreed with Bushra that the new constitution would be an improvement. But he sounded more cautious. He hoped what was written on paper would be applied in practice. He worried that some politicians might try to bring back elements of Sharia. Not to impose what they claimed was God's will, but to use – abuse – Sharia to enhance their own power.

'We certainly don't want a theocracy,' he said. 'We can be guided by God through our prayers, as can our religious leaders. But if our politicians fail to rebuild the country, people will turn more to God in the hope He will. Yet it's human hands that build dwellings, grow food, raise children, make medicine and care for the poor and sick. God is our guide. He shows the way. But we must do the legwork.'

His words stopped any debate for a few moments, allowing all to absorb and interpret them in their own way. Meanwhile Natcoo and Ali presented the evening's main dishes, batter-coated chicken and a plate stacked ten inches high with crispy Moghul parathas.

The political discussion was filibustering the one question on everyone's mind and remained unasked: Ayesha, how did your exams go today?

Previously, after an exam, Ayesha would spend the evening having a lively discussion with her father. She'd be checking if this answer would have been better than the one submitted. Was that the right term, Abba? Should I have added...? Perhaps if I'd answered...? She'd have cross-checked all her answers with her textbooks to the questions in the papers. His patience – always astonishing to Mrs Rahman and Bushra – endless. Abdur Rahman recognised that to be a competent doctor one needed intellect. But to be a great physician one also needed boundless enthusiasm, energy and compassion. His daughter possessed the full suite of attributes.

But tonight, with father to her right at the table end, and Ben to her left, Ayesha responded only in monosyllables. Everyone was thinking she is either tired or disappointed in how she tackled the exam papers. Perhaps both. She ate quietly, eyes fixed on her plate, her shoulders hunched forward, wrapping herself in herself. The aura Ayesha radiated was clear: don't ask. Everyone, even Bushra, who would usually cut through such barriers, respected Ayesha's right to a period of introspection.

FROM THE DINING room, they could hear a car's engine ticking over outside the front garden, but couldn't see it. The gate bell rang and everyone at the table waited to see who the visitor was. No one was expected, but Ben had always been pleasantly surprised how many friends and neighbours casually called in. All were made welcome, tea and refreshment generously provided every time, even when the timing was inconvenient. No invitations are required here, Dr and Mrs Rahman said, it's the traditional way. But on this occasion, whoever it was in the car, declined to stay and drove away.

A few moment later Natcoo entered the dining room with a large brown oblong cardboard box.

'It is for you, Miss Ayesha. Shall I open big box for you?'

Ayesha, compelled to break her silence, replied 'Yes, please, Natcoo.'

All eyes were on him as he lifted out three gift-wrapped presents, ornately tide with ribbon. Natcoo pushed to one side Ayesha's dinner plate and placed the first parcel on the table. A small envelope was tucked under the ribbon of the larger box. For now, she declined to open it. Natcoo left the room taking the outer box away.

She turned to Ben. 'Have you sent this?'

'No.'

She crunched her eyelids, not convinced by his answer.

'Amma, Abba, did you?'

'No, my dear.'

269

'I've a great idea.' Bushra sprung up and pointed. 'Sister, dear, why don't you just open that little white envelope there and see who the present is from. I think it will be much better than this guessing game. And I can tell you now, they're not from me.' She sat back down in her chair with a sigh and her usual sardonic smile. Mrs Rahman gave her younger daughter the usual look of exasperation.

Ayesha read the note, first to herself, then aloud:

Dear Miss Rahman, no words can adequately express my deepest gratitude to you. But for your swift, decisive and expert action following the shooting at the wedding, I would not be alive to give you my thanks. Khalida tells me you would not expect nor welcome a reward. But I trust you can accept these small grossly inadequate tokens of my grateful thanks.

May Allah keep you safe,

Farook Hussain.

PS: I trust today's decision also meets your approval.

'Hmm, don't know what that refers to,' Ayesha said before being loudly interrupted.

'Swiss! Swiss chocolates. A huge trayful,' Bushra yelled as Ayesha ripped away the bright green wrapping. 'Let's open them now.' Bushra rushed around the table to stand behind her sister. 'We all should have at least one...'

Mrs Rahman intervened. 'Bushra, don't be impatient. It's for Ayesha to decide when she wants to open the box. And she might decide not to give you one.'

'What do you think, Ben?' Bushra asked. 'Chocs now or later?'

'I agree with your mother.'

'Scaredy cat! You dare not disagree with Ma.'

'I also always agree with you, Bushra.'

'Touché!'

'But we have Ali's paesh to come,' Ayesha said turning to face Ben. 'Your favourite.'

'Rice pudding will keep for tomorrow,' Mrs Rahman said. 'And it's equally nice cold.'

'We could have pud *and* chocolates!' enthused Bushra.

Unwrapping the smaller parcel, Ayesha said, 'I think I know what this will be.'

'Oh, it's beautiful,' Mrs Rahman observed as Ayesha draped the headscarf over both arms.

'This is even better than the one I wore to Khalida's wedding reception.'

'And in the large box?' asked Bushra.

Ayesha opened it to see a beautiful sari, no doubt to replace her blood-stained one, which had to be destroyed. But her initial instinct was to give it away: she didn't wish to be wrapped in clothing from Hussain.

Natcoo returned to the dining room, his flip-flops as always announcing his approach along the tiled floor. Everyone expected to see him with his large tray with the pot of paesh. But instead he was carrying his small round silver tray. Ben had only seen it used for the post and the newspapers.

'It is for you Mr Ben,' Natcoo said. 'Special delivery from minister. Driver said must give to you. Came with box for Miss Ayesha, but I left in kitchen. Sorry for delay.'

Ayesha took in a deep breath. She clutched her chest, still holding the silk scarf. The room fell silent. Bushra returned to her seat.

Ben removed the envelope thanking Natcoo, who took one step back and stood still. He too was anxious to hear the news.

For a few moments, everyone froze in anticipation. The grandfather clock's ticking the only sound, and it was still. December evenings in Bangladesh rarely needed the fans to stir the air. Ben recalled Ayesha's words from months earlier, the tick-tock of the clock made her remember *there is a past, a present, a future…*

'This is it then,' Ben said. 'The moment of truth. I'm either allowed to stay or, in five days, I have to leave you all.'

Ben lifted his unused dinner knife to slit open the envelope. Before removing the letter, he paused. 'May I say, whatever the decision, I cannot thank you enough for your amazing, generous hospitality and kindness over the past six months. You've all welcomed me into your home and hearts, I'll be devasted to leave you. And I don't know what the future holds…'

Impatient as always, Bushra quipped, 'It would help if you read the letter.' Everyone, except Ben, shushed her.

'Even you, Bushra, have made me feel at home, part of the family.' They exchanged twisted smiles. Ben turned to thank Natcoo. He was surprised to see that Ali and housemaid Buna had slipped into the dining room and stood next to Natcoo awaiting his news. 'All three of you have been so kind to me too.'

'You welcome, Mr Ben,' Ali said. 'I make special gulab jamun tomorrow.' He smiled exposing his missing tooth.

'My sister – just for once – is right,' Ayesha said. 'It would be useful to know what Hussain's letter says.'

'Yes, I know. But I just wanted to say…'

Dr Rahman interrupted, a rare event. He usually allowed everyone to finish speaking before speaking himself. As always, with his natural authority, everyone listened attentively.

'My dear Ben, we thank you for your thanks and gratitude. When you first stepped into our home – remember the monsoon rain was pounding down – you became part of it. Of course that night was soured by the horrible news about Abi's fiancé, Jonny.

'But the next day none of us will forget you put your life on the line to protect us by confronting those thugs. God knows what would have happened if you hadn't been here.'

'I suspect they'd have cleared off after breaking a couple of windows,' Ben said.

'I must disagree, Ben,' Mrs Rahman intervened. 'It was clear to us that, until you went outside, they were intent on doing far more than that.'

'And I must agree with my dear wife,' added Dr Rahman. 'And since that dreadful night there has been no subsequent attack, no threatening notes.

'There was also a special moment, and we all recognised it, when it was as clear as the midday sun that you and Ayesha had clicked. And over the years, one lesson I have learned is that love knows no boundaries. Nor should it.

'I will admit, Raina and I had our worries, particularly over whether any relationship would interfere with her medical studies.

Happily, if anything, she's concentrated even harder on them – apart from the unavoidable consequences of Khalida's situation.'

Ben unfolded the letter and glanced at the decision. Maintaining a neutral expression, he handed the letter to Ayesha.

Ayesha hugged Ben. Everyone except him saw her beaming smile. Ben felt awkward and embarrassed: it was the first time they had displayed physical contact in front of anyone. Ayesha also realised she'd crossed a line. It was hard to gauge what her father and mother thought. Bushra's happy damp eyes however showed sisterly solidarity. Natcoo, Ali and Buna added their smiles of approval too. Not that anyone now needed words to reveal the contents of the minister's letter. Nevertheless, Ayesha gleefully announced, 'Hussain has had the home minister rescind his expulsion order. Ben's staying!'

FORTY-FIVE

'The hospital called, Tom, he didn't make it,' Pete Conan announced in Womach's suite at the Intercontinental. 'They couldn't revive him. Some big artery coming out of his heart just burst wide open, the doc said.'

Womach had his back to Conan while feeding his leopard danios and dwarf gourami.

'It's his own fault,' Womach scoffed, continuing to watch his fish. 'Never took exercise. Ate like a pig. Drank like one of these.'

'Do fish drink?' quizzed Conan.

'Have you let his wife know?'

'I think she'd appreciate a call from you, Tom, rather than me. Not that she'll be too upset, she'd already filed for a divorce. They've not got on for years. Giving her a dose of clap was the last straw.'

Womach laughed. 'Yeah, Bob was never too choosy. Some of those girls in Haiti…'

'I'll miss him, though,' Conan said.

'Jesus Christ, Pete, don't go all goddam sentimental on me.'

Robert Beck had worked for Womach since he established his charity business. He was one of the inner circle, a handful of trusted associates. Womach's 'consultants' received generous compensation packages, lived a lavish lifestyle of luxury hotels, private yachts and first class flights. In the US, the company's jet was at their disposal. *For executive efficiency to help even more impoverished people around the world,'* was the PR spin. Americans understood and accepted this practice. Elsewhere, even in Europe, charity workers using anything but basic hotels and economy class travel were frowned upon.

Nobody could deny Aid International provided food, medicines, blankets, clothing and emergency accommodation for thousands of the world's poorest. When disaster struck – floods, hurricanes, earthquakes, tsunamis, famines, refugee crises – AI would be one of the first charity organisations at the scene. They routinely beat UN agencies to the front line. That wasn't hard. The voluntary aid sector was generally disappointed in the tardy bureaucratic response of the UN agencies in humanitarian crises.

But alongside AI's aid work ran the business closest to Womach's ambitions: high political office. Correction: the highest political office. And because those closest to Womach – his lawyer, accountant and the consultants – received extremely high rewards, they were not going to kill the goose that laid golden eggs. Womach's top team also knew even greater rewards were to follow once he came into office, first in New Mexico, then, possibly, Washington DC. Several long-standing senior senators, whom he had generously supported over the years, constantly advised Womach on how best to climb the greasy political pole. It was pay-back time for them.

The public relations firm Womach used in New York suspected there was more to AI than pure altruism. Certain commissions, such as arranging meetings on privately-owned islands in the Caribbean and the Philippines, didn't appear to match a charity's role as a humanitarian aid agency. But when over eighty per cent of your income comes from this one client – and unlike most clients AI pay their bills on time without quibbling – it's best not to ask awkward questions. If they want the best wines, champagne, genuine beluga caviar and hostesses flown in to ensure AI's events go smoothly, fine. It's not a PR company's job to challenge the client's inventory of requirements. Why shouldn't a charity use the same marketing techniques as movie studios, fashion houses and global corporations?

Womach turned his attention away from the tropical fish and paced the office. Conan sat playing with Newton's cradle, Womach's executive toy, swinging the outer steel balls onto the others.

'You know Hussain let that Brit stay here,' Womach said.

'Yeah, you already told me.'

'I advised him not to. Told him Altringham was a trouble-maker.'

'Why do you let that guy bother you so much? Tom, he's a nobody. He's out of our hair. You're flying home tomorrow, not back here for what... two... three months?'

'Pete, no one talks to me like Altringham did and gets away with it. Came in here demanding money for that girl. Jesus Christ, Pete, I hardly touched her. I made a quick pass. She didn't play ball. Threatened to scream the house down. I backed off and left it at that. No big deal. Stupid bitch.'

'So?'

'So, Pete, I don't want him spouting his mouth off about me.'

'No one will take any notice of what he says, Tom.'

'Problem is, you and Bob – bless his newly committed soul in hell – said he asked a lot of questions about me and our operations. You thought it was as if he'd been tipped off, asked to ask. What if he goes poking around further?'

'If what I hear is right, he's shacked up with that doctor's family in Tungipur. My driver says he's into one of the doc's daughters.'

'What? You mean really into her? Screwing her?'

'Yup.'

'What, in a Muslim family? Here, in this country? In that backward place, Tungipur? That's playing with fire, isn't it?'

'Sure is.'

Womach, deep in thought, walked to the fridge and took out two bottles of American beer. After opening them, he handed one to Conan and sat on the sofa. Conan stopped playing with Newton's cradle and came to join him on the sofa opposite.

'This driver of yours...'

'Syed,' Conan confirmed.

'He still lives in Tungipur, right?'

'Near enough. Some village.'

'He must know a few hotheads, a mad mullah or two who'd kick up rough if they knew a white English Christian was having it away with a lovely local girl. And they're not even married, right?'

'Right.'

'Tut, tut. Naughty boy. Deserves a spanking.' Womach took a mouthful of beer and swilled it around like mouthwash before swallowing. 'Get your driver to spend a day or two letting the local mullahs and all those sex-starved young hoodlums know the situation. Offer him a bonus – on condition Altringham runs into a little trouble. Some of those louts and the local mullah would appreciate a contribution too. Damn sure his mosque or house needs a bit of repair work. And those fanatics are good at whipping up their congregation into a God-loving man-hating frenzy.'

'Consider it done.'

'Your driver, can he be trusted?'

'Sure. He likes money.'

'Whatever you arrange, make absolutely certain the girl he's screwing is unharmed. If anything happened to her, Hussain would make inquiries. He'll remember I don't like Altringham and he might put two and two together. Hussain also reckons Altringham's girl saved his life. All she did was get his son to plug his bullet hole with her scarf. But she's also a close friend of his new daughter-in-law.'

'I will be discreet. As always.'

'Wait for a couple of weeks until I'm out of this shithole. Jesus Christ, Pete, this country's in a fucking mess. I can't see them ever getting on their feet. This place is going to ride the aid train for ever. But it's good for business, eh?'

'As you've always said, Tom, charities love poverty.'

Womach walked over to the fridge and took out two more beers, removed the tops and handed one to Conan.

'Every politician here wants a slice of the action, Pete. But most of 'em aren't as clever as Hussain. We have to select our partners carefully. If Farook does become prime minister, that could be even more profitable for us. But once he's banked a few more million overseas he'll resign and piss off out of the place – or get shot in a coup.'

Womach crossed the room to finish feeding his fish.

Sat back in his chair with his feet on the coffee table, watching his boss, Conan said, 'Tom, instead of all those little fish you got in there, why don't you get a nice big piranha?'

'Don't need a piranha, Pete. I got you.'

FORTY-SIX

At midnight, Ayesha knew for sure she was in love. Now, two hours later, in the deepest darkness of night, she thought she was in love. And that was the problem: she *thought*. Perhaps there is always uncertainty surrounding love. As with religion, love needs faith more than fact, heart more than mind. Or is love purely a delusion between two people, mutual self-deception, desire driving affection?

Where is the empirical evidence of love's existence? Or does love not need verification. The evidence is the experience.

Tired but restless, unable to sleep and sat bolt upright in bed, is not the best time to ask, 'Am I in love?' Friends would say, if you must ask that question, the only answer is, 'No'. In true love, one could not accept any cross-examination, any challenge, any doubt. Love is blind, isn't it?

Before the war, Ayesha went with Bushra to the cinema at Dacca University during a season of international films. Unfortunately many scenes were clumsily cut by the Pakistani censors: even a married couple couldn't be seen kissing. In *Les Enfants du Paradis*, she remembered the line, *'C'est tellement simple, l'amour'*. But love isn't simple. She also recalled some old English poet penned, *'Love's a malady without a cure.'* Indeed, Ayesha accepted she wouldn't find any reference to a disease called love in the medical textbooks.

Ayesha could faintly hear the grandfather clock tick-tocking in the hallway: perhaps love needs time. Without question she loved Amma, Abba and Bushra. Several uncles, aunts and cousins. She loved Khalida. Even Safa, Fatima and Dahab. But they had a key advantage over Ben, one element in common: time. She'd known them all her life. And they her. They were part of her being, her identity, linked by experience and memory, happiness and sadness – the bond of relationships. But loving one man, for life, hopefully for children, is different.

Being an arranged marriage, surely father and mother couldn't have loved each other when they first met? However, to use Abba's old-fashioned word, they apparently 'clicked' at their first meeting. They even managed to 'click' surrounded by all their parents and a handful of other relations. Abba had laughed when telling his daughters of their 'engagement' meeting, set up by the ghotok, the matchmaker. Ayesha was not surprised they instantly saw eye to eye: Ma was – is – beautiful, Abba handsome, and both intelligent and caring. But they must have had doubts. It was time, time itself, that changed thinking 'I like you' into saying 'I love you'.

The clock chimed the Westminster notes before striking twice. Only four hours sleep before Buna would rattle her door at six and bring her 'good morning' tea. At eight, at Dacca Medical College and Hospital, she would collect an envelope revealing the results of her end of term exams. She was not hopeful and the worry delayed her sleep further.

Earlier that evening her family, including Ben, had welcomed in New Year 1973. Dr Rahman casually mentioned during the evening however that, for Muslims, it was 1392, and not yet the Islamic New Year. Bushra quipped that this 'Christian' New Year's Day was established by European Catholics, specifically Pope Gregory, nearly four hundred years ago. Ben and her family were constantly surprised with, as Mrs Rahman put it, 'the things you come out with'.

A week earlier the Rahman household celebrated Christmas. Ben assumed the celebrations had been arranged for him. He was wrong. Very wrong. Ayesha told him so. Throughout childhood Abdur and Raina had enjoyed Christmas in Calcutta; the tradition continued with Ayesha and Bushra. Decorations were hung and presents exchanged. Bushra had received a Christmas card from her pen-pal, Sarah Goodwin, in Heswall, England. Dr Rahman received cards from friends in Britain, the United States and Australia. Ali cooked roast goose – turkeys are American, Bushra casually mentioned, although everyone was aware of that fact – and Christmas pudding and cake, without sherry or brandy. Crackers pulled contained the usual paper hats, plastic toys and corny jokes.

Dr Rahman explained to Ben on Christmas Eve while everyone helped with the decorations, 'Muslims believe Mary – Maryam in Arabic – as a chaste virgin who miraculously gave birth to Jesus. We consider Jesus not as the son of God but as the penultimate prophet, Muhammad – peace be upon him – being the ultimate, which allows me to say "peace be upon you".'

DR RAHMAN DROVE Ayesha to college to collect her exam results at eight o'clock. Ben travelled with them. He had secured an interview with the International Committee of the Red Cross. They were interested in his work with Biharis, many of whom wished to be flown from Bangladesh to either Pakistan or to the state of Bihar in India, where many Bihari families came from when Pakistan was established in 1947. But Pakistan nor India wanted ethnic Biharis from Bangladesh. Tricky negotiations needed to take place: political and economic bargaining over hundreds of thousands of lives. In Pakistan, there were also Bengalis who now wished to live in India's West Bengal or Bangladesh. Everyone seemed to know someone who wanted to traverse the subcontinent, including the Rahmans who had aunts, uncles and cousins in Karachi.

Dr Rahman said he would need a couple of hours talking through the result of any final year students who had failed their exam, or not achieved the marks they expected. Then he had a 'quick procedure' to perform on a patient at the hospital. 'Just a tonsillectomy on a young fellow who suffers recurrent bouts of tonsillitis,' he said easily. 'His father is a better surgeon than I am. But ethically, of course, he can't under normal circumstances operate on his own son. And when it comes to operating on your own child, one fears one's hand might shake with the scalpel.'

Ayesha said her lectures for the day ended at two o'clock. So it was agreed they would pick her up at two-thirty. She wished Ben good luck for his interview with the ICRC; he reciprocated regarding her results.

'Not that you need it,' he added. 'I know you've done well.'

'It's kind of you to say so, Ben,' she replied, 'although totally illogical because you have absolutely no idea how I responded to the questions.' There was a sharp edge to her tongue – a very rare cut. Was it him, something he's said, or exam results anxiety? Neither of them could tell.

'Sorry,' she said immediately. 'I didn't sleep well.'

As they watched Ayesha walk towards college through the gardens, clutching textbooks and her notepad, Dr Rahman turned and said they needed to talk. Ben agreed.

There had been growing unease over Christmas and New Year in the household. It couldn't be put stronger than that. There were no arguments, no tense silences, no unpleasantness of any kind. Everyone rubbed on well with each other as they had always done. But there was 'something in the air'. Ayesha at times was a little despondent about her impending results. But she had returned to her usual study regime following the 'distractions' of Khalida's flight to Jessore, Ben's arrest and the shooting. Bushra remained her bouncy bubbly irrepressible self.

Life became a little easier for Ben when, through a friend of Mrs Rahman, who owned a small private school, he started teaching English. He began on Monday, two days after the country celebrated its first anniversary of 'liberation' on Saturday the sixteenth of December. The job took him out of the house Monday to Thursday, eight to midday, and he thoroughly enjoyed teaching. He'd been given guidebooks for teachers and he followed the curriculum. He remembered his former wonderful English teacher and used him as a role model. The children – he was firmly informed never to call them 'kids' in front of them or their parents – were delightful, aged from eleven to sixteen. ('Kids' are young goats, the vice-principal, peering over her half-moon spectacles, had sternly informed him.)

With Ben living in the household, Dr and Mrs Rahman, understandably, wanted to know what Ben's hopes and ambitions were for the future. The current state of limbo couldn't continue. There was discomfort about the future. The word 'marriage' had been assiduously avoided. Apart from the impromptu hug Ayesha gave Ben on hearing his expulsion order had been rescinded, they had continued maintaining a respectful distance when others were present. Dr Rahman and Ben both realised decisions had to be taken, the future outlined, discussed at the very least.

'If we meet at, say, eleven-thirty,' Dr Rahman said studying his watch, 'we could enjoy a spot of tiffin at that restaurant over there.' He pointed to a dark-glass fronted establishment frequented more by medical staff, lecturers and senior administrators than students. 'It's cosy and quiet and serves excellent food.'

'Not as good as Ali's, surely?'

'They'd give him a run for his money. But, no, because Ali blends in his love for us as well as all his ingredients. He's served our family since he was a boy, and his father my father. Eleven-thirty then, inside the Sultan's Khaddyo.'

'WELL, BEN, DON'T keep me guessing.' Dr Rahman was already seated in the restaurant when Ben arrived.

'Once they check out my references, then, yes, I've got the job.'

Dr Rahman stood and offered Ben his hand. 'That's wonderful. And your position?'

'Nothing special, simply a field representative with the International Committee of the Red Cross.'

'And you're not required to fly to Geneva for any further process?'

'No, it would have been nice to have flown to Switzerland, though. I could have bought another box of chocolates.'

They placed their order with Sultan's Khaddyo's manager, who greeted Dr Rahman as an old friend.

'Before you ask,' Ben said despondently as the manager turned away towards the kitchen, 'I don't know the answer to your question,'

'That's very prescient of you, Ben,' Dr Rahman said gently. 'Pray tell, what is my question?'

'What are my…' Ben hesitated, 'my intentions regarding your amazing, beautiful daughter?' He fingered air-quotes around the word 'intentions'.

'Have a guess.'

'I can't answer simply because I don't any longer know what Ayesha wants. At one time, early on, before all the fiasco over

Khalida, the future seemed clear. I wanted to marry her; she wanted to marry me. But now?'

Tears welled in Ben's eyes. He dabbed them with the back of his hand. He swallowed deeply.

Dr Rahman paused briefly to allow Ben to recover.

'Has Ayesha said anything recently to provoke this impasse? If, indeed, that is what it is.'

'No. That's my difficulty,' Ben said. 'Perhaps it's because she's worried about this exam. At least we'll know the results later. That might clear the air. Maybe not. I just don't know. Has she said anything to you, or Mrs Rahman? She may have confided in Bushra. We know she acts silly sometimes, but we also know she's extremely intuitive when she wants to be.'

'So true. So true. It will be a very brave man who marries Bushra, eh?' Dr Rahman smiled. 'Of course, in today's modern world, perhaps she won't marry at all.'

Dr Rahman paused to sip his tea and Ben emptied his glass of lassi. Dr Rahman caught the attentive eye of the waiter to signal Ben would enjoy another drink.

'Regarding Ayesha,' Dr Rahman said, 'no, she has said nothing, certainly not to me or Raina. We have always shared any information about our daughters. Ayesha keeps her own counsel. She thinks very deeply about things. You have learnt that already.'

'Yes, it's one of the many things I admire about her.'

Dr Rahman's next question temporarily stunned Ben. He instantly knew the answer. It was simply that he didn't expect the questions to be put so directly.

'Do you love Ayesha?'

'Yes, absolutely,' he said decisively, but after a pause. He explained his hesitation when he saw doubt on Dr Rahman's face. 'Sorry, I was just surprised by your question. But of course it's the right question. It just took me by surprise. Yes, yes, I love Ayesha and, I think it's traditional, I should ask you, her father, if I may ask her to marry me.'

Dr Rahman laughed a little. The waiter arrived with Ben's lassi and a jug of fresh iced water, which interrupted the discussion.

'Kasem say food ready in five minute, Dr Rahman,' he said before greeting more customers at the door. A group of four men and two women acknowledged Dr Rahman, and he felt obliged to stand and introduce Ben to them. He stood too.

'Some of my colleagues from college and the hospital, Ben.' They all shook Ben's hand, including both women, who volunteered their greeting. 'You're in good company, Ben. If you have a heart attack this lunchtime, these chaps are cardiac specialists. Rumana is a neuro-surgeon, who, I hope, will one day tutor Ayesha…'

'Oh Abdur,' Rumana cut in, 'within a few minutes in theatre, Ayesha will be putting me to shame. I've watched her working on brain tissues, Ben. She's deft and delicate and with one distinctive advantage for a neuro-surgeon – a young pair of eyes!'

'And Nadeen,' Dr Rahman said, 'is a psychiatrist. But don't worry, we all know she's the most crazy one of all us physicians.'

They laughed and joked and said their goodbyes and went to their table.

'Sorry about that interruption, Ben. Perhaps I should have chosen another restaurant away from here.'

'It was good to meet your colleagues. It was lovely to hear what Rumana said about Ayesha.'

'Not quite true, of course. It will take Ayesha at least twenty years to get to Rumana's level of experience.'

'Now, my dear Ben, back to the matter in hand. As you have witnessed, Ayesha and Bushra are very much in control of their own lives. Raina and I have raised them to be independent, free-thinking, open minded. It's very good of you to ask me for her hand. I appreciate the respect it demonstrates. But Ayesha's hands are her own. It will be her decision into which other hands she places them. But, as you kindly asked, Raina and I would be delighted if you became our son. The decision, you understand, is however entirely Ayesha's.'

FORTY-SEVEN

Ayesha approached her father and Ben in the college's car park. They stood next to the doctor's white Volkswagen Beetle awaiting her arrival. She was nearly half an hour late. Ben interpreted this as a bad sign: I was wrong, she has dropped marks, although she can't possibly have failed. Her father appeared sanguine.

A group of students came through the gardens chatting happily and excitedly, sharing their exam results. Ayesha peeled away from her friends towards the car. She walked, elegant as always in her white blue-bordered sari, but slightly hesitant, head drooped. Ben feared the worst. He realised she would be in no mood to be formally, officially, asked if she would marry him. Certainly not on this day.

'Sorry, Abba, for being so tardy. But, you know how it is, everyone wanted to share their marks with everyone else.'

'Yes, my dear, I had predicted you'd be later than planned.'

'How did your interview go?'

Ben looked quizzically at her. Come on, Ayesha. Spill the beans. Forget about my interview. What the hell are your results? He remained on tenterhooks.

She teased, knew what he was waiting for.

'I passed!'

Ben desperately wanted to hug her. Even stepped towards her. But there were far too many students and parents around the car park. He pulled back.

'Told you,' Ben said.

'Congratulations, well done, my dear.'

'Abba, don't pretend. I know you already knew my results. Professor Huda told you this morning.'

They all laughed.

'Abdur,' Ben said, shocking Ayesha by using his first name, which he rarely did, 'you never told me! And I've been worrying all day!'

'Ah, Ben, a pleasure delayed becomes a greater pleasure when delivered. But Ayesha has more to tell you.'

She pretended to be annoyed. Stamped her foot, exhaled loudly, pursed her lips and looked sullen.

'Come on.'

'I came equal top! I'm to share the top student award for my year!'

'That's wonderful news. Let's celebrate. Ice creams all round,' Ben declared.

'The first paper was tough. Not one of us reached eighty per cent. The second paper on the CNS – that's the central nervous system, Ben – focussed on the twelve cranial nerves.'

'Just up your street,' Dr Rahman said.

'That reminds me, Mr Benjamin Altringham,' Ayesha said happily, 'I've been meaning to ask – what were you doing here on the day of my exam wandering around out here like a lost puppy?'

'I came to wish you well, what else? But how did you know?'

'I saw you. From up there. That window. Perhaps your well-wishes worked.'

'After ice creams, let's get home to share the double-good news with Amma and your sister,' Dr Rahman said. 'We also need to get ready for tonight.'

'Hmm, "double-good news"?' quizzed Ayesha. After one second thinking, 'Ben! You got the job!'

'Sure did. Start soon.'

'I'm so pleased for you, Ben.' Ayesha said, and it was her turn to restrain herself from stepping forwards into a hug. 'If you knew I would pass my exams, I was even more certain you'd walk your interview.'

'Interviews are far harder than medical exams,' Ben joked.

'You're very lucky, Mr Altringham, we're in a public place – otherwise your ribs might have caught my elbow.'

Turning her back in fake protest from Ben, Ayesha asked, 'Father, where are we going this evening?'

'Lucky House. Where else? I booked a table with Mr Ong last week. Seven o'clock. So we need to get our skates on.'

'Funny expression for here,' Ben laughed. 'When was the last time there was ice in Bangladesh?'

'Ben, my dear, haven't you heard of roller skates?'

FORTY-EIGHT

It promised to be the perfect Sunday. Dawn's sharp sunlight sliced through the Rahman's garden exaggerating the contrast between areas of light and dark. Long shadows cast by the tall palms quickly shortened as the tropical sun raced higher. Daybreak provided crisp air to breathe helping the mind think clearly. Night-scented stocks surrendered their perfume to the day flowers, as their petals unfolded to seize the sun's rays.

All was still, apart from outbursts of crows' caw-cawing and squabbling sparrows. Lemons and limes hung in the trees, many ripe for picking. Ali enjoyed a rich supply for kitchen use, especially lemon juice, lebu pani. Such is the climate and richness of Bangladeshi soil that many trees deliver fruit all year round.

Following his conversation with Dr Rahman, Ben decided to discuss with Ayesha their future. If, indeed, there was a future. He didn't know what exactly he was going to say. Nor when he would say it. He was certainly uncertain as to how he would approach the subject, what tone to adopt.

When is the right time to raise a debate impacting the rest of your life, especially if you're fearful of the outcome, hearing what you don't want to hear? But not knowing, limbo land, was the most unnerving place to stand. Stranded in no-man's-land on the battlefield doubles the danger: bullets come from both sides.

Ayesha, still questioning her feelings for Ben, also sought resolution. That niggling question: do I, do I not, do I, do I not love him spun in her head. Also repeating itself: if you need to ask, then the answer must be No.

Because both held these unspoken thoughts, perhaps that's why they found themselves having breakfast at the far end of the garden away from Abba, Amma and Bushra. Without talking, they knew it was time to talk.

Natcoo was happy to bring breakfast to them as they sat on the cane chairs. A few routine lines were exchanged, like an opening gambit in chess, a set pattern of moves and counter-moves. Love the smell of jasmine. Gardenias are my favourite. Pass the salt, please. Going to Tungipur later? More toast? Then, after a minute's silence, a change of atmosphere and the silence broken. Ben made the first move.

'Ayesha, I don't know what to say. Or how to say this.'

She looked at him nervously; he became more anxious.

'I also have something to say to you,' she said.

'You go first then.'

'Well, no, as you spoke first, Abba would say "you're the opening bat".'

While he prepared himself, rehearsed in his mind his first line, Ayesha added, 'I don't know what you're about to say. I have a hunch. But I should tell you, I don't really know what I'll say in reply. Although I should know.'

Ben wondered if Dr Rahman had alerted his daughter to this impending and necessary conversation. But he'd promised Ben he wouldn't say a word to Ayesha about what they'd discussed in Sultan's Khaddyo. 'Bloody hell. This is difficult,' he blustered. Then he regretted swearing because he knew Ayesha didn't like bad language.

Her silence, that beautiful but enigmatic face she deployed, didn't make it easier.

'I want... no, I need... to ask a question. But I'm afraid of your reply.'

'Well?' Even her voice, flat, level, toneless, gave nothing away. There was no hint of hope, nor any sign of despair.

'I want to ask... I want to ask if I can ask you something.'

'Ben, this is getting silly.'

'Er, yes. You're right. Okay, here goes. Can I ask if I can... if I can marry you? Or should I say... will you marry me?'

For several seconds Ayesha retained her dead-pan expression. Ben feared the worst. Then she sighed heavily and a slight smile spread across her face. 'I must say, Ben, at least you avoided clichés like "Will you do me the honour" and so on. And you're not even down on one knee!'

'Well?' he pleaded.

'Hi, you two.' Bushra, still in her pyjamas, came bouncing across the grass. 'Natcoo's bringing some more tea and toast. Don't worry, I won't need to share yours.'

Ayesha and Ben turned together and eyed Bushra with such a look that she instantly spun round and started returning to the house.

'Oops, sorry. Interrupted.'

But after a few steps she turned again and bounded back to stand bolt upright a yard in front of them, hands on hips.

'No, I won't go away until I've had my say. Ayesha, you love Ben. Ben, you love my sister. I can't see what the problem is. Just get married. Have some babies. Then I can practice my nurturing skills on your kids before I have mine.'

Ayesha and Ben were left stunned and speechless.

'Okay, I'll leave you to sort yourselves out. I'll have my tea and toast and scrambled eggs with Ma and Pa. Bye.'

As in the still silent aftermath of a hurricane, Ayesha eventually asked, slowly, 'Did I just hear my baby sister ordering me to marry you and you to marry me?'

'Without a shadow of a doubt, yes, that's what she said.'

They burst into a fit of laughter. Through it, Ben struggled to say, 'I... I... think she's... she's right.'

Ayesha managed to spurt out, 'So do I.'

When they recovered their senses, Ayesha presented Ben with her most serious face, although he recognised her playacting.

'Now Mr Benjamin Altringham, get down on one knee. Give me a naff corny proposal because, if you don't, you'll regret it for the rest of your – sorry, our – married life.'

AYESHA AND BEN, hand in hand, delivered the news on the veranda as Natcoo carried in the Sunday newspaper on the silver tray. Dr Rahman, Mrs Rahman and Bushra were overjoyed at the news. Natcoo clapped his hands. Bushra, literally, jumped up and down for at least a minute. Dr and Mrs Rahman stood and hugged their daughter and future son-in-law. Natcoo trotted to the kitchen and told Buna and Ali about the announcement. They arrived with beaming smiles to offer their congratulations. Bangladeshis love a wedding. Ayesha had often described all Bengalis as a very romantic people.

'Best special dinner tonight, yes doctor?' Ali asked.

'Yes, Ali, thank you,' he confirmed.

'I do all your favourites Miss Ayesha Mr Ben.'

'Everything you make is my favourite, Ali,' he said.

'I go now, start prepare.'

'I'm pleased you've taken my advice,' Bushra said imperiously, addressing her sister and Ben. 'Amma, Abba, you won't believe it, I had to virtually bang their heads together earlier. Honestly, if I hadn't chivvied them along, they'd have been dithering until… until… until they were too old to give you grandchildren.'

'You're wise ahead of your tender years, my dear,' Mrs Rahman said. 'Now, having finished breakfast, I think it is time you went upstairs and changed out of your pyjamas into something more respectable.'

'Yes, Bushra,' Dr Rahman said, with an expression that left no doubt he wanted her to scarper. 'We grown-ups have certain matters to discuss.'

'Well, if that's all the thanks I get for making this wedding happen…' She hugged her sister and kissed her cheeks. And, for the first time, she felt able to do likewise with Ben. 'Let me know if you need any more help from me.' She sauntered away singing a song.

Mrs Rahman shook her head with affection for Bushra. Looking at Ben, she said, 'It's her father's fault. He's been far too lenient with her.' She smiled at her husband.

Dr Rahman said, 'Ben, you'll find once you're married husbands get blamed for everything.' He smiled at his wife.

It's almost certain Ayesha and Ben at that moment thought exactly the same thing: if we can be as happy after twenty-eight years of marriage…

'I don't wish to spoil the moment,' Dr Rahman said. 'But we all know we have to discuss how we are going to handle this. Let me start by saying your marriage has my unreserved support. I have no doubts you're made for each other.'

'That goes for me also,' Raina Rahman said. 'But let's not kid ourselves, let's not deny the fact that you, Ayesha, are a Bangladeshi Muslim and you, Ben, are a British... I don't think you've expressed any views on religion.'

Ben dreaded this moment. He wouldn't lie. But he certainly couldn't tell the whole truth. The Rahmans were devout Muslims, although not pious. They believed in God, but were not evangelists. Islam, to them, was the one true faith, yet they accepted there were other faiths and tolerant of them.

'Mrs Rahman, Dr Rahman, I'm afraid I find it hard to believe in...' Ben wanted to say some omnipotent, omnipresent being. He believed belief in God or gods was bunkum. He thought unscrupulous religious leaders peddled superstitious nonsense to needy people and exploited their vulnerabilities. But truth hurts and insults, so Ben censored himself. 'I fully accept the right of others to believe in their chosen faith. Religion is just not for me.'

A moment of reflection followed, the Rahman family interpretating Ben's statement, aware all was not told, and assessing the possible implications.

'Ayesha, did you know Ben's view?' Dr Rahman asked.

'No, although I suspected his position. We've had many conversations about religion, especially ours. But no. I suppose after all this time we should have done.'

'Serious question, my dear. Now that you do, does it affect your decision to marry?'

'Absolutely not, Abba. I have my beliefs, Ben is entitled to his, or no belief in God whatsoever.' Gradually appearing upset, she added, sounding increasingly alarmed. 'You and Amma raised Bushra and me to accept diverse opinions. You can't start pulling up the drawbridge, reneging on those views now they come to be challenged...'

'Ayesha, Ayesha, my dear, there's no need to get upset.' Dr Rahman went to place his arms around her shoulders. Softly, he said, 'As you didn't know Ben's religious beliefs, I simply wished to see how you felt now you have heard them, that's all. My view remains, each and every one of us is entitled to his or her belief, or no belief in God or religion at all.'

Ayesha calmed herself. 'Sorry, Abba. Don't they say "love conquers all"?'

Mrs Rahman, seeing that Ayesha needed a break, stood, leaned forward with her hands resting on the table and suggested they discuss details later, perhaps after dinner. She added, 'We must consider practicalities, especially when and where the marriage can take place. As you discovered, Ben, with that ridiculous idea of marrying Khalida to extricate her from the Hussains, our marriage laws in Bangladesh are unclear at best and in a state of flux at worst. We must think about this very carefully.'

'I agree, and there's no rush,' Ben said. 'One thing we have decided already is that we'll wait until Ayesha qualifies as a doctor next year.'

'*If* I qualify,' she said.

'Top of year, year after year…' Ben said.

'Only equal top, this year,' Ayesha interrupted.

'Ayesha, you're equal to no one,' Ben said sincerely. 'Considering what you've faced the past few months, even days before your exam, the shooting, you're top all the way.'

'What a lovely thing to say,' Mrs Rahman said. 'And true!'

'Dr Rahman, serious question to you now: if Ayesha had taken this year's final exams, those you invigilated, would she have passed?'

'Don't answer him, Abba.'

'Honestly, Ben, yes. I believe she would have scraped through with her current level of knowledge and skills. But you will find, if you haven't realised already, scraping through is not our lovely daughter's way.'

'Yes, I had noticed,' Ben said. 'And my new job with ICRC means I'll be going away regularly over the next year. They told me I'd be travelling to Islamabad and Karachi, where most Bangladeshis are in Pakistan, and to New Delhi and Patna helping to persuade India to accept at least some Biharis.'

'Good luck with that,' Mrs Rahman said. 'You'll need it. Pakistan nor India want Biharis – well, not many. And they'll want paying for taking them in. I doubt it will be resolved in the next twenty-five years. If not fifty. If ever.'

BEN REGRETTED LEAVING his teaching job after just four weeks. He felt embarrassed giving notice after such a short time. It was a stop-gap, after all, and he was not trained to teach. He was sure Mrs Rahman had arranged the post with its principal, her friend, to get him out from under her feet. It also restored some pride being in work after summarily losing his job with Aid International. The money helped too; his modest savings wouldn't last indefinitely.

Mrs Rahman had adamantly refused to take a taka from him for 'my keep'. Ayesha gave him a subtle but firm telling off for even making the offer. You should have told me what you were planning to do, she had said. We never, never, never take money from guests. Bushra had a less than subtle pop at Ben. Offering to pay? That's almost an insult, she ranted, possibly an outrage.

Ben insisted however on paying for the family's weekly Chinese meal at Lucky House. Compared with the amount he had received living with the Rahmans – shelter, food, laundry – the weekly meal at Lucky House amounted to little more than a token gesture. And Jimmy Ong, with his perma-smile, always whispered in Ben's ear, 'I give you discount'. Ben never worked out what the discount amounted to.

'I hear you become half Bangladeshi soon.' Jimmy had intercepted Ben on his way to the bathroom. Ben didn't understand at first until Jimmy continued, 'Congratulation. When wedding? I set up Lucky House tent for best food. Bangladeshi don't know how to make noodle proper.'

Ben should have realised that Natcoo, Ali, Buna, the night guard or the dhobi, the couple who do the washing twice a week, would have gossiped. Bushra too was bursting to tell all her many friends, despite the family pact of secrecy for the time being. Keeping wedding news from spreading in Bangladesh would be like trying to stop water escaping through a sieve.

Delivering humanitarian aid was Ben's long-term career choice; helping eradicate poverty his ambition; no destitution his dream – a pipedream perhaps. Even after a mere three years working amongst the poor, he understood it would take more than UN agencies, non-governmental organisations and charities to end poverty. And the same questions dogged him almost daily. Do politicians and those who have plenty genuinely want to end inequality? Is that even possible? Will there always be winners and losers in the game of life – rich and poor, lucky and unlucky, smart and inadequate? And, as his future father-in-law observed, there's always some power-hungry territory-grabbing war-mongering despot desperate to disrupt the peaceful happy lives of others.

AYESHA AND BEN accepted they would face prejudice on several fronts.

'It won't be easy, Ben,' Ayesha said. 'Many here will despise me for marrying a non-Muslim. Some of my aunts and uncles, even friends, will believe it's wrong. Ridiculous, I know. But, as Amma said, we must face facts.'

'We'll get through all that,' Ben said.

'Yes. Yes we will. But we mustn't ignore what we might meet on the road ahead.'

'Some of my family in England will find it... find it strange I've married a Bangladeshi too. But I promise you, Ayesha, my mum and dad and sister will love you to bits. I've already told them lots about you. They can't wait to meet you. And when they saw your photograph, they all said how beautiful you are. My sister said you looked far too classy for me.'

'Your sister, clearly, has excellent judgement. Although she sounds as if she could be as annoying as Bushra, right?'

'No way. When it comes to irritating, Bushra is in a league of her own.'

'One or two of our relatives might boycott the wedding because I'm not marrying a Muslim. As I've said many times, marriage here is as much between two families as between two individuals.'

'I'm not going to,' Ben said, 'but for the sake of argument, what if I converted to Islam? Your father told me it's easy. All I have to say in front of two witnesses is: *"There is no god but Allah. Muhammad is the messenger of Allah"*.'

'There's a catch, Ben. You must *believe* what you say,' Ayesha said. Looking disappointed, she added, 'And I don't think you should make light of Islam, and certainly not our Prophet, peace be upon him.'

'Sorry, I didn't mean to offend,' Ben said. 'In many ways I admire people who have a faith in religion, believe in some god or other. I just can't.'

'Conversion, sincere conversion to Islam, might appease some. But we have cultural aspects too. Bangladeshis – in fact all Bengalis, here and in India, Hindus, Sikhs and Muslims alike – consider that we're unique across the subcontinent, in the world. We are. In our language, music, poetry, customs and practices, even the way we think. By marrying you, some will believe I'm abandoning my cultural inheritance, diluting the purity of… what shall I call it? Let's try "Bengalism".'

'Nice word.'

'Many Tamils consider themselves Tamils before being Indian, likewise Gujaratis. There's still loads of Sikhs in Punjab, both Pakistani and Indian Punjabis, who want Punjab to be an independent state, like many Kashmiris.'

Ben raised a similar situation in the UK with many people in Northern Ireland, Scotland and Wales wanting independence.

'Even in England,' Ben said, 'there are those who want to be free from London's rule, especially people in Cornwall and Yorkshire.'

'And Northern Ireland is where Catholics and Protestants are fighting each other, right?'

'Yes, there's the Irish Republican Army and the Ulster Defence Association, among other groups and paramilitaries, all claiming right is on their side…'

'And God,' Ayesha added.

'True enough. It's odd how every side in a war claims God backs them.'

'Same here in our conflict,' said Ayesha, sadly. 'I believe Allah cried when he heard prayers pleading for His backing – from Pakistanis and us. Allah wants peace, not war. If warmongers listened to God's voice, they'd lay down their weapons. Better still, they wouldn't have weapons in the first place.'

THEIR CONVERSATION PAUSED. Fragments of reflection descended, falling as leaves off a tree buffeted by a breeze, thoughts swaying one way and then another.

For Ayesha, painful memories of friends and family killed and injured during the nine-month war. Abba's limp, still painful at times, although he hides it without complaint; Khalida's father, tortured then hung; cousins killed in Khulna and Saidpur; school friends gone, some their destination unknown; three of her professors at Dacca Medical College and Hospital bayonetted in the grounds, their blood oozing into the earth where the memorial now stands.

Ben saw the sadness on Ayesha's face. In that moment her eyes had lost life, their sparkle, as the curtain of a teardrop closed over them.

Ayesha accepted Ben would never – could never – fully understand her nation's pain. No one would know the war's true death toll. If no one was left in a village, there was no one to count the corpses. The rats and dogs and vultures and crows feasted on bodies. Worms and insects cleared the crumbs. Lush, leafy, quick-growing jungle fauna soon covered bodies allowing flesh and bone to sink into the soil. Rivers washed bloated bodies into the Bay of Bengal for the sharks to bite and the fish to nibble.

Ben's thoughts turned to the millions of people displaced as nearly one in three houses had been destroyed. Although rarely mentioned, and then only in whispers, up to half a million women were raped. For Bihari girls and women, Ben knew only too well such attacks continued almost daily.

Ayesha broke the silence. 'I suppose we'll just have to live with bigotry, on whatever grounds – race, ethnicity, religion, culture.'

'Sure, we'll always remember that most people most of the time are not so… so ignorant.'

'Our race, your skin colour here, my skin in England, will upset some people.'

'Yes, it will. But that's their problem, right?'

'Right.'

'And kids? Oops, children,' Ben said, remembering the reprimand from the school's vice-principal.

'We're getting ahead of ourselves,' cautioned Ayesha, affectionately. 'But, yes, it may be harder for them. Anglo-Indians across the whole subcontinent generally formed their own community. Still do. They were – are – viewed as having one foot in both communities, but not fully accepted by either. Hopefully the world is changing.'

FORTY-NINE

Housemaid Buna heard the knock. She jumped, startled, always wary since the war: the soldiers had banged on the door before crashing into her home in Saidpur.

She peered through the living room window to see who it was. She didn't recognise either of the two women, their headscarves pulled further forward than traditional and across their faces. They appeared furtive, agitated, as if being watched. The Rahman family had gone shopping in Tungipur. Buna turned to call Natcoo, then remembered he was buying fish in the market. Ali was out the back busy preparing meals.

But they must have a proper reason for calling, otherwise the gatekeeper would not have allowed them in.

Tentatively, Buna opened the door. Just slightly, enough to talk through. She believed they were Biharis, or at least half Bihari. Buna didn't like Biharis: after the Urdu-speaking Pakistani soldiers bayonetted her father and brother, they did vile things to her mother and younger sister before dragging them off – never to be seen again. Crushed and blood-soaked under her brother's body, Buna played dead to survive.

Occasionally, in desperation, people called to see Dr Rahman for treatment and she expected them to ask for him. She would tell them to go to the hospital, although being Bihari they'd be sent to the back of the queue, if treated at all. Knowing the camp at Mohpur had been all but bulldozed, if they had walked from the new camp, they'd walked a good five miles.

The younger of the two women lowered her scarf to reveal a beautiful, thin, kindly face, devoid of malice. She spoke first. Buna's

English was fast improving and she fully understood the question put to her. 'Is Ben, Mr Altringham, here?'

'No,' Buna replied. 'He gone Dacca.'

'Oh, that's unfortunate.'

Buna had not learnt the word un... fort... u... nate. But the tone spoke clearly. She opened the door wider accepting these women posed no threat.

'You leave message. I give him,' she said.

Then, in pure Bengali, the older woman asked when he was expected back. Buna said she'd overheard him saying he'd be home around lunchtime. Approaching one o'clock, that could be soon. But Buna was not in a position to invite the callers into the house.

'We'll return later,' the older woman said, disappointed, but understanding Buna's dilemma. They turned to go away.

'No,' Buna murmured, correctly sensing what they had to say would be important for Ben, 'you wait in garden at back.' Buna pointed the way along the gravel path edged by shoulder-high flame-red and lemon-yellow cannas. Pulling their scarves further around their faces once more, they shuffled swiftly through the garden keeping their heads low, shoulders arched, eyes watchful.

NEARLY SIX MONTH'S pay for one day's work was a reward beyond his dreams. A bundle of dollars, in crisp clean bills; one-tenth now, nine-tenths when the job's done satisfactorily. Syed had asked for half up front, but Womach's henchman Pete Conan drove a hard bargain.

Ishaaq, Syed's cousin at the garage in Tungipur, had 'friends' who would be willing to punish the Englishman. Ishaaq's two guard dogs strained their chains lunging at the strangers scurrying down the side passage in single file late at night. He silenced his animals by threatening them with the long spanner he brandished.

Syed, Ishaaq and his gang of four gathered around a campfire on scrubland at the back of the station. It was an untidy scrapyard, littered with rusty shells of cars, engine parts, old axils and torn seats. Several goats, tethered to the cars' carcases, bleated, their sleep disturbed by the gathering. The men huddled behind head-high columns of clapped-out tyres, the rubber ready to be cut and shaped into cheap sandals. It was a profitable side-line for the three Bihari women Ishaaq enslaved in his compound's breezeblock outhouse – in addition to servicing the desires of men.

Syed outlined their task. The men contracted to do the deed agreed with him, helping traitorous collaborating Biharis was bad. But much worse was for a foreign infidel to take a local girl. Bangladeshi girls are for Bangladeshi men, Syed said while plying them with more locally distilled bootlegged spirit. Alcohol was haram. But the rich drink it – imported, from Scotland, good whisky – so why shouldn't we? Sat on their haunches around the fire, the gang nodded their approval of the grog. And if it makes you feel better, less hungry, alcohol is not forbidden when used as medicine to quell pain.

The thugs asked for fifty dollars each, but accepted thirty after ten minutes of hard haggling. When you earn only two dollars at most for a fourteen-hour day, thirty dollars for a few minute's work is still a good deal. Make it look like a robbery, Syed said. All foreigners carry cash. Some have good watches and gold rings. They should take these as a bonus. If the guy struggles, a machete will make light work of a few fingers or his hand, as easy as a chicken's neck.

The woman, if she's with him, must not be harmed, Syed stressed. Although she is sinful, allowing her unmarried body to be defiled by a non-Muslim, her punishment must be left to others, ultimately Allah. If she gets hurt, we get no money. Understand? He made them repeat the command. They slurred acknowledgement of it.

BUNA RUSHED OUT as he paid the taxi driver. She spoke with urgency. 'Mr Ben, Mr Ben,' she whispered, looking left and right quickly, nervously, 'you have visitor. I tell go in garden at back.'

'I find that hard to believe,' Ben said after listening to Faiyaz and Sana. 'Why?'

'Because someone is paying them many dollars. Hundreds, he claimed,' Faiyaz said.

'And some men think it wrong you are… you are… close to local woman,' Sana added. 'She unmarried, you not Muslim.'

'Are you sure or is this just idle talk, village gossip?'

'My friend said she heard man boasting of money he get. Very many dollars, he said, and take gold watch.'

'I don't have a gold watch, just a cheap one.' Ben squeezed a smile trying to reduce the melodrama his former pharmacist and her cousin had outlined.

'Please, please be careful,' Sana said.

'Perhaps best you go away. It is only way,' Faiyaz pleaded. 'You're a good man. You tried to help me after… after… well, you know, that bad man.'

'Abi and I were threatened a few times before. Faiyaz, you remember that. Nothing happened. It was just bravado, just lads showing off.'

'Yes, but this much different. This man been prison many times. Has bad friends. Get drunk. Beat wife. Beat kids. Kick dogs.'

'Thanks to you both for your concern. But I don't intend going anywhere.'

'But you staying puts Miss Rahman in much danger too,' Faiyaz said.

This stunned Ben. He immediately condemned himself. Why had he been so selfish? Why hadn't he thought about what this man – or his pals – would do to Ayesha?

'NO. NO. I won't let you go,' Ayesha cried.

'I must. It's the only way to keep you safe.'

'It's just a rumour…'

'That's what I argued at first. But Faiyaz and her cousin convinced me this guy was not bluffing. He's a string of convictions for violence and has some pretty despicable friends. They've been offered a lot of money – in dollars.'

'Who would do that?'

'I'll give you one guess.'

'If they're talking dollars, I'm thinking Womach.'

'Spot on. After all, local lads would beat me up for free.'

'That's not funny,' Ayesha said sternly to Ben's quip. 'Look, let's see what Abba thinks. He'll confirm it's just another idle threat.'

'You've forgotten, Ayesha. A few months ago your family…'

'*Our* family…'

Ben paused, took in a lungful of air, slowed down his speech. 'This house was attacked. Windows broken. Those guys are still out there. Hussain was shot in his own garden, surrounded by hundreds of armed police and soldiers. Khalida was drugged, raped, abducted – I was there when she was grabbed, remember – imprisoned. There's a lot of nasty guys out there who do more than make idle threats.'

'Those were all different. Nothing to do with this gossip.'

'I must move out. For now, at least. Of course I'd prefer to stay here, close to you. But it's not safe – for you, the family, even for me because they know I'm here. I'll find a room in Dacca. Perhaps a small hotel. Somewhere near ICRC's office. I'll be travelling to Pakistan and India soon anyway to help sort out this displaced persons mess. I'll be less of a distraction for you too in your final year at college.'

'You've worked it all out, haven't you?' Ayesha said sadly, realising Ben was adamant about moving away.

'It's for the best. You know it makes sense. We can see each other after college some days. Maybe at weekends we can still all go to Lucky House. Can't miss out on Jimmy's discount!'

PETE CONAN'S DRIVER, Syed, told him that Ben Altringham appeared to have moved out of the Rahman's house. Syed's cousin in Tungipur had boys watch the property for nearly two weeks, day and night. Altringham hadn't come or gone. Not once.

Ishaaq had slapped the boys, but they insisted they had never fallen asleep while watching the house. There had been no routine to observe, no opportunity to plan an attack. The gang became restless, eager to receive their American dollars, angry they had been let down. Ishaaq worried they'd turn on him, perhaps torch the garage or demand payment. He had appeased the men by giving them free access to his three Bihari women.

Conan was suspicious, the timing of Altringham's absence more than coincidence. Had he been tipped off? Were Syed's contacts up to the job? Had these boy spies been stupid, too blatant, observed observing the place and alerting the Rahmans?

Within the close-knit community of aid workers in Dacca, after a few inquiries, it wasn't long before Aid International heard that its former employee in Mohpur Camp had secured a post with the International Committee of the Red Cross.

Conan ordered Syed to have ICRC's office watched, particularly at the end of the working day. Get Altringham followed. Find out where he's staying. Tell your cousin's guys to do what they need to do down here in Dacca.

'Remember, make it look like a robbery and just a beating. Break an arm or smash a kneecap. Kick his bollocks. No need to kill him. Is that clear?'

'Yes, Mr Conan.'

'And, if she's with him, the woman must not be harmed. If I hear one finger has touched her, no pay. Not a dollar. Not a cent.'

FIFTY

As the chromosomes arranged themselves into the embryo, Khalida resented the fact that Maz had determined the baby's gender. His X or Y chromosome will have lodged itself into each cell. He, not me, determined my pregnancy. He, not me, determined my child's sex.

The ovum, following fertilisation, would have taken around a week to descend the Fallopian tube and implant itself in the endometrium. My endometrium, not his.

But as the collection of cells developed, pregnancy became more than textbook theory. Khalida experienced a change of mind, a change of heart. She was fully aware of the physical and psychological changes that pregnancy brings. She knew the power of hormones to drive emotions. But the overwhelming feeling of love for her child had become as real as life itself. Mother-love was not self-deception, nor coercion by circumstances.

Khalida was not simply resigned to her condition, but positively pleased with it. She deeply regretted asking Ayesha to perform an abortion. She felt ashamed and embarrassed that she even considered a termination. She was eternally grateful that her closest friend refused to perform the procedure. Ayesha made the right call, as she so often did.

Despite the despicable sins of Mazharul and Farook Hussain, her child was innocent. She hoped her girl or boy would never discover how they were conceived. The story of the spiked mango juice, her initial desire for an abortion, her imprisonment at the hands of the child's grandfather, would never be revealed... certainly not through her lips.

Approaching five months, she could feel movement. An elbow, knee, or a foot had just pushed. Beno Hussain insisted on feeling and laid her fat hand on Khalida's bare belly. Khalida wished the hand had been that of her own mother. On Fazana's next visit, she hoped the baby would be as lively so her mother's delicate hands could feel her grandchild. Through those laid-on hands would come a blessing of love: pure, free, unconditional – not tainted and biased in favour of being a male heir to evil men.

The doctor said the baby's heartbeat was strong. Khalida already knew. She'd listened every day for weeks with her own stethoscope.

Khalida believed her child could hear her singing, sense the comfort it brings, feel the love. For a few weeks after marriage, angry with her husband, Khalida when alone often softly sang the traditional folksong *Amar gaye*.

> *Do what you wish, my cruel love,*
> *as long as I can suffer it.*
> *It was witnessed by the moon and stars.*
> *When the time comes you will be judged by them.*

Now, with another phase of anger towards Maz over, Khalida sang other Bengali songs. With its rich repertoire, especially with songs of the river and of the land, Khalida had many lyrics to choose from.

> *I gaze at the sails of the riverboats, full of hope, I await someone.*
> *One day I'll flow like a river and be free in the sea.*

'I'M SO VERY sorry,' Maz had said, many times now. He seemed sincere. But sincerity can be faked. Trust may be restored in time, although time lasts forever, beyond a lifetime. 'Sorry' is simply a word. It will be how Maz behaves that will determine its veracity, his candour.

'Can you forgive me?' he also asked.

No. Never. But Khalida replied, 'Perhaps, in time.'

Maz had been attentive, patient and gentle. A model husband. A week after the attempt on his father's life, he had returned to college. He appeared diligent and studied most evenings. Khalida started to take a keen interest in his subject, business economics, and enjoyed discussing matters arising during his day. They lived together as husband and wife, but not united in trust.

Khalida noticed that impending fatherhood had driven Maz to act more maturely. His beard had added ten years to his appearance. She preferred him clean shaven, but didn't express her opinion. She avoided expressing a view on almost everything of importance. Because on almost everything of importance she held a strong view.

But strength mustn't be shown. For now. She stuck to trivia: the shade of new curtains, the choice between a sari or salwar kameez for the day, plain or spicy rice with her fish. It was safer to appear content, although it took concentration, patience and discipline. Khalida maintained her own counsel, constantly vigilant with Maz, her mother-in-law and to servants, whose loyalty were not to her.

To her relief, Khalida had hardly seen her father-in-law. For the first month of marriage, he had remained in PG Hospital recovering from his gunshot wounds. Beno Hussain did not think it 'appropriate' that Khalida should visit him. As if Khalida didn't know, her mother-in-law declared hospitals are full of dangerous infections and, in the early months of pregnancy, these are best avoided. And since Farook Hussain's return home, recuperating, most days he had dined alone in his bedroom.

On the few occasions she unexpectedly encountered her father-in-law, she almost flinched – recalling the crack of the prison guard's lathi. Her stomach turned, unable to forget the stench of the cell.

And Hussain knew, he really knew, she was biding her time, waiting her moment, playing the long game. Beno and Mazharul may be fooled, but not him. What Hussain didn't know was what she would do and when. Would she escape? Go to England, Australia, Canada? Would she stab him? Poison him? When old, push him down stairs? It would be either flight or fight. One day, she will make that choice. He would remain vigilant. Or after my grandson is born…

Despite her demure acquiescence of the marriage and appearing to become a dutiful wife, she possessed her father's eyes: the mouth lies, behaviour deceives, but eyes tell the truth.

Khalida was free to roam the extensive house and grounds. After all, she was now Mrs Khalida Hussain, married to Mazharul, daughter-in-law of a minister of state, possibly the next head of state. On occasions she had been shopping in central Dacca with her mother-in-law, maid and bodyguards. But it was unwise to spend too much time outside, Beno Hussain had said, rest was best. Khalida did not disagree.

Farook Hussain in recuperation was not well enough to walk far. He had however insisted on attending cabinet meetings and running his affairs of state from home. Since the assassination attempt, security surrounding him had been increased.

News of Khalida's pregnancy remained withheld from family and friends. Normally it would be shouted from the rooftops at the earliest opportunity. Rumours were rife though amongst the servants; key household staff knew it as fact. Tittle-tattle cannot be stopped, Beno constantly told her husband. It will be known, but unspoken, she said.

KHALIDA HAD REQUESTED a year's break from Dacca Medical College and Hospital, which had been granted. Unknown to her, the principal had checked with minister Hussain to see if that arrangement was acceptable. Thanks to a weekly visit from Ayesha, who came armed with textbooks and copies of lecture notes, Khalida maintained her study regime. Whatever the Hussains had in mind, she fully intended to qualify as a doctor: years of study would not be wasted. If independence for Bangladesh was important, independence for self was equally so. Her father fought and suffered for the former; she must do likewise for the latter.

'You're looking really well,' Ayesha said, hugging Khalida. 'Positively blooming. Even better than last week.'

'Thank you. But it's getting harder with the humidity increasing by the day.'

'I know. It will be better once the clouds break.'

Khalida's maid served tea and two small bowls of sweet and sour dried noodles, rice flakes and peanuts – khatta meetha. She lingered in the background, busying herself with trivial tidying of objects on shelves and sideboards. Although Khalida and Ayesha spoke mainly in English, Khalida was sure the maid understood English. She had claimed that, apart from a few words, she didn't speak it.

To secure a few minutes of private conversation – without arousing suspicion – Khalida had deliberately left a textbook in her bedroom and asked the maid to fetch it. It would buy a few moments to speak freely without, as she joked, nosy ears. Still, the maid would have an ear to the door some of the time. Anything suspicious would be reported to Mrs Hussain; anything spicy shared with other servants.

'Is everything really all right?' Ayesha asked, lowering her voice, although the servant had left the room.

'Yes, really. The pregnancy is fine. Maz is being surprisingly nice. Beno? Well, as you'd expect, she's the mother-in-law stuck with a woman who's not good enough for her son, her only son.' Khalida laughed slightly. 'And you? You said on the phone Ben had moved to a place in Dacca. Have you two fallen out?'

'Absolutely not. It's closer to the ICRC's office, that's all.'

Khalida always knew when Ayesha wasn't spilling the whole can of beans. 'And?'

Ayesha didn't try to deceive. 'Nonsense, really. Just rumours. But he's moved away for me and the family.'

Khalida widened her eyes demanding more.

'He was told there was a gang out to get him. They're being paid by someone, as if there's a price on his head.'

'What? To kill him!'

'To beat him up.'

'Why?'

'A combination of things, they'd heard.'

'Who's "they"?'

'Faiyaz, the pharmacist who helped Abba in Mohpur's clinic. Her sister's husband heard one of the gang – nasty types, former jailbirds – boasting about the money they were to get, in dollars, for "teaching him a lesson".'

'For what?'

'Helping Biharis, for one thing. Then being friends with me. Then…' Ayesha hesitated. 'Then what happened with you.'

'Me?'

'Somehow these guys heard of him taking someone – they didn't know it was you – for an abortion. Probably assumed it was me.

I think the main reason is that these yobs resent the fact this Englishman is in a relationship with me. You know what it's like, Khalida, many of these backward guys think we should "stick to our own kind".'

'That's the line from that song in *West Side Story*, right?'

'Right. But staying in Dacca has advantages for both of us. Besides being closer to his office, it does allow me to focus on my final year. We talk every day on the phone. We still meet at Lucky House most weekends. And he'll be flying to India and Pakistan regularly soon on the repatriation programme.'

'Does absence make the heart grow fonder?' quizzed Khalida.

'So far, yes, it does.' Ayesha returned Khalida's smile. 'Now, I want to know everything – all the details – that has been happening with this baby. All the changes, a full analysis, please.'

'Why, Ayesha, are you thinking of specialising in obs and gynae instead of neuro?'

FIFTY-ONE

It was a slim victory. A handful of votes bagged it. But you only need a majority verdict to determine the difference between winning and losing.

He recognised that many about to listen to his victory speech disliked him. Some hated him instinctually, although they were not quite sure why. In politics you make enemies. You need someone to blame. And if anyone presents a threat they must be discredited, demoted or silenced.

Newly elected Mayor Thomas Womach milked the applause. The cheerleaders had earned their bonuses. But it was time to raise his hands and calm the throng. Then wait. Wait for church-like silence.

He remembered reading an analysis of great speech-makers. Some started softly. It made the audience listen harder, enhancing the value of each word heard. Hitler whispered. Slowly. A phrase here and there. Pausing. Then a long crescendo before exploding into a rant – against the Versailles Treaty, the Poles, the Jews, the Roma, homosexuals and the disabled.

Then make the universal politicians' promise since the dawn of time: a better future, a wonderful world, Utopia, everyone's rich, nobody's poor. He'd proved over the past twenty-five years operating Aid International that you can fool most people most of the time. They keep giving money to eradicate poverty. But the world witnesses more poverty, relatively and absolutely. People want to believe that one day, just one day, politicians' promises will be fulfilled. Let them have their pipedreams.

Dressed in white, including his shoes, Womach addressed the people of Santa Fe, New Mexico. The magnificent state capital building, popularly known as the Roundhouse, was barely ten years old. At its centre the Rotunda, sixty-feet high, carried Womach's opening whispers well.

'Thank you. Thank you. And thank you again.'

He looked left, right, then centre, pausing between each 'thank you'. Stagecraft was important. Remember you're really talking to just one person, not thousands, his media coach had taught him. On TV, Thomas, you're a guest in someone's home, imagine you're talking from their armchair. On radio, Thomas, wrap your voice round the microphone. Look at it. Lean in. Love it. Always prepare what you're going to say – never make an impromptu comment.

'You,' Womach continued to the audience of around three thousand, 'the fantastic, generous, kind-hearted people of Santa Fe, have put your trust in me to make this city the greatest of great cities in America. I promise…'

The standing ovation lasted long enough to satisfy his election team.

In the limousine driving back to Womach's ranch, his campaign director said, 'Next stop in two or three years, Thomas, 1600 Pennsylvania Ave, Washington DC. I already got a slogan that'll make you stand out from the drab crowd.'

'Sock it to me.'

'White suit for the White House…'

'That's shit.'

'I'M GOING TO call the British high commissioner's office first thing in the morning,' Ayesha said firmly.

'Perhaps he's travelling, on his way to Delhi or Islamabad,' Dr Rahman said in the hope of quelling his daughter's anxiety.

'He wasn't expecting to go there until the end of next week.'

'Maybe the meetings were brought forward,' suggested Mrs Rahman.

'He'd have called before leaving for the airport.'

'There's still a possibility he may call tonight,' Dr Rahman said.

'Abba, it's after eleven. Ben wouldn't call this late for fear of waking us. I could understand missing a day if he's on the move, but not two.'

Bushra shared her sister's unease over Ben. She stood and wrapped her arms around Ayesha. They held each other tighter than ever before.

IN WHITEHALL, LONDON, following a round of mayoral elections across the USA, the Foreign and Commonwealth Office requested intelligence reports from Century House. It was standard procedure for the Secret Intelligence Service to monitor 'significant persons' should they be elected to high office.

MI6's file on Thomas Womach – cross-referenced to Aid International – had more or less gathered dust. At one time his organisation had been considered a front for the Central Intelligence Agency: it was an open secret that agents embedded themselves with UN agencies, international aid organisations and US charities working overseas. They provide an effective cover for spying operations.

Intelligence officers had investigated several AI projects over the years, including those in Haiti and Kenya. They uncovered clear discrepancies between the reported funding and the results on the ground, and unsavoury links to corrupt regimes.

Although analysts at Century House concluded these findings amounted to 'financial irregularities', they posed no threat to UK security. A 'No Action' order was stamped on the file.

A junior officer suggested that the Charities Commission should be alerted because AI's UK operation was registered in England and Wales for its fund raising activities. Her superior was dismissive: 'We don't share our intelligence with all and sundry.'

The latest attachment to the Thomas Womach-Aid International file came from an intelligence officer in Dacca, Bangladesh.

In summary, three points.

First, incoming funds publicly announced appear not to have been fully invested in AI's operations. There have been improvements, but far short of what could be expected.

Second, at one AI site in the Tungipur district, where the land is officially allocated for internally displaced persons (IDPs), a large private dwelling is being constructed within the area now marked 'private land'. Approximately eight thousand Biharis, the IDPs, have been moved southwards to land even more prone to flooding.

Third, in line with submissions from elsewhere, it appears AI's Womach has a penchant for women and girls. I interviewed one victim of a sexual assault by him at Camp Mohpur. I deliberately omit the caveat 'alleged' because I have every reason to believe her account: her suicide note expressed the 'shame' of the assault. NC: F241052.

After reading the report, the minister made a note on the file: *This intelligence currently has little value. However, should Womach be in serious contention for higher office, this information may prove useful. It could in future help persuade the White House to our way of thinking on key strategic positions. Review in six months.*

FIFTY-TWO

The doctor called the British High Commission soon after eight. It had been a long, hot, humid night, made worse when the theatre's back-up generator failed mid-operation after another power cut in Dacca's Imamganj district. Treating patients using paraffin lamps, candles and torchlight is far from ideal.

Dr Sheikh asked to speak to the ambassador 'on a matter of grave importance'. The receptionist put him through to his personal assistant, senior secretary Stephen Sykes.

'Do you employ a Mr Nowel Cribb?'

'Yes, Dr Sheikh.'

'May I ask if he is present today?'

Sykes became cautious. It was a strange question. Why didn't he ask for Nowel directly? Dr Sheikh appeared genuine, well-spoken, authoritative. Echoey metallic hospital noises could be heard in the background. But caution and confidentiality were second nature to staff at the Foreign and Commonwealth Office, never haste and openness.

'Dr Sheikh, please allow me to ask the nature of your inquiry?'

'Of course,' he replied without hesitation. 'At around ten o'clock last night a man – a white gentleman – was left outside our hospital's main entrance. Some rough-looking fellows had been observed unceremoniously dropping him on the road and running off. By the time medical staff reached him there was, I'm sad to say, no hope. Far too much blood loss.

'If medical assistance had reached him earlier, perhaps he could have been saved. His femoral artery – I'm sure you know, Mr Sykes, that's the one supplying the leg – had been completely severed. If a tourniquet or direct pressure on the wound had been quickly applied, there may have been a chance of survival. Alas, Mr Sykes, I have reason to believe the victim is your Mr Cribb.'

'Well, Dr Sheikh, I'm terribly sorry of course for this man who has died. But I can assure you it is not Mr Cribb – I said good morning to him not ten minutes ago. So how…'

'Ah, it is good we can eliminate him. But the deceased had Mr Cribb's card in his shirt pocket.'

'I see,' Sykes said slowly, thinking. 'How old would you say the man is – was?'

'Hard to tell. He had been badly beaten. I would guess late twenties, perhaps early thirties.'

'Did he have any other possessions? Watch? Ring?'

'No. His shirt was made by St Michael and trousers at Burton – well-known British brands I know from my time working at The Royal London Hospital in Whitechapel.'

'So, Dr Sheikh, we can assume that, coupled with carrying Mr Cribb's card, that this unfortunate chap is British.'

'I have informed the police, as is my duty. And because Mr Cribb's business card is the main clue to his identify, the police will obviously ask him to help. It seems highly likely that Mr Cribb will know him.'

STOOD OVER HIS naked body in the hospital morgue, Nowel Cribb confirmed it was Benjamin Altringham. The police inspector wrote the name slowly, carefully, without comment. Nowel said he would phone through details as soon as he returned to the office and checked his registration file. His next of kin in Britain would need to be informed, and his employers, the ICRC.

Nowel also thought of Ayesha, the Rahman family, and Khalida. But he would contact the Rahmans directly: Ben's death is a matter of personal grief, not police investigation. If the Rahmans wish to contact the police later to furnish them with further information, that would be their decision.

Ben's contentious relationship with Aid International also flashed through Nowel's mind. But surely that couldn't be linked to this murder. Unless… unless Womach… the argument over Faiyaz… Ben's knowledge of Womach's nefarious predilections…

Nowel had seen many casualties in post-war Bangladesh and at his previous posting in Saigon. But those victims of violence, suicide and traffic accidents were strangers. This was different. He knew Ben. Liked him. Admired the aid work he was involved in, despite being very naïve about the good it would do. Nowel hid his grief.

'It looks like a simple robbery gone wrong,' inspector Iqbal Subhan said. He then made a full circle around Ben's body on the cold, chipped and cracked ceramic slab. Subhan occasionally paused to lean in taking a closer look at the bruising and blood-stained slashes.

'Hardly simple, inspector,' Nowel said blandly. 'And what do you mean by "gone wrong"?'

'My suspicion is that, when challenged, instead of simply handing over his wallet, and perhaps a watch or gold ring, he foolishly resisted the miscreants. Street robbers don't usually resort to this level of violence – once they have a person's money and possessions.'

After the inspector finished scrutiny of Ben's corpse, Nowel turned to address the morgue attendant. 'Do you think we could cover him up?'

Appearing not to understand English, the inspector translated into Bengali, aggressively, issuing an order rather than making a request. The attendant rushed away.

'If I correctly recall a report from several weeks ago,' the inspector paused, raised a forefinger to his lower lip and strained his brow, 'this Mr Benjamin Altringham is the same fellow who was arrested and jailed for some time.'

'Your memory is impressive, inspector,' Nowel said. Nowel could not know that Iqbal Subhan had also been in charge of a team searching for Khalida Chowdhury. 'But he was only inside for a few days and the charges were, I believe, concocted.'

'Concocted?'

'Invented. Fabricated.'

'Yes, yes, Mr Cribb, I know what concocted means. But the Bangladeshi police has been swept clean with a new broom since the birth of our new nation. Such things no longer occur.'

To argue against such a blatant falsehood would make fools of both men, so Nowel maintained a diplomatic silence. Breaking the impasse, the orderly returned and spread a white sheet over Ben's body.

'I wonder,' the inspector said after the attendant retreated to the back of the morgue, 'if this was an attack after he upset some fellow prisoner. Something like that?'

'No, definitely not. I visited him in jail – that's where I gave him my card.' Nowel had no intention of revealing Ben had been in contact prior to his imprisonment.

'Mr Altringham had a prison cell alone and didn't associate with any of the inmates, most of whom couldn't speak English. Mr Altringham's Bengali was limited. No, inspector, there had been no trouble with anyone inside.'

'Then I must return to my first impression,' Subhan said. 'Instead of handing over his money and valuables straight away, Mr Altringham foolishly decided to fight the thieves.'

'No, inspector,' Nowel insisted. 'He would have given all his money and possessions without resisting. He may have been naïve, too idealistic, but he wasn't stupid. And I doubt he had much to give.'

EPILOGUE

In 2021, at a world-renowned teaching hospital in central London, a doctor died after contracting SARS covid-19 in what the World Health Organisation declared a pandemic. A brass plaque in the main reception reads:

Professor Ayesha Rahman-Altringham, BSc (Hons), MBChB, FRCPE, FRCS, born 1950 in what was then East Pakistan, now Bangladesh, died after serving a long and distinguished career.

Recognised globally as a specialist in neuro-surgery, she lectured as far afield as Australia, Canada, China, South Africa and the USA, where she held the post of Honorary Professor at Harvard Medical School in addition to teaching roles at London and Cambridge universities.

For over 25 years Professor Rahman-Altringham served this hospital. She saved countless lives, gave hope to the traumatised, provided inspiration to every one of her colleagues.

END

FOOTNOTE

During the year *Red on Green* is set around 750,000 Biharis lived in Bangladesh. Because some of the majority Bangladeshi community turned against them, more than seven out of ten Biharis fled their homes from persecution. They flocked together in colonies to feel safer, although safety was far from guaranteed. In these extemporized camps Biharis became, to use the official jargon, 'internally displaced persons' – effectively refugees in their own country.

Today, fifty years later, many of this minority group still struggle to survive. They continue to subsist in around seventy squalid shantytowns, settlements established in 1972.

The largest, known as Geneva Camp, in the Mohammadpur district of Dhaka, contains around twenty-five thousand residents. Conditions in the shanty are atrocious, the facts bleak. Nine people on average occupy one small room; there is one latrine for ninety people; only one in twenty has any formal education. Many insist on calling themselves 'stranded Pakistanis'.

Sheikh Mujibur Rahman – still today revered as the Father of Bangladesh – became the country's first prime minister. Yet within a few years resentment grew against his leadership. On 15 August 1975 he was assassinated alongside his wife, two sons, other family members and servants at their home in Dhaka. The coup d'état was spearheaded by Major Farook Rahman of the Bengal Lancers.

For years this beautiful lush land was then beset by more mutinies, treachery and coup attempts. Mujibur Rahman's daughter, Sheikh Hasini Wazad, is the current prime minister. She was, fortunately, in West Germany at the time of her family's massacre in 1975 and escaped the carnage.

Bangladesh remains one of the world's poorest countries with a population of around one hundred and sixty-eight million, with an annual birth rate of nearly three million. It regularly suffers natural disasters: cyclones, floods and tornadoes.

As storms become more frequent and extreme and sea levels rise because of climate change, this low lying country will suffer more than most. Millions of Bangladeshis live in flood plains or just a metre or two above sea level, particularly in the southern flatland area known as the Sundarbans.

ACKNOWLEDGEMENTS

Where does one begin thanking all the people for their help and advice over many years that results in writing novels? Family? Teachers? Friends? Colleagues? All have had, to a greater or lesser degree, some influence on shaping each and every one of us.

All can't be named, but these can.

My wife and best friend, Kathy, must come first. Without her *Red on Green* could not have been written. Her endless patience, understanding and support made possible my work on this story. She also read the initial draft: it received approval. And that's from someone who is an inveterate reader of novels and a candid critic.

Daughters Jemma and Eva continue to provide encouragement. Their energy and zest for life is a constant inspiration. Eva deserves additional thanks and praise for designing the book's stunning cover.

Special acknowledgement must go to Lesley Anslow and Pramodrai Unia for reading the draft manuscript. Their eagle-eyed expertise, respectively in the fields of journalism and international aid, provided invaluable comments, much-needed criticism and essential corrections. But, as the writer and final arbiter, any remaining errors are entirely mine.

Thanks too to many people across the Indian subcontinent from Karachi to Chittagong, Islamabad, Delhi and Dhaka, some of whom welcomed me into their homes and provided the kindest hospitality and insights into their history, faith, beliefs and culture.

Although the novel's storyline is critical about certain aspects of international humanitarian aid programmes, that does not imply the majority are tarred with the same brush. Far from it. Appreciation of the excellent work many charities and organisations undertake should be recognised, especially when dealing with the consequences of failed politics and policies.

Kathy and I take particular interest in Médecins Sans Frontières, who deliver outstanding medical and nursing care in often dangerous and difficult situations.

Finally, the team at Grosvenor House Publishing could not have been more helpful, especially Melanie Bartle and Dean Zaltsman.

Steve Ellis